CORNERSTONE

Peter Michael Diamantopoulos

Copyright © 2013 by Eastern Estate Publishing
All Rights Reserved
Printed by Amazon CreateSpace
ISBN-13: 978-0615838236
ISBN-10: 0615838235

Maps by Peter Michael Diamantopoulos
Cover Art by Filtered Focus Productions
Edited by Rebecca Heyman

To Dortha Samuelson:

I'm still writing.

Contents

Now	*Then*
One 5	Fifth Summit 9
Two 21	Ten Seconds 23
Three 29	Alkali 31
Four 43	Reassignment 45
Five 53	Porcelain 55
Six 69	Education 71
Seven 83	Ballabor 85
Eight 97	Echoes 99
Nine 109	Catalyst 111
Ten 133	Demon 119
Eleven 151	Most Dangerous Path 137
Twelve 165	Sins Best Forgotten . . 153
Thirteen 185	Severance 167
Fourteen 223	Answers 187
Fifteen 239	Surge 197
Sixteen 249	Spider's Claw 209
Seventeen 269	Starlight 225
Eighteen 285	Epitaph 241
Nineteen 301	Angel 251
Twenty 317	Ransom 271
Twenty-One 335	Ruined 287
Twenty-Two 353	Dichotomy 303
Twenty-Three 381	Epiphany 319
Twenty-Four 389	Esker 337
Twenty-Five 399	Del Solae 355
Twenty-Six 413	War and Death 371
	The Last Option 383

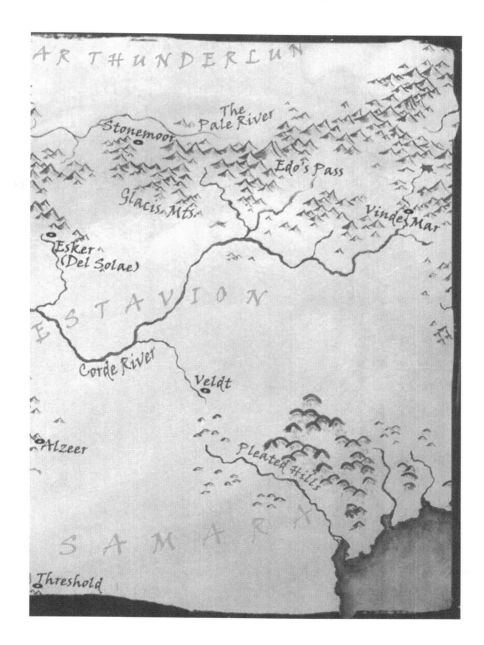

One

"Good morning, lieutenant. Come in."

I enter as the door closes behind me.

"I'm the royal arbiter, Rehoboth." The woman motions to the older man beside her. "I assume you know General Uriah."

I tilt from habit as the general nods.

Rehoboth indicates a nearby chair. "Please, sit."

I glance at the chair. It seems comfortable and inviting, a simple chair in a cozy room, and the other aesthetics around me complete the illusion. Warm tapestries depict lazy, rural life. A plush carpet cushions the stone floor. An intricately carved door shields us from interruption.

But it's a thin veneer. I know there are unyielding granite walls behind the tapestries and two sentries posted outside the heavy door. I wonder what treachery lurks behind Rehoboth's relentless smile and immaculate attire, and I stay standing.

"As you wish," Rehoboth concedes. With perfect poise, she sits beside Uriah behind the cedar desk that separates her bench from the judgment seat. "Can we fetch you anything?"

I don't answer.

"Tea, perhaps?"

"This isn't going to take that long," I finally say.

Her smile widens. "I'm sorry. You *do* know why you're here?"

"I read the summons."

"Then—"

"You've made a mistake, your grace," I cut in. "You think I'll incriminate him. But I won't."

"Lieutenant, please." She speaks soothingly, like she's trying to convince me there are no dragons under my bed. "You're only here to fill in the gaps."

"You have the wrong man. You should question Abner."

"We already did." She lifts a neat stack of parchment sheets. Her notes, I'm guessing. "Captain Abner left most of the gaps."

"Interview Damascus, then."

"He has refused to defend himself."

I don't believe that, not for a moment, but I just shrug and ask, "Can't you force his compliance?"

The arbiter chuckles. "Even if we could, I doubt he'd provide straight answers."

"And you expect something different from me?"

Rehoboth's smile cracks. She glances at Uriah.

Like a trained dog, the general growls. "You're an experienced soldier, Mordecai. A Vanguard agent. Surely you're capable of some professional objectivity."

I approach the desk. "You want my report, the story of my redemption. My life is forever changed, and you expect objectivity?"

"We expect the truth," Rehoboth tries again.

"The truth?" It's my turn to laugh. "Then why are we behind closed doors?"

Rehoboth raises an eyebrow. "Would you rather we open an official investigation? Start a trial? Call witnesses?"

"That would not end well," Uriah assures me. "You instigated a war. There are many angry people who need someone to blame."

"If you think I'm responsible, just execute me. Don't waste my time."

Rehoboth leans closer. She asks something I didn't expect: "Are you responsible?"

Good question.

But I don't reply. Instead I scan the room again. My eyes settle on the long desk that separates me from my interrogators. I notice

One

the objects lying there, Rehoboth's collection of evidence. Her research has produced impressive results thus far. She's already gathered samples of the strange alkali powder. She's confiscated the cursed obsidian armor, white shards from the porcelain horse and those delicate lace gloves. There's something else too—a small object wrapped in a folded scrap of velvet.

No! Rehoboth, you fool!

My pulse throbs. My hands tremble and sweat. I bite my tongue to stem curses that demand release, but Uriah notices my mania.

"Lieutenant?"

I inhale deeply, and when I look up to his earnest eyes, I find an anchor against the inner storm that threatens to drag me away. He's playing his part well—I'll give him that. For the briefest moment, I actually believe the general cares about my fate, and maybe he does. Perhaps if he hears the story—the whole story—he'll understand why my actions were necessary. Maybe he'll even absolve me. I was acting partially under his orders, after all.

Rehoboth will be harder to convince. I could probably rearrange the stars sooner than change the condemnation behind that smile, but I don't have a choice. I can't remain quiet, not if the stone is here. No, she must be warned. Otherwise she may try it herself, and I can't allow that.

I sink into the comfortable chair. I swallow the spines in my throat and gather my thoughts. There can be no mistakes. I must be absolutely precise. I must say the right things in the right sequence for the right reasons, or they might draw the wrong conclusion.

Soon I'm ready. "Very well, I'll speak."

"Thank you," Rehoboth chimes.

"But I won't just fill the gaps," I add. "If you want the truth, then you must hear it. All of it."

The Fifth Summit

My involvement in this catastrophe started in late summer, about five months ago. It was the kind of day that had once left me feeling blessed to be alive, but on that particular morning the sun was too hot and the air was too dry. The heat left my nostrils raw and my skin leathery. Besides that, my stomach was knotted and my throat was parched, both afflicted by the devastating drought that was then entering its fourteenth year, by most accounts.

I hardly noticed the discomfort, though. I was focused on my work. I was standing in the citadel's auxiliary training yard with about twenty recruits, brave and loyal soldiers handpicked from the regular corps for the Vanguard elite. These exceptional men were entering the last stages of their initiation, and as their instructor I was finally teaching them the most advanced tactics. I stood opposite the class leader, an impressive man named Caleb who was dressed, like me, in a loose-fitting canvas sparring suit.

Caleb was perhaps the best recruit I had ever trained, undeniably my favorite of that group. He was decisive, lean, dedicated and fiercely loyal. For whatever reason, he wanted nothing more than to join the Vanguard, protect Estavion and serve the king. I had chosen him specifically for a demonstration to test his quality, and he was circling me without sword or spear, watching carefully. His classmates, meanwhile, listened to my instructions.

"Misdirection," I was saying, "is your ultimate weapon. Your enemy may possess better armor and training. He may even have sharper instincts and reflexes. Nevertheless, all those advantages can be nullified with a deliberate feint. If you lead your opponent wrong, make him believe you've made a mistake, and then strike when he least expects—"

But at that moment, someone interrupted my lesson. From behind, a young voice cried, "Lieutenant!" I turned away from Caleb to answer the messenger, and my student attacked.

It was a good move. A fair move. I hadn't officially paused the exercise, after all. I had only looked away, so he capitalized on the distraction. He hadn't been truly paying attention, though. While I had been speaking to the other recruits, Caleb had been watching for an opening. He hadn't heard my caution against misdirection, so he surged forward, leapt into the air, and thrust his leg toward my unprotected back.

I was waiting for this. Expecting it. Hoping even. It didn't matter that I couldn't see him. I heard his bare feet scuff against the sandy pavement, I noticed him grunt as he leapt into the air, and I knew he would strike center mass because I had taught him that tactic. So I shifted left, twisted sideways, dodged his attack, and caught his leg while he was still flying through the air. Then I redirected his momentum downward, slammed him into the granite tiles, and finished with my knee resting against his chest.

The class murmured its approval of the demonstration while Caleb rubbed a bruise forming on his skull. "You won't be so lucky next time."

"If we weren't practicing, there wouldn't be a next time." I smiled at his gall, though, and offered my hand to help him up.

Then something else occurred to him. His mouth fell open. "You arranged for the messenger to interrupt, didn't you?"

I laughed. "No, I merely took advantage of an unexpected situation." I turned to the messenger. "Isn't that right?"

"I don't know nothing 'bout that," the boy gasped. "You're Mordecai, aren't you?"

"That's right."

The Fifth Summit

The frantic servant pushed a folded parchment note into my hands. It was sealed with a smear of black wax imprinted with two long swords crossed in an X.

"A letter from the high general?" Caleb peered over my shoulder. "What's it say?"

"Never mind that. Dismiss the class. Go get washed."

Caleb obeyed begrudgingly, and I couldn't blame him. Most soldiers never see Uriah's seal in their life. Fewer still receive personal messages. I myself had only received one once before on the day I had been reassigned from Veldt to Tel Tellesti, so I opened the note cautiously, hoping I would not find new orders that would take me hence.

As I read, sweat trickled into my eye. "Are you certain about this?" I asked the messenger. "It's most unusual."

The boy lowered his voice. "I think it's because of Masada."

"He's finally arrived?"

"Yes, but he broke the terms. Instead of the expected number, he brought an army."

My stomach tightened. "How many?"

"A thousand. Maybe more."

"I see. Then tell Uriah we'll report at once."

The messenger nodded and dashed away across the pavement toward the keep. I paused a moment, my eyes pressed shut, until I remembered that I had dismissed my students.

"Wait!"

To a man, the twenty recruits paused in the training yard.

"Change of plans," I announced, stepping before them with my arms folded behind my back. "You are all aware of the drought and famine that have ravaged the Inheritance these past years. You have also heard rumors, no doubt, of the secret Summit convened by our king with the other estate leaders."

Heads nodded around me. Men exchanged nervous glances. Then Caleb spoke. "Doesn't the Summit start soon?"

"It starts today, actually. Over the past week, the various leaders have been arriving with their delegations and escorts, and everything is ready at the Foundation," I said. "Lord Masada of Near Thunderlun, however, delayed his journey and arrived only this morning, and instead of bringing one hundred guards, as specified, he brought one thousand."

A second round of anxious glances passed among my men.

"One thousand ghosts?"

A good question. I checked the letter again. "It doesn't say."

That didn't help the mood.

"King Everett has proven gracious," I added, "and Uriah has been accommodating. He's exercising caution, though, and with the Vanguard spread thin on relief efforts, he feels that citadel defense is lacking." I took a deep breath. "So you're being pressed into service early."

Caleb smiled. Other heads and hearts rose proudly. Only one man asked, "Are you sure we're ready?"

"It doesn't matter what I think," I countered. "You're to visit the armory, dress in uniform, and report to the eastern narthex. We'll reinforce the sentries there, and our added presence will hopefully deter the Glacians from anything rash. Understood?"

Twenty heads nodded in unison.

"Good. Then dismissed. I'll meet you there."

When my men ran from the training yard toward the armory, I turned in the opposite direction. I didn't need a new uniform. As a Vanguard lieutenant, I already had the standard apparel stored under my bunk in the barracks. I still wished I could go with Caleb and the other recruits, though. I wished I was like them, inexperienced and ignorant of what the day meant.

I wished I wasn't so scared.

They only knew the basics, the rumors and "facts" recorded in our annals. They knew this drought and the resulting famine was the longest and most widespread epidemic in the history of the Eastern Estates. They had seen how the heavens had denied us all but the scantest spatters of rain. How the rivers had run dry. How entire harvests had turned to dust and reserves had dwindled until fear of starvation crept into the hearts of every man, woman, and child in Estavion.

They didn't know the deeper truth, though. Caleb and the others—no, the whole nation. No one knew about the raids that had followed in the south. No one heard the rumors of ghosts stirring in the north. But I did.

I thought it pathetic, actually, how quickly we had regressed. I hoped we were beyond such belligerence. After discovering the Inheritance so many centuries ago, we had enjoyed unrivaled prosperity for generations. Each estate had found cities vast enough to house its growing population. We had terraced fields and irrigation systems that could guarantee bountiful harvests year after year, and I had assumed such consistency would have transformed us, made us better somehow. But I was wrong.

On the contrary, once the drought started we reverted within years. Instead of tightening our belts, we stole from our friends. Our cities raided each other for resources, and even worse, they reached across our borders and attacked our neighbors. In less than a decade, we undermined every good relation and betrayed every ally. Soon we were clawing at each other's throats again, like dogs fighting over scraps in the gutter.

Then the Samarans violated our southern border and sacked Veldt. Threats of war emerged. We faced a continental crisis that threatened to tear the Inheritance apart.

Peter Michael Diamantopoulos

The sole point of pride in this whole disaster was our king, who had wisely intervened before the crisis became common knowledge and spiraled out of control. He had hoped, I suppose, that if he sent messengers and invited the other leaders of the Eastern Estates to his citadel, they could then talk honestly, reach a compromise and avoid armed conflict. Such was his devotion to peace.

From the hushed rumors that saturated the Vanguard ranks, however, I knew the other estate leaders did not share our king's optimism. They viewed his invitation to Tel Tellesti as a stalling tactic, meant to distract them while Estavion reinforced its borders and mustered its armies. It took months to convince the Samarans to attend. In the distant north, Lord Masada of Near Thunderlun also seemed suspicious. For the better part of a year, he delayed the Summit by disputing the terms, and now that he had finally come, he hadn't even followed the allotment he himself had specified. Instead of one hundred soldiers, he had brought one thousand. He knew our Vanguard were spread thin, and he dared to enter the ageless citadel with enough strength to threaten those that remained.

That's why my recruits were being stationed in the narthex.

I was anxious, therefore, because I knew what this Summit meant. I understood the stakes. I knew that if the conference failed, the Estates would once again plunge into war. Caleb might see a battle for which he was unprepared. Indeed, if the Summit did not go perfectly, each of my men might die that very day.

I tried to push that thought from my mind, though, and focus on the simple tasks at hand, so I rushed to the barracks and my bunk. I didn't have time to bathe or shave, but I unfastened the wide leather belt, stripped off the canvas pants and tunic, and donned my uniform. Ignoring the heat, I pulled on the leather pants and tall boots. I slipped my gambeson over my head before adding gold-plated chainmail, a polished breastplate and studded bracers. The belt returned to support the folded-steel broadsword hanging in its scabbard, and last of all I added the vermilion mantle, my favorite item. I wrapped the heavy cloak around my shoulders and arranged the red fabric so that it draped over half my chest and accented the gilded mail and silver armor.

Appropriately dressed, I left the barracks, crossed the training yard again, and entered the central complex of Tel Tellesti's citadel. I strode through crowded stone corridors and up twisting staircases, and soon I reached the great hall's eastern entrance.

My men had arrived ahead of me, and they were busy finding places among the other fifty sentries already posted in the expansive narthex. Some carried spears and shields, according to their expertise, while others only carried swords. They were each dressed like me, though, and my heart swelled unexpectedly at the sight. I had thought I would not see them thusly arrayed until their commencement, so I was ill prepared for this day. It had come too soon. Their first Vanguard assignment was already upon them, and I had no proud words for the occasion.

But there was no time for speeches. Not one minute after I arrived at our station, the trumpets and drums resounded within the hall. A hush fell over the sentries in the narthex, and I assumed a place beside Caleb near the middle of my men. Then I looked left through the great doors and witnessed the start of the Summit.

From my post, I had an unrestricted view of the cavernous hall. Under the flickering lights of fifty high candelabras, I could see Everett preparing to welcome his guests as they entered through the main doors at the opposite end. I could see General Uriah too, standing close to the king, and many more Vanguard lining the walls.

But there were Glacian soldiers inside as well. Hundreds of them clustered in the corner, a resolute host cloaked in white.

Caleb's voice spoke in my ear. "Ghosts?"

"I don't think so," I whispered back. "You wouldn't see ghosts until it was too late. Those are regulars."

"They don't look so fearsome."

"That's because you can't see what's under those robes," I cautioned. "Just hold your position and stay alert."

As I spoke, a herald began announcing the delegations. The Samaran Empress came first with a few dozen attendants, and she warmly greeted our king and high general. The Celadon Council arrived next in a discombobulated mess, with all their numerous dignitaries jostling in line. For the better part of fifteen minutes, each patriarch filed past Everett, and each tried to flatter him with a joke, compliment or morsel of savory gossip.

Then at last, the Lord of Thunderlun arrived. Masada entered the vast hall with far too many bodyguards and vassals. The herald announced his title. A deafening shout rose from the Glacian soldiers, and my hand instinctively grasped my sword.

"This is it," Caleb whispered.

Nothing happened, though. With surprising grace, Masada calmed his cheering men and humbly bowed before our king. He presented General Uriah with a mysterious gift in an ivory box. He introduced some other members of his procession, and then he strode past to meet the other estate leaders before taking his assigned place at the Foundation, the ancient table of arbitration that dominated the center of the hall.

The setting was then gradually prepared. The roar of so many boisterous voices settled to an anxious murmur. Servants appeared from every corner and pattered across the granite floor to fill glasses, bring decadent foods, take cloaks and deliver messages. It was a painting of harmonious chaos, like wind rustling fields of wheat, and all these sights and sounds coalesced with sweet smoke from the scented candles to create an astonishingly majestic scene.

The Fifth Summit

But I didn't like it. My hand stayed on my hilt. I couldn't bear the sight of so many Glacians so close to our king. I didn't understand why Uriah had posted most of the Vanguard outside the hall and not within, and despite the prevalent atmosphere of comradere and cooperation, I still felt some underlying tension, like a heavy odor of sweat that even the strongest perfume could not mask.

The estate leaders felt it too. I could see it in their shifting eyes and vacillating hands. On every face I clearly saw the heavy burden of rule, the clear understanding that if they couldn't develop a solution to the drought, every nation would suffer the bitter consequences, and they would soon see each other again. Next time, though, they would not meet in an ancient Ascendant citadel, but on the bloody battlefield.

That's if we were lucky.

If we were unlucky, the war might start in that room, perhaps that very day. Indeed, at the slightest provocation, Lord Masada or one of his advisors might lose his temper, lash out, and murder whatever unfortunate fool happened to be closest. He may command his one thousand men to attack. And then? I didn't want to think about what might happen then. My men and I were in the narthex at least thirty paces from the Foundation. We were fast, I knew, but we would still require at least ten seconds to reach the king and assist General Uriah, and a lot can happen in ten seconds.

As the preliminary affairs continued, I grew more nervous and wished I could have moved closer. I even started questioning Uriah's wisdom. My men also grew restless, and despite their discipline, I heard whispers all around me. I didn't bother to quiet them, though. I let them talk. I let their nerves slowly fray. It would keep them alert and ready, I knew, and better prepared for the unthinkable.

Then the whispers abruptly ceased. A hallowed hush fell over the narthex. In the sudden silence I heard light, padded footfalls, almost silent, like those of an assassin, and I turned fast, my fingers still tight around the hilt of my sword.

But when I saw her, the young heiress named Amethyst, my apprehension vanished. Indeed, all my trepidation evaporated as I beheld that small girl for the first time.

I can hardly describe that hypnotizing moment, and at the time I wasn't sure what mesmerized me most. I thought perhaps it was the shimmering alabaster gown that cascaded around her, or the golden curls that framed her focused eyes and fair complexion.

Now, however, I know exactly what captured me, because it was the same thing that captured everyone else in the narthex. It was her confidence. Her poise. She was slender and frail, and she couldn't have been more than sixteen, but when the herald rattled off her complete title (which I somehow didn't catch), Amethyst entered the great hall with the authority of a revered queen. The gathered dignitaries fell silent and rose respectfully. The many soldiers, Glacian and migrant alike, snapped to attention. The world held its breath.

Then Amethyst approached the raised dais, stepped behind the podium, and faced the gathered host. In a strong voice that echoed throughout the ancient citadel, the heiress delivered the Summit's opening address.

"Gathered lords, great empress, my gracious liege," she said, tilting respectfully to Everett, "I thank you for coming. At this time of such incredible peril, you have offered your hearts and minds to the trials facing our peoples. Before we set to the task, however, I thought it fitting to pause and reflect—to consider where we have been, so that we might remember best where we should go. Therefore, if you will indulge me, I will remind you of our proud history. I will take us back into myth and legend, to the foundation of our existence."

Grunts of consent rose from the Foundation.

"I must start at the very beginning, when the Ascendants discovered this realm so many eons ago. Our predecessors found an expanse devoid of life but teeming with possibility, and from that barren wasteland they fashioned a new world—a grand legacy. With

The Fifth Summit

unsurpassed wisdom and foresight, they raised the mountains and excavated valleys. They carved arteries and veins through the deserts and planted lush forests to border the plains. They cultivated endless fields and anchored the islands in the sea. They built vast cities, erected monuments and sanctuaries, and laid a network of granite roads to connect the four estates. Some even say," Amethyst added with a smirk, "they flung the stars into the sky."

That particular comment produced splashes of laughter.

"And then, after exhausting their miracles, they left," Amethyst continued. "At the pinnacle of their civilization, after achieving unparalleled peace and prosperity, the Ascendants rose into the heavens to fashion a new paradise. They became the first angels, and from their new home they watched and waited.

"We eventually followed. Chasing the promises of the blessed realm foretold by our prophets, we ventured over the oceans and crossed the frozen tundra. We braved the Impasse, and we all discovered a bountiful gift—an Inheritance greater than anyone imagined. A new world where we could grow and prosper. A whole continent prepared for us, complete with cities, roads, fields and homes, all empty and waiting, ready for us to claim and make our own. So we did.

"Sadly, our bliss was short-lived. Like children squabbling over scraps while ignoring the feast on the table, we fought over territory and prestige. Instead of embracing each other as lost siblings, we clashed with swords and spears for centuries. With selfish hearts, we nearly tore ourselves asunder, and we almost ruined the legacy.

"But then, a thousand years ago when all hope seemed lost, the Peacekeeper appeared. The great King Viticus called an assembly in the ancient Ascendant citadel of Tel Tellesti. In this very city, in this very room and *at this very table*, he convened the First Summit. He united Glacians, migrants, clansmen and nomads. He laid the Foundation. He forged the First Alliance. On that day, Viticus brought peace to the Inheritance, and from that moment on we've stayed strong.

"The path has been perilous. Our fragile harmony has been threatened by insurrection, betrayal and plague. After a few prosperous centuries, even the First Alliance dissolved, and our nations separated into the four distinct estates again. Despite these challenges, however, we've remained committed to peace, and whenever tribulation threatens, we've remembered our proud history. When all else fails, we've convened the Summit and emerged victorious, and we shall again.

"Therefore, on behalf of my gracious lord, the High King Everett Viticus of Estavion, I welcome you to the Fifth Summit. From the northern estate of Near Thunderlun, I welcome Lord Masada." Amethyst smiled warmly at the Glacian lord. "From the Chersonese clans, I greet our eastern allies, the Celadon Council. From the south, from the Samaran Empire, I welcome our dear sister-in-arms, the Empress Yuridonna. To all of you, I extend my deepest gratitude, for you are here, united under one roof, for one purpose. You have answered the summons. You have come to rescue our Inheritance again from doom. And for that great service, I commend you."

The great hall erupted with applause. At the Foundation, the leaders of the Eastern Estates rose to congratulate the heiress and pledge support of her ideals, and for a split-second, for a delicious moment, far too brief, even I believed the Summit might succeed.

Two

"Pardon me, lieutenant," Rehoboth says. "I'm sorry for the interruption, but I must ask, why are you calling her Amethyst?"

"Who? The heiress?"

"Yes."

"That's her name," I say simply.

Rehoboth glances at Uriah, and she's not smiling.

"That *is* her name," I repeat. "Isn't it?"

Uriah leans toward Rehoboth and whispers just loud enough so I can hear. "Damascus calls her Amethyst. For her protection."

"*Who* does he call Amethyst?" I spent nearly half a year with the girl. How did I never learn her true name?

"That does not concern the case. Or you," Rehoboth says. "Now please, if you would, lieutenant. Continue."

Ten Seconds

It was a superb performance, especially for one so young. Never mind that Amethyst glossed over a few unsavory points in her romantic version of history, like the fact that Viticus had to crush the Glacian horde before they agreed to attend that first summit a thousand years ago. She spoke strong and loud in that great hall, and her speech transformed the prevalent tension into determination. It also prompted instant admiration. Even Lord Masada seemed impressed, and before the Summit commenced he left the Foundation long enough to climb the dais, grasp her hand, and whisper something that made Amethyst blush.

Then as our king read the orders of business and as the estate leaders settled themselves for the difficult task ahead, the young heiress dismissed herself, slipped out the eastern entrance and passed my station in the narthex.

She didn't speak to me, of course. I doubt she even noticed me or any of my men, and why would she? We were adornments to her, a few soldiers guarding the narthex. She was an heiress, the teenage daughter of some nobleman, no doubt chosen from a host of rivals for the honored privilege of addressing the estate leaders and commencing the Fifth Summit.

Besides, the profundity of her accomplishment had finally struck, and angst had replaced her confidence. She had somehow bottled all the burdens from the great hall and carried them hither on her shoulders, so now she was sweating and hyperventilating, trying to catch her breath after so momentous an experience, perhaps the greatest of her life. I felt compelled to say something encouraging, but before I could think of anything appropriate, someone else rushed to her aid. From down the hallway, an elderly man approached.

Her grandfather, I presumed.

He was ancient, I must say. I've never seen someone so old, with wrinkled hands and a creased brow. Still, he had kind eyes, thin lips curled in a gentle smile, and a properly trimmed beard to match. He wore pressed linen robes and possessed a youthful energy that defied his age, and when Amethyst noticed him, her entire body relaxed. Indeed, his mere presence proved more comforting than anything I could have mustered, and she reached out for him.

"Damascus? Damascus! Did you see?"

"Splendid, my dear child! Splendid," the man proclaimed, his arms outstretched in victory.

"I was so nervous," she said, grasping him, "and the whole time Lord Masada just sat there, daring me to make a mistake."

"But you didn't. You were perfect!"

"I never imagined he'd be so large and pale—and *intense*."

"He's as terrible as you expected, then?"

"Much worse," she giggled.

"I'm curious." Damascus stepped closer. "What exactly did he whisper in that pretty ear of yours?"

She looked down and the clarity returned. "He said I must make my tutor very proud."

The old man's smile deepened. "Well, he was certainly right about that."

So he wasn't her grandfather.

I wasn't certain I had heard him right, and it didn't help that as he spoke, Damascus reached out and pulled a silk ribbon from Amethyst's hair so the glowing strands could cascade around her slender shoulders. This was an intimate, personal act that he reinforced by softly caressing her cheek. I distinctly remember thinking they didn't appear like student and teacher, and I coveted their intimacy.

Ten Seconds

In fact, their actions stirred unexpected tremors in my heart. Painful memories I thought I had buried long ago surged into mind. My chest tightened and my mouth grew dry, so I turned away and tried to focus again on the Summit proceedings. I couldn't stop my ears without breaking form, though, so I had no choice but to overhear when their conversation resumed.

"Damascus," she said anxiously.

"Yes, Amethyst?"

"Do you think my speech was enough?"

"Of course! I wrote it, didn't I?"

"No. I mean—" She glanced at the floor as if she had dropped something, like her confidence.

"Amethyst?"

"Did my speech inspire anyone?" she finally said. "Do you think the Summit will succeed?"

"Ah. That is the question of the day, isn't it?"

"Father said the outcome is predetermined," she commented, her eyes still downcast.

"Did he now?"

"He said the Glacians are desperate because the famine is so much more severe to the north. He said Masada's people are suffering worse than ours."

"That probable. Near Thunderlun has always been a touch less hospitable. And your father's sources are usually accurate."

"So?"

"So…what?"

She locked onto his gray eyes. "What does that mean?"

Damascus sighed while Amethyst awaited his answer. I waited too, hoping his next words might dissuade the common panic. We were both disappointed.

"My dear," Damascus eventually said, "these are difficult times. They are among the worst I've ever seen, and while a wise man must always remain optimistic, a wiser man should also remember that men, at their core, are still men. They are not gods or angels. They are not Ascendant. If they are desperate enough, and if they can validate their actions, then even the best men, with the best intentions, can commit the greatest of evils."

Amethyst didn't respond. She studied the granite floor underneath her padded slippers. As for me, I held my breath and glanced back through the open doors and into the great hall, where Lord Masada was already standing and arguing with three of the Chersonese patriarchs. Behind him, the Glacian soldiers drifted from their assigned place in the corner.

"But that," Damascus continued, "is a concern for a later day. Not today. Not while the sun shines and the Summit might succeed. Hmm?"

"I suppose."

"Why don't we go out?"

She hesitated, confused. "But—but my lessons."

"Oh, I think we can skip your lessons. Just for today."

Her face brightened.

"How about a walk? Hmm? Some fresh air? It's rather warm, but we could wander along the canal. Visit the fountains."

"And Avram," she added. "Could we visit Avram?"

"Avram?" Damascus straightened. "I suppose. But why—"

She turned away, suddenly blushing again.

"Why Amethyst, my dear girl. You haven't acquired an unhealthy interest in Avram's son, have you?"

"I lent him my bow," she explained. "I want it back."

"Indeed."

"It's been almost two months. I need to practice."

Damascus only nodded his head. "You know, he's not of noble birth."

Amethyst rolled her eyes and turned to leave. Damascus called after, instructing her to meet him in the atrium once she changed out of her formal regalia, but she only waved a hand in acknowledgement

Ten Seconds

before disappearing down the ancient hallway. A moment later, Damascus chuckled to himself, sighed happily and left in the opposite direction.

I was glad to see them go.

Their whole conversation had made me uncomfortable. They were so trusting and intimate, a cruel reminder of the simple things I had abandoned for the sake of duty. They were also distracting me from the Summit. But I had my instructions, so I remained at my station with my men. During their entire discussion, half of which made no sense to me, I said not a word for fear I might remind them of my presence, and when they finally left, I breathed easier.

Then I noticed the white ribbon lying on the granite floor.

Amethyst must have accidentally dropped it after removing it from her hair, and she would surely miss it. I paused long enough to glance through the eastern entrance, but once I saw that Lord Masada was no longer verbally assaulting the other diplomats, I did something I've never considered before, not even in my most irresponsible moments.

I left my post.

My sudden movement confused the other Vanguard and drew concerned stares. Caleb even said, "Where are you going?"

"Just stay here. I'll be back in a moment."

I don't know what I was thinking. Maybe I wasn't thinking at all. I just knew Amethyst would want her ribbon, so I scooped up the silk band and chased the heiress down the hallway. It didn't seem proper leaving my men in the narthex, but I thought I could find the young lady, return the ribbon, and resume my post before anyone else noticed I was gone. I was certain, too, that nothing would happen at the Summit, not in the ten seconds my errand would require.

The first part of my assumption did prove true. I did find the heiress down the hallway, around a corner, and opening her chamber door. When I showed her the lost ribbon, she did smile and compliment my thoughtfulness.

But then I heard something unnatural and horrifying, like a tempest funneled through a narrow window. I felt a blast of heat emanating from inside her room, and I hurled myself against Amethyst as a billowing fireball tore through her doorway and engulfed us both.

Three

"You're a brave man."

"I did my duty, your grace. I did what any other Vanguard would have done."

"I doubt that," Rehoboth says, flattering me with that hollow smile. "Most men would have stared stupefied while the explosion ripped the girl in half. They would have never acted so quickly."

"We're just lucky I was wearing armor," I say.

"Yes. Lucky."

"And she's lucky she dropped that ribbon," I carefully point out. "Otherwise—"

"I was listening, lieutenant."

ALKALI

At the time, I didn't think Amethyst was fortunate. As the flames consumed her room and flashed into the hallway, I threw myself against her, hoping my vermilion cloak would shield us both. Her bare right arm somehow slipped out from behind my protection, though, and the heat instantly stripped the hair and skin from her forearm. Then we were falling backward, her beneath me, and to cushion the fall she reached down with her other arm, but it didn't work. Maybe if she only had to support her own weight, the effort would have sufficed, but I landed on top of her, so instead of breaking her fall, she broke her wrist.

Shrieks of agony followed. By the time the flames dispersed and I rolled off, Amethyst was hyperventilating again. Her right arm was scorched black and mangled from the elbow down, and her opposite wrist was bent unnaturally. With one glance at her contortions, I knew she was going into shock, so I grabbed her shoulders and shook gently. "Hold on, girl. Hold on!" Then I scooped her into my arms and ran for the infirmary.

She was rather light and the medical ward wasn't far away, but curious crowds were already congesting the granite hallways. Spectators and concerned guards rushed toward the sound of the explosion, and moving against that tide proved difficult. I had to scream at them to clear my path.

Once we reached the infirmary, I cried for help and lowered the trembling girl onto a bed as two maids and a physician rushed over. One of them asked what happened. I told them. I don't think I made much sense, though. The memory was too fresh and muddled in my mind, and I couldn't concentrate with Amethyst weeping and shivering, but she at least possessed the clarity to repeatedly cry someone's name.

"Damascus! DAMASCUS!"

One of the maids abruptly left to fetch Amethyst's tutor, and after I finished my fragmented explanation, the other maid started soaking bandages. The physician spread some kind of slimy balm over Amethyst's charred skin, but when she noticed me still standing there with mouth agape and legs locked, the doctor shoved me from the room.

"You've done all you can, lieutenant," she explained. "We'll let you know when she's stable." Then the physician shut the infirmary door and left me alone in the hallway.

For a long moment, I didn't move. I couldn't yet fathom how the girl, that strong heiress who had captivated the Summit just a few minutes ago, was now wailing on an infirmary bed. Her arms were broken or burnt. She might never use either again, at least not properly. Her life was forever changed.

I should know.

I've seen similar situations before. I've watched men writhe in unquenchable flame. Those poor bastards had been soldiers, though, men who were cognizant of such risks and had pledged their lives to serve king and country. Seldom had I witnessed such violence against children, and I wondered who could do such a thing, and on the first day of the Summit no less.

I wondered then about the assassin that had left the firebomb in Amethyst's room. Did he know whom he was targeting? Was he acting alone, or was someone else directing him? I wondered, too, if he knew how precarious that day was, but that question at least quickly answered itself. Maybe Amethyst was an accidental target, and maybe the assassin had indiscriminately picked her chambers, but the timing was not random. Whoever planned this attack knew exactly what day it was, and he knew that if word reached the Foundation, baseless accusations would soon follow. The Summit might fail.

But that wouldn't happen. Not while I could stop it.

So I left. Since I couldn't observe Amethyst, I backtracked through the corridors and staircases that led to her room. Somewhere along the way, I passed Damascus and the maid rushing in the opposite direction toward to the infirmary. I also noticed, as I passed, a crowd of Vanguard, servants and officials already gathering outside Amethyst's charred chambers, so I stopped long enough to position guards at the door and give them specific instructions not to allow anyone inside. To detain the crowd, I pulled Caleb and my other men from the narthex and posted them at either end of that hallway. An extreme measure, perhaps, but necessary. I couldn't have those people wandering off and spreading rumors. Not yet, anyway. Not while our fate hung in the balance.

With Amethyst's chamber thusly secured, I passed through the half-empty narthex again and slipped into the great hall. The Summit proceedings were still underway, thankfully, undisturbed by the explosion. Perhaps they hadn't even heard. They were discussing something rather passionately, and Lord Masada was standing and arguing loudly again, this time with the Samaran Empress, but I didn't listen. Instead, I scanned the hall, thinking the assassin was hidden among the dignitaries or soldiers. Maybe I could spot some consternation, a faint trace of emotion that might betray some underlying treachery. Surely if the guilty man was there, he had noticed my abrupt entrance and guessed what I had witnessed. His lips might curl in satisfaction or fear.

Unfortunately, I detected no such suspicious emotions. Every eye was trained on Lord Masada's outburst, and no one paid attention to me, so I started looking for someone else, the only person who could help me.

I found General Uriah right where I expected, seated beside the king at the Foundation, and he likewise noticed me. With his squinted eyes, he told me I shouldn't be in the great hall. He silently asked why I wasn't at my post, and what happened to my uniform and hair. Why were they burnt? But I ignored those questions. I moved closer and leaned toward his ear. In a whisper meant only for him, I told him, "There's been an attempt on Amethyst's life." Then I watched the color drain from his face.

He held his expression well enough. Somehow he managed to politely excuse himself and casually follow me from the great hall without arousing suspicion or interrupting the Summit. Once outside in the narthex, though, his eyes hardened and his smile vanished. He grabbed my arm and whispered, "What happened, lieutenant?"

I told him everything. About Damascus and Amethyst talking in the narthex. How she had dropped the ribbon and I had chased after her. How her chambers had been consumed, and especially how her arms might never be the same again.

"What about Damascus?" Uriah interjected. "Did someone move against him too?"

"I don't think so. I saw him headed to the infirmary to check on Amethyst."

"Good. That's good," Uriah said, suddenly relieved. "He'll fix her up nicely. That leaves her chambers to us."

We returned to the grisly scene, where Uriah commended my initiative to contain the curious crowd. He also addressed the numerous complaints that arose the moment we reappeared, and with impressive clarity he spoke to the detainees. "I'm sorry," he announced, "but we cannot allow anyone to leave. Not yet. This is a sensitive matter, and it must not become public knowledge, so please, wait a little longer."

With their concerns thusly addressed, General Uriah and I entered Amethyst's blasted quarters, and my heart sank.

The room was a total loss, much worse than I expected. I've never seen anything that compares, and I've witnessed more than my fair share of arson. Every surface in that chamber—the slate floor, the granite walls, the high ceiling—was charred black and infused with a foul, unnatural stench. The blaze had also vaporized every shred of fabric, from the silk bed sheets and the satin upholstery to the heavy tapestries and plush carpets. Even the resilient cedar furniture had been burned beyond repair.

It was overwhelming. I remembered Amethyst's face, when she had been lying under me in the hallway, her arms burnt and broken, her hazel eyes wide with shock. Was that how I looked then? I didn't like that thought. I couldn't bear feeling so far beyond control.

There was something else disturbing too, something odd I couldn't at first identify. Something unnatural that reminded me of the hissing sound the fireball had made before it burst through the doorway and reached out to devour me. After standing there for perhaps five minutes and sifting through the blacked pieces of furniture that littered the room, though, the aberration finally hit me. It was the furniture, the tables and chairs. They were all scorched, as expected, but they weren't sitting in the usual places were they had been before the blaze started. They were strewn about, and most of the smaller pieces were smashed to bits as if some rabble of thieves had hurled each piece against the walls.

At first I guessed this anomaly was indeed caused by thieves. Maybe the timing was coincidental and this wasn't an assassination attempt after all. Perhaps the firebomb was only meant to conceal some much simpler crime, like a theft. But no. The dispersal pattern didn't support that assumption. If some person had done this, the furniture would have been tossed about erratically as he moved through the room in search of his prize. There was a pattern, though, and now that I recognized what was bothering me, I could clearly see how all the furniture had been thrown outward toward the walls by some great vortex focalized near the doorway, perhaps only three or four paces inside the room.

Still, I couldn't imagine what could have caused that effect, so the first words from my mouth weren't especially insightful. I just said, "I've never seen anything like this."

"Nor I," Uriah admitted.

I sucked in some air to calm my quavering heart but choked on the lingering smoke instead. I surveyed the debris field again, imaging how the fireball must have radiated outward and surged throughout the room. It reminded me of the whirlwinds I'd witnessed over the fields near Veldt when I was stationed there. "What would it take to do this?"

Uriah thoughtfully stroked his speckled beard. "A few cord of wood. A few barrels of oil. A candle."

"But that would've burned slow and long. It would've burned everything to ash," I pointed out, noticing another chair that had been hurled against the wall of Amethyst's chamber with force enough to reduce it to kindling. "This was sudden. Violent."

"I know."

We stood there a few minutes longer, silently studying the incomprehensible damage. We searched for ash or oil, for any evidence of arson, but we found nothing unusual except some sprinklings of gray powder that I dismissed as dust particles blasted loose from the ceiling.

"Any ideas?" Uriah eventually asked.

"No." Then I tacked on, "What will you tell the king?"

He turned and looked at me, and for the first time I detected a trace of amusement. "You think I'm going to tell the king?"

I didn't answer. I was too confused.

Uriah didn't wait for me to gather my thoughts. "In case you haven't noticed, lieutenant, I'm a general. Everett didn't promote me because I'm good at filing reports. He promoted me because I'm good at fixing problems."

I still didn't answer.

"Don't worry," he added. "I *will* notify Everett, but not yet. Not until I have answers for the questions he'll ask. I must first know who did this and why."

Suddenly I was glad I had trusted Uriah. Despite the chaotic moments following the bomb, I had somehow picked right and chosen the clearheaded general as my confidant. I still wasn't as calm as he. I wasn't sure how we could keep this disaster secret for the next few days while the Summit continued, especially with so many witnesses detained outside in the hallway, but for the first time since Amethyst's speech, I relaxed a little and breathed easier. Maybe the Inheritance wasn't doomed. Maybe the assassin hadn't won.

Then Damascus arrived on the scene.

His presence surprised me. I had assumed he would stay by Amethyst's bedside for the foreseeable future, but perhaps she had been sedated and Damascus felt useless waiting by her side. His temperament contradicted that hypothesis, however. He was, like the general, remarkably calm considering the circumstances, but Damascus took his detachment one step further. He seemed almost excited to be there, and had I not known any better, I would have never guessed a senseless tragedy had befallen his student just minutes prior.

"I came as soon as I heard," he explained as he threaded the guards stationed at the entrance. "Well actually, I visited the infirmary first. Then I came as fast as I could."

"It's all right." Uriah smiled at the tutor's enthusiasm. "You needn't have come at all."

"Oh? You've already determined the cause?"

"No, but—"

"Then I've arrived just in time," Damascus announced.

Uriah narrowed his eyes and gave Damascus the same look he had given me when I had approached the Foundation, the look that said, "Isn't there someplace better for you to be?" Then he uttered almost exactly those words. "Surely you'd rather be with your pupil."

"Oh, she's fine. Just wonderful. No need to fret. I expect a full recovery." Damascus waved off Uriah's concerns. "She's resting comfortably now, so I may as well lend a hand."

"As I said, that's not necessary," Uriah persisted.

"Nonsense," Damascus replied as he surveyed the blasted room. "Someone tried to murder my student. Why shouldn't I be here?"

Uriah opened his mouth to provide such a reason.

But Damascus kept going. "Besides, who do you have that's more qualified? Who else has devoted his life to knowledge and science? Hmm? Do you have another world-class historian on call? Someone else who's explored the farthest reaches of the Azure, or sailed past the Islands?"

"I've been to the Azure," I blurted out, eager to shut him up.

And with a sideways glance that could have launched spears through my chest, Damascus considered me suspiciously.

In that uncomfortable moment, it suddenly occurred to me that Damascus hadn't directly addressed me since his arrival. He had only interacted with General Uriah. Perhaps he hadn't even realized I was there, and now that he did notice, he didn't appreciate my presence. He glared at me as if my very existence were a stain on his conscience, a blemish he'd rather ignore, and he asked the general, "Uriah, who is this?"

"The name's Mordecai," I answered.

"He's a Vanguard lieutenant," Uriah clarified.

"I can see that," Damascus responded.

"And I *have* visited the Azure Forest," I repeated to highlight my usefulness.

"Have you?" Damascus smiled politely. "You mean you've been to the border. The Line."

"Yes."

"But you've never ventured *into* the forest, have you?"

"A little."

"A little? How delightful," he said with feigned fascination. "How far did you dare? A day? A week?"

"I—I don't know," I said, though I knew precisely. I had explored fifty paces before turning back, scared for my life.

Alkali

"You don't know?" Maybe Damascus read my mind. I don't know. It didn't seem beyond him. He knew I was lying, though, and in his gray eyes, I detected no trace of the compassion that had comforted Amethyst. There was only defiance. "I do know, lieutenant. I've been *three months* in. I've been lost in that endless forest. And do you know what's back there?"

I shook my head, reluctant to speak again.

"There's a city," he whispered. "A lost, Ascendant city. Can you believe that? Yet another city. Forgotten. Empty. Sleeping. Full of ancient wonders and mysteries. Just waiting for us."

"Another city?"

"Yes," Damascus nodded, "and that's just one of a million things I know that you don't, so please, from now on, stay quiet."

With his point made and me silenced, Damascus returned to the investigation. Without a hiccup, he resumed where he had left off, and with that same eager detachment he said, "Now, when I spoke with Amethyst, she mentioned an explosion."

"Yes," Uriah answered.

"And she was most specific about that. It wasn't a slow burn or a dull *whoosh*. It was a *boom!*" He clapped his hands and glanced at me for confirmation.

"That's correct," I admitted.

"But there's nothing here to create that affect," Uriah argued. "That kind of blast would require a dozen barrels of oil. There's no way anyone could have smuggled all that in here, not with the extra security I added for the Summit."

"True," Damascus admitted, stooping and reaching toward a puddle of water that had curiously collected on the smooth slate, "but what if something else caused the explosion? Something far more potent," he continued, shifting toward the nearest corner while scrutinizing every surface.

"Like what?"

"Aha!" Damascus announced victoriously.

Intrigued, Uriah stepped closer. I drew nearer too, though I stopped a comfortable distance away from Amethyst's teacher.

"Here we are!" Damascus pointed at a smear of gray powder, the same dust I had dismissed a few minutes before. He pressed his index finger into the powder and lifted a sample for us to see. "This is rather special," he explained like a professor broaching his favorite topic, "something I haven't seen in a long time. It's called alkali. It's quite fascinating, most amazing and incredibly rare. It's only found in one place in the entire world, far as I know. It seems innocent enough before it's processed, looks something like opaque chalk, but if you grind it into a fine powder, it's a powerful accelerant."

"That will burn?" Uriah asked skeptically, and I'm glad he did, for I was about to say the same thing myself.

"Oh, not by itself. It still requires an ignition source."

"Like a flame."

"No," Damascus said, shaking his head and wandering back toward the small puddle he had noticed before. "Water."

Then, before our very eyes, Damascus rubbed his index finger and thumb together, dislodging a few specks of the mysterious powder. These particles floated down like snowflakes alighting on a frozen pond, except when they touched the water, they burst into crackling flame. With a sharp pop and a puff of smoke, the water and the powder annihilated each other.

"Incredible." I heard myself say unintentionally, regretting I had ever doubted the old man's usefulness.

"Indeed," Damascus echoed, "and quite inconspicuous, I dare say. Even if your sentries had noticed the arsonist when he entered this room, they would have never guessed he possessed the components for a firebomb. It probably looked like he was carrying a bag of gray flour and a jar of wine, or perhaps a sack of granite dust and a jug of water. It's not until the ingredients are combined that anything disastrous happens, and by then it's too late."

Alkali

No one spoke for a few moments as we stared at puddle on the floor where we had just witnessed an alkali reaction. I don't know about the others, but for my own part I remained silent because I was trying to imagine how such a bomb might have been triggered. The tiny puddle remaining on the slate floor also confused me, though now I suppose that perhaps the explosion burned so rapidly that it didn't have time enough to vaporize all the water.

In my efforts to imagine the firebomb's design, I eventually settled on a theory that an alkali sack had been placed on the floor a few paces from the door at the focal point I had noticed earlier. Then a tall pitcher of water had been set next to it. That pitcher, in turn, could have been connected to the latch with a string so that the opening of the door would yank on the line, pull the pitcher, spill the water onto the alkali, and spark the reaction.

Unfortunately, there was a flaw with that theory, a problem I recognized as soon as I glanced at Amethyst's door, which opened inward, not outward. Any line connecting the latch and the water pitcher would just go slack once the door was opened, so my design must have been wrong.

I set at the puzzle again, but Uriah interrupted my thoughts before I made any progress. Apparently something else had stumped him, because he didn't ask about the firebomb's design. Instead, he said to Damascus, "Wait. You said alkali can only be found in one place?"

"Yes," Damascus said, resuming his informative lecture, "an extraordinary Ascendant construct. An ancient volcano, still active. The Glacians call it the Crucible of El'Shadon."

"The Glacians?"

"Of course. The volcano is in the north, the far north across the vast tundra, almost to Thunderlun itself. In fact, when I visited—"

But then Damascus stopped, and he didn't have to explain why. I knew exactly what he was thinking, because I had reached the same conclusion, and so had Uriah. The general now had his suspect, the name he must report to the king.

"Lord Masada."

Four

"Lieutenant, you *do* realize this isn't important."

I glance up, confused.

"You only need to fill in the gaps, remember?"

"That's not enough," I explain, irritated by the interruption, "and this *is* important. I'm sorry it's taking so long, but I'm only telling you what's absolutely necessary. I'm leaving out many details. I'm not describing the citadel or the—"

"I've noticed," Rehoboth interjects, "and I do appreciate that, yet you just explained a conversation in which General Uriah was present."

My eyes shift to the general, who is still sitting beside the arbiter. Uriah awkwardly waves back.

"Hello, lieutenant."

"Uriah's already provided his testimony, including that entire conversation," Rehoboth continues, lifting her notes. "He even provided a sample of the alkali." She points to her small collection of gray powder on the cedar desk.

I remain focused. "I just—I thought it necessary to emphasize what Damascus did."

"Emphasize?"

"Yes."

The smile falters again. "And what exactly did Damascus do?"

"He identified the alkali. He pointed us in the right direction," I stress. "Why do such a thing? If he is responsible, as you've assumed—"

"We've assumed no such thing."

I fall silent. I know Rehoboth's lying. I know she's only listening for certain things, the evidence she needs to prove her version of the truth. It's despicable, really, how she's abusing the system and manipulating the facts to support her predetermined conclusion, but I can't blame her. I'm doing the same thing.

So I say, "Of course, your grace. Forgive me."

Reassignment

It's sickening, when I think back on it.

At first, I thought the firebomb was devastating enough, but what happened afterward—after Damascus identified the alkali and fingered Masada—that was the real catastrophe. Uriah finally had a suspect, one that couldn't be ignored, so he had no choice but to inform the king. Then a whole different kind of bomb went off. Once Everett learned that someone from the north had detonated an explosive inside his beloved citadel, he rashly accused Lord Masada in front the other estate leaders. Enraged, the Glacians abandoned the Foundation and promised retribution, and sickened by such dissent, the Samarans and Chersonese departed soon after.

For the first time in written history, the Summit failed.

The following days plummeted into chaos. Suddenly another northern invasion seemed unavoidable, and this time our southern and eastern allies would not reinforce our ranks. To prepare for the impending conflict, therefore, the king recalled the Vanguard and mustered our reserves. Despite the ongoing drought, he hoped to gather our full strength to counter any offensive Near Thunderlun might launch in the coming months.

I wasn't involved with those decisions, of course. I'm simply a lieutenant, an insignificant cog in a great engine, but I played my part. I worked with Caleb and my other men, finalizing their training. I prepared my gear for the unlikely event that I'd be sent to the front. I sharpened my sword and swapped my burnt uniform for something new, but all the while, I was distracted. There was a question, you see, writhing inside my head, refusing to die.

Why would Masada sabotage the Summit?

This question nearly drove me mad. True, the pale Glacians were mysterious and dangerous, lurking behind their indomitable mountains. They've always been an enigma, and we've never had good relations with them. In the last major war that preceded the First Alliance a thousand years ago, the Glacians had attacked without provocation, explanation or warning, and their defeat had required the combined might of Estavion, Chersonia and Samara. I wasn't expecting their motives to make complete sense. Nor was it difficult to believe that they would prove devious once again.

But still, something didn't measure up. I couldn't imagine what motive might drive Masada or any official in his delegation to attack anyone in Tel Tellesti. His people were starving, just like ours. He needed the Summit to succeed. Surely he would have known that any violence would result in dire consequences, so why dare the risk? Perhaps he could win the coming war, but only an imbecile would choose that path before exploring the alternatives.

And even if Masada harbored some unforgivable grudge that demanded retribution, why use a firebomb when the Fifth Summit was only a few hours underway? A poisoned wineglass or a dagger in the back could achieve the same result without scaring off other potential targets and enraging the gathered Estates.

Furthermore, why target Amethyst, of all people? After exerting such effort to research a supposedly untraceable firebomb and smuggle it into Tel Tellesti, why not attack the king or any of the visiting emissaries of infinitely more significance than a young heiress?

So as I said, these thoughts were consuming me. The riddle threatened my sanity. For days I could hardly sleep or eat, and in the end I decided I must speak with someone.

I chose Amethyst.

It didn't seem right, approaching her with such questions so soon after the attempt on her life. Her wounds would still be fresh, and I couldn't guess how she was coping emotionally. It wouldn't have surprised me if she couldn't speak about the event, but I didn't see

Reassignment

much choice. She was the only person who could shed light on Masada's motives. Well, the only person besides Uriah or Damascus, but I wasn't about to visit Damascus, not after our previous interaction, and speaking to Uriah didn't seem proper either. So, as I said, I decided to speak with Amethyst.

There was just one problem. I couldn't find her.

I visited her chambers first, but that didn't help. I only found a repair crew that couldn't tell me anything except that the heiress had been issued new quarters somewhere else. Likewise, the people in the infirmary proved useless. When I went by, I saw neither the physician nor the maids from that fateful day, and when I asked the replacement staff about a burn victim named Amethyst, none of them had any knowledge of her.

And that was it. Though my investigation had only just begun, I had already reached a dead end, and there remained only one remaining course. I had to visit Uriah.

The idea made me nervous. I was bypassing the chain of command, going directly to the general, but I hoped Uriah would make an exception. After all, the alkali powder wasn't common knowledge, so I didn't want to mention it to my commanding officer, and furthermore my questions had such weight. Such gravity. What if Masada was innocent? What if someone was framing the Glacians? What if we were risking war over a faulty assumption?

As it turned out, however, someone else narrowly beat me to the general. Indeed, as I approached Uriah's office to voice my concerns, Damascus appeared from the opposite direction. My jaw clenched as I remembered his annoyance with my previous behavior, but I adjusted accordingly. This time, I was not so presumptuous. I acted as a respectful soldier. I opened the heavy door for my elder and followed him inside.

And in so doing, I precipitated a disastrous chain of events.

Uriah was reviewing some reports when we entered, if I recall correctly, and he was annoyed by Damascus's unsolicited visit (though he didn't even notice me), so he only glanced up long enough to say, "Not now, Damascus."

"I'm sorry, general, but it's about Amethyst."

Uriah lowered his papers, suddenly concerned. "Is she well?"

"Oh, yes. Quite well. She's healed up rather nicely."

This news baffled me. Amethyst had suffered a broken wrist and severe burns just a few days before. Surely she couldn't have healed so quickly.

The revelation barely registered with Uriah, though. He only shrugged and asked, "Then what's the problem?"

"Well, someone did just try to murder her."

"So I heard."

"The attack has left her rather rattled," Damascus explained. "I'm quite shaken as well."

"I'm sorry to hear that."

"She's barely left my room. She's hardly eating. She refuses to visit the atrium or the vault. I've had to conduct her lessons in my personal chambers."

"Damascus, we've stationed extra security throughout the citadel," Uriah reminded him. "We've provided her a continual escort. We've changed her schedule. I'm not sure what else we can do."

"Exactly! That's why I'm here." Damascus approached the general's desk. "I was hoping to take her away again."

"Another field trip?" Uriah tilted back in his chair. "That's not a terrible idea. Get her out of the citadel. Out of the city. Away from harm."

"Exactly."

"You couldn't take her anywhere north or east," Uriah thought aloud. "In fact, I would avoid the highlands altogether."

"Quite right. I was thinking we should go someplace entirely different than our usual trips," the old man suggested with a mischievous twinkle in his eye. "Someplace where the ghosts of Thunderlun could never reach us, like, oh, say, Ballabor?"

Reassignment

At that word, Uriah's eyes narrowed. A sly smile crossed Damascus's lips. This seemed like quite the idea, though I couldn't tell if it was genius or insanity. From the half-chuckle that escaped Uriah, I could tell he didn't know either.

"Oh, come now," Damascus pressed. "Please?"

Uriah raised a hand in protest. "You cannot take her to the king's refuge. No one's allowed there. He'll never agree to it."

"Not if I asked," Damascus admitted. "He'd laugh me out of court. He might even banish me for suggesting such a thing. But what if, perhaps, a close friend asked instead? What if the king's favorite general humbly suggested that this might be in Amethyst's best interests?"

"You've got some nerve, playing Everett like that."

"I did learn from the best."

Uriah coughed out a guilty, nostalgic laugh. "Fine. I'll ask, but no promises."

"Thank you!" Damascus exclaimed, clasping his hands. From such a reaction, I assumed the king's permission was mere formality at that point. I was certain Damascus would get his trip to Ballabor.

The men said a few additional words to each other after that. Damascus made sure he still had permission to commandeer a ship for his travel needs, and he asked if Uriah wanted any extra advice about the Glacian threat. Soon enough, though, their conversation finished, and Damascus turned to leave, only to pause halfway out the door.

"Something else?" Uriah asked.

"As a matter of fact—" Damascus shut the door again. "Whenever I've taken these excursions with Amethyst, you've always insisted on a Vanguard escort, but now I was wondering if that requirement still applies. It is most unnecessary. Amethyst and I are quite capable alone."

"It stands," Uriah confirmed. "You're not stepping one foot outside the citadel without a Vanguard agent."

"Very well, but if that is the case, I need a recommendation. If you recall, in the past we've always taken Captain Avram."

"The blacksmith. I remember."

I remembered too. Avram was something of a legend—a venerated Vanguard blacksmith who had traded his hammer for a sword and subsequently risen through the ranks at record pace. He had made lieutenant even faster than I did, and this man had connections with Damascus? I wondered if the erudite tutor had somehow affected the blacksmith's meteoric rise.

"Yes," Damascus was still saying, "Avram's been the perfect traveling companion, most accommodating, but recently—" He stalled again. He lowered his head, tempered his voice, and asked, "Did you, by chance, hear the news about his wife?"

Uriah froze. "No."

Damascus held his breath. "She died. In childbirth. Two months ago."

The general swallowed uncomfortably. "I see."

I saw pain in Uriah's eyes, and I remembered another rumor I had heard many years earlier, a rumor about how the mighty general had lost his own wife suddenly to some mysterious disease. How she had left him with two young boys.

I felt for him, of course. Uriah isn't the only person who's ever lost a wife and had to care for his children alone. Damascus must have pitied him too, because the tutor paused respectfully before continuing. "Avram has taken a brief leave of absence, obviously, to care for his newborn daughter and his son, and—well, I doubt he'll accompany me on this trip, even if I asked."

"You need someone else," Uriah guessed.

"Precisely."

The general nodded, and his squint deepened. Then he finally noticed me standing near the door, patiently waiting to voice my concerns about Amethyst's near assassination, and he said unexpectedly, "Take Mordecai."

Reassignment

My stomach churned. This was the last thing I wanted, to leave the citadel at such a crucial time with war brewing, famine spreading and Caleb's education unfinished. Fortunately, when Damascus turned toward me, I saw he shared my distaste for the idea. Indeed, I dare say my very existence still incensed him.

"He's a touch young," the old man pointed out. "Wouldn't you rather send someone with more experience?"

"He *is* young," Uriah admitted. "He's one of the youngest lieutenants in the Vanguard, actually, but he's talented. He's an expert swordsman, a master tactician, and he's seen more action that most men twice his age. And do you remember the reports about Veldt?"

"Yes."

Uriah nodded at me. "He's the sole survivor."

Damascus scrutinized me like a jeweler searching for imperfections in a ruby. "So he's a good man?"

The general shrugged. "He's a good soldier."

"That's not the same thing," the old man answered.

"Maybe not, but he did save your girl's life. If nothing else, you owe him for that."

"Very well," Damascus sighed. "Meet us in the harbor at dawn tomorrow. We'll sail on the *Sole Solution* at morning's tide." With that, he swung open the door and slipped out of Uriah's office.

Five

"Something wrong?"

"No, your grace."

"I don't have any additional questions. Not yet."

I shift in my seat. "I have a question, actually."

Rehoboth lifts her quill slightly without breaking her smile.

I take that as permission. "There's an academy in Tel Tellesti, isn't there? A private institute for all the children of dignitaries and ambassadors and so on?"

"That's correct."

"The academy is quite renowned, as I recall."

"I should say so. I went there myself," Rehoboth boasts as if I should be impressed.

I'm not.

"Why did Amethyst have a personal tutor, then?" I say instead. "Why wasn't she enrolled in the academy?"

"That's a good question."

Of course it is.

"And furthermore," I add, "why was Amethyst allowed on these expeditions? Why did her parents allow her to tour Estavion with naught but her old tutor and a single escort?"

"Another good question," Rehoboth replies.

I wait for a better explanation, but when it doesn't come I lose my patience. "So?"

"I said they were good questions. I didn't say I would answer them."

Porcelain

"Lieutenant?"

I turned from Uriah's door, where Damascus had just exited. The general waited expectantly, no doubt wondering why I lingered in his office.

"Is there a problem?"

There were multiple problems. I thought back to the narthex, where Damascus had complimented Amethyst's performance and dismissed her fears about our uncertain fate. Their intimacy had caused me such discomfort and hesitancy. Was I the best person to accompany them to Ballabor? Could I endure so many months in their presence? Should I inform Uriah about my own tragic history? About the family I lost? Shouldn't he take that into consideration before reassigning me?

I also thought about the investigation in Amethyst's room and the terse interaction that had just occurred. In both cases, Damascus had barely tolerated my presence. Would he ever accept me as a suitable replacement for Captain Avram?

And what about my men, the Vanguard agents I was still training? Caleb and the others needed my guidance. My sudden disappearance might disrupt their education.

"Mordecai?"

My mouth opened to explain my doubts, but then I recalled something else. I saw Amethyst broken on the floor beneath me, one arm blistered, her other wrist wrenched back, her eyes gushing with tears. I remembered her screams of agony, and how there had been no one to carry her to safety. No one except me.

So I said, "No, sir. There's no problem."

Uriah squinted. "You're certain?"

"Perfectly."

"Good. Then follow Damascus's instructions, and speak of this to no one." He paused for a solemn breath. "It will be safer if no one else knows your destination."

"I understand."

He nodded, feeling better about the situation already. His shoulders relaxed and he leaned back in his chair. "Now then, what else did you come to say?"

"Sir?"

"You didn't come with Damascus, did you?"

Right. I had almost forgotten.

I expressed the numerous questions that had plagued me over the previous week. For the next fifteen minutes, I told Uriah my concerns about the firebomb, Lord Masada's doubtful motives, the curious timing of the attack, and the absurdity of targeting Amethyst. I also cautioned against declaring war with Near Thunderlun despite the evidence justifying that decision, and through it all Uriah listened graciously. He didn't chastise me for bypassing the proper channels. He even took some notes, and after I finished he thanked me for my insights and promised to investigate matters.

In the meantime, however, my instructions were clear. Pack whatever gear I deemed appropriate. Tell no one of my orders. Escort Damascus and the heiress to Ballabor. Keep the girl safe.

A simple task, I thought foolishly.

That night I prepared for the coming mission, a process that took mere minutes. We weren't traveling on foot or horseback to some remote retreat. We were taking a ship to a well-supplied island for-

Porcelain

tress, so I packed only the essentials. I brought my Vanguard uniform, my sword, some spare clothes, and my favorite knife tucked into my boot, just in case.

Following Uriah's orders, I spoke with no one, not that I had any friends to bid farewell. When a man spends as much time as I do with new recruits, he doesn't have opportunities to socialize with peers. I did long for one extra day with my men or at least ten minutes to explain where I was going and why I couldn't personally oversee the final stages of their education, but I knew that was impossible, so I avoided the training yard and didn't see Caleb that night or the following morning.

I left the barracks at first light, determined to impress Damascus or Amethyst with my punctuality. I left the citadel, took the famous stairs and descended the cliffs. When I arrived at the harbor far below, I approached the biggest piers where our largest warships were anchored. I assumed that Damascus acquisitioned the best vessel possible for Amethyst's protection, something like the *Reticent Majesty* perhaps, but I didn't find the *Solution* among those warships. When I asked for directions, I was instead pointed back toward the fishing boats and ferries, and by the time I found the boat moored to a short pier, I was very late and nearly out of breath.

And when I beheld that ship, the rest of my breath escaped.

She was small, yes, perhaps only twenty paces from bow to stern with a dozen crewmen to count, but she was tall, with three masts and nearly a dozen wide canvas sails. She was sleek and streamlined too, all clean lines and low profiles, with minimal room beneath deck for storage and only one small cabin at the stern. She wasn't mighty, perhaps, without troops or armament, but she looked fast and nimble, capable of soaring swiftly over the Mediate Sea through waters too shallow for larger craft. It wasn't hard to imagine how she won her name, and I felt honored to look at her.

Damascus had chosen brilliantly, I realized then, and so much better than I would have. True, the *Solution* could never defeat any larger frigate or warship the Glacians might send after us, but she could do something far better. She could indefinitely outrun our enemies. She could slip through ambushes and evade capture. Indeed, as long as Amethyst remained on that ship, I knew she would remain safe, and that was a boon sorely needed at such a time.

That revelation was followed fast by another encouragement, a booming voice that embraced me and lifted my spirits.

"Lieutenant Mordecai?"

I glanced up at the squat man waddling down the gangplank.

"Ha! Knew it was you. Damascus said you'd have that dumb look. He's always right, the ol' fox." When the short man came near, he slapped my shoulder hard enough to leave a bruise. Then he eyed my pack. "That all you brought?"

"Yes."

He snatched it from my hands before I could protest. "Best I take that. I'm Abner, captain of the *Sole Solution*."

"I see," I said, though I had trouble imaging him as captain of anything except maybe the king's jesters. Regardless, I tilted and said, "Permission to come aboard, sir?"

My formality made him laugh and slap my shoulder again even harder. "Ha! Good! That's—ha ha! Good one, pup. You're gonna fit in nicely. I can see it."

I wasn't yet convinced, especially when he carelessly swung my pack and tossed it up the gangplank without aiming.

"Something wrong?"

"No. I just—" I paused to collect my thoughts. "I assumed this was a Vanguard ship."

His smile widened. "This *is* a Vanguard ship."

I highly doubted that.

"No! Take that back. It's better," he continued, shoving me up the short gangplank. "We're a freelancer reconnaissance ship, number eighty-seven. A kite runner. And we're all Vanguard, or used to be. Half of us retired. The others were discharged."

Porcelain

I'd bet Abner was among the latter.

"But we're still brothers," Abner reassured me as we reached the deck. "You're with family here. That's still the code?"

"That's the code," I echoed.

"Right!" Then the captain did something else unexpected. He grabbed a coiled rope from the banister and dumped it into my arms. "Take a line then, pup! Tie down the plank."

His request seemed fair enough, but when I quickly scanned the *Solution*'s deck and the busy crew preparing to cast off, I noticed a glaring omission that gave me pause. "What about Damascus and Amethyst?"

"They're in my cabin," Abner answered. "Been there for hours. We only been waitin' on you. Best be more punctual next time. Wouldn't wanna soil the Vanguard name, would we?"

He wailed on that same shoulder before sauntering off. He moved to where my pack had landed on the deck and picked it up, only to drop it again down a nearby open hatch and into the lower cargo hold. Then he started shouting orders and curses at his able crew, spurring them to action like a plowman driving his oxen before the cart, and I readily joined that team.

It seemed unnatural at first. My hands were more accustomed to swords than ropes, and my legs were more comfortable in a stone courtyard than on a listing wooden deck. But it felt good to work, to just follow orders and focus on a simple task, like dragging up the gangplank and securing it against the railing so the *Solution* could clear her moorings and depart the harbor. For the first time in weeks, I didn't think about the looming war or the unsettling fact that we were fleeing for Amethyst's life. I wasn't thinking about anything. Instead, I was assisting the crew, learning names, acquainting myself with these new brothers, and doing whatever I was told. I even started to appreciate Abner's abrasive humor.

As we slipped away from Tel Tellesti's cliffs for the next few hours, I volunteered wherever I could. Having never sailed before, not even on a civilian craft, I knew little about the job, but I could at least tie knots and pull lines when given instructions. The crew was patient enough, and though they laughed heartily at my novice mistakes, they were also forgiving and quick to clarify directions and offer second chances.

Best of all, they let me assist with the kites.

I had heard Abner call the *Sole Solution* a kite runner while coming aboard, but I hadn't understood what he meant. Once we cleared the last harbor buoys and entered Adis Bay, however, and once the captain steered us into a favorable wind, Abner suggested I assist the kite master, and he pointed me toward the ship's bow.

There I learned the secret to the *Solution*'s speed. I met the first officer, a lanky sailor who called himself Gideon and said little else, and I watched as he unfurled billowing sheets of reinforced silk. With my help, he secured these to stiff cross braces and strong lines, and soon we had a kite that could have been mistaken for the kind any child might fly high over the barley fields on a windy day. The only difference was our kite's ludicrous size.

Once assembled, the kite was about four paces wide, nearly half the width of the *Solution*'s deck. It was difficult to maneuver around the spider web of lines that crisscrossed the bow, and it was even more difficult to launch. We had to wait for the proper wind with just the right strength and direction, but Gideon was a true master, and following his lead we released at the right moment. Then we turned to the anchor line, looping the ropes through a wrought iron winch that was secured to the *Solution*'s deck with iron bolts as thick as my wrist.

Slowly and carefully, we released more line so the kite could steadily climb, and at first I was disappointed. Despite the grand buildup, the resulting affect seemed minimal. Almost useless. I even wondered why Gideon bothered with such a contraption. As we fed more rope through the winch, however, and as the kite rose higher above the ocean, the airborne sail entered a powerful trade wind.

Porcelain

Then the line stretched tighter, and Gideon clamped down the winch, securing the kite at its current altitude and eliminating the slack. A second later the iron bolts groaned, the weathered floorboards buckled and the *Sole Solution* lurched under my feet.

I fell, actually. So sudden was the acceleration, I tipped onto my back, but I wasn't hurt. Instead I laughed, and when Gideon reached down to help me up, I begged for more. "Tell me we can do that again!"

The first officer just smiled.

We launched additional kites after that. I think we finished with about ten suspended above us. It was difficult maintaining such an array, keeping all the lines taught and untangled, but the benefit was well worth the hassle. With so many sails pulling from such heights, we sometimes skipped across the waves like a flat stone over a lazy pond. My heart skipped too, knowing that no pursuer could match our speed.

Then the petite heiress emerged from the captain's cabin, and the day got even better.

I noticed Amethyst almost the moment she appeared, and I watched as she greeted Abner's sailors and navigated the listing deck toward my station near the *Solution*'s bow. I had seen her before in the citadel, but I had been distracted by other concerns then and hadn't yet realized her significance, so I had given her minimal thought. On the ship, though, in such close proximity and better light, I paid better attention and saw far more. I noticed that she was younger than I had assumed, perhaps only fourteen, with delicate features and silky skin to match. She was simpler too, wearing only a long satin dress and padded slippers, both a vibrant purple, with no ornaments except a mirrored, silver bracelet around her slender wrist and the ribbon in her hair.

As she drew closer, I detected more aberrations that gave me pause. First there were those slender wrists, so soft and delicate, the same wrists that had been hopelessly burnt and broken when I left her in the infirmary. How could she have healed so quickly and without the slightest scar? There was also the matter of her shimmering hair, which was a deep auburn. Hadn't she been blonde before? Or had the golden sunlight tricked my eyes when she had stood on the dais and given that speech?

The most significant change, however, was her demeanor. Gone was the terrified little girl who had wept bitterly in the granite hallways and screamed for Damascus. In her place again was the resolute woman who had so effortlessly captivated the Summit leaders. In fact, had I not known any better, I would have never guessed Amethyst had almost died a week ago and was now fleeing the citadel for her life.

Her reappearance and approach bewildered me, and before I could make sense of it all, she was standing at the bow. Then my nose detected roses and myrrh, despite the salty air. And that tension? Those few doubts and fears that still remained? She banished them with her piercing blue eyes and angelic voice as she said, "It's a fine day, isn't it, lieutenant?"

"Yes, I suppose it is."

"It's good to see you again."

"Likewise. Of course."

"Are your accommodations satisfactory?"

"Perfectly," I answered, though in truth I couldn't say. I had no idea if I had been assigned a bed, a bunk or a hammock. I only knew Abner had dumped my pack below deck.

She indicated the adjacent space on the bench. "May I sit?"

"Please."

With practiced form, she positioned herself next to me, her hands in her lap, her back perfectly straight, her eyes focused and clear. Then she said, "I wanted to thank you."

"For what?"

"For saving my life. Have you forgotten?"

I lowered my eyes. "I was just doing my duty."

Porcelain

"Still, it's appreciated, and I'm glad you've joined us."

"And I'm glad you're all right," I answered. Then I noticed her hands, her elegant hands, still folded in her lap. "How is your arm, if I may ask?"

Suddenly self-conscious, Amethyst covered her right wrist, the one that had been burnt, with her opposite hand. "It's fine."

"Shouldn't you have it wrapped?"

"I'm a fast healer," she explained hastily.

Sensing her discomfort, I dropped the matter, but somehow even her awkwardness entrapped me. She was still a teenager, after all, despite her noble upbringing, and it was comforting to see her fidget like a normal girl.

Her awkwardness only lasted momentarily, though. After a breath her confidence returned, and she said, "Tell me about yourself, lieutenant. Have you ever seen Ballabor?"

"No. I haven't been around much at all."

Her brow furrowed. "Damascus said you visited the Line?"

"Once. A long time ago."

"But nowhere else?"

I shook my head and offered a condensed biography. "I never had much chance. I'm just the son of an architect. I was born up north, past Esker. Moved around a bit, but never really went far until I joined the corps. I transferred around more after that. Saw some action in the Hills before being reassigned to Tel Tellesti and joining the Vanguard."

"What about the Battle of Veldt?" Amethyst pressed. "Is it true? You defeated the marauders all by yourself?"

Damascus needs to learn how to hold his tongue, I thought, but rather than insult her tutor, I shrugged. "I just did what I had to survive after the garrison was killed."

"And then you ingeniously ignited the parched barley fields and caught the invaders in the blaze. You sacrificed an entire harvest and city rather than watch them fall into enemy hands."

Her detailed knowledge surprised me. "I don't remember Uriah mentioning that part."

"He didn't. I've read the reports."

At that, I didn't answer. I couldn't. My jaw was locked shut. The tension had returned.

Those reports were classified. The Battle of Veldt had been the first act of aggression directly caused by the drought, and it was a siege we decisively lost. As such, it had never been publicly announced for fear of widespread panic. Even as the sole survivor, I could never get permission to read the reports, not before being promoted to general or appointed as a royal advisor, so how had Amethyst seen them? Had Damascus given her access? Or was there something else about her? Something that would justify the attempt on her life? Was there enough reason for an assassin to chase her to Ballabor?

Before I could verbalize these concerns, though, Amethyst pressed again. "What else have you lied about?"

I swallowed nervously. "I'm sorry?"

"You lied about not being around much," Amethyst teased. "Seems to me you've been everywhere."

"That's not a lie. It's a matter of opinion."

She smiled. "I suppose that's true."

I breathed easier again.

"Well, I hope you've satisfied your lust for adventure. You won't be seeing much action anymore. Not with us. I've been on dozens of trips like this with Damascus, always with the same purpose."

"Spying on the clans?" I jested.

She smiled again. "No. Researching the Ascendants. Before Damascus became my tutor, you see, he was a historian, specializing in the Ascendant period, and he loved it so much, he never truly gave it up. Whenever an opportunity arises, he takes me away to one of the sanctuaries to study stonescript. That's why he asked about Ballabor. There's an ancient construct there, a monument called the

Testament. It's the only Ascendant site he's never been permitted to visit."

I stifled a laugh. "You travel around Estavion visiting ruins just to read the ramblings of a dead civilization?"

Her smile faded. "They're not *ramblings*. The inscriptions document all their accumulated wisdom and learning. All their secrets. You could do well to read a bit yourself."

I leaned back. "You believe in the Ascendants?"

"Don't you?"

I couldn't answer right away. No one had ever asked me such a direct question like that. I was taken aback and had to consider my next words. My response was complicated by the fact that I was speaking to a superior, not a casual acquaintance, and it wasn't proper for me to question her. In fact, I may have already overstepped my bounds.

"I believe they existed, I suppose," I said ruefully. "I mean, *someone* built all those cities and sanctuaries."

"What about the Ascension?"

"Amethyst—"

"No, I'd appreciate hearing your thoughts."

I bit my tongue. I couldn't believe she still clung to the old superstitions. It seemed even more unbelievable that she valued the opinion of her bodyguard. I had saved her life, true, but that hardly seemed reason enough for this endeavor to win my trust, and I still didn't think it appropriate to share my perspective.

She was asking, though, and I don't refuse open invitations. "I don't believe the myths."

My answer didn't faze her. I suppose she'd heard it before. "Did you ever?"

"When I was a child, maybe."

"But not anymore?"

I shook my head.

"Why not?"

I sighed. How could I put something like that into words?

"Lieutenant, please. This is important. After we arrive at Ballabor, you'll spend countless hours looking over our shoulders at the last words of the greatest civilization the world has ever seen. We might even request your help with the analysis, so I'd like to know where you stand."

I held back another moment. I didn't want to shatter this young girl's faith, but I had no choice, so I took a deep breath, softened my voice, and slowly started. "I think the myths are wonderful," I admitted, "but they're just that. They're myths, nothing more. They're fables, fairy tales to entertain children and teach them how to behave. I don't think the Ascendants ever rose into the heavens. It's more likely they were wiped out by war."

"Then why did we find the Inheritance? Why were their cities left empty for us?"

"Maybe they had some custom about only fighting in the fields and leaving their cities intact," I theorized, "or maybe they abandoned their lands because of another drought like ours. Maybe they all drowned in a catastrophic flood that washed them away but left their cities intact."

"That's not what the records say."

"Those records were written by men. Historians. Men like Damascus. And I know he seems ancient," I said, checking to make sure the old man wasn't within earshot, "but he wasn't there. No one was there. All we have is speculation. Theories that fit the facts. And I know it's fun to believe the legends. It's fascinating to hear the fantastic stories about why we're here and who came before us. It's wonderful to believe that this world was meant for us. That we have a purpose. But sooner or later, we all have to grow up. We have to accept the fact that only observable reality matters. The truth may not be pleasant, but at least it's real. At least we don't have to believe in the mystical to make sense of it."

Porcelain

During my speech, Amethyst said nothing. She only watched with sad eyes, as if I was the one to be pitied for my perspective, and when I paused to catch my breath, she just asked, "I don't suppose you believe in magic, then."

I laughed outright. "No. No, I don't."

She nodded pensively then rose without another word. She left me on the bench, strolled across the *Solution*'s deck and slipped into the captain's cabin.

My heart ached as I watched her leave, and I almost regretted my words. She had to learn eventually that the world is not the wonderful place from her childhood stories, but was this the best time? Was I the right teacher? Couldn't I leave that bitter lesson for Damascus? She was still a child, after all. She hadn't yet suffered, like I had. She hadn't watched her dreams die or felt her heart break. She was still blissfully ignorant of the crippling emptiness that awaits us all. Who was I to rush that epiphany?

Before my doubts solidified, though, Amethyst unexpectedly returned. She wasn't angry or disappointed. She came confident as ever, and in her hands she now cradled a small figurine—a white porcelain horse and rider frozen in a ferocious charge.

"That's rather lovely," I blurted out, eager to reengage. "Is that a draft horse? From the Line?"

"Yes. Damascus gave it to me a few years ago. He knew how much I love horses, so he commissioned it for my birthday. It's completely unique. There's not another one like it." She smiled nostalgically. "It is my favorite thing in the whole world."

I was about to say something else, perhaps to ask about the quality of the porcelain, when Amethyst held out the fragile horse at arm's length. Then, defying every ounce of common sense I assumed she possessed, she did something unimaginably careless. She dropped the figurine.

It tumbled down, spinning as it fell. When it struck the deck, the horse's neck snapped off. Horrified, I sat there with my mouth hanging open and my eyes wide with shock, but I couldn't guess what kind of temporary insanity might have prompted such recklessness. It also didn't help that the *Solution*'s crew took no notice of Amethyst's odd behavior. And as for the heiress? She remained smiling and indifferent to the tragedy.

Then she turned toward the cabin and cried, "Damascus!"

Almost at once, her aged teacher emerged from the captain's quarters. He meandered slowly across the listing deck, dodging crewmen and swaying lines all the way. As he came, Amethyst's complexion melted so that by the time Damascus reached us, she had conjured up an impressive act that would have fooled anyone who didn't already know she had dropped the porcelain horse on purpose and was now faking the tears.

"Damascus!" She lifted the broken figurine. "I'm sorry. I was showing it to him, and it slipped—"

"Come now, my dear. It's quite all right. You'll see." With a gentle smile, he collected the pieces from her outstretched hands. For a few moments, he studied the irreversible damage before carefully fitting the two pieces back together.

Then Damascus did something extraordinary. I expected him to say something encouraging or perhaps scold Amethyst for her carelessness, but instead he whispered something indistinct, some foreign words unrecognizable, and he rubbed his fingertips along the cracks. As I watched, the white porcelain melted together like splinters of ice, and when he returned the horse to Amethyst, the cracks were gone. The horse was whole again.

"There you are," the old man said. "Better than new."

Six

"I'm sorry, lieutenant," Rehoboth says, her smile wider than normal as she lifts a white shard of porcelain from the cedar desk. "You expect us to believe that the girl broke her porcelain horse—this horse—and Damascus miraculously repaired it?"

"I know. I honestly have trouble believing it myself, your grace, and I was there. I saw it with my own eyes. I—I touched it."

She drops the shard back among the other pieces. "You know these details aren't corroborated by anyone. Even Captain Abner."

"I assumed as much."

"Couldn't it have been some kind of trick? An illusion?"

"Perhaps," I admit. "Except—"

"Except what?"

"If that was it," I stress, "if Damascus *only* repaired a broken horse, maybe I could convince myself I was mistaken. Maybe I could believe that it was just the sun getting to me, or the salty air, or something. But—"

Rehoboth guesses where I'm going. "There's more?"

"Just a bit."

Education

The alkali powder was the first hint. That should have tipped me off. But the horse? The porcelain horse was the undeniable evidence that I had been pulled into something mystical, something I wasn't yet willing to believe and for which I was sorely unprepared. Perhaps I'm still not ready.

Amethyst didn't rush the matter. She left me with the horse, and for hours afterward I stared at the porcelain figurine as if I could penetrate its mysteries with my eyes and discover how it had been so miraculously repaired. I even considered breaking it again, to test if Damascus was truly a magician, but something told me he would not offer me the same courtesies he freely gave the girl, and I started resenting him for that.

Part of me, a small part at least, was glad Damascus offered Amethyst such grace. No doubt that love had helped mold her into the incredible girl she was. With such a man believing in her and entrusting her with all the mysteries of the Ascendants, it was no wonder she could address the Summit with such resolve and recover from an attempted assassination without the slightest psychological or physical damage. But still, as good as I felt for her, a spark of jealousy ignited that day.

Why her, and why not me?

I shouldn't have felt that way. I knew it wasn't his conscious choice. He didn't intentionally pick her over me. Circumstances just happened. Life unfolded in its arbitrary, inequitable fashion. Still, I couldn't help but think how different my own life might have been if there had been someone like Damascus investing in me. Would I be better? What if I had grown up with a personal tutor who predicted my every need, with a ship and crew that could take me wherever my heart desired? What if I had grown up sheltered from harm?

As I considered that alternative, though, I realized something else. If I had lived Amethyst's life, I might have never lost my family. I probably wouldn't have joined the Estavian army or participated in the Battle of Veldt either, and I certainly would have never made lieutenant or been reassigned to the citadel. I wouldn't have trained Caleb, and on that first day of the Summit, I wouldn't have been in the narthex. Amethyst would have been burned alive. We'd all be in the same place then, or maybe someplace worse.

I was left hurt and confused. I didn't want to explore the possibility that my pain perhaps had some greater purpose, so I didn't. I turned my attention elsewhere. I focused on the job and forced everything else from my mind. I joked around with Captain Abner, and on favorable days I assisted Gideon with the kites. I volunteered for other duties as well, like fishing for the evening meal or scrubbing the *Solution*'s deck. Above all I avoided Damascus.

That at least proved easy. For the majority of each day, Damascus sequestered Amethyst inside Abner's quarters, no doubt reviewing history or policy or something like that. He was her personal tutor, after all. He didn't suspend her education during the journey to Ballabor. He took full advantage of their time away from familiar distractions to cram her head with as much information as possible. He only let her out during the early morning, when the wind was calm and the sea still as a mountain lake. As soon as she ate her breakfast and filled her lungs with salty air, though, he beckoned her into the private cabin, where she vanished from my sight and thoughts.

Despite my involvement and Damascus's relative absence from the deck, I still suffered too much unstructured time. The *Solution* was a small ship with an experienced crew, and once we cleared the Straits of Nore Mere and entered the southern Mediate Sea, the men settled into an efficient groove that left me nearly useless. As days stretched

Education

into weeks, my thoughts ventured into uncomfortable territories with more frequency. I carried along well enough during the days when I could find distractions, but during the long nights below deck, I worried constantly and always awoke the next morning more exhausted and far less capable of combating the doubts and resentment clawing at my heart.

As this cycle spiraled deeper, I started fearing for my sanity. To combat the ever-increasing inactivity, therefore, I resorted to the one thing that always makes sense—my training. On rough days when the tumultuous waves pitched us back and forth, I stood on the listing rear quarterdeck and lifted barrels, sandbags, and anything else heavy I could find to strengthen my legs and test my balance against the swaying ship. On calmer days I brought out my Vanguard broadsword. With my sharpening stone I made the folded steel sing, keeping the razor edge sharp, and after confining myself to a corner where I wouldn't accidentally strike one of the crew, I practiced my favorite routines. I paid close attention to my form, imaging myself as the student instead of the teacher, and I tried to guess what criticism might best improve my technique. After a few days of this schedule, fatigue finally overpowered my fear. I slept better and my mood improved.

My new regimen also attracted spectators, though. Gideon in particular fancied my sport, and on one especially uneventful day when I paused to rest, the first officer approached me and tossed a few long strips of canvas into my lap.

"What's this?" I asked.

He didn't offer a response. He just wrapped his fingers and wrists with the stiff scraps of bleached cloth. Either he wanted some friendly competition, or this was a rite of passage every man suffered when traveling aboard the *Solution*.

I considered the quiet man's physique, a sight I had seen dozens of times already, but on this occasion I focused on his taut biceps and his lean frame, which stood a full head taller than I. Almost instantly

I calculated his fastest speed, his longest reach, and his maximum power. I found them all impressive but insufficient, so I said, "Don't the kites need tending?"

Gideon just shrugged.

Tickled by his confidence, I picked up the canvas strips and started wrapping my own knuckles. "You won't win."

He nodded casually, almost as if he understood that fact better than I. Then Gideon did something he'd seldom done since I'd know him. He spoke. "That's not the point."

How could I argue with that?

So Gideon and I fought. We sparred like young men, jabbing and laughing and circling each other around the quarterdeck. We created an entertaining scene, and a small crowd soon gathered. It seemed the *Solution*'s whole crew stopped their chores to watch our match, and I wondered why Abner wasn't berating them for neglecting their posts…until I noticed the captain among the spectators, cheering on his first officer. The stout man even bet twenty shekels against me.

Gideon was the heavy favorite among the crew, and I must admit he was fairly formidable. If the fight was indeed part of some initiation, the crew chose wisely putting him up first. He had a long reach, and his hard profession had made him strong and resilient. Still, he was sorely unpracticed, and though he had obviously received extensive training during his stint with the Vanguard, the decades since had dulled his reflexes. He seldom hit me, while I never missed.

For the sake of our audience, I went easy on him and slipped into my instructor's mode. I called out half of my shots before I made them, and I offered unsolicited suggestions, telling him to watch his footwork, keep his chin down, raise his right arm. Regardless of these pointers, I bested him easily, wearing him down with repeated jabs to his abdomen as I ducked under his wide, high swings, and eventually, after a rare uppercut to the chin, Gideon raised his hand in defeat.

A smile lingered on his swollen lip, though.

"You all right?" I asked between long breaths.

Education

The first officer nodded and started unwrapping his wrists.

I started pulling off the canvas too, glad I passed Gideon's test, but Abner stopped me with a wail on my shoulder.

"You're not getting off that easy, pup," he said, taking Gideon's place.

So I fought Abner too.

I was winded from the previous match, but the captain lacked Gideon's reach, so I bested him even quicker. As soon as Abner surrendered, though, another sailor volunteered, confident he could defeat me since I had been weakened by my previous two opponents. I proved him wrong, however. For the next hour, in fact, I sparred through the *Solution*'s crew, finding each man's skills lacking. I was still thankful for the practice and the distraction. During that afternoon, I never once thought of Damascus or Amethyst.

Eventually, though, after knocking down one last man, there was no one left. After waiting a few moments in vain, I grew impatient, and I even cried out, "Is that all?"

To my delight some did shout, "I'll fight you," but as I turned toward the voice, I saw not another crewman, but the heiress and her tutor climbing the quarterdeck stairs.

Amethyst sauntered toward me, and at her promise the crew started snickering. Though they each sported bruises from my fists, they chuckled quietly as if privy to some wonderful joke I hadn't yet heard. The few who weren't already watching dropped what they were doing to witness the coming spectacle, and even Damascus seemed amused.

"I'm—I'm sorry," I sputtered, pretending to lose my breath. "I didn't mean you."

"Why not?"

A silly question. I blubbered something about impropriety and weight disparity.

"Come now," she said, using her tutor's favorite phrase, "you're not the only one who needs practice."

I looked to Damascus, expecting him to discourage her, but he only cocked his head and said to me, "This must happen eventually. Now is as good a time as any. But I'd prefer some protection, if that's acceptable." He turned to Abner. "Do you still have that heavy armor on board?"

The captain winked at Damascus. Then he nodded to three nearby crewmen, who ran off and disappeared through the main hatch into the cargo hold below. They reappeared seconds later with various sections of plated armor, which they brought to the quarter-deck and laid at my feet.

I thought this provision unnecessary. I had defeated everyone else without injury, and Amethyst was by far the smallest of the lot, but at Damascus's request I secured each piece as it was brought. I fitted a hardened breastplate and set steel faulds across my thighs. I slipped vambraces over my forearms and a helmet on my head. With all this I felt perfectly safe, ready to confront a dragon, and I turned to see what armor Amethyst had brought.

To my surprise, though, the girl had added almost no armor whatsoever. Instead of layered steel, she had fastened only a leather cuirass over her shimmering satin dress, and she had replaced her silk slippers with tall suede boots fastened with multiple buckles. She had restrained her hair with a white ribbon, but instead of wearing leather gauntlets or something else appropriate, she only slipped on an elegant pair of elbow-length lace gloves.

She looked at me inquisitively. "Ready?"

I nearly laughed at her attire, especially her poor choice of gauntlets. She seemed dressed for a masked ball, not a battle. "Don't you have anything better to wear?"

"This will do," she smiled deviously. Then she hit me.

I let her hit me, actually. She was a teenage girl, barely half my weight. I could probably hoist her off the ground with one arm. What harm could she do? But when she slammed her fist against my breastplate, I didn't feel the feeble punch of a frail girl. I experienced

Education

the jaw-rattling crash of a battering ram that raised me off my feet and hurled me backward. When I landed, I bounced and slid across the wooden deck until crashing into the railing, and when I lifted my head, I noticed something absurd. Her gloved fist had dented my steel breastplate.

"Are you hurt?"

I shook my head as a nearby crewman helped me up.

"Good." Then she came at me again.

"Wait!"

She stopped two feet away, her fist raised for another strike. At such proximity, I could see the intricate lace pattern, flawless and untorn, and her skin underneath, soft and pristine. There was no blood or bruise on her knuckles despite the violent impact from moments before.

"What's this? More magic?"

Her lips curled. "Lieutenant, please. I thought you didn't believe in magic."

I answered her with a quick jab. I aimed low, avoiding her face, but my effort was wasted. Without armor weighing her down, she easily slapped aside my arm and ducked under the following swing. Then she spun behind me and planted another hit center mass, sending me sprawling across the quarterdeck.

I bounced up, adrenaline surging, and with no further words Amethyst came again, giving me ample opportunities to redeem myself. I swung fast and often, throwing jabs and uppercuts quicker than I thought possible with such armament, but she moved faster and more frequently. I could have snatched a fly out of the air before landing a punch on her, and the whole time she struck back, slamming those gloves at my shoulders, chest, and thighs with devastating results.

I soon abandoned my offensive and focused on defense, but even that proved difficult. I avoided her best I could. I dodged and deflected her punches. I danced around the quarterdeck, forcing her to make constant adjustments. I even moved among the crewmen who were still nearby, watching and laughing. I used them for cover, placing the unarmed men between my opponent and myself whenever possible. But Amethyst was too quick. She darted and struck like a cobra, and whenever she made contact, no matter how slight, I was thrown backward, knocked down, or launched off my feet. Every hit left me rattled and gasping for air, and I found myself silently thanking Damascus for the armor. If not for his foresight, Amethyst would have shattered every bone in my body.

Despite this vicious beating, though, I couldn't help but feel she was holding back. I first suspected this during one exchange when I raised my right arm too high, which in turn shifted my breastplate upward and exposed my lower abdomen. Amethyst could have taken advantage of this mistake and taught me a painful lesson, but she aimed low. Instead of hitting my stomach, she struck the padded faulds that protected my thighs and merely threw me off balance, and as I regained my wits, Amethyst offered a suggestion, imitating my didactic tone. "Watch that arm, lieutenant."

Her overconfidence gave me a fresh spurt of blinding energy, and I might not have noticed what was happening, but Amethyst repeated herself. Whenever I dropped my guard, in fact, she avoided hitting me anywhere unprotected and waited to strike someplace safe. It became evident that she was exerting a mere fraction of her strength. She was toying with me, and all the while she parroted back the suggestions I had given Gideon minutes before. "Keep your chin down! Good, lieutenant. Now hold your guard. Here I come!"

When I realized what was happening, I grew angry, and the longer I endured that beating—that humiliation at the hands of a novice—the madder I grew. Most men would have shrunk in fear, perhaps, or admitted their match. After a few minutes, a better man would have perhaps graciously admitted defeat.

But I am not a better man. I am the famous Mordecai, the survivor of Veldt. The pride of the Vanguard. And who was she? A

Education

spoiled child? The protégé of some old scholar? I could accept that life was unfair, that she had enjoyed luxury and advantage while I suffered and struggled, but I would not let her win a fight, not while she was cheating. I would beat her, no matter the cost. I just needed to even the odds.

At the next opportunity, I raised a hand in mock surrender.

She straightened up. "Done so soon?"

I started pulling at my breastplate straps. "I'm just getting a little warm."

"We can stop."

"Nonsense." I lowered the armor, trying not to wince at a hot pain shooting through my shoulder.

The girl glanced at Damascus, then at Abner, then back at me, but she didn't back down. Better yet, she started pulling off the lace gloves.

I still feigned confidence. "That's all right. Leave them on."

She huffed at my lunacy. "One wrong hit could kill you."

"There are worse ways to die."

As I stripped off my armor, she removed the delicate gloves, one finger at a time, and gave the terrible gauntlets to her teacher. He tucked them into his robe, but also he leaned closer and whispered something into her ear, so quiet I didn't hear.

I heard her response, though. She told him, "I know. Don't worry. I'll be gentle." Then she turned to face me again.

The game was different now. Pure. I wore no armor, but neither did she except for her leather cuirass and boots, far more vital now that she lacked her mystical advantage. She seemed no less confident, though. With a set jaw and fierce eyes, she raised her arms in a fighter's stance. She didn't curl her hands into fists, like I did, but she did extend her fingers toward me, her digits pressed tightly together like slats on a fence, and she tucked her thumbs against her palms in a unique style that I instantly recognized, even though I've witnessed it only once in my life.

Like before, Amethyst attacked first. She aimed for center mass, and again I let her connect. It hurt more than I expected, with all her momentum condensed into her strong fingertips, and against my bruised sternum she might have produced a paroxysm that would have left me incapacitated. But I knew this second technique, so I flinched left, making sure her fingers struck muscle instead of bone. The searing pain pierced my chest and surged through my left arm, but no farther, and instead of flying back across the quarterdeck, I only shifted one foot to recover.

Then the adrenaline rushed anew, and I counterattacked. To my horror, however, I found that Amethyst was no more vulnerable than before. Her insane strength had vanished, but she was still surprisingly fast, and some master had taught her the martial arts of redirection and pressure attacks. Whenever I threw a punch, Amethyst's one arm automatically deflected my blow while her other hand sent pointed fingers into my ribcage. If I kicked, Amethyst would dodge like a rabbit and answer with lightning fast attacks aimed at any nerve points she could find. It I tried to entrap her with my arms and wrestle her to the ground where I would at last have an advantage, she would twist and writhe out of reach and knock me off balance with swift kicks to the knee or shins.

This second match was going wrong. If anything I was losing worse than before. At least then, with those gloves, Amethyst had weighed each blow carefully before making her move. Now she was unreserved. Unleashed. From the glint in her eye, I knew she seldom enjoyed opportunities like this, when she could test the true limits of her abilities and attack without fear of killing her sparring partner, and I knew she would not stop of her own volition. She would keep coming faster and harder. She would never relent, not unless I asked for mercy.

So I didn't.

I waited. I played the part. I winced after every hit and retreated like a coward. I endured jabs to the stomach and ribs. I nearly threw

Education

my shoulder out of its socket swinging high over her head. I took a hard blow to my knee and started limping, and through it all the *Solution*'s crewmen spurred on their heroine. Empowered by their cheers and emboldened by my ineptness, Amethyst grew reckless. She danced around me, striking out with her slender arms and pointed fingers, but eventually she even tired of that game. I stumbled a little, and then she came at me, cocking her arm back, her fingers finally curled in a fist meant to take me down.

That's when I reacted. I exploded forward, throwing my arms around her tiny waist. Once my hands clasped behind her, I arched back and twisted, whipping her body over my shoulder.

Her head cracked against the wooden floor, and a sharp cry escaped her lips. The rest of the quarterdeck fell silent. Abner's men suddenly stopped cheering as terror replaced excitement. The captain shot a look at me, wondering if I had lost my mind. Maybe I had. Only Damascus still thought clearly, and he rushed to Amethyst's side.

I stood frozen, unable to move. "I'm sorry! I didn't mean—"

"It's all right, lieutenant," came a reply.

I exhaled at last. It was Amethyst's voice that spoke.

With her tutor's help, the girl sat up, blood dripping from a deep gash on her forehead. "I asked for it, didn't I?"

Seven

Rehoboth picks up the lace gloves and turns them over as if searching for a stray thread. "These enhanced her strength?"

"Damascus made them," I explain. "He learned the method from some Ascendant inscriptions he discovered in one of the sanctuaries they visited."

"How significant is the effect, would you say? Ten-fold?"

"Try one hundred," I scoff.

Rehoboth skeptically pulls a glove over her left hand, but her hand is too large. She can barely squeeze her fingers inside the narrow sleeve. Nevertheless, once the glove is on as far as possible, she makes a fist and slams it on the table.

But the cedar desk stands fast, unscathed.

She smiles, "Have they lost their charm?"

"They don't fit you."

"Still, they should do something, shouldn't they?"

I don't justify that with a response.

Rehoboth removes the glove, consults her notes, and mentions casually, "You arrived at Ballabor next, correct?"

"Wait."

Rehoboth glances up at me, her smile frozen. She doesn't appreciate the delay. "Yes?"

I don't speak to her, though. I turn toward Uriah. I think of Amethyst's second style, how she struck with pointed fingers instead of clenched fists, and I ask a question I've been harboring for months. "How long did you train her?"

"I don't train anyone anymore, lieutenant," the general answers. "You know that better than anyone."

I do know. Uriah transferred me to Tel Tellesti specifically so he could ignore that aspect of his duties. "Then how did Amethyst learn your technique? The style you personally developed?"

"First of all, Damascus developed that technique based on his Ascendant research. I only perfected it. But that's not what's bothering you."

"No?"

"No. You're embarrassed you lost to a little girl."

Ballabor

Amethyst didn't claim victory after our little exhibition. She only complimented my nerves and clarity, adding that she had never been bested, not since completing her training. She also dismissed my counterattack as an instinctive reflex, never suspecting it was actually vicious premeditation. "The Vanguard are trained to use deadly force," she reminded Damascus when he berated me. "I should have been more careful." She was right. She was lucky I didn't kill her. We were both lucky.

Damascus didn't let us push that luck any further. As soon as Amethyst could walk straight, he helped her down the stairs and into the captain's cabin beneath the quarterdeck so he could tend her wounds. At the same time, the captain ended the recess and sent his crew back to work. Soon everything returned to normal with the wind in our sails, Gideon manning the kites, Abner humming at the helm, and the *Sole Solution* skipping over the waves toward Ballabor. Everything seemed exactly as it had been a few hours before…except me.

I felt as if I had been trampled by a stampede, and as the adrenaline wore off, new pains emerged. I found scratches on my arms and tears in my pants. My wrist swelled so badly I could feel each heartbeat throbbing through my veins. My lips bloated and the vision in my left eye blurred. After a few minutes of rest, it dawned on me that I had come much closer to losing than I had realized. Amethyst had nearly knocked me unconscious. Then I started doubting my status among the Vanguard. It didn't seem right, my holding the rank of lieutenant after a thin girl bested me so effortlessly, but I didn't blame her for that disillusionment. I blamed Damascus, and the resentment almost resurfaced.

Fortunately, I was too broken to care. I could only think of my hammock below deck. It was a thin, uncomfortable sheet strung between two bulkheads, and it always left my back bent in unnatural alignments, but at that point anything was preferable to standing, so I stumbled down the quarterdeck stairs, through the hatch, and into the cargo hold. I collapsed into the hanging bed and passed out.

I don't know how long I lay unconscious. Maybe it was only a few hours. Perhaps it was a day. I'm not certain. But I awoke when a violent lurch tossed me from the swinging hammock and onto the floor. The fall gave me new bruises and a fresh concussion, but desperate to see what trouble had befallen us, I scrambled up the ladder. When my head poked through the latch, Abner's voice shouted at me, "Best grab hold of something, lieutenant! These are treacherous waters!"

Then behind him, perhaps only a stone's throw off starboard, a jagged cliff drifted past as we entered the forbidden islands.

I knew we had no choice. Abner had already explained to me that Ballabor lay hidden in the heart of the Oorameres, and the only course to the remote fortress lay through the tightly clustered islands. He had also shown me on his map how the islands stretched out from the Chersonese peninsula and curled inward toward the Inheritance, sheltering the southern Mediate Sea from the ocean beyond, but I had envisioned the Oorameres as flat, tropical atolls with sandy beaches and inviting lagoons. As I stumbled out of the cargo hold and grasped the nearest railing, though, I realized I could not have guessed any further from the truth.

Ballabor

In reality, the Ooramere Islands were perilous, and our course suddenly seemed suicidal. The isles shot out of the water around us like the precipitous peaks of some great mountain range drowned long ago by a jealous ocean. There were no white shores, no gentle slopes, only vertical walls stretching upwards into the clouds above. On every side, sharp boulders threatened to shred us apart and devour us piecemeal. Between the islands, waves crashed and ricocheted against immutable granite only to refract and collide with other swells that followed after. The churning sea created swirling eddies and rip currents that often spun the ship. Sometimes we were even pulled backward.

Nevertheless, with her kites retracted and her sails at half, the *Solution* dared those ominous heights. The ship sometimes felt like a piece of driftwood bouncing through a labyrinth of rapids, but Abner maintained his course through that chaos with a jolly grin plastered to his face. His crew worked like a well-oiled machine around him, trimming the sails or adjusting the rigging at a moment's notice to climb a swell or avoid a cliff face, and at the bow, through the spraying mist, I noticed Damascus standing with Amethyst, his open hand stretched forward. I wondered if the old man was somehow redirecting the winds or parting the waters with some ancient trick, because I can't understand how we arrived safely otherwise.

But we did arrive. Eventually we rounded one final corner, skirted one last island, and before us rose an ancient fortification hewn high into the cliffs.

"There's the damned wench," Abner proclaimed. "Ballabor!"

If I had a hundred lifetimes, I could never imagine a place more impenetrable. This was not some castle constructed on an island, but a mountaintop transformed into a fortress, with wide battlements and commanding towers perched atop sheer walls that reached down into the depths beneath us. There were no beaches fit for landing an invasion, nor any safe cove where enemies might anchor their ships and mount an assault. There was only foaming surf beneath high ramparts, atop which archers and catapults waited to rain death upon whomever opposed them.

Wisely, Abner did not directly approach the island. Instead, he circled to the western side and maintained a safe distance. There we found Ballabor's only weakness: an immense pair of iron doors built into the cliff face. If opened, they would provide an entrance large enough for our greatest warships, but they still seemed poorly designed. Could any helmsman, even one so skilled as Abner, ever thread this needle with his ship, especially through such a turbulent causeway?

Thankfully, that was not the plan. Abner didn't approach the entrance. He merely steered the *Solution* close, within a bowshot or so, and signaled the all-stop. Then Gideon blew a ram's horn, trumpeting an unfamiliar call that echoed against the walls of the watery canyon. Indistinct shouts answered from high above, and soon I saw the welcome silhouettes of Vanguard soldiers peering through alcoves on either side of the floodgates. Moments later, though, I noticed something less inviting. I saw the sentries readying ballistae, aiming the giant crossbows right at us.

I almost cried a warning, but when I turned toward Abner, he seemed calm. Expectant. Damascus and Amethyst also appeared unafraid, though they watched the catapults with keen interest, so I held my tongue as the ballistae launched grappling hooks toward the *Solution*. Instead of smashing through our hull, these missiles landed harmlessly on our deck, and the crew tied off the attached tethers. Once the lines were taut and our sails lowered, the great iron doors creaked open on pillar-sized hinges, and we were towed into Ballabor's spacious belly.

Inside that harbor, once the floodgates closed behind us, everything changed. The water grew calm, and the foreboding fortress suddenly felt inviting. The walls that had previously locked us outside now shielded us like a mother's embrace. We found sisters there, other Vanguard ships ranging from small reconnaissance craft like the *Solution* to colossal warships, and I noticed brothers as well. Vanguard by the dozen watched from the battlements, and many more approached the docks.

When our momentum dissipated, Abner ordered the towlines removed. Then he called for oars, and the crew paddled toward the nearest pier. Once we pulled close enough, my soldier's discipline took over; I dutifully leapt down with Gideon to moor the ship. Other nearby Vanguard offered help, and we soon secured the vessel and lowered the gangplank so Amethyst and Damascus could disembark in appropriate comfort.

No sooner had they descended to the pier, though, than Damascus cried out in delight, "Talsadar! You bumbling bureaucrat, is that you?"

I looked, and I saw perhaps the most annoying and ridiculous man I've ever seen. He was old, not nearly so old as Damascus, I suppose, but well advanced. He was tiny too, unbefitting his big name, though he wore tall boots and thick furs that puffed him up like a strutting peacock. He approached us alone, favoring an ebony cane as he traversed the pier, and at first I disregarded his status since he lacked any escort. Then I remembered where we were and thought perhaps bodyguards weren't necessary here, so I took my place behind Amethyst just in time to appear respectful. I soon regretted that decision, though.

Talsadar answered Damascus's jest in kind, calling him a "sniveling owl."

"You overgrown tumbleweed," came the retort.

"You incompetent wizard," snapped Talsadar.

"Obsequious goon!"

"Sordid scab!"

The two men chortled and embraced.

"So this is where you've been hiding," Damascus said. "I thought they took your head."

"They had to move me somewhere. They couldn't exactly demote me, now could they? I may not be citadel material, but I served my time, thank you. You can be sure of that. Fifteen years in the fleet, twenty in the margins. Twenty years!" As he spoke, Talsadar buzzed around Damascus like a mosquito determined to fly into his ear.

"And now you're a steward here?" Damascus asked. "Seems a bit generous."

"I am the garrison general, thank you," Talsadar squawked, poking his cane at Damascus. "Remember that, or I'll hang you from the bulwarks by your whiskers!"

Damascus straightened up. "You'd have to reach them first."

The little man could have reached Damascus's beard, at least if he stood on his toes, but he didn't try. Instead, he spat and said, "Ridiculous." Then he pushed his stubby nose into Amethyst's face. "Can you imagine anyone more ridiculous?"

Amethyst shot me a telling glance. Yes, she could imagine someone more ridiculous. He was speaking to her now.

"You've finally tricked Everett into letting you see the Testament, have you?" Talsadar continued. "Took you long enough. I suppose you'd like to start at once, or would you rather see the guest quarters first?"

"Come now, you're not getting off that easy. We want the grand tour. I insist."

The general's face fell, and for the first time I suspected he wasn't faking the annoyance. "That will take hours!"

"It will take all day if I want."

"All day? Ha! You neophyte, how about a week?"

With a vindictive snarl, Talsadar pivoted and started toward the fortress keep, hobbling on his cane across the pier. Damascus strode after, taking only one long step for each of Talsadar's two. Amethyst followed close behind, already bored as the general began his elucidation in tortuous detail, highlighting the profound significance of every tower, window, plank and pebble. I turned to Abner, though, my eyes begging for deliverance.

The captain just laughed. "Have fun, pup!"

I noticed my clothes, still torn from my bout with Amethyst. My eye was still swollen too. "Shouldn't I change first?"

"You think Talsadar will notice?"

He had a point.

As I hurried to catch up, I wondered why Damascus didn't bother to introduce Amethyst or me. I was just a Vanguard agent, so it didn't matter that Damascus ignored me, but it seemed odd he would discount the heiress. It also struck me that Amethyst didn't protest this oversight and instead played the assistant. Even more concerning was the fact that Damascus didn't share the true purpose of our mission or the escalating tension between the Estates, but at least there I could imagine a justification. Perhaps he was just saving that delicate conversation for a better time and place, like Talsadar's office, where dozens of soldiers couldn't overhear and perhaps panic.

Once I caught the others, I pushed those concerns from my mind. I also ignored the onslaught of "interesting" facts that Talsadar launched at his hapless audience. Since this was to be Amethyst's refuge for the uncertain future, I instead studied the retreat's impressive fortifications, which were, best I can tell, comprised of three distinct sections.

The first was the harbor, surrounded by tall granite walls on three sides. The fourth side opposite the floodgates boasted an inviting dock with piers, boardwalks, and a rocky shore littered with stones perfect for skipping over the placid waters. But Ballabor's true personality reemerged beyond that point. The only escape from the harbor was a brutal climb up steep stairs, and then another wall separated the harbor from the next section. This barricade was shorter than the outer bulwarks, but still high enough to thwart most catapults, and it offered only one passageway—a gatehouse guarded by thick, reinforced doors.

"Imported from the Azure," Talsadar rambled as we neared the entrance. "The Ascendants carved each door from a single beam. The iron bands and hinges came from Edo's Pass."

"They mined granite at Edo's Pass, you indolent insect," Damascus sighed. "The iron ore came from Sul Nissi."

Talsadar responded with more insults, but I stopped listening and instead considered the armaments positioned atop the two towers that flanked the gatehouse. I counted thirty-seven archers and two ballistae before our tour resumed.

The next section was a courtyard, where gardens and springs encircled a monolithic sphere molded from metallic rock. The scene resembled a manicured graveyard or perhaps an orchard, and I wondered what honored king might be buried underneath the spherical tombstone that dominated the center of the square. Adjacent to the courtyard were various other features like the guest quarters to the south, the stables to the north (which seemed rather superfluous), and the great hall to the east.

Behind the courtyard and farther up, Talsadar showed us a final section that I'll call the complex. This was mostly utilitarian and functional, much less spacious and imposing, with crowded buildings and narrow alleys. It housed the barracks, some kitchens, a few cisterns, and storehouses stocked well enough to endure a yearlong siege.

There were many Vanguard soldiers in the complex too. In fact, during our tour I noticed guards at every choke point and patrols throughout the fortress. Archers and catapults watched our every move from the ramparts and towers. From all this I estimated a garrison numbering around four hundred. Even the servants performed their duties with swords strapped to their belts, and I specifically remember thinking that Ballabor rightly deserved its reputation. It *was* nigh impregnable. Even if the ocean froze and the vast Glacian armies marched across the Mediate to lay siege against the bulwarks, the fortress would never crack.

Ballabor

Convinced of Amethyst's safety, I finally started paying attention to our guide, and just in time, for the last stop proved the most memorable. Ballabor was a fortress, after all, a strong-hold hewn directly from a granite mountain. With the exception of the gardens, everything was expectedly stark and gray. It was magnificent, rivaling any natural or artificial wonder I've ever seen, but it was barren and cold. The few decorations I noticed were appropriately functional. Therefore, when Talsadar brought us through the great hall to the chamber beyond, I was duly surprised by its shameless extravagance.

"This is the royal reception area, which will stay strictly off-limits during your stay, thank you," Talsadar insisted, pointing at Damascus. "I only show it so that you know to stay out. It must be preserved for the king's visits, infrequent as they may be."

Talsadar didn't allow us beyond the threshold, but from the double doorway I could see chandeliers hanging from a cathedral ceiling. There were tapestries, rugs, and a throne studded with silver accents. This wasn't left behind by the Ascendants, I knew. Some other decorator had visited centuries later and converted the empty space into something more appropriate for Estavian royalty. Whoever he was, he had spared no expense, but he had still failed to overshadow the only piece of Ascendant architecture remaining in the room.

Against the back wall behind the throne, I saw something like a mural glowing with iridescent paint. After another look, however, I realized it was stained glass, a window spanning the entire width of the room. Light poured through this marvel, bathing the hall with hues of crimson and gold. I had seen glass before, mostly in the citadel, but never had I seen anything so wondrous. Never had I imagined such splendor and color, and I was so awestruck that it took me a moment to realize the shapes and lines were intentional. They depicted a scene from history, a noble woman dressed in ceremonial armor and riding a magnificent horse, with a young boy seated behind in the saddle.

"That's Estelle Migra discovering the Inheritance," Amethyst explained when she noticed my mouth agape. "The migrants landed here first. Did you know that?"

I shook my head.

"This is where it began," she whispered reverently. "Estelle led the refugees across the seas, searching for the blessed realm, the fulfillment of a prophesied birthright, and she found Ballabor and the Testament. This was the first glimpse, the guarantee of the promise to come."

A chill tingled my spine. The island suddenly felt different, hallowed, and I wanted nothing more than to stay in that room and stare at that window all day and into the night.

The tour was winding down, though, and Talsadar seemed eager to dispose of us, so he guided us one last time across the large courtyard and up a wide staircase to the guest quarters. He showed Amethyst a lavish chamber with a private bath and a window overlooking the lush gardens, but he stuck Damascus and me next door in something he dubbed the servant's residence. It looked like a closet with only a thin cot and a rickety chair added for appearances.

Talsadar shrugged as Damascus ducked into the tiny space. "This is the best I can do. Try to freshen up. Dinner's in an hour. Don't be late." Then he snuck off, chuckling to himself.

Inside the servant's residence, Damascus stretched out his arms. He could touch both walls simultaneously.

"I'll sleep in the barracks," I offered.

"You'll sleep on the floor outside Amethyst's door, and you'll be happy about it," he snapped.

I expected that sentence to finish the day's excitement. After spending so many weeks on the *Sole Solution*, I assumed Amethyst would take advantage of her accommodations and perhaps enjoy a hot bath. No sooner had Talsadar disappeared, though, than the girl's head popped out her door. "Is he gone?"

"Finally," Damascus sighed.

"Can we see it then?"

"Of course."

Without another word of explanation, we were off again. As the bright afternoon faded into evening, Damascus led us once more to the courtyard, only this time we didn't pass through. He strode across the polished granite floor to the center of the square, to the spherical tombstone, and he abruptly stopped.

That's when I realized the sphere wasn't a tombstone.

It was a monument, a perfect sphere of rusted metallic rock covered with ancient stonescript. It stood twice my height and balanced on a circular base, yet somehow the globe rested not on its supports. It floated slightly, hovering high enough that I could have slipped my fingers underneath (if I believed it would stay suspended, that is), and while this anomaly baffled me, it tickled Amethyst.

"Can I try it?" she begged.

Damascus nodded. "Take it slow. Be careful."

Giddy as a birthday girl, Amethyst reached out her trembling fingers and touched the floating sphere. She pushed slightly, and the monument moved. Though its mass must have far exceeded that of our largest warships, the thin girl could rotate the globe as easily as spinning a raft in a shallow stream.

"What is this?" I gasped.

Amethyst narrowed her eyes. "It's the Testament. Weren't you paying attention? It's the first Ascendant construct ever discovered by the migrants. Well, the first besides Ballabor."

"And it floats?"

"It's magnetic," she explained.

"Magnetic?"

Amethyst opened her mouth to clarify but then stopped, apparently stumped. When she turned to Damascus, though, he proved unhelpful. "Don't waste your time, my dear. He won't understand, not without hours of explanation. Best call it magic," he said. Then he intently spun the sphere himself as if searching for something specific.

"Magic," I huffed. "Again with the magic."

"Come now, lieutenant, don't be so cross," Damascus chided. "This is the chance of a lifetime, being here now."

"So you've really never been here before?"

Damascus pretended he hadn't heard me.

"No historian has ever visited this place," the girl explained instead. "When the migrants landed here, they couldn't guess what the writing meant. They couldn't decipher the language. It wasn't until centuries later that anyone translated stonescript, but by then Ballabor was off-limits, annexed by the royal family, so the Testament has never been studied by anyone."

Until now, I thought. Until an assassination attempt failed and Damascus capitalized on the situation. Then I said aloud, "I guess it's fortunate, in a way. Just think. If that firebomb hadn't gone off, you might have never been allowed this visit."

"Yes," Damascus growled, "how fortunate."

Eight

"He actually said that? 'How fortunate'?" Rehoboth inquires, her quill poised in midair. "Those were his exact words?"

"Yes."

"Interesting." She jots a few notes. "Was that your first doubt?"

"Excuse me?"

"Was that when you started suspecting him?"

I don't answer. I just stare at the cedar table, at the fold of velvet sitting beside the lace gloves. So close.

"Lieutenant?"

Her voice jerks me back. She's still waiting for a response. "No. No, I didn't have suspicions at that time."

"None whatsoever?"

"We were making conversation, your grace. I was distracted by details. So no, I didn't suspect him. I didn't suspect anything. I was just trying to follow orders. Stay out of the way. Protect Amethyst."

Rehoboth cocks her head, her smile never breaking. "It's a shame you didn't do better."

Echoes

Despite their enthusiasm, Damascus and Amethyst didn't begin their survey of the Testament that evening. They managed to tear themselves away for dinner and behave like appropriate guests for Talsadar and his officers. I accompanied them, of course. I ate with Gideon and the rest of the *Solution*'s crew, and we tried not to snicker too loudly as Damascus and Talsadar berated each other incessantly. Then darkness fell, and rather than try the research by candlelight, Damascus suggested starting the next morning. So Amethyst retired to her spacious room, Damascus squeezed into his closet, and they both settled down for the night. I left the heiress long enough to visit Ballabor's barracks and find a fresh uniform, but then I was back at my post outside her door. I remained there throughout the night, seldom sleeping and desperately trying not to think about the reasons why I was standing guard in such a strange, old place.

At first light, Amethyst awoke and sent me to the kitchen to fetch a hot breakfast of porridge and salted pork, meager rations necessitated by the drought still gripping the Estates. After we ate, she sent me on another errand to the ship to collect reference scrolls, parchment, rubbing chalk, and the various other supplies Damascus would require. Then we returned to the courtyard, to the Testament, where she finally settled down beside her tutor and began that long anticipated research—after about twenty minutes of which, I grew rather bored.

They couldn't have been happier, I imagine, staring at that rusted construct and meticulously studying every inscription as if the fate of the Inheritance hinged upon their accurate translation. Damascus would lean close, squint seriously, and mutter to himself. His student would hover nearby, parchment and quill in hand, ready to record every utterance for later review and reflection. Occasionally they would grow excited, as if they had found something that could revolutionize life as we know it, but then they would realize they had mistranslated a phrase or missed a character, and the dull process would resume.

I found it tedious. I wished I had followed my first instinct and asked General Uriah to assign someone else for this task. I wondered what was happening in Tel Tellesti. Were they still preparing for war with Near Thunderlun? Had Caleb and the others finished their education? I even found myself wishing I were back on the *Solution*, where I could watch the sails or the kites or the ocean. In the courtyard there were no such distractions. There was only an old man and a young girl staring endlessly at an immense metallic sphere.

At least their intimacy no longer bothered me.

My legs grew restless after a few hours of inactivity, so I left the Testament and walked circles around the courtyard. I counted the apricot trees in the orchard and drank from the fountains that bubbled up from springs far below. I explored the gardens and watched the patrols that crisscrossed the square. When that failed to satiate the monotony, though, I expanded my route into larger circles. Then I noticed a steep, narrow staircase carved into the southern granite wall, and I glanced back at Amethyst and Damascus. Would they mind my absence? Would they even notice? Probably not.

I climbed the stairs to the ramparts atop the barrier wall that separated the courtyard from the harbor. I found more patrols and soldiers guarding those high walkways, but I also discovered a vantage point that overlooked both the courtyard and the docks beyond. From that place I could have taken a narrow ledge along the harbor cliffs to the floodgates, but I chose to climb up another flight of stairs, around a tower, to reach an even higher rampart that the soldiers there called the skywalk.

Echoes

The view nearly made me dizzy. I looked north first, where I could see the entire harbor, complex, and courtyard, with two long walls separating the three sections. I could spot Damascus and Amethyst by the Testament too, oblivious to my absence. They seemed like ants from such heights.

When I turned south, however, a sense of awe overpowered my vertigo. There was a short granite parapet, no higher than a handrail, but past that safety barrier there was only a sheer drop that plummeted into raging white-capped surf far below. I could see the Ooramere Islands spreading before me too. In the morning mist, they seemed like jagged mountain peaks clawing through the clouds, and if not for the salty air stinging my eyes, I could have believed I was standing on top of the world. It was far beyond words. I only remember thinking that perhaps this post wasn't so bad. The guard work was mind numbing, true, but the scenery was matchless, the historical significance unprecedented.

Then I sensed a buzzing nearby, and the moment was ruined. "Terrible view, isn't it?"

I turned toward the voice, but I noticed nothing except a few Vanguard who were farther along the skywalk and too distant to be the source of the interruption. Then I looked down and saw Talsadar. Was he tall enough to see over the parapet? I didn't insult his height, though. I complimented his vista instead. "I can see why you left Tel Tellesti."

"Didn't have much choice, and I wasn't there long. I was only transferred when the council was considering me for high general's position," Talsadar rambled. "Then the king promoted Uriah. There wasn't a place for me there after that."

"I'm sorry," I said automatically. I honestly didn't care about his past, but I did try to imagine the little general in Uriah's place, perhaps standing by the king's side during the Summit and pointing his cane at the dignitaries. The thought brought a rare smile that was hard to suppress.

"It's better this way," Talsadar went on. "The capital's too crowded—all those puppets looking over your shoulder. I'll gladly take the islands, thank you. Better to stay out here where it's safe and boring."

I couldn't fault that logic.

"But speaking of the citadel," Talsadar said, finally reaching his point, "I've been meaning to ask, is it true what they're saying?"

I stepped back from the parapet. "You'll have to be more specific."

"Abner tells me the Summit was cancelled unexpectedly, and then you launched the next week. No one ever told him why, but he did hear rumors of an attack by Near Thunderlun."

I was honestly surprised Abner didn't know more. Why had Damascus not yet informed him or Talsadar of the recent events?

"So what of it, lieutenant?"

I remembered that Uriah had sworn me to secrecy, but only about Amethyst's destination, which Talsadar already knew. Uriah had never mentioned the war. Besides, Talsadar was a general too. What harm could the truth do? So I told him everything. I told him about the firebomb, the alkali and the new northern threat. I even mentioned Masada, though I included my own personal doubts about the Glacian lord's involvement.

"You're right about Masada," Talsadar interrupted. "He's not your man. Trust me. I spent three years in northern command, met him twice, and this doesn't sound at all like him."

"Too brutal?" I guessed.

"Quite the opposite. The Glacians are barbarians, the whole lot of them. Masada's the worst. He'd castrate his own son if he had reason. But he wouldn't hide it. He's too impatient and proud. If Masada wanted Amethyst dead, he wouldn't use a bomb. He'd crush her little skull with a war hammer." Talsadar mimicked the murderous blow with his cane. "He'd have done it right in the Summit too. There'd be none of this sneaking about."

Masada had opportunity, I remembered. He had been close enough to whisper compliments into Amethyst's ear. How easy would it have been for him to reach forward and snap her neck?

"Masada may still be involved," Talsadar added. "The whole Glacian horde might be working as mercenaries. Someone else is playing them, though, someone much more treacherous and devious. There is some evil villain at work here, and that's who you must be looking for."

"Who?"

Talsadar smiled. "If I knew that, you think I'd be stuck out here?"

I smiled back, impressed by his intuition. Perhaps he would have made a good high general after all.

Talsadar left the skywalk after that, but I lingered longer, staring out over the islands and considering his suggestion. I searched my memories, thinking back to the many staff meetings I had endured as a lieutenant, recalling all the reports and gossip about the drought and the raids that had followed. I didn't find a suitable name, though. I instead realized I had been gone from the courtyard for far too long, so I descended the stairs, passed the guards and returned to the Testament, only to find my haste wasted. When I asked Damascus if they had missed me, he only stared blankly. No, he hadn't noticed my absence, and he didn't appreciate the current interruption.

The rest of the day passed much like that morning. Monotonous. Slow. We stopped for a midday meal, then Damascus and Amethyst continued the research for another few hours. We had dinner with Talsadar and Abner. We slept. We woke and repeated the process the next day, and the next, and four more. Sometimes the *Solution*'s crew joined us for dinner. Sometimes they didn't. Sometimes the hours passed easily, but usually they dragged on. Occasionally I trained in the courtyard, and often I escaped to the skywalk. Each visit to that vantage point seemed less and less profound, though, and soon the fortress no longer felt like a wondrous Ascendant construct or a sacred chapter of migrant history. It felt like a prison. The only benefit was that the boredom eventually became all-consuming, drowning away my other concerns. I no longer cared about Lord Masada or the war. I didn't ponder the identity of Amethyst's assassin. I just wanted something to happen.

"I warned you," Amethyst teased one evening when she paused for a drink and noticed me counting the rivets in my mail. "Not much action."

"I'm amazed you can stay focused."

"I have the easy part. Damascus handles the translations. I just copy the information and maybe help if he gets stuck."

My eyes widened slightly. "You can read stonescript?"

"Damascus taught me during our visits to the other sanctuaries. And even when we're not visiting sanctuaries, I can still study the language. See?" She unrolled the fragile parchment scroll in her hands, and I saw what she meant. The scroll contained row after row of Ascendant words copied from the Testament in precise detail.

"Seems like a waste."

Amethyst rolled up the scroll as if to shield the ancient words from my heresy.

I quickly backtracked. "It's just—it seems that someone like you might have better things to do."

"Someone like me?"

"Someone of your stature—I mean *status*, and—"

Her nostrils flared a little.

"Shouldn't you be studying economics or politics? History? Something worth your time? Something relevant?"

"There is *nothing* more worth my time," Amethyst insisted, "and there is *nothing* that compares. We're the first people to read these words in thousands of years. Do you realize that?" Her voice softened with reverence. "Think about it, lieutenant. Haven't you ever wondered what was so important that the Ascendants bothered to carve it in stone? What secrets could possibly be worth immortalizing for all time?"

"They're just words," I argued, perhaps overstepping my bounds again. "Echoes of a dead nation."

"Just words?" She pointed at Damascus, whose face was pressed close to the sphere again, his lips moving silently as he translated. "How do you think he learned to repair porcelain?"

"A near-useless trick."

"Perhaps, but the inscriptions hold other tricks, other secrets. Together the monuments and sanctuaries comprise a vast library, a record of everything the Ascendants learned during their corporeal existence. And that knowledge is power," she said, her voice quivering, "power to help the world, not just fix porcelain. Power to amplify lace a hundred fold. Perhaps there's even some way to—" But she stopped. Unable to stem the rising emotions, she lowered her eyes and breathed deep.

She truly cared, I realized.

This wasn't just a distraction or an apprenticeship. There was a rationale behind her obsession, a profound motive driving this passion. And that intrigued me. What was she hoping to find? What answers could be hidden here? I still didn't believe, not really, even despite the porcelain horse and her lace gloves, but I did wonder what hope was driving her persistence.

"Amethyst? What is it?"

Her answer was rather indirect. "I suppose you heard about Near Thunderlun."

"Yes."

"And the southern threat? Did you hear about that?"

"What?" I asked with fresh concern. "No. What happened?"

Her eyes grew glossy. "During the Summit, after the king blamed Lord Masada for the bomb—well, the Samaran Empress didn't appreciate the accusation either, so when the Glacians left, the Samarans did too. The Impasse has been spreading for years, you see. There have been riots in Threshold. Severance is overflowing with refugees. The Empress can barely feed her own imperial guards. They're growing desperate, just as desperate as the Glacians. Their herds are dying, their farms have turned to dust, and just north they see an easy fix. A narrow strip. The most fertile estate in the Inheritance, along the Corde River."

She was describing Estavion. Our country. Our home.

"The tribes won't move. Not again. Not after what happened in Veldt. They won't risk anything while our strength matches theirs. But if the Glacians attack and pull our attention north, away from the river…"

Her voice trailed off again, but she needn't continue. I had already grasped the implications. All those weeks I had feared the northern threat, but now I knew our situation was much worse. If the Glacians attacked from the north, then the Samarans might strike again from the south, and in the middle Estavion would be mercilessly crushed. Perhaps the Chersonese clans would honor the old alliance, but even if they did, the outcome wouldn't change. The ensuing conflict would leave millions dead, and the migrants would lose their birthright. At best, we would be forced from our homes and banished from our cities. At worst, our entire estate might be exterminated.

Suddenly, Amethyst's research didn't seem unwarranted. Indeed, as I lifted my head I saw the Testament as if for the first time. I remembered that when Estelle had arrived three thousand years ago, her situation hadn't been all that different. Her people had been driven from their homes across the seas. The migrants had been desperate enough to brave the Ooramere Islands and find Ballabor. Estelle had likely stood in my very spot, and when she had first glimpsed the Testament, she hadn't seen an old, useless monument. She had seen her salvation, an Inheritance left for her people.

It did seem intentional, I had to admit, that ancient construct being there, and for the first time I sincerely wondered if the stories were true. Maybe the Ascendants had lived here in eons long past. Perhaps they didn't just die out. It's possible they were mystical and somehow knew we would follow, and they intentionally left something for us, something even more extraordinary than the Estates.

It had to be important, then. The inscription carved into that construct. Some eternal king had spent years, decades maybe, choosing every sentence, every word, always knowing his message would long outlast his corporeal existence. What secret could be worth such sacrifice? The key to their immortality? The meaning of life? Some method to pull rain from the heavens?

It was exciting to consider such possibilities, but frustrating as well. Almost as soon as my heart rose, it plummeted again. I was well accustomed to disappointment, and while it did seem possible that there was some solution to our dilemma graven on that rock, I knew it was far more likely we would never find it. There was no use tending my hopes, so I tempered my spirit.

But then Damascus cried out, and his excitement lifted me. "Amethyst! Quickly!"

The heiress wiped her tears and returned to her tutor's side.

"Here!" Damascus pushed a fresh parchment sheet and some charcoal into her hands. "Make rubbings. Right here!" He was already busy making his own.

"I can copy it down."

"No! The light is fading. I need copies now. We must record this tonight!"

"Why tonight?"

"Come now, my dear! Quickly!"

Amethyst began her task. She pressed the brittle parchment against the spherical stone and ran the charcoal lightly overtop so a shadow of the inscriptions appeared on the page. From her eyes, however, I could tell she didn't understand her teacher's urgency, so I asked the question she wouldn't.

"What's the matter? What's so important?"

"We found it! I can't believe, after all these years, we've found it at last," Damascus exclaimed. "A catalyst!"

Nine

"A catalyst?"

I nod absentmindedly while sipping some steaming tea one of the guards brought.

"You mean the Cornerstone," Rehoboth suggests.

"Damascus didn't call it that."

"And you didn't suspect he meant something else?"

I don't answer because I've just noticed the guard depositing a tray of hayberries and crusty sourdough on the desk, and my stomach growls painfully. How long have I been in here? Why does Rehoboth use interrogation rooms without windows? I dismiss those thoughts, lower my teacup onto the desk and reach for a sliver of bread.

"Lieutenant?"

Right. Her question about my suspicions.

"Your grace," I explain between bites of the warm sourdough, "before that very day I had no idea what a catalyst was. Can you understand that? I had never imagined such a thing might even exist, and I had certainly never heard of the Cornerstone before."

"But he *was* talking about this," Rehoboth says. Then the arbiter does something incredibly stupid. She reaches for the folded scrap of velvet.

Instantly, of its own accord, my hand drops the bread, shoots forward, and clamps around Rehoboth's wrist as I scream, "Don't touch it!" Just as suddenly, something hard strikes my temple, scrambling my vision and leaving me dizzy. I jerk my head toward the attack and see the closest guard heaving his sword over me. I see, too, my blood on his pommel.

He's too slow, though. Before he can land another blow, my foot comes out, catches his kneecap, and sends him sprawling to the floor. Then I'm on my feet, my hand reaches for my boot, and I grasp the dagger hidden there. All this happens in the blink of an eye, before anyone else can react. The whole time, I haven't released Rehoboth's wrist, and now I have a blade at her throat.

"Don't you ever, EVER, touch that thing!"

Somehow, the arbiter shows no fear. She just smiles—always that damn smile—and she says, "Remove your hand, lieutenant."

I glance at the guard, who's picking himself off the floor, but he doesn't seem eager to attack. I glance, too, at General Uriah, who hasn't moved from his chair behind the desk. I'm not sure he even flinched when I threatened Rehoboth's life. Does he still trust me that completely, even after everything? Or was he silently hoping I would kill the arbiter?

My hand starts to hurt, though. My knuckles have gone white. So I release Rehoboth's wrist and let her fall into her chair. Once I'm content with her distance from the stone, I return the knife to my boot. I settle back into my chair.

Then I notice my sliver of sourdough lying where it fell to the floor. I pick it up and blow off the dust. "Where was I?"

Catalyst

It *is* true, as I've said. Before that fateful day, I had never heard of a catalyst or the Cornerstone. Why would I? I wasn't a historian, like Damascus, who had spent his life studying the Ascendants. I wasn't an heiress, like Amethyst, with the means and opportunity to travel the Estates. I was a soldier, a lieutenant. I was no one of consequence.

Still, the old man's haste concerned me. In my brief tenure as Amethyst's guardian, I had never seen him so fraught and elated. Even when Amethyst had nearly perished in the firebomb, he had conducted himself with restraint. Why the sudden impatience?

"Damascus?"

"This is no time for queries, lieutenant."

"Why? It's not like the Testament won't be here in the morning."

Damascus didn't answer. He finished one parchment sheet and snatched another, pressing it against the ancient sphere's inscriptions as he furiously rubbed the page with charcoal.

I glanced at the fading evening sky. They had mere minutes of daylight left. "Should I find some torches then?"

"We're not spending the night in the courtyard," he snapped. "Now please, either keep quiet or help."

I kept quiet.

Amethyst didn't speak either, though I'm not sure if she shared her teacher's passion or just knew better than to interrupt. She also seemed to have forgotten her fears about Estavion's fate. With singular focus, she produced page after page of rubbings from the Ascendant construct.

A few minutes later, the sun slipped behind Ballabor's high walls and a darkening shadow fell upon the Testament. Almost immediately after, Damascus stopped.

"I can still work," Amethyst said. "There's light enough."

"That's quite all right, my dear. We have what we need." He rolled up his parchment rubbings and gently deposited the scrolls into my arms. "Take these to her chamber, would you?"

I obeyed without objection, carrying the dozen or so scrolls across the courtyard, up the stairs and into Amethyst's guest chambers. I dumped the research materials on the nearest table. Damascus and his pupil followed presently and carefully laid their own scrolls and rubbings on the table, the bed, the chairs, the windowsill, and whatever other flat surfaces they could find. Then they ignited a few lanterns and surveyed the chaos.

"Now," Damascus asked Amethyst, "where did I put that first page?"

"Shouldn't we stop for dinner?" I asked.

"You can go," Amethyst said dismissively. "We'll be along shortly." But we both knew she was fooling herself.

I wasn't terribly starving myself, given the excitement, but I left all the same. It wasn't wise to skip a meal during a drought. Once I arrived at the great hall, though, I felt ashamed letting the heiress go hungry, so instead of taking a seat near Talsadar or the *Solution*'s crew, I grazed around the long tables. From one I stole some hard rolls. From another a small cheese. I took some olives, a half-empty jar of wine, and three tumblers, and with my arms fully laden I turned toward the exit.

Talsadar noticed my behavior, though, and called from a nearby table, "That's all right, lieutenant. No need to leave some for the rest of us."

"It's for Damascus and Amethyst," I explained. Then I slipped out the door before Talsadar could answer.

Catalyst

I returned to Amethyst's chambers triumphant and laid my offering on the crowded table, but the food was ignored. Neither Amethyst nor Damascus acknowledged the meal or even my presence. They remained glued to the parchment rubbings, so I stopped helping. I snacked loudly on an olive and interrupted instead, finally asking my question outright. "What is this—what did you call it?"

"A catalyst," Damascus replied without rising from his notes.

That didn't help. "What's a catalyst?"

I directed my inquiry at Damascus, but this time he didn't respond. He only glared briefly at me with that deep irritation before returning to his research.

Amethyst answered for him again. "It's hard to explain."

"You have time."

The heiress tore her attention away from the parchment and stared out the window, almost as if she expected the explanation to float in from the dark courtyard. When that didn't happen, she glanced around the lavish room. Then she noticed the meal I had brought, and she broke off a crust of bread. The food provided new inspiration.

"I should start with something more basic," she said between bites. "From all the inscriptions in the sanctuaries and on monuments like the Testament, we know the Ascendants learned to manipulate their world on supernatural levels, and with this knowledge they wrote spells and enchantments, which they called *artifices*. These artifices vary significantly in scope and complexity, however. Some are relatively easy, like shifting the direction of the wind, or changing your appearance, or—"

"Or healing a broken wrist?" I guessed.

She bit her lip but eventually answered, "Yes."

"How is it done?"

Amethyst fingered a second crust of bread. "It depends. For something simple like a broken wrist, you need only a few words and a certain wave of your hand. Someone with more experience and skill might need only to *think* the necessary incantation."

By "someone", I'm certain she meant Damascus.

"But other artifices are more complicated," she continued. "They involve specific emotions, not just words and actions. These artifices require impossible levels of concentration and focus, far beyond average human capability, so the Ascendants devised a solution, a *catalyst* that amplifies and clarifies thought. With such a device, they could accomplish the truly miraculous."

"Such as?"

Amethyst filled a tumbler with wine. "How do you think they erected the mountains? Carved the rivers?"

"No one is certain they did," I reminded her.

Damascus shot me a detestable glance, but said nothing.

"The point is," Amethyst added, "with a catalyst, anything is possible. *Anything*. Damascus could thaw the tundra. He could forge new streams through the deserts or soak the Impasse with rain. He could stop the drought."

"I might even bring a person back from the dead," Damascus added absentmindedly.

"You could prevent a war," I realized, my voice cracking.

"Exactly," Amethyst said before returning to the rubbings.

At such a revelation, I had to sit down. Overwhelmed, I sank into a chair as the innumerable implications raced through my head. Suddenly I understood why Damascus had begged General Uriah for permission to visit Ballabor. I knew why he had risked the king's favor and ordered the *Solution* through the Ooramere Islands to this ancient fortress. If Amethyst was right, if such an ancient device survived, it could alter the course of history.

My thoughts surged fast after that. How would it work, I wondered? What would it be like if we could fix whatever was wrong with the clouds? What if we could stop the drought? Surely the old alliances weren't yet beyond repair. If the rains returned tomorrow,

Catalyst

Near Thunderlun and Samara would relent, wouldn't they? There would be no reason for conflict.

Just as suddenly, though, another thought entered my mind, one far less noble. As I remembered why we had fled to Ballabor in the first place, the familiar anger and resentment resurfaced, and I realized there was a vile part of me that didn't want our enemies to back down. I wanted the famine to end, yes, and I wanted Estavion to return to her former glory, but I didn't want the Glacians as allies, not after what they did to Amethyst. It was their turn to burn. I even pictured myself facing them in battle, and though I didn't yet know what the catalyst looked like or how it functioned, I imagined wielding it like a flaming sword, scorching the ghosts of Thunderlun like chaff in a wheat field.

Then my wits returned, and my breath stalled. Shame seized my heart. How could I want such things? Why did I rush toward such brutality? I wasn't even certain the Glacians were the true threat, yet I was already fantasizing about their destruction.

That's when it made sense, why a catalyst was necessary. Amethyst had explained that the most powerful artifices required perfect concentration and singular focus. And I didn't have that. I had remained focused on the drought and the solution for...what, ten seconds before my mind veered into murderous territory?

Then I wondered if Damascus was the same as I. Did he need a catalyst just as badly? When he fixed that porcelain horse or repaired Amethyst's arm, how focused was he? How close did he come to losing control and making everything worse? Is that why he was so determined?

I didn't dare pose that question, though, so I asked something else, something safer. "Why search for a catalyst at all? Why not just make your own?"

"Ha!" Damascus erupted in a fit of laughter. "Just make my own? Of course. How silly of me! The catalyst is the unrivaled masterpiece of Ascendant technology, the epitome of eons of development, but surely I can make my own. Why not?"

I raised a hand. "Damascus—"

"While I'm at it," he continued, "why not forbid the sun to shine? Hmm? Command the tides to retreat? Why not—"

"Damascus!" Amethyst suddenly squeaked.

This time the old man stopped. Perhaps it was the urgency in her voice or the delight in her eyes. Whatever the case, he paused long enough for Amethyst to blurt out, "I found a description!"

"What?"

"Yes!" She giggled and pointed to a parchment rubbing lying on the bed.

Her tutor leaned over, forgetting his previous tirade. I approached as well. "What does that mean?"

"In all these years," Damascus mumbled while scanning the inscriptions Amethyst indicated, "I've found countless references explaining *what* a catalyst can do and *why* it's necessary. But a description? Never have I found an actual description of how it works, how it's made, or even what it looks like."

"What does it say?"

"I was getting to that, thank you," he barked. Then, after Amethyst brought an extra lantern, he started reading aloud. "*In his hand, the Author held*—What is that? The Touchstone?"

Amethyst leaned over the bed, trying to follow along.

"With the Catalyst," Damascus continued, his fingers tracing the words, "the Prefex birthed fire and water. He tore corporal and ethereal, fractured reality and time, traded eternity for death. The stone, black as night, penetrated his heart and—and manifested desire. The foundation?—no—The Cornerstones. The shards of—"

But there, Damascus stopped, nearly dropping the lantern onto the parchment. His gray eyes drifted from the inscriptions. He gazed out the window and over the courtyard, paralyzed by some long-forgotten memory. "The Cornerstone."

Catalyst

"Damascus?" Amethyst asked, her hand on his shoulder.

"The catalyst. A black shard." He wasn't reading anymore. He was babbling, grasping at some murky details from his past. "Of course. A Cornerstone. *Irrideous*."

"What?"

"Irrideous," he repeated, though not to answer my question. "If Irrideous possessed a Cornerstone, then—" He took a sharp, agonizing breath. "Oh dear. What have I done?"

"Who's Irrideous?" I asked Amethyst.

"I don't know," she answered. Then she asked Damascus, "Does he have a catalyst?"

Damascus didn't respond. For perhaps a whole minute, he continued staring out the window, his expression vacant and his mouth hanging open. Then he stood to leave.

Amethyst chased after. "If Irrideous has a catalyst, we should go looking for him."

"We will do no such thing," he snapped.

She flinched. "Damascus, *please*. This is the solution we've been searching for."

"No, Amethyst." He grasped her shoulder. "The Cornerstone is not a solution. It's damnation. It is certain death."

"Is that what happened to Irrideous?"

Damascus would say nothing more. He shuffled out the door, leaving Amethyst bewildered and hurt.

I almost followed. I nearly chased after him, but at that exact moment something else distracted me. From somewhere outside I heard a rumbling crash, like a demon shaking the foundations of the earth.

Demon

That crash wasn't the first warning. Thinking back, I can remember other omens. There had been some indistinct alarms shouted from the harbor, followed by distant screams of terror. Then I had heard soldiers rushing past Amethyst's door. I didn't heed those signs, though. Distracted by Damascus's sudden horror about the Cornerstone and someone named Irrideous, neither Amethyst nor I realized something was happening outside until that first thunderous crash.

There was no ignoring the threat after that, and we rushed to the window overlooking the courtyard. Night had fallen by then, and we couldn't see everything clearly, but from the torchlight we could make out hundreds of Vanguard flooding the square below. The entire garrison had responded, it seemed, and Talsadar was there too, pointing his cane to position his men behind the gatehouse that separated the courtyard from the harbor beyond. Around those thick doors he stationed perhaps one hundred pikemen in a rough semi-circle to surround whatever intruders might penetrate Ballabor's defenses, and behind them he placed twice as many soldiers armed with gleaming swords. Then the garrison general shouted to the archers stationed atop the two towers that flanked the gatehouse. "What is it? What do you see? Answer me, damn ingrates!"

If the archers answered, I didn't hear. I could only watch as they launched countless arrows over the wall at some enemy below. Then the crash sounded a second time, the gatehouse doors buckled, and the archers stumbled as the granite ramparts shuddered beneath them.

Something was on the other side trying to break through, I guessed. Our unknown enemy had followed us. Under cover of night, Amethyst's assassin had somehow navigated the tumult and slipped past the floodgates into the harbor, and he hadn't come alone. This time he brought an army and a battering ram to smash down the ancient gates.

Such foolishness, I thought as the crash resounded again.

I wanted to let them come. They had dared so far and risked so much. At great cost they had tracked us through the Ooramere Islands to our fortress, so why not open the door? Why not allow them in where our soldiers waited to greet them with sharpened steel? Let them enter the hornet's nest. They were all so eager to die. Why deny them any longer? Why wait while they pounded away at that impenetrable gate?

Before I could verbalize this boast, however, one final crash resonated. For the fourth time something smashed against the entrance, and the doors suddenly failed. Though they should have stood steadfast for days, the thick gates exploded inward, hurling wooden shrapnel and twisted iron bands into Talsadar and his waiting men.

Then, into the courtyard, something truly horrific came.

It wasn't an army. It was a single warrior—no, a demon. A harrowing creature from the underworld, if there is such a place. It resembled a man, perhaps, as a war horse resembles a mongrel dog. It had two massive legs, two strong arms, and a helmed head between its broad shoulders with perhaps a cruel face behind a skull-like mask, but it towered half a length taller than our defenders. It stood indomitable, encased within an impenetrable exoskeleton of overlapping black armor plates that shimmered like ink in the torchlight. From behind a morbid helmet, its eyes blazed with yellow bloodlust, and its heavy steps quaked the earth. This demon wielded only a glaive—a pole weapon with a cleaver blade fixed atop a long

Demon

shaft—but that dreadful sickle tore swathes across our lines. It shredded chainmail like paper and cracked steel armor like eggshell.

This fiend had broken the door by itself, I finally realized. Using only its shoulder as a battering ram, the juggernaut had smashed through reinforced timber, and though it now faced hundreds of heavily armed Vanguard in the courtyard below, I knew such opposition meant nothing. Whatever counterattack we offered, the demon would advance. It would kill Amethyst.

So I firmly seized her shoulder. "Stay here!"

"What? No!"

"Stay out of sight! If Damascus returns, hold him here too," I ordered. Then I bolted out her door to join the battle.

I had no other choice. From our tour with Talsadar, I knew there was no escaping Ballabor. There were no back doors or secret exits, only high skywalks overlooking sheer drops and swirling surf. There were no safe places either, no hidden vault where Amethyst could endure the storm. I suppose we still could have run somewhere, the cisterns perhaps, but that would only have delayed the inevitable, and I couldn't just hide, not while my Vanguard brothers sacrificed so much for our safety. No, if I wanted to keep Amethyst alive, I had to destroy that demon.

I bolted into the hallway and unsheathed my sword, filling the corridor with the resonance of folded steel. I turned west toward the staircase and ramparts above. I avoided the courtyard since it was already jammed with too many soldiers pressing against that deadly adversary, and instead I climbed atop the barrier wall that separated the harbor from the inner square.

From the high ramparts, I could see the juggernaut below, decimating our forces. I saw the lavish courtyard already littered with the dead and the polished granite floor stained with blood. I saw Vanguard attack simultaneously from every direction with pikes and broadswords, all without causing injury, and I witnessed the demon's onslaught tear them asunder.

Then I noticed our archers standing petrified atop the wall, their crossbows at their sides, and my blood boiled. "You callow vermin! Fire!"

One of the pallid archers dared to protest. "We still have men down there!"

"You'll soon have no one left at all if you don't intervene. Now shoot!"

"It's no use! The armor—"

I twisted the crossbow from the soldier's hand, snatched a bolt from his quiver, and took aim. It was an easy shot from that high vantage point, even in the dim torchlight. The massive demon hardly moved, preferring instead to hold its ground as Vanguard reinforcements surged against it. I fired with total certainty, knowing beyond doubt I would strike my target, and following my lead a few dozen archers sent bolts to follow. I screamed a warning too, and the men below leapt aside to avoid the barrage.

The deadly volley failed, though. Perhaps two shots found gaps in the demon's armor and sunk into whatever lay beneath, but they made no difference, and the other arrows bounced off the black scales like hail on cobblestones. We didn't stop the demon. We hardly even annoyed it. The beast only glanced up at us briefly before it resumed slaughtering our men, and why not? Why bother climbing the stairs to swat fleas off a wall when there were so many closer targets of opportunity?

Infuriated, I hurled the crossbow away and looked for something larger, a spear perhaps. Then I saw the ballistae.

"You there!" I shouted to another Vanguard lieutenant, an armory officer. "Can you pivot that machine around?"

He gawked open-mouthed as if the idea had never occurred to him, but he nodded his head all the same.

"Do it!"

The armory officer gathered his wits and barked some orders to his crew, and while they spun the ballista inward, more Vanguard reinforcements swarmed into the courtyard below to contain the threat. Their valiant efforts were wasted, though. With its long glaive, the demon effortlessly sliced through armor and flesh, and each step brought it closer to the guest quarters.

"Hurry! Faster!"

The ballista crew rotated the machine and cranked back the torsion bundles, twisting the taut ropes that powered the massive crossbow. They wedged granite blocks under the back end so the ballista could fire downward instead of lobbing its shot across the harbor. After an eternity, the siege weapon was positioned and loaded, and then the officer looked to me for permission.

"Fire!"

He gave the signal. The ballista launched. With a loud groan the torsion ropes snapped, hurling the harpoon fast and true. The missile struck the demon almost center mass, and as the beast toppled backwards, I screamed victoriously along with the ballista's crew.

But the demon rose again, and our voices fell silent. We hadn't killed it. We hadn't even penetrated its armor. Though the ballista could have pierced the hull of a great warship, it only knocked the demon off its feet and dislodged a small section of armor. We only succeeded in one aspect: we had finally earned the demon's undivided attention.

"Again! AGAIN!" I urged the ballista's crew.

The terrified soldiers worked fast, frantic to launch a second shot before the demon could climb the stairs and reach our location atop the barrier wall. Our adversary had no intention of waiting that long to retaliate, though. While the armory men cranked back the torsion bundles again, the demon reached for a nearby corpse and curled its gnarled fingers around the man's ankle. Then it spun and heaved the dead weight toward our rampart like a boy tossing a stick.

I cried a warning, but I was too late. In an instant the body cleared the distance, crashed into the ballista's crew, and sent men sprawling in every direction. Most fell with only superficial injuries, but a few others, like the armory officer, were knocked backwards, over the parapets, and off the wall. I don't know if they survived the drop. I only knew that the ballista remained intact. It was even loaded and ready for another shot.

The demon saw that fact as clearly as I, though, and it sent more missiles after the first. From that endless quiver, that courtyard littered with the dead, the juggernaut hurled body after body at the ballista, and when those lifeless shots failed to damage the machine, the demon offered something else. Quite by accident, I think, the demon found a long splintered beam—a piece of the wooden gates blown inward by the breech. This was more solid than a dead body and larger by far, but with little extra effort, the demon hefted the beam like a javelin, hurled the missile toward the barrier wall, and struck the ballista center mass.

That collision was catastrophic. When the siege weapon was struck, the crossbeams and side supports snapped like kindling. Then the coiled torsion arms unraveled, releasing their stored energy like wound springs. In the blink of an eye, the machine tore itself apart, and since I was standing nearby, I was caught in a shower of planks and splinters.

Instinctively, my hands rose to shield my face, but they offered little protection against the rain of timber. Planks and bolts peppered my arms, and something bigger struck my chest, broke my ribs, and knocked me backwards against the parapet. I was weightless a moment, just long enough to realize I had tripped off the wall and was tumbling through the air. Then I slammed into the courtyard floor below.

I passed out for a few seconds, or maybe the shock scrambled my memory of those next few moments. I only know that when I awoke, my vision was blank and I could taste blood in my mouth. My lower back burned insatiably, I couldn't feel my legs, and I couldn't move. My right arm was broken too. I couldn't do anything to protect Amethyst anymore, not that it mattered. It never really mattered. The

Demon

whole Vanguard garrison and the protection of the Ooramere Islands didn't matter. I could have stayed in the girl's chambers all along. We could have stayed in Tel Tellesti. I could have even stood back and let her perish in the firebomb. Such a terrible end would certainly have been preferable to whatever torture that demon had planned for her.

The demon!

It was still alive, wasn't it? The realization sent jolts of pain through my chest. I was the best the Vanguard had to offer, the consummate soldier, yet I lay broken on the polished granite floor while it continued uncontested. It had slashed through our armored soldiers like reeds and shrugged off our arrows like rain. What would happen next? Would it wait in the courtyard until the entire garrison was spent, or would it climb the staircase to the guest quarters? Would the demon find the heiress or an empty room?

I didn't want to know the answer to that question, but again I had no choice. I couldn't save Amethyst, but if she was to die, I had to at least watch. Perhaps I would hear something from the demon that I could report to General Uriah. Perhaps I would glean some clues about who wanted Amethyst dead, and why. So I stirred. I still couldn't move my legs, but I found strength enough to raise my head and open my eyes. At first I saw only vague images, a blur of flashing light, a flickering blaze, and then suddenly everything came into dreadful focus, and I cried out with new terror.

The demon had burst into flames.

How could this be? What dark sorcery was this? I blinked and focused again, desperately wishing my eyesight deceived me, but the facts endured. A fiery cloak danced over the demon's armor, and from its smoking throat a screeching cry resounded throughout the courtyard. Then it raised the long glaive overhead and took another heavy step that shook the fortress.

But it stepped back.

I blinked a third time, longer still, and propped myself higher with my one good elbow. Then I looked again with fresh eyes and realized a welcome truth. The demon wasn't advancing. It was withdrawing. The dreadful glaive in its hands was raised in defense, and the demon retreated another step away from an old man who was approaching from the far side of the courtyard.

At this new adversary, the demon finally spoke with a low growl that reverberated behind its forbidding mask. "Step aside, prefex!"

Damascus didn't step aside, and from underneath his pressed robes he produced a small ceramic flask. This vial he hurled straight at our adversary with impressive speed and accuracy for such an old man. The demon tried to swat the container away, but when it missed the little vial struck its target, shattered, and spilled its liquid contents. Then the flames came bright again, and the demon shrieked in agony, spinning and flailing and slapping its hands against the black armor to smother the fire.

Like a living torch, the demon offered new light to the dark courtyard and illuminated more welcome sights. I saw Vanguard still standing. They gathered behind the Testament and crowded the alleys that led to the complex beyond. There were perhaps a hundred or more reinforcements waiting in the margins for an opportunity, and even after watching their brothers perish under the demon's glaive, these survivors bravely advanced, bolstered by their enemy's agony.

Damascus warned them off, though, waving his hands. "No! Stay back! He is far beyond you!" The Vanguard kept their distance. It pained them to hold fast, but they only watched as the demon stifled the oily flames and addressed the teacher.

"Stand aside! It is not your time!"

"That is not your choice to make," came the brash answer.

Enraged, the demon surged with fresh vigor and raised its glaive to hew Damascus in two. In response, the old man only reached into his robes again, into some interior pocket, and he produced a fistful of some granular substance, like sand, which he tossed into the air so the particles could twinkle like stars in the sky. At first this seemed an inadequate counter to the mighty glaive, but before the demon could strike, the particles cracked into glowing embers. Then they burst forth, crashing against the demon's armor like a myriad whistling meteors, and the juggernaut stumbled back again.

But Damascus hadn't won—that much I knew. He had only angered the demon, and I could do nothing to help.

Without a word, the fiend attacked again. With seemingly inexhaustible strength, the demon charged. Damascus retreated and offered more Ascendant artifices, each one more wondrous than the last, but still his nemesis rallied. Protected by that accursed armor, the demon weathered the assault and even made headway. Relentlessly, the enemy swung the glaive in wide arcs, forcing Damascus backwards. With methodical precision, the demon herded Damascus across the courtyard and backed him into a corner.

Then Damascus stopped. Resigned to his fate, the teacher's hands fell. He did nothing to oppose the demon as it strode forward, raised an arm, and cracked a clenched fist against the old man's head.

"No!" I screamed. Others screamed too. I even heard a young girl cry out desperately.

The demon ignored our words, but it didn't kill the old man. Instead, it reached down with the glaive and poked Damascus like a boy prodding a fallen bird to see if it was truly dead. Then it opened its mouth again, and hot smoke belched from its gullet. "Don't you die. Not yet. Not until you watch."

Whatever the demon meant to demonstrate, though, I didn't see. No one saw exactly what happened next, actually, because at that moment, the dark island fortress suddenly shone bright as day. A surge of blinding light, beyond intense, illuminated the whole courtyard, and stunned by such white radiance, the demon dropped Damascus and stumbled back. With my one remaining good arm, I shielded my eyes as something arced toward the demon and landed near its feet, like a burning fleck of the sun thrusting itself between the wolf and its prey, and from that resplendent glory, like an archangel descended from heaven, Amethyst appeared.

She still wore her satin gown, though it now shimmered in the brilliance, but in the few minutes since I had left her, she had changed into her tall boots and pulled those lace gloves around her clenched fingers. With only those armaments, she assaulted an invincible foe. Without a moment's hesitation, she hurled herself against the demon before I could shout warning or rebuke. Without a sword or even a shield, Amethyst smashed into that armor with her fists just as she had assailed me on the *Solution*—only this time she didn't hold back.

I was amazed, I must admit, watching her battle a beast three times her mass. Silhouetted by the burning radiance, Amethyst seemed a shining goddess waging war against a black shadow, an inky stain on humanity. The demon still far outmatched her strength, but she was a faster and smaller target. As the demon raged and lashed with its pole cleaver, Amethyst danced and spun, keeping herself beyond her opponent's grasp and pounding away at its plating with her powerful gauntlets. As the blinding light faded, Amethyst drove her enemy away from her teacher and across the courtyard. She even managed to catch and wrench away the demon's glaive, and had she pressed in that moment, perhaps she could have ended the battle.

For whatever reason, however, the heiress didn't capitalize on her advantage. Whether from youthful inexperience or unfounded mercy, Amethyst tossed away the glaive and instead redoubled her efforts. Sadly this wasn't enough, because unlike the demon, Amethyst wore no armor. Therefore, when her foe finally made contact, the momentum instantly shifted. The first devastating blow the demon landed, in fact, sent Amethyst tumbling like a stone skipping across a pond until she slammed against the interior wall, and when she picked herself up, she was heavily bruised and bleeding from a deep gash on her forehead. From then on, she focused on defense. She decided to retreat from the demon, to lead it away from the ravaged courtyard and the defeated garrison, and unfortunately her only course lay up.

Heedless of the inherent danger in such a path, Amethyst limped to the staircase and scrambled toward the skywalk. Undeterred, the demon hounded her up the stairs to the narrow ramparts above the courtyard, and there it cornered her. Amethyst had no escape, no options, so with her back against the low wall, beyond which laid only a long drop into cold oblivion, she fought desperately. She fought well. She fared better than I would have guessed considering the atrocities I had witnessed at the demon's hand. She dodged many blows that would have left her dead, and she ducked devastating punches that smashed apart the granite parapet behind her.

Eventually, though, even her luck ran out. The demon caught her off balance with the back of its hand and hurled her against the battlement again, and this time, when she didn't pick herself up, the dark bohemoth provided cruel assistance. It reached down and curled massive claws around her neck. Then it lifted until her boots dangled above the floor. With a snarl, it held her close, so close she could probably feel its hot breath on her face and smell its foul stench, and it spoke. With a low, guttural growl, it gloated, "You're the best he can do?" Finally, as I cried her name and as the surviving Vanguard watched in horrific disbelief, the demon tossed Amethyst over the parapet, off the skywalk and to her death.

Then the enemy turned and started its long descent.

My heart pounded even harder than before. My mind raced. I knew what was coming next. It seemed predetermined. The demon would return to the open courtyard and engage the remaining Vanguard. Maybe the soldiers would strike first, hoping to overwhelm the demon before it could retrieve its glaive. Maybe they would retreat and hide, hoping the enemy would let them live now that it had accomplished its primary mission. I doubted that mattered, though. Whatever their choice, I knew the demon would exterminate the survivors and finally kill Damascus before leaving the proud fortress of Ballabor utterly decimated.

I had to somehow survive that plan. Though I had failed to protect the heiress, I had to at least live long enough to report back to Tel Tellesti. I had to inform Uriah about our new enemy, one more fearsome than the Glacians and Samarans combined. So I decided to disengage. If I played dead, perhaps the demon would let me be. Perhaps behind that stony mask, it wouldn't notice my labored breathing or smell my fear. Once it left, I could escape. Despite the broken bones I had suffered, maybe I could still crawl back to the *Sole Solution* (if the ship wasn't already sunk in the harbor) and leave this wretched place. Maybe I could even manage to navigate the Ooramere Islands without dashing my ship upon the rocks.

I never had the chance to tempt my fate, however, because the demon never reached the courtyard. Before it descended halfway down the staircase, in fact, something massive struck from behind, and the demon spun around to see the impossible.

Amethyst was alive.

She had indeed fallen, I assure you. She had been knocked insensible before being hurled from the skywalk, and had she remained unconscious, she would have crashed into the raging surf below. But halfway down, Amehtyst had regained her senses. After plummeting perhaps a hundred paces, she had reached out for the granite walls and dug her gloved fingertips into the solid stone. It had been easy, she later told me, no harder than poking into tightly packed snow. She had nearly wrenched her shoulder from its socket, and her downward momentum had carried her farther than she would have liked as her laced fingers tore long gashes into the ancient cliffs, but eventually she had stopped falling.

Then she had clawed her way back. She had leapt up onto the skywalk where the demon had bested her, and she had seen her damned adversary descending toward the courtyard, confident of its victory. Fuming, she had picked up the nearest piece of debris, a

Demon

heavy slab of granite dislodged from the parapet by the demon's fist, and hurled that rock downward. Launched from her amplified arm like a catapult missile, the projectile had smashed into the demon's armored head.

It caused incredible damage, I'm pleased to say. Struck from behind, the demon stumbled and tripped down a few stairs, and when it turned back and realized who had dared such an assault, it bellowed at Amethyst's reappearance. Forgetting its glaive, the demon lumbered back up the stairs as Amethyst fired more missiles. Though its hard armor fractured under the assault, and though it fought an uphill battle, the demon still made steady progress. In the last few yards or so, it even sprinted toward the heiress, and for a petrifying moment I feared it would throw itself into her and hurl them both from the skywalk to guarantee her demise.

At the last second, however, Amethyst ceased her missile attack, leaned down, and reached for its waist. Mimicking a move from my book, she lifted fast and arched her back, using her enemy's momentum against itself. She twisted the demon over her shoulder and off the skywalk.

Ten

"We need to stop for some clarification," Rehoboth interjects. "Do you mind?"

"Course not."

"First," she says, reviewing her notes, "you mentioned a flare, a blinding light Amethyst used to distract this *demon*."

"Yes."

"How did she create such light?"

"She didn't. She used an artifice, a star fragment from a meteor. She showed it to me later on the way to Severance. It, um—" I pause and scratch my temple. "It looks harmless, like a melted rock, but when exposed to a heat source—a torch, for example—it burns bright as the sun at noonday."

"She acquired this from Damascus?"

I nod.

The arbiter consults her notes again. "So she ignited this *star fragment* and tossed it between the demon and Damascus before she intervened?"

"Correct."

Rehoboth makes the necessary corrections and flips the page. "Also, you called the monster a demon."

"Is that a problem?"

"Yes, actually. Yesterday I interviewed an archer named Reuben, another survivor. I think he's the man whose crossbow you took. Regardless, he called the assailant a *dreadnaught*."

"He's correct. Damascus identified the intruder as a dreadnaught after the event."

"Then why are you calling it a demon?"

"Because *at the time*, I thought it was a demon. It was huge and strong, and it had those crazy eyes." Then I add dryly, raising my wrist as evidence, "It snapped my arm like a twig."

Rehoboth glances dubiously at my forearm, which is completely healthy.

"I got better, obviously."

She doesn't appreciate the humor. "Please call it a dreadnaught from now on. For consistency. Understand?"

"Very well."

She checks her notes one more time. "I think that does it. You may continue."

I remain quiet, though. I glance at Uriah and then at the additional guards now stationed inside the doorway because of my previous outburst.

"Lieutenant?"

"Your grace," I eventually answer, "may I ask a few questions of my own?"

"I can't guarantee answers."

Fair enough. "It's just—well, we never found out how the dreadnaught arrived."

"It probably arrived the same way it left," she says without consulting her notes.

"How?"

"We don't know," Rehoboth admits. "That archer, Reuben? He was the first to notice the dreadnaught, but he claims it didn't come from anywhere. It didn't arrive on a ship. It was just suddenly *there*, standing on the pier."

"It just appeared?"

She nods.

I swallow nervously. "Then it's possible it just disappeared too, isn't it? Perhaps it's not dead."

Ten

"Perhaps," Rehoboth allows, "although it's far more likely that Reuben was neglecting his duties and invented that part of his story to protect himself."

How perceptive. Does she suspect I'm doing the same thing?

Rehoboth raises an eyebrow at my silence. "Is that all?"

"I was also wondering about casualties. We left Ballabor soon after, so I never heard the final report."

Rehoboth consults her notes again. "One hundred nineteen."

"Really?" The number seems low.

"One hundred nineteen dead," she clarifies. "Nearly another two hundred wounded, though from the testimonies I've heard, I'm surprised the number isn't higher. Fortunately, all the casualties were just soldiers."

I grit my teeth. "Just soldiers?"

"Yes," Rehoboth says. "Just soldiers."

The Most Dangerous Path

Amethyst remained on the skywalk for a few minutes after hurling that dreadnaught over the ledge. I don't know why. I never bothered to ask. Perhaps she didn't want to repeat her enemy's mistake, and she peered into the crushing blackness to ensure the demon would never rise again from the depths. Maybe she needed to catch her breath. I suspect, though, she lingered on that high rampart for a different reason. She wasn't ready to return. She couldn't bear the sight that awaited her below.

I don't blame her. I could hardly stomach it myself.

Hundreds of dead and dying men lay strewn about. Ribbons of chainmail littered the courtyard. I saw broken pikes, bent broadswords left where they had fallen in puddles of blood, dismembered arms and legs still wrapped in crumpled, twisted armor. Worse than that, I heard haunting wails drifting through the shadows, the dirge of survivors suffering from their wounds or lamenting the dead.

I feared I would soon die myself, still lying where I had fallen from the barrier wall. I couldn't feel my legs. Everything below my chest was numb, in fact. My arm was surely broken, and my eyes were failing again.

The various shapes in the courtyard were already fading into indistinguishable blurs, but I could see well enough to recognize Talsadar nearby, his body half crushed under a splintered section of Ballabor's gates, a gaping gash across his chest, his ebony cane snapped in two. I found Gideon's body too, and I wondered why he hadn't returned that night to the *Sole Solution*.

Then I saw Damascus.

He didn't seem much better off than I. He had suffered a concussion, I suspect, from the blood matted in his hair, and he walked with a painful limp, but at least he was moving. He had mind enough to sidestep the dead and kneel beside the living, and he had kind words enough to comfort the survivors. He never stopped for long, though, and whenever he rose again, he set his gaze on his destination. He locked eyes on me.

But when he eventually reached my side and stood over my broken body, he offered no sympathetic words. He glared down, his eyes brimming with anger. Betrayal. As if this carnage were all my fault. He even said, "Are you quite satisfied?"

Such a strange choice of words. He must have hit his head harder than I thought.

No further accusation passed from his lips, though. Instead, Damascus sighed with sad resignation and knelt beside me. He considered my numerous injuries, poking and prodding without concern for my comfort. He ignored my groaning and wincing, and then? Well, I'm not sure exactly what he did next.

While I lay motionless, Damascus clapped his hands together and rubbed his palms briskly until they grew hot from the friction, and with those warm hands, he reached under my armor. He spoke too, muttering something ancient and indistinct as his fingers kneaded my dark bruises. He pushed at broken bones under my skin until I screamed out in agony.

But then he stopped. He stood up, reached down, and yanked me to my feet, and when he removed his supporting hands from my arm, I didn't fall down. I could walk again.

"How is this possible?" I gasped. "What did you do?"

Damascus didn't answer. His attention had already shifted elsewhere. The heiress had finally descended from the skywalk, and she was shuffling toward us.

Like everyone else in that courtyard, Amethyst looked worse for wear. Her confidence, her humanity, had disappeared. Her satin

The Most Dangerous Path

gown was soiled and torn. Her exposed skin was a patchwork of gashes and bruises. Her bleeding lips hung open, and her unblinking eyes—

Her eyes. Those endless hazel eyes. They were bloodshot, like an autumn harvest consumed by brushfire. Gazing into that pain, I forgot where I was and the miracle that had just occurred. Suddenly, I was back in the citadel when the flames had licked the skin off her arm, and those eyes asked the same questions. Who could have done such a thing? What reason could justify such hatred and violence? Is there no place secure, no hallowed ground?

I couldn't answer those questions, and Damascus didn't try. He still embraced her, though. With warm hands and an ancient whisper, Amethyst's teacher stroked his thumb across a gash on her chin, wiping away the blood and leaving no trace of crimson, not even a faint scar. In similar fashion he healed the rest of her wounds, brushing away the scratches and bruises as easily as he might sweep a tear from her eye, and soon he had Amethyst's body good as new.

Then Damascus turned his attention deeper, to her heart, that white porcelain. He leaned close. He embraced her and spoke softly into her ear, "You did well, my child. So very well." With mere words, he reduced the girl to a weeping heap.

And I left.

My presence wasn't needed there. Damascus had already fixed Amethyst's body. The damage to her psyche would take longer to heal, I suspected. After all, she wasn't a soldier. She was a teenager. A girl. She hadn't endured the training and developed the discipline necessary to endure combat, yet she had taken a life that day and seen so many others callously tossed aside. She had confronted oblivion, and despite her survival I doubted she would ever truly recover, no matter what secrets Damascus whispered in her ear.

That was not my primary concern or responsibility at the moment, however, and regardless I wasn't comfortable seeing her like that with Damascus, so I pushed her situation from my mind and focused on the task at hand. That undertaking was no more agreeable, though, so please forgive me if I don't provide ample details.

Suffice it to say, I helped the other survivors move Ballabor's wounded from the courtyard to the infirmary. Then we focused on the dead. It was a morbid, miserable affair during which no one spoke. The only happy note occurred when I visited the harbor and discovered the *Sole Solution* miraculously unscathed. The demon, it seemed, had focused entirely on the fortress and ignored targets outside the main wall.

That blessing barely lifted my spirits, though. Since Talsadar and many of the other officers had perished, the survivors looked to me for leadership. Under my direction we gathered the fragments of the ancient doors, those heavy gates the demon had so effortlessly shredded, and in the courtyard we built a great bonfire to provide light and warmth and comfort as we worked through that long night.

We wrapped and carried the dead to the harbor, where they would eventually be loaded on ships and sent home to their wives, children, siblings and families. We gathered up weapons after that. Many of the pikes and crossbows had been broken during the attack, so we used those to fuel the bonfire's blaze, but we sent home the steel tips and arrowheads since they could be melted down and reforged back in Tel Tellesti. We also collected and returned the discarded broadswords, which had mostly survived intact, and my heart lightened a little. Those old blades would be allocated to new Vanguard soldiers, and I felt better knowing that at least those swords would live on.

With the courtyard thusly salvaged, we finally set to work mopping up the blood, scrubbing the crimson stains from that ancient pavement. After working through the night, we held a short memorial service early the next morning so the Vanguard of Ballabor could bid farewell to their brothers. Many men came forward, offering kind words and fond memories. A few spoke of General Talsadar, often ignoring his acerbic nature and instead focusing on the shrewdness that had won so many admirers (and a few enemies). There was a private affair held for Gideon too, I'm told, aboard the *Sole Solution*, but Damascus and Amethyst attended neither.

I tried to ignore that offense. I tried to excuse the girl who had already suffered too much, too early. I focused on my duties. I even closed the funeral with a little speech. "As Vanguard," I proclaimed, "we honor the valiant who have followed the code without question. We remember those who willingly surrendered their lives for Estavion. For our home. For us. We promise never to forget their sacrifice." The words felt hollow as they tumbled from my mouth, though, because Talsadar and Gideon didn't die for their estate. They didn't die protecting their homes. They died for a girl, an heiress who didn't even attend their memorials.

Afterwards, with the cleanup finished and the distractions gone, the shame and guilt came fast. The anger rose unabated. What was the point of all this? The running? The hiding? The research? I didn't let my emotions show. I visited the great hall for a much overdue meal and ate slowly in a corner by myself. I wore a mask of stoic apathy, but inwardly I raged at Amethyst and Damascus, though I wasn't sure how or if it was their fault. I hated the Glacians for their part, whatever it was. I even hated the Ascendants for leaving us that fortress, for luring us into such false assurance.

More than all that, though, I hated myself. Why was I so ready and willing to blame Amethyst and her tutor? How could I harbor such hatred for Lord Masada despite doubting his very involvement? Most of all, why couldn't I accept my own role? I was just a Vanguard agent. A lowly lieutenant. A bodyguard. A man who had previously enjoyed his anonymity and minor status. These mysteries were not my concern or responsibility to solve, and I had many superiors who were much more capable and equipped to handle such dilemmas, so why couldn't I trust their judgment and focus on my duties?

Because they didn't know the answers either, that's why. I knew that when word of this attack eventually reached General Uriah, he wouldn't know how to react. The whole royal court wouldn't know what to do. They had no more clue what was happening than I did, and because of their incompetence, more of my Vanguard brothers would die. The whole Inheritance would plunge into war.

So I put my mind to it, determined to solve this puzzle. I finished my breakfast, left the great hall, crossed the courtyard and climbed the stairs to the skywalk. Once I reached that high vantage point, I paused to appreciate the scenery and solitude, but then I set my mind to the riddles.

I first tried again to figure out *why*. Why had the dreadnaught slaughtered Ballabor's men? Had it really come for Amethyst? I had doubted her significance before. When the firebomb exploded in Tel Tellesti, I had dared consider that Amethyst was only a random victim. Now I knew better. It couldn't be a coincidence that the demon's attack had occurred mere days after we had arrived. Amethyst was the only probable target.

That only led to another *why*. Why kill Amethyst at all? I was ill-equipped to answer that question, though. I still knew nothing whatsoever about the heiress, her family history, her life. I didn't even know her real name, apparently, so how could I guess why someone wanted her dead?

I turned my attention, therefore, to the *how*. How did the dreadnaught navigate the perilous Ooramere Islands and reach Ballabor? Immediately after considering that question, though, I disregarded its importance. That *how* didn't seem necessary. After witnessing Damascus perform so many miracles, and after seeing that single demonic warrior decimate our entire garrison, I had little trouble believing the dreadnaught could have steered through the tumult.

The Most Dangerous Path

Besides, there was another *how* distracting me, another question more disturbing than all the rest.

How did the dreadnaught know where to find Amethyst?

I knew her escape was probably no secret. After the firebomb and the Summit's resulting failure, I'm sure the whole estate had heard rumors of the heiress fleeing for her life. Few knew her exact location, however. There was me, of course, and General Uriah. Amethyst's father had undoubtedly been informed, and the king, since Uriah had asked permission for our visit. But that was it. Wasn't it? Captain Abner and his crew had only been informed of our destination *after* we left port.

That left only two conclusions. We were either followed from Tel Tellesti (an unlikely scenario, given the *Solution*'s matchless speed), or someone had betrayed us.

At first, I didn't panic. I thought perhaps someone had just bribed one of the *Solution*'s crewmen to drop a message in a bottle. That didn't seem likely, though. Any ship hoping to retrieve such a breadcrumb before it disappeared on the rolling waves would have followed us closely, and we never detected any vessels trailing us.

Perhaps someone at Ballabor had committed the deed. There were hundreds of soldiers stationed there. Any of them could have discretely released a carrier hawk from the skywalk under cover of darkness. That didn't seem likely either, though. It would have taken days for the message to reach its destination and weeks for the recipient to travel out to Ballabor, but the dreadnaught attack had occurred mere days after our arrival.

That left only one possible conclusion. The demon had been dispatched before we ever arrived. Someone knew exactly where we were going, and when. There was a traitor among us.

At the thought, my fists clenched. Panic and anger coalesced in my racing heart. I actually snatched up a small hunk of granite broken from the parapet and hurled it over the edge, where it tumbled and fell into the churning waves far below. I vowed vengeance and justice on that villain, whoever he was.

But before I could do anything else, a small voice interrupted me. "Lieutenant?"

"What?"

I spun and noticed a man behind me, the young archer who had lent me his crossbow. He seemed terrified to speak with me. No doubt he had witnessed my outburst, but all the same he held his ground and spoke. "Excuse me. I only meant to ask what we should do with these."

At his statement, I realized the youth was holding two objects for my consideration. In his left hand, he held the dreadnaught's glaive. In his right, a section of that cursed armor.

"We found them during salvage," he explained. "No one knows what to make of them. What should we do? Doesn't seem appropriate to keep them as trophies."

I sighed impatiently. "Why don't you ask Damascus?"

"He's been busy in the infirmary, or the lady's chambers. Didn't seem like he wanted to be disturbed."

"Fine," I relented. "Let me see."

Reluctantly, I took the glaive from the soldier's hand. Up close, I saw it was longer and heavier than I expected, much too ungainly for any normal man to wield, so without another thought I pitched the dreadful glaive over the parapet, and I let it fall into the sea below where it would be forever buried and forgotten. Then I reached for the armor, fully intending the same treatment.

Once I held that section of armor and looked closer, however, I couldn't discard it. On the contrary, I found myself baffled, intrigued even. When I had first noticed the dark armor during the battle, I had guessed it was molded from blackened steel or perhaps polished iron, but in the morning sun I realized the truth was much stranger. In my hands, I held a *vambrace*—a section of armor that wraps the forearm, perhaps knocked loose when we had fired that ballista harpoon—but this vambrace was unlike anything I had ever seen before.

First off, the armor was not forged from steel. Rather, it was carved from some lustrous stone, like obsidian or maybe onyx. It was also remarkably heavy despite being one of the smallest pieces of the armored suit, and I marveled at how strong the demon must have been to even stand under such crushing weight. Most disturbing of all, though, I noticed strange writing graven across the outer surface of the armor, and with a twinge of trepidation, I recognized the language. It was stonescript.

The doubts and fears returned fast after that. And the anger. With horror, I realized that this traitor, this villain Talsadar had warned me about, was much more clever than I had assumed. Not only did he somehow guess Amethyst's secret refuge, and not only could he summon minions like that dreadnaught, but he could interpret Ascendant writings. He knew how to construct artifices like Amethyst's lace gloves.

There was only one hint of good news in all this. If our enemy possessed knowledge of the Ascendants, then maybe he was known to someone else. Just maybe.

I didn't consider any other alternatives. I just acted. I thanked the young soldier, left the skywalk, and descended the stairs. With the dreadnaught vambrace, I went looking for Damascus, and I eventually found the old man in Amethyst's guest quarters.

He looked exhausted, and he still wore the same clothes. He had probably been up all night, like me, perhaps spending his time in the infirmary and offering his healing to the wounded and injured while the rest of us had salvaged the courtyard. Now he was taking a break, I suppose. He was bent over a table staring blankly at some parchment notes from the Testament, and a plate of food sat untouched beside him.

Amethyst was there too, looking no better. She had changed out of her torn gown and into a linen frock, but her expression remained the same. Lost. Scarred. When I entered, she was sitting reticent on the wide granite sill and staring vacantly out the window at the blood-stained courtyard below. Had she sat there all night? Had she refused to sleep for fear of reliving those horrid memories in some nightmare?

I was too angry to care. I burst in without knocking and tossed the vambrace onto the table before Damascus. I didn't hide the accusations in my voice. "Explain this."

Amethyst glanced over but said nothing. At the sight of the armor, though, Damascus paused his research. Very slowly, as if choosing the headstone meant for his own gravestone, he lifted the vambrace and muttered a word under his breath. "*Nephilim.*"

"What? Speak up!"

He ignored my question. "Where did you find this?"

"Where do you think?"

That was not the answer he wanted.

I kept pressing. "You know what this is, don't you?"

"Come now, lieutenant. What kind of bumbler do you take me for? Of course I know. It's dreadnaught armor," he answered, "and it's quite an amazing artifice, when it's not used against you, that is. It works somewhat like Amethyst's gloves, only it's far more sophisticated and potent. Each piece is custom made, and it affixes to the warrior, vastly increasing his size, strength, and endurance."

"Wait. *His* size?" I stammered. "You mean that demon—that dreadnaught was a man?"

"An incredibly strong man, no doubt, to wreak such havoc," Damascus clarified, "but yes, a man all the same."

"That's not possible."

"No? Why don't you see for yourself?" Damascus offered me the vambrace. "Put it on."

I hesitated. I even glanced at Amethyst, hoping she would shake her head or otherwise contradict her tutor's suggestion, but she was staring out the window again, ignoring our conversation. I didn't particularly trust Damascus or this cursed armor that had just decimated an entire garrison, and I was skeptical since the armor seemed designed for someone much larger than I. It even lacked the usual straps and buckles to secure it in place. Still, my curiosity overcame my concerns, so I slipped the vambrace over my forearm.

As soon as the obsidian armor touched my skin, my doubts vanished. The vambrace stuck fast like glue. My veins throbbed and my skin turned dark and cold. My muscles bulged painfully, far exceeding their design and limits. Somehow my arm swelled to fill the armor, and the rest of my body also grew so my forearm seemed proportional despite its increased bulk.

And all the while, for as long as I wore that armor, *something else* surged through my bloodstream. I know not what it was or from whence it came (Damascus never explained that particular effect), but the exhilarating elixir possessed and empowered me. The heavy vambrace grew light, almost negligible, like leather padding, and I felt invincible. Indeed, once the transformation finished, I felt insanely strong, answerable to no one.

Before I could embrace these effects, though, Damascus peeled off the armor. He saved me from actions I would have deeply regretted.

"That—that was—"

"Yes," he nodded gravely, dropping the vambrace onto the table, "and that was but one piece. You experienced a fraction of the dreadnaught's power."

I said nothing else. I stood in stunned silence, and I tried to imagine what it might have been like from the dreadnaught's perspective, facing so many Vanguard while equipped with such armaments. We must have seemed like crickets to him.

Once I caught my breath, however, my wits returned and I finally asked the question I'd been waiting to pose. "Who made that armor, Damascus? Who sent the dreadnaught?"

"It's not that simple."

I rolled my eyes at his cryptic response. "The vambrace is covered with Ascendant stonescript. You must have some idea."

Damascus pursed his lips and narrowed his gaze. From such an awkward reaction, I could tell clearly that he did know. He knew exactly who had made the armor, but he wouldn't say. This was some awful truth, some secret from his past he would never willingly admit.

So I set my jaw, crossed my arms, and blurted out the only other name I had heard in the past few days. "Was it Irrideous?"

His eyes snapped up. Amethyst turned as well.

"Who is he?" I asked.

"That's a long story, I'm afraid. Perhaps another time."

I conceded that point. "What's he after?"

He answered with a reluctant sigh.

I grew petulant again. "Can you at least say if he'll try again? Is Amethyst safe here?"

"No," Damascus admitted. "If Irrideous is after her, then no, Amethyst is not safe anywhere. None of us are."

My hands physically trembled, but I fast proposed a solution. "We should leave then."

Damascus shook his head. "That won't do any use. Irrideous has eyes everywhere. He'll find us wherever we go."

"He'll find it harder to strike a moving target," I argued.

"Yes, but we have orders to remain here."

"Forget Uriah's orders," I lashed back. "The situation has changed. We can't just sit here and wait."

"This is still the safest place."

"And if he sends another dreadnaught? What then?"

"Better to face him here than someplace else," Damascus countered. "Here, we have allies. Here, we have endured."

A wise rationale, of course, but I suspected he was harboring a different motive. "Better to stay with the Testament, you mean. It would be a shame to lose the opportunity."

The Most Dangerous Path

Damascus set his jaw and leaned close as if to strike me. "There are already enough lies in this world, lieutenant. I would prefer you not make up any more, especially about me."

"Then start packing."

The old man glared at me, deadly serious, and for a second I regretted my boldness. I had no idea what ancient tricks he had hidden within his flowing sleeves. Despite the Vanguard sword hanging from my belt, he could probably incinerate me before my blade left its sheath.

I never discovered what Damascus intended, though, because at that moment the heiress finally spoke. "Quiet, both of you," she snapped from the windowsill. "All you ever do is argue. It's like you've been at it forever."

"Tell him to back down, then," I said. "He knows I'm right."

At my words, Damascus snorted and sputtered, but when he glanced at Amethyst, he noticed something that gave him pause. The vacant stare had vanished, and while her usual confidence had not yet returned, there was something else in its place.

"Amethyst?"

"Mordecai is right, Damascus," she said. "You're right too, in a way. It's not much safer without than within. And I know you wish we could stay," she apologized. "I want the same thing. The Testament is so mysterious, and we've only just started, but—"

She glanced down again out the window, and she didn't need to explain. She couldn't continue here, not anymore. How could she stand at the Testament and focus on any research after such an event? Could she ever push those memories from her mind? Could she ever forget the terrible price this opportunity had cost?

"You think we should leave," Damascus said.

She nodded sadly.

"And what of Uriah's orders? We don't have permission to go elsewhere."

Amethyst only shrugged. "I can override him, if I must."

149

I almost gagged on her words. Who was this girl? How could she contradict orders from Estavion's highest-ranking general? Maybe these attempts on her life had a logical motive after all.

Her comment fell unnoticed by Damascus, though. He only asked, "Then what does my lady command?"

She considered her next words carefully. "If Irrideous knows how to construct an artifice, if he's studied the Ascendants, and if he can build dreadnaught armor, then do you think—I mean, is it possible he knows where a catalyst is?"

Damascus swallowed uncomfortably. "It's much worse than that, my dear. Irrideous probably has a catalyst already."

My heart palpitated. My teeth chattered. I thought back to our conversation at the Testament and in that very room the previous evening, and I recalled Amethyst's explanation of the catalyst's powers, how it amplified thought and enabled the impossible. That same stone, I realized, might already be in the hands of Irrideous, and he was determined to kill Amethyst.

Suddenly, my previous suggestion seemed all the more relevant, and I wondered why Amethyst delayed. This was not a hard choice. It was a terrible, awful choice, to be sure, to leave that ancient fortress with such comfortable accommodations and interesting research, but the decision was simple. Either remain at Ballabor, or depart on the *Sole Solution*. Either wait for death incarnate to return, or begin a desperate flight toward some other harbor. Either stay and die, or flee and live.

Amethyst chose soon enough, and when she did, I nearly bit my tongue. She didn't pick the safer path or the foolish path. Instead, Amethyst settled on a third option I hadn't considered. The teenage girl recklessly chose the most dangerous path imaginable.

"We're finding Irrideous," she declared. "We're going after the Cornerstone."

Eleven

"You actually left," Rehoboth says. It was not a question, but a declaration of guilt. "You defied orders."

"It wasn't my choice," I stress. "Amethyst took charge."

"Following *your* suggestion," Rehoboth stipulates.

That's a stretch, but I don't argue the point.

"You could be discharged," Uriah adds. "Do you realize that?"

The comment only makes me laugh quietly.

"You'll be fortunate if it ends there," Rehoboth chimes in. "We could intern you for insubordination. Really, lieutenant, what were you thinking? Putting that idea in such a young girl's head?"

I toast my interrogators with my teacup. "I'd hold off on the trial, if I were you. Insubordination is merely the first of my crimes, and the least."

Sins Best Forgotten

That same day, we embarked on our new mission. With fresh urgency, Damascus gathered his research. A few soldiers packed up Amethyst's belongings and carried them down to the harbor. I readied my own gear, but to my satchel I added one important addition: the dreadnaught vambrace. I stowed away that cursed artifice. I thought it might prove helpful in some way, though I hoped I would never find use for it. I only knew I couldn't leave it behind or destroy it. I needed the reminder of what might still be chasing us.

Once our things were carried off and our goodbyes said to Ballabor's Vanguard, we left the fortress ourselves. Damascus, Amethyst and I left behind the lavish guest quarters. We passed the ancient Testament still floating majestically on its magnetic supports, and we crossed over the courtyard still tainted with blood and terrible memories. We passed through the gatehouse that now stood without gates, and we descended the granite stairs to the harbor where we found the *Solution* prepped and waiting.

Her captain waited too, standing near the gangplank and chewing on his patchy beard. "Leaving already? I was just starting to like the place."

Damascus ignored Abner's sarcasm and issued new orders instead. "Take us out, captain. Set course for Severance once we're clear of the Islands."

Then the old man and his student climbed the ramp, entered the captain's cabin and shut the door. I didn't see them again for many hours.

Abner didn't mind this rude behavior. He just issued orders to his crew and to me. We raised the gangplank, cast off from the pier, brought out the long oars and rowed through the crowded harbor. Then the sentries opened the immense iron floodgates and towed us through Ballabor's only exit; we slipped out among the treacherous Ooramere Islands again.

Our course didn't seem so risky this time. Maybe the Islands didn't frighten me as much since we had already passed through unscathed, or perhaps I was distracted by thoughts of Irrideous and the suicidal chase Amethyst had initiated. Whatever the reason, I hardly noticed as we maneuvered through the narrow causeways among those towering cliffs, and I didn't realize we had exited the Oorameres until Abner ordered the sails out full.

Then the captain called to where I was leaning against the quarterdeck railing. "I could use you on the kites, lieutenant."

It was strange, the way he spoke. Sober. No jokes. He didn't seem the same person. Then I remembered who usually manned the kites, and with a lump in my throat I nodded my assent. I approached the *Solution*'s bow, swallowed nervously, and tried my best to recall my few lessons and make Gideon proud.

And suddenly, I was glad to be moving again, even if the course ahead did seem hopeless. There was still a chance, wasn't there? A slim chance to make that villain pay for what he'd done? I found myself eager to be on the offensive. We were no longer sitting idle and waiting for tragedy to strike. We had taken our destinies into our own hands.

I set to work with new conviction, spreading the kites across the deck, raising them along the tethers at various altitudes, and securing them tight through the iron winch. I didn't work as fast as Gideon, I suspect, but I was competent enough and pleasantly surprised by how much I remembered. By the time night fell that first day back on the southern Mediate Sea, I had all the white kites flying high.

Still, something didn't feel right. The boost never came. Our speed hardly increased. The kites seemed useless, despite the easterly winds filling our wide canvas sails.

Sins Best Forgotten

The answer soon appeared behind me. Footsteps approached on the wooden deck. I turned to see Amethyst, her loose cotton dress fluttering in the breeze, her chestnut hair tied back with her white ribbon, a silver bracelet around her slender wrist, and her confidence focused on my array high overhead. "Nicely done, lieutenant. Gideon would be impressed. Now for the final touch."

The girl raised her hands before her as if pushing against an invisible wall. She closed her eyes. She moved her lips, silently forming words of a forgotten language, and the *Solution* lurched forward under my feet.

"What did you do?" I asked after regaining my footing.

She smiled and shrugged. "I told the wind to blow higher."

"And it listened?"

"When you speak the right way, in the right tongue."

I didn't ask for a better explanation, and even if I had, I doubt she would have obliged. She seemed intent on another purpose. "Are you finished?"

"I think so."

"Then come along," she said. "Damascus is ready to talk about Irrideous."

"And he wants my company?"

"*I* want you present," she stipulated. "Another pair of ears might benefit us all."

Her reason made sense, but I glanced up at the quarterdeck, where Abner stood at the helm. Was I free to leave my post?

"Don't worry," Amethyst said, reading my thoughts. "He'll manage without you. Abner's been captain of this runner a long time, and Gideon isn't the first man he's lost."

Hardly a justifiable excuse. All the same, I couldn't refuse the heiress who could overrule a general's orders, so I followed her across the deck, past the swaying lines and tall masts, through the only door and into the captain's cabin.

Inside, I found a cramped, modest stateroom. A narrow bed hugged the back wall under the window, with a mess of blankets and furs nested nearby on the floor. Was that where the old man slept all those weeks at sea? On the floor beside Amethyst's bed? There was a small octagonal table too, covered with a cracked vellum map of the Eastern Estates held down at the corners with numerous oil lanterns and an old, dusty leather-bound book fastened with a buckle. Finally, I noticed some plain wooden chairs, three of them, all without upholstery or cushions. Even so, Amethyst took one of the empty seats, I sat next to her, and we waited for Damascus to speak.

The tutor occupied the third chair, his frame weary and spent, his face downcast. I suspected that, like me, he still had not slept since the previous night, and since he lacked my youth and strength, he wasn't coping as well. Either that or he was about to confess some heinous crime, and the fear of such exposure had driven him mute. I was right on both counts.

"Should we come back?" Amethyst eventually asked.

"No, it's all right, my dear," he sighed, obviously lying. He followed up with something true, though. "I just don't know where to begin."

"Start from the beginning," Amethyst said.

"The beginning." He smiled sadly and glanced at the dusty book. "I'm not sure I remember anymore where this all began."

"Start with Irrideous, then," I suggested.

The idea seemed to make some sense. The old man sucked in a long breath, gathered his thoughts and started his tale, though his eyes remained downcast. "I met Irrideous a long time ago—a *very* long time ago—when the world seemed young. He was an Ascendant scholar, like me, always searching out sanctuaries, cities, temples. You could have even called us partners at times, though we seldom worked together. He was always a touch less cautious, shall we say? Less reverent. He was always pushing the limits. Always trying to experiment. It wasn't enough for him to just observe and learn. He wanted to experience, to taste the miracles described in the script.

"And that can be dangerous," Damascus cautioned. "Even a good man can be sorely tempted if he knows too much. Tempted to meddle with things he shouldn't. Tempted to believe himself beyond certain vices, as if learning breeds character.

"Still, I respected him. He was driven. Passionate. Incredibly intelligent and knowledgeable. Widely proficient in various disciplines. He was even a good influence on me, in some ways. He dared me to test for myself if the Ascendant artifices were possible. Without him, in fact, I doubt I would have ever learned the tricks I know. For that, and for many other reasons too numerous to mention, I considered Irrideous a good friend."

"Until you found a catalyst," I guessed.

Damascus nodded.

"What happened?" Amethyst asked.

There was another pause, followed by a weary sigh. When Damascus finally spoke, I nearly missed his words. "I made a mistake, my dear. I made a costly, terrible mistake."

We didn't push further. We just waited for the old man to gather his nerves. It was a long wait.

"We found the Cornerstone quite by accident. We were in the Ascendant city of Essence. You remember, my dear?"

"The city lies submerged under the northern sea, near the Sinnus Ines," Amethyst answered automatically, almost as if responding to a test question.

"Yes, exactly. That's the one," Damascus said, perking at her enthusiasm. "It's a fascinating place, full of gravitational anomalies. I really must take you there someday soon—but as I was saying, we were conducting the typical research, Irrideous and I, just exploring a new place. We were the first to investigate that site, I believe, and no one has returned since. It's not easy to reach, deep beneath the waves. Even with the bubble, it's—" But then he stopped. "Well, that's not important. Not yet."

I glanced at Amethyst. I guessed that particular lesson would have to wait for another time.

"As I was saying, we were exploring a conservatory, taking notes. And then—" Damascus took yet another sharp breath. "Then we found it. *I* found it. Sitting on a granite table. A mere trinket among a dozen other artifacts blanketed by eons of dust. I didn't think it special, considering its context. It was only a small flat stone, no larger than a button, but black as the abyss. It had four sides, two of them straight and smooth, the other two jagged, almost as if it were the broken corner of some larger, perfectly square testing stone. It seemed entirely irrelevant, lying there like the discarded slag of some greater project, but when I touched it—"

He trailed off again. We endured another long wait.

"When you touched it?" Amethyst eventually prodded.

He didn't exactly continue, though. "You must believe, my dear, *I didn't know.* When we found it, I never imagined that shard was a catalyst, *the last Cornerstone*! Why would it be left there unguarded? Of all the places! I thought it some cruel trick."

"What happened when you touched it?" I steered him back.

"What happened?" The teacher shook his head. "Touching that shard felt like touching my own heart. I'm not sure I can describe it, but imagine—imagine, for a moment, your every fear and passion amplified, as if you lost control. Imagine every conscious thought vanishing, replaced by pure impulse." He closed his eyes momentarily. "Imagine your heart pounding and your mind racing. Imagine believing, sincerely believing you could do *anything*. Be anyone. Whatever you wanted, you could have. Whatever you desired, you could make happen, and no one could stop you. Or judge you. Your most vile and terrible thoughts could be realized. Your deepest dreams, no matter how impossible or selfish, could be instantly granted."

As he spoke, as he described the possibilities the catalyst embodied, I suddenly understood this Cornerstone in a whole new way. It wasn't just a tool or a weapon. It was power. In his clumsy, ineloquent fashion, Damascus was describing power, pure and simple. That's what the Cornerstone was—the ability to satisfy any wish or thought. With such a device, forget carving the mountains or stopping the drought; a person wielding the stone could possibly reshape reality to his whim. He could create his own personal paradise.

"Doesn't seem so bad," I quipped.

"Then perhaps your heart is better than mine, lieutenant," Damascus snapped.

I didn't answer that.

"I didn't want to keep the shard," Damascus continued. "It was too overwhelming. Too terrible. Whenever I touched that black stone, I couldn't control myself. I couldn't think clearly. I felt reckless. Lost. And I could only ever touch the stone for mere fractions of a second. I could never hold it long enough to form a clear thought and *do* anything. I always dropped it long before I accomplished anything.

"But Irrideous," Damascus added. "Irrideous was different. He was fearless. Unrestrained. Where I shrank back, terrified by what I might do, what my heart might wish, Irrideous pushed forward. He believed he could manage the catalyst."

"And you let him take it," I guessed.

"No."

I leaned back, surprised.

The tutor's weariness returned. "I fought him for it."

Sickened by the thought, Damascus hung his white head in his hands, but in response, Amethyst drew nearer. She rose from her chair and knelt beside her mentor. Lovingly, she reached out and squeezed his withered hands. She smiled at him, as if that simple act could somehow absolve his crimes.

"If I knew then what I know now, I would have never done it," Damascus gasped. "You must believe me."

"I know," Amethyst whispered. They paused a moment longer, their heads bowed together as if visiting the grave of some dearly departed friend. Then Amethyst changed the subject momentarily. "Why did you never tell me this before?"

"Oh, I had my reasons, some better than others," Damascus answered. "I long thought you weren't ready, though perhaps it is I who wasn't ready. Most of all, I hoped this was behind me, that it would never surface again. I hoped perhaps Irrideous had renounced his revenge. Part of me even thought that he had forgotten all about me. About what happened."

"What did happen," I interrupted again, "when you fought Irrideous for the stone?"

"Well, I was passive at first. When I realized his lust for the shard, I took it away. Far away, where I thought he would never find me. But I underestimated his resolve, and he chased me for years. For half my life, it seemed—always demanding that prize. He lashed out at my friends too. He hurt my relatives and my old acquaintances, always hoping to flush me out. And it worked.

"Eventually, I realized a confrontation was inevitable, so I visited his home and waited for him. I thought in the presence of his parents and sister, he might demonstrate some restraint and listen to reason. But I was wrong. Irrideous was past words, past apology. He attacked me, and in the struggle that followed, his family perished. We ruined that entire place."

It was a vague, unsatisfying explanation. On this particular point, however, even I couldn't push Damascus, so great was his sorrow. I also couldn't help but identify with the chilling details. When he mentioned Irrideous's sister dying, I shuddered, thinking of my own sister and her untimely fate.

Sins Best Forgotten

I couldn't face that painful memory, though. Not then. So to distract myself, I tried to imagine what it would have looked like when those two Ascendant scholars clashed with magic and fury. I remembered how Damascus had confounded the dreadnaught temporarily with brimstone and meteors, but then I faltered. Had Damascus been holding back? Had he withheld his full potential, fearing the destruction he might cause? Knowing his pupil stood ready and willing to engage with her lace gloves if he failed?

Once again, I didn't ask. I just waited for Damascus to find strength to continue.

"After that—that *accident*, my resolve vanished. My heart failed me, and Irrideous seized the Cornerstone."

"And he didn't kill you," I blurted out.

"A welcome surprise, I assure you," Damascus answered. "I expected swift retribution, but for all his fortitude and wrath, Irrideous proved no more capable with the shard than I. If anything, his passion proved more detrimental, more costly, and it drove him far away. He left me there. Left his murdered family. He rejected civilization and ignored his other research. He focused solely on the Cornerstone. He retreated to some far corner of the world and explored the cruel depths of his nature. He tried the catalyst over and over, pushing ever further into his psyche. Eventually, he lost himself in that relic."

"Lost himself?"

"The stone drove Irrideous mad."

A welcome boon, I thought. The first good shred of news in the whole confession. Perhaps Irrideous was no longer a threat.

"I nearly lost myself as well, I must confess. At any rate I swore off my research and abandoned the cause. I burned my books and scrolls. Forgot about the supernatural. I wandered throughout the Inheritance, trying my hand at other trades and failing miserably. Eventually I ended up at Tel Tellesti, where I started a foundry. I met

Avram," he pointed out for Amethyst's benefit, "and taught him how to hammer."

"And then you became my teacher," Amethyst smiled.

"How did that happen?" I asked, getting off track. Why had Damascus started researching the Ascendants again despite his tragic past?

"Oh, I don't think we have time for that. Not now. Let's just say I was given an opportunity I couldn't refuse. A chance for redemption." As he spoke, Damascus finally lifted his head. He gazed straight into Amethyst's eyes, and for the first time during that whole conversation, he truly smiled.

"Then what about Irrideous?" Amethyst pressed. "What's the last you heard about him?"

"It's been a long time since I heard anything. Twenty years, if I recall correctly. But I heard rumors that Irrideous had abandoned his research and returned from isolation. He settled in Severance and even started his own family. Can you imagine? I thought he would never again have the stomach for such a thing, but he did. He married some delightful woman named, um, Diana? No, that can't be right. Dana, perhaps?"

He glanced at me as if I knew the answer. I only shrugged.

"That's why we're visiting Severance," Amethyst guessed. "Irrideous might be there. He may still have the stone."

"It's possible, yes."

"This could also be a trap," I interjected, more to Amethyst than Damascus. "Maybe Irrideous is there. Maybe he abandoned his revenge. But if he didn't, and if he *is* behind these attacks, he might have anticipated our next move. The next time he strikes, we might not be so lucky."

"Lucky?" Damascus actually laughed. "You think we've been lucky?"

"We're still alive."

"Lieutenant, let me make one thing perfectly clear. Irrideous is many things, but he is never incompetent. If he is planning these attacks, we are not still alive because he failed or missed. No. If we are alive, it is only because he wants us alive."

"Then why send the dreadnaught?" I argued.

"The dreadnaught was nothing," Damascus countered. "It was but a taste of his powers. If Irrideous is involved with this, he's planning something terrible, mark me. Worse than a drought or famine or even another war. And the dreadnaught? The firebomb? They're just warnings. He's sending a message."

"What kind of message?"

"He thinks I can't stop him," Damascus said.

I must admit, Irrideous seemed right. I couldn't imagine how Damascus could stop him, even with our help. We had hardly survived the dreadnaught, and if what Damascus said was true, that demon was only the beginning. There could be greater terrors waiting in Severance. Our mission already seemed suicidal, but now it felt pointless. And what could we possibly do even if we did find Irrideous? What plan did Amethyst have? Surely she didn't intend to knock on his door, introduce herself and ask politely for the Cornerstone.

And even if we succeeded, what then? If we somehow won that prize, that ancient relic that had driven Irrideous beyond insane…I doubted Damascus would touch it again. Could I try it then? No. Damascus had clearly explained that the stone would amplify my desires and emotions, and I could never bear that. My heart was already burdened with anger, resentment and guilt. I struggled enough keeping all that bottled up. The last thing I needed was a catalyst. So why was Damascus allowing us forward? Why chase the Cornerstone at all?

Then it struck me. The answer. It was Amethyst. She was the reason. Damascus didn't have any vain idea he could use the stone, but Amethyst did. She had sent us after Irrideous. She must believe she could use it somehow, or at least wrest it from our enemy's grasp. For some reason, she was willing to risk everything for the slim chance that she could protect her family. Avenge our friends. Stop the drought. Prevent the looming war.

And Damascus, I realized. He believed too. He must think there was some chance we could succeed, or he would constantly argue against our current path. If he truly believed we had no hope, he would endlessly press his case until Amethyst relented and changed our course. Since no such argument took place, he must have thought Amethyst was capable of something he was not.

How foolish.

Suddenly I felt utterly powerless. Impotent. There I was, charged with Amethyst's safety, yet I hadn't shielded her from the dreadnaught, and I couldn't veer her away from Irrideous. I could only watch and wait as we followed that madman into the abyss where we would either perish or watch our world descend into chaos.

There was one other possibility as well, one even more terrifying than all the rest. There was a chance—a slim chance, mind you—we might succeed. We might find Irrideous and the Cornerstone. We might steal away that catalyst. And then? Then Amethyst might try to use it. She might not react the right way. The stone might corrupt her, amplify her adolescent passions and make her a greater threat than Irrideous.

And then I would have to kill her.

Twelve

"That seems an extreme assumption," Rehoboth chides. "You truly believed you might have to kill her to protect Estavion?"

Considering what actually happened, I don't see the point in answering. Besides, I'm starving again, so I chew the inside of my cheek and wonder when more food will come.

Rehoboth smiles at my silence. "At least you learned why Irrideous was targeting Amethyst."

I don't respond to that statement either. I'm growing to hate these interruptions. If she's not going to feed me, she can at least let me talk. "May I continue, please?"

"In a moment. I am curious about one other thing now that you've explained about Irrideous. It's the armor." Rehoboth reaches for the dreadnaught vambrace sitting on the table. "You said before that Irrideous invented it."

I nod. "He derived it from his research with the Cornerstone."

"How?"

I know the answer, but I only shrug. She wouldn't understand if I explained, so I don't bother.

Rehoboth sighs and consults her notes. "So then, when the dreadnaught attacked Ballabor, was that Irrideous in his armor?"

"No. Damascus later explained that Irrideous had a servant, a collosus named Edo who often accompanied him. It was probably him wearing the armor."

"I see." Rehoboth makes the necessary corrections in her notes. "Did you ever meet this *Edo* again?"

"Why don't you let me talk? I'll get to that."

Severance

For the next few weeks, the *Sole Solution* skipped southeast through the tropics toward the sandy Samaran coastline. The late summer air grew warmer. The turquoise waves beneath our hull turned clear. The white kites flew high in a cloudless sky that stretched over us like a seamless curtain of cobalt, and we settled into a lazy rhythm.

Abner spent days on end tilted against the helm, transfixed by the churning sea, counting the gulls overhead and noting their size and numbers, and watching for the first telltale signs of land, or of another ship shadowing us. His crew, the eleven retired Vanguard that remained, meticulously manned the canvas sails, harnessing every last whip of speed from Amethyst's obedient winds. The heiress remained in the stateroom with Damascus to continue her education, only venturing out for meals and the occasional recess, and I tended the kites, trying my best to improve our pace…and forget my fears.

But early one morning after a particularly restless night, a disturbing dream about Irrideous shook me from my swaying hammock. Quietly, so as not to wake the snoring crewmen, I crept through the dark cargo hold, up the ladder and through the folding hatch. In the final minutes before dawn, I wandered the main deck, filling my lungs with salty air. I tried to clear my troubled mind and calm my anxious heart.

Then I saw Amethyst.

She stood near the bow, leaning against the railing. Her back arched, her satin nightgown fluttering in the breeze. Her tiptoes were bare on the weathered floorboards, her hair golden. I suspected she came there every morning to welcome the day. I just never noticed before because I always slept late.

I said nothing. I didn't even move for fear of interrupting her meditation. I only watched, and when the sun breached the horizon with streamers of emerald and scarlet, Amethyst breathed deep. She seemed not a girl then, but a frail blossom embracing the radiance, and I shuddered to think what the future might hold for her—how she might be plucked before reaching her full height.

More than ever before, I wished we could turn aside. I wished she would delay our arrival until we knew with certainty where Irrideous lived and what schemes he had laid up for us. I half thought to speak with her, but that was not my place, and I doubted my words could ever change her mind anyway. I had no choice but to follow and obey.

She had no choice either, I suppose. For some reason I could not guess, she had already decided to maintain her course no matter the cost, to follow the Cornerstone wherever it led. We were both already trapped, pulled along not by kites on long tethers but fate, and there was nothing to do but hold on tight.

I let her be. I returned to my hammock and my dreams.

Two full days later, on a cloudless, sweltering morning, we entered the bay near Severance. The waters grew calm, the wind changed direction against us, and Abner ordered the sails down and the oars out. We rowed for many long hours, skirting the sandy coastline east and then south until we reached the Rapha`Dim delta and arrived at Samara's capital port.

It was a disappointing mess.

Severance

I shouldn't be so critical, I suppose. Severance is a manmade city, after all, and much younger than the Ascendant constructs like Ballabor and Tel Tellesti. It wasn't molded from seamless gray granite in ages long past, but rather it was built, brick by brick, by the Samaran tribes after they crossed the Impasse and settled the southern estate only two millennia ago. Since then the city grew organically, district by district, with streets that snaked about randomly with no clear direction or purpose. At some point the Samarans built a wide outer wall around Severance, but that had been nearly destroyed during the last Northern Invasion when the Ghosts of Thunderlun swept down in their vain attempt to seize the whole Inheritance, and the wall never returned to its former grandeur despite the constant restoration efforts. It stood half ruined and half rebuilt around the city, like old tattered rags hanging limp on an even older man.

Still, I expected more, so I despised all of it, and Severance made no effort to change my mind. First, the city stretched out under the murky waters and grasped the *Solution*'s hull with a submerged sandbar, nearly scuttling us. Then it lured us into a confusing labyrinth of wooden piers, pontoon jetties and depth buoys spread across the mouth of the Rapha`Dim. It sent ships against us too, a tightly packed crowd of tiny fishing boats, swift skimmers and lumbering frigates. To avoid collisions, we had to reduce our speed to a near crawl, stretching our approach from mere minutes into hours, and when we finally reached the harbor, we spent even longer searching for an empty slip among the congested piers.

Eventually, though, the city reluctantly presented us with an open mooring. Abner steered the *Solution* alongside a dilapidated wharf at the harbor's southern terminal, and once we drew near enough, I leapt down onto the jetty with some other crewmen to secure the boat.

With that chore complete, I studied the city again, hoping that perhaps a closer view would change my initial impression. Like before, though, I only saw a decaying maze that paled in comparison to our Ascendant citadel. Instead of polished granite, Severance had narrow cobblestone streets and a stumpy outer wall built from red clay bricks. Instead of elegant architecture, I noticed short square buildings, each cube only one story high and nearly identical, as if stamped from a mold and packed tightly together under the baking sun like pots in a kiln.

The only features worth mentioning stood tall in the distant northeast toward the city's center. These were the Towers of Samar, the home of the Empress Yuridonna and her extensive imperial family. The three towers were the tallest manmade structures in the entire Inheritance, I knew, but even they failed to impress. They reached only a few hundred paces high over the surrounding red brick buildings. From such a distance, they resembled short, twisting stumps in a poppy field more than the proud Samaran capitol.

Then the city offered one last insult. As we finished securing the *Sole Solution* and surveying the adjacent boardwalk that ran the length of the harbor, a group of about ten soldiers emerged from the crowds and approached us.

These were imperial guards, I guessed, from their stringent black turbans and tunics. They each wore thick beards and bushy eyebrows that concealed most of their dark faces. They came well armed mostly with tall spears, though a few carried composite bows and curved knives tucked into their silk belts. They were well protected too, with sheets of interwoven lamellar armor draped over their shoulders and thighs like a patchwork of rectangular metal scales. They approached with long, purposeful strides, and at the sight of them, I thought to fetch my sword.

Thankfully, the captain's cheerful voice spoke behind me before I could act. "Ah! I was wondering when the welcoming committee would arrive."

Without a shred of fear or disappointment, Abner stepped past me and greeted the imperial officers. Then he endured a barrage of questions ranging from "Where are you from?" to "Are you expecting an audience with the Imperial Empress?" He shrewdly answered each question in turn, usually honestly, and somehow he convinced the committee that we were neither spies nor soldiers—we were merely merchants coming to purchase wares. No doubt his ruse was helped by the fact that his small ship was a *freelance* reconnaissance craft and his crewmen were *retired* Vanguard. As such, his vessel lacked the usual Estavian design features, and his men didn't wear the gold-plated chainmail and vermilion mantle typical of Vanguard. I also appeared inconspicuous. By sheer luck, I had failed to dress appropriately that day. Because of the heat, I wore thin pants and a loose shirt instead of my uniform.

Nevertheless, the committee proved remarkably thorough. They questioned Abner for the better part of an hour, and they searched the entire ship, including the captain's private cabin and the cargo hold. What they asked Damascus and Amethyst, I can't imagine, nor can I guess whether they noticed my Vanguard uniform or the dreadnaught vambrace stowed below deck in my satchel. I only know that they soon left the *Solution* untouched, though they charged Abner the required toll for renting the pier. They also informed the captain that he might endure additional inspections and fees if he remained at port longer than two days.

Despite their professional demeanor, I breathed easier once the committee left, especially since I knew we would be long gone before they returned. My relief was short-lived, however, because as soon as the imperials departed, Damascus emerged from the stateroom, and I immediately noticed something amiss.

I couldn't quite place the problem. At first glance, he seemed the same as every other time I had seen him. He wore the same pressed linen robes as before. His white hair still laid slick across his head. His beard remained short and trimmed, though he had obviously groomed recently. A leather document tube hung from his shoulder, and in his hand he held a buckled book, but those didn't seem out of place. I had noticed both those accessories in the stateroom when he had spoken about Irrideous.

It was his company, I finally realized, or lack thereof. For the first time since we had left Tel Tellesti, the heiress was not close by her teacher's side. Damascus was leaving alone.

"Where are you going?" I asked as he stepped onto the pier.

"Come now! There's no use delaying the inevitable. I'm off to the Towers and the imperial archives. With any luck, I may find some official record about Irrideous."

"And you're going alone?" Didn't he remember where we were? Who might be chasing us? Did he not know how the Samarans currently felt about their northern neighbors?

The old man sighed. The familiar irritation returned. "Please, lieutenant. Please think before you speak. Estavion and Samara teeter on the brink of war, remember? And we're in Severance, the Samaran capital! Do you think the imperials would tolerate an heiress anywhere near the Towers? Hmm? What about her Vanguard escort? Please! They would imprison you both as spies. Demand a ransom! We're fortunate enough they've let us dock safely."

He had a point.

"No, it's far better I go alone. I'm just a harmless old man, and I may still have some friends in the archives. I did visit there from time to time, in years past, and I suspect I can gain entrance once more if I'm careful with my words. They shouldn't suspect me, and with any luck, I'll be back before dusk.

"But you," he added, pointing cautiously, "you stay here. Is that understood? Keep the girl here too. Practice that swordplay, if you must. Let her chase you around the quarterdeck, but stay on the ship. Do not take her into the harbor or the city. *Especially the city*. That would be most dangerous, most foolish. There's no telling what might happen to her if you venture into that place."

He was warning me about Irrideous, I knew, and he was wasting his breath. I already understood the risks we were taking. I thought to point out that his caution was immaterial—that if Irrideous was still living in Severance and if he did want the heiress dead, then staying on the boat wasn't going to stop him—but I didn't see what good that could do, so I just told Damascus, "There's no need to worry. I understand perfectly."

"Good," he answered. Then, after a deep sigh, he left the pier and disappeared into the crowds mingling on the docks.

I was jealous to see him go, I must admit. Part of me wanted to leave with him. I still didn't care much for his company, but anything seemed preferable to sitting around and waiting. I had spent too much time waiting already. Waiting to reach Ballabor. Waiting while the tutor and his student researched the Testament. Waiting to hear about Irrideous. Waiting for Irrideous to attack again. Now I wanted to do something, anything, and Damascus was off doing it alone.

I quickly pushed the disappointment from my mind, though, and focused on my duties. I double-checked the knots securing the *Solution* to the pier, and after finishing I climbed the ramp onto the boat, but once on deck I noticed something else amiss.

Amethyst was waiting for me.

She had changed her clothing, I immediately noticed. She had pulled on her leather boots with those buckles that rose up to her knees, and instead of the usual satin gown or flowing dress, she wore a drab linen frock with a scarlet sash wound about her tiny waist. She had another scarf wrapped around her neck and draped over her brown hair. Her attitude had changed too. The confidence was still there, but now it mingled with something else, like anger perhaps. She looked ready to tear the city apart, and with her disguise it was possible no one would suspect her until it was too late. She might blend in perfectly.

I already knew the answer, but regardless I asked her almost the exact same question I had asked her mentor only minutes before. "Going somewhere?"

"I'll never find Irrideous if I stay here," she shrugged. "Care to keep me company?"

I thought she'd never ask.

Following Amethyst's lead, I borrowed some clothes from Abner's crew to so I could pass as one of the city's inhabitants. I chose some loose, faded pants; short boots; and a long, drab tunic with a thick sash for a belt. I brought my Vanguard broadsword, though. I couldn't justify leaving it behind. I only wrapped the distinctive sheath and hilt with strips of leather so no one would recognize the signature weapon unless I drew the folded steel. Then Amethyst and I slipped into Severance.

It was tense, venturing into that dusty city, much more nerve-wracking than I expected. I had followed Amethyst so readily, but as soon as we left the pier and approached the docks, I fast doubted my previous resolve.

The docks were crowded. That was part of the problem. Sailors, fishermen and merchants moved to and fro, unloading their cargo or discussing their business with their associates. City residents mingled about bartering for old fish, stale bread, thin livestock, and bruised vegetables. There were imperial soldiers everywhere as well. Archers patrolled the ruined city walls with composite bows and packed quivers. Guards stood at every corner with long spears. Cavalry officers rode about on fearsome black horses with curved swords hanging from their saddles.

And we did not blend in. That was the other part of our problem. Despite our efforts to appear inconspicuous, Amethyst and I stood out like hawks among buzzards. Our attire was drab, yes, but it was still clean and new, much unlike the tattered rags that clothed many of the Samarans. Our lighter skin also betrayed us. Against the tanned complexions surrounding us, Amethyst's skin shown like milk, and my naked face won its own attention among so many dark beards. That all paled in comparison to our voices, though. With her verbose expressions and polished accent, Amethyst attracted attention whenever she spoke, and try as she might, she could never mimic the terse, precise southern dialect.

I doubt anyone ever suspected the real truth, that I was a Vanguard agent and Amethyst was a highborn heiress, but they knew enough to identify us as migrants, and they despised us. We quickly became unwelcome guests in a city that was never known for its hospitality in the first place. People bumped and jostled us without apologizing. Pickpockets struck on at least three different occasions, though thankfully they always left empty-handed since I carried nothing of value except the sword that I held against my chest with both hands. Suspicious eyes constantly followed us, and I feared that some of them belonged to the enemy's spies, or perhaps to Irrideous himself.

If all that wasn't bad enough, the Samaran soldiers watched us too. Indeed, not three minutes after we left the *Solution*, a female officer approached on horseback.

"Migrants! Halt there! Who are you? State your business."

"My name is Amethyst," the heiress answered politely. "I'm from Tel Tellesti."

The woman pointed her long spear down at me. "And who are you? Her father?"

"My escort," the girl explained honestly. Then the lies came. "My parents died, so he's brought me to find an old kinsman."

"And who is that?"

"My kinsman, you mean?"

"Yes."

"His name is Irrideous." Amethyst said the name effortlessly, without fear or hesitation. "Do you know him, by chance?"

The imperial woman did know the name. A dark shadow fell over her. "You're related to Irrideous?"

"He's my uncle." Amethyst perked a little. "Where can we find him?"

"He is dead," the soldier replied, and that was it. No apology. No extra trimmings. Just a blunt fact.

Amethyst recoiled a little, not sure how to answer, so I spoke instead. "Are you certain about that? It's just—we've heard from him recently. He sent us a message."

"Irrideous *is* dead," the woman repeated as she turned her horse away. "Make no mistake. Don't waste your time. Go back home. And I would not ask anyone else about your uncle, if I were you. Irrideous is not beloved here. The mention of your relation may cause trouble."

As quickly as she had approached, the woman rode off to question someone else who had caught her eye. She left Amethyst and me alone on the crowded docks.

"That was encouraging," I joked.

"I'd say so," the girl agreed.

"Do you think she meant what she said? About Irrideous being dead?"

"No. She's trying to scare us off."

"It's working," I admitted. "Do you want to go back?"

Amethyst glanced at me, a little surprised. "Do you?"

The comment made me smile. Was she really so fearless?

"We should leave the harbor, though," Amethyst continued. "We might have better luck in the poorer districts, and there will be fewer eyes watching us."

I didn't argue.

We soon found a wide gate that led through the outer wall, and once inside the city, we entered a large cobblestone square packed with merchant carts and various street venders. This market was even more crowded than the docks, though, so we circled around and found a narrow side street that led deeper into Severance. Finally, the crowds thinned and we made better progress. We also noticed fewer soldiers in those winding streets, and best of all we found people more willing to overlook our strange appearance.

We met one old baker in particular sitting on his front stoop and smoking his pipe, and when Amethyst introduced herself, he jumped at the opportunity to talk. He chatted eagerly about the unusually hot weather, the never-ending drought and the terrible rumors about a war. The moment Amethyst mentioned Irrideous, though, the old baker doused his pipe and pushed himself up.

"Don't know nothing 'bout that devil," the baker hissed. Then he slipped into his shop and slammed the door in her face.

Our luck did not improve. After a cursory glance, few people willingly spoke when we approached, and those who did always reacted negatively to the name of Irrideous. Many just walked away like the baker, leaving our questions unanswered. One man actually spat on Amethyst's frock.

The scenery did not improve either. I thought it couldn't get much worse than the crowded, uninspired docks or the chaotic market, but the farther we pressed into the baked city, the closer the insipid red clay buildings pressed around us. The cobblestone streets narrowed into twisting alleys only a few paces wide, and the people…

We soon realized that the harbor was the city's center of commerce where money and power still mattered, and among that hubbub and activity and prying eyes, the drought felt less prevalent. Once we ventured deeper into Severance, however, the reminders came fast and frequent, and I finally understood what Amethyst had meant earlier when she told me about refugees flooding the city. Homeless families lived in the streets. Packs of ragged and emaciated children wandered the alleys. We even noticed one decrepit man prostrate in a puddle of filth; I'm quite certain he was dead.

Most disturbing of all, though, was the ever-present idleness and apathy. Starving men sat on windowsills and stared at the cobblestones. Listless women leaned in doorways as they warily watched Amethyst and me pass by. It seemed the whole city had given up and was waiting for something, for death probably, and why not? Why work for a wage if there was no food to buy? Why struggle against adversity if the bitter end cannot be prevented?

"It's worse than I expected," I lamented.

Amethyst didn't comment.

Despite all these negatives, we pressed forward, and I admit the credit for that must lie with Amethyst. If I had searched for Irrideous alone, I would have certainly turned back from fear or despair at the pitiable sights that greeted us. I almost did turn back on occasion, in fact, but whenever the doubts rose, I only had to glance at Amethyst's face and read the confidence and determination written there, and my spirits would lift.

I shouldn't have been so easily encouraged. The facts were certain. The hazards were real. And she was hardly a teenager. Perhaps she knew something I didn't that gave her strength, but it was more likely that she was blinded by inexperience. She had that air of youthful invincibility, that foolish faith that insists all the dangers of the world are mere obstacles to overcome. Never did she consider the possibility that she might meet her match, that here, in a foreign city far from home, her life might end.

I should have been irritated that she wasn't taking the risks seriously, but I wasn't. On the contrary, her confidence somehow bolstered me. I even started believing we stood a chance. Despite the numerous eyes watching us, despite the poverty and squalor, and despite the heat and the constant refusals to our inquiries about Irrideous, I couldn't help but believe we might find our target and escape alive. Half of me even wondered if Amethyst could convince Irrideous to see reason and abandon his revenge.

"I must thank you," I blurted out after a few hours.

The heiress glanced at me curiously. "For what?"

Severance

"For everything," I shrugged, not sure how else to say it. "For taking me here. For trusting me."

"I couldn't well have gone off alone," she responded. "Can you imagine what Damascus would have said?"

I stopped to picture Damascus sputtering and fuming at Amethyst's disobedience, all without the authority to even slap her wrist for such recklessness. The thought made me smile.

"Still," I continued, "you've been most gracious. Ever since I boarded the *Sole Solution*, you've been kind and patient." Then, though I shouldn't have said it, I dared to add, "You've been much more accommodating than Damascus."

It was Amethyst's turn to smile. "He does seem to despise your very existence, doesn't he?"

We shared a slight chuckle. Then we paused for a break. I slipped into an empty side alley, out of sight from the poverty and grime, out of the hot sun, and I leaned against the red bricks walls. Amethyst followed me.

"Why does Damascus behave that way, if you don't mind my asking?" I asked after a moment's rest. "Is he always like that?"

"It's mostly you," she admitted with another distant smile, "but I wouldn't take it too personally. Damascus is an old man with many responsibilities and duties. He has much on his mind and more in his memory. And just so you know...he's never been particularly fond of meeting new people. They're all just more names to learn, more faces to recognize, and he's already far past the point where he forgets more than he can remember."

I could understand that. I wasn't fond of making friends myself. They always seemed to die anyway. Best just to focus on my duties.

"It probably doesn't help that your assignment is temporary," Amethyst continued. "To someone like Damascus, why bother even learning your name? Once this whole mess is over and we return to the citadel, Avram will probably resume his place as my guardian, and you'll be transferred back to the training yard."

She was right. No wonder Damascus hardly tolerated my ignorance. That realization only reinforced the gratitude I felt toward the girl, though. I understood much better why she shouldn't have trusted me, shouldn't have invested such kindness and patience—but she did. And she was still trusting me, despite my inability to protect her against the dreadnaught. She was trusting me with her very life.

"Well," I winked at her, "I'll just have to do my best to make our time memorable."

She laughed a little and, feeling refreshed, I left the alley to continue our search. As I stepped into the narrow cobblestone street, though, and as I glanced at the people mingling around us, my feet faltered. All at once, I realized I couldn't remember which direction we had come from. We were lost.

"Wait. Where were we going?"

At my question, Amethyst stepped out behind me, glanced around, and pointed up one of the winding streets. "We were walking that way, weren't we?"

I couldn't remember. I turned in the opposite direction and pointed down a different street. "Then is the harbor that way?"

"No, the harbor—"

Her thoughts probably mirrored mine, trying to remember. We had been in the city for hours by that point, though, and we had stopped often to ask about Irrideous. We had turned left and right, wandering wherever our instincts guided, never giving much thought to our location or direction. It didn't help that every red brick building seemed identical, and they pressed tightly around us. The streets seemed more like deep trenches from which we could only see the cloudless sky if we looked overhead. We could not spot the Towers for reference. We could not see the sea or any other landmarks. We could only see buildings and windows…and people. A mounted solder rode past, his horse clopping on the cobblestones. A beggar stooped at a nearby intersection, his hand outstretched in a statue-like pose. A few refugee children eyed us curiously from a nearby window.

Finally, I spied a glint of hope. Just down the street, near the beggar, I saw a wooden sign hanging over a large door. The bold letters on the sign were completely illegible, worn away by years of weathering, and a layer of red dust obscured half the door, but I could still see that the boards had once been painted white—the Samaran color that indicated an inn.

"Come on," I said to Amethyst. "Let's try in there. I could use a drink anyway."

Amethyst followed me to the intersection, and I pushed open the creaking wooden door. Inside, we found a small tavern, I guess, though I couldn't imagine how it still survived. The main room was nearly empty. The tables stood undusted, the rickety chairs unused. A large man stood behind a counter with his back toward us, and he didn't turn when the door opened.

There were only three customers in the whole place, all squatting over a corner table with one jar of wine between them. If they were talking before we entered, I can't say, but when they noticed Amethyst and me, they eyed us suspiciously without a word. They stared unceasingly at our clean clothes, our washed, pale faces, and the wrapped sword clutched in my hand.

I ignored them best I could and pulled out a nearby chair for Amethyst. Once she was seated, I spoke quietly. "I just remembered I didn't bring any money."

She slipped her hand under the wide sash that served as her belt, drew out a fat purse, and pushed it into my hand. I couldn't help but smile. She had somehow warded off the many thieves, I realized, though I had never seen her respond to their sly fingers, but that's not what amused me. No, it was the heavy weight of the purse in my hand. It was completely excessive, just like the lace gloves. Amethyst had brought enough money to buy the whole tavern.

With a grin spreading, I shook my head and left Amethyst at our table. Then I approached the large man and rapped on the wooden counter with my knuckles. The man (who was also the owner, I'm guessing) turned and slowly looked over me, and I returned the favor, noting his dark eyes, untamed beard, and the tattered towel slung over his broad shoulder. He did not seem prepared for customers or willing to oblige strangers. He didn't even welcome me. All the same, I plopped the purse on the counter. "Just some water, please, for me and my companion."

The request brought a slight curl to his lips. "Water?" Then he raised his voice loud enough to the other three customers in the corner could hear. "They want water!"

His words produced a chorus of snickers.

I glanced back at Amethyst, but she didn't seem to mind. Maybe the owner's comment was just a joke about the drought. Perhaps water was hard to come by in Severance despite the Rapha`Dim flowing wide and deep along its northern edge.

"I suppose some wine would suffice instead," I said with a polite smile. "Or mead, if you have that. We'll pay, of course."

The owner crossed his arms. "There's no wine here either."

My smile vanished. Now I knew the man was lying. His other customers were drinking something. Surely they didn't bring that in from outside. And besides, there were numerous ceramic jars behind him on a shelf. There was one within reach, in fact, and I could see clear liquid staining its gray spout.

But I swallowed my anger and changed the topic. "Perhaps you could help with some information, then. My companion and I are visiting on personal business. We're looking for a friend, an old acquaintance named Irrideous."

At the name, a stool squeaked against the floorboards. The three customers straightened in their seats.

Severance

The owner's face changed too. The loathing remained, but now it mingled with fear. "Why look for the prince of darkness? You mean to join him?"

"Join him? What do you mean?"

The large man tightened his jaw. "You'd best leave. Now."

I only leaned closer. "What's happening? Is Irrideous alive? Is he here? Is he building an army? Is that it?"

The owner didn't respond.

"Speak!"

That last word was a mistake. The man detected the authority in my voice, and he guessed my motives. His fear vanished, and the defiance returned. "I don't answer to migrants," he spat. "Not now. Not ever."

That was it. Finally, I understood the man's actions, how some deeply rooted prejudice drove his refusal to help. It didn't matter what Irrideous might do. The large man probably didn't even care about the people starving and dying outside his very door. He just wanted to see us lose. He would rather watch the whole Inheritance collapse rather than risk Estavion recovering faster than Samara. He would damn us just to hinder an old rival.

And I did not dissuade his bias, I'm sorry to say. On the contrary, I gave him another reason to hate us. As soon as I realized he would never help, a swelling rage overwhelmed me. My fingers curled, my arm shot out of its own accord, and my clenched fist found the owner's nose.

Thirteen

"Unbelievable," Uriah growls through his speckled beard. "You assaulted an innocent civilian?"

"Hardly innocent," I shrug. "He was withholding important information. He's lucky I didn't kill him."

Uriah clenches a fist as if to strike, but in the end he only points a finger instead. "You're a Vanguard agent, Mordecai. He was a Samaran citizen. You had absolutely no authority in Severance. No justification! Don't you know better?"

I laugh lightly.

"This is funny to you?"

"No. It's just—that's almost exactly what Amethyst said."

Answers

I was wrong. I know that. I knew it then just as I know it now. I couldn't help myself, though. I could only think of the firebomb. The dreadnaught. The Cornerstone. Caleb. Talsadar and Gideon. The drought and the looming war. All those fears and regrets melted into a delicious moment of perfect wrath, and I unleashed that brutal fury at the tavern keeper. He knew the answers we sought. He could tell us about Irrideous and give the information that might end this.

I just needed to beat it out of him.

So I hit him, and I relished the moment, the control, the feeling that at least there, in that tavern, I was not some helpless whelp against the whims of fate. My fist instantly erased that smug smile from his face, and as my knuckles crushed the man's nose, I heard cartilage break. Blood trickled down my hand, and I saw him stumble, thrown back by my mighty arm. He crashed into the shelf behind him and crumpled to the ground.

Then I leapt over the counter, stood over him, grabbed his collar, and pulled him up. "Speak! Answer me!"

He didn't respond. He had already lost consciousness.

"What do you know about Irrideous?"

The other three customers in the tavern answered for him, though not with words. They rose and tossed aside their stools. They flashed knives, eager to avenge their tribesman. They stepped forward, as if the three of them were a match against me.

To encourage them, I raised the stakes. I reached for the sheathed sword still clutched in my left hand. I drew fast, filling that tavern with the ring of tempered steel. I lifted the glinting blade high, daring them to come. I offered death to whomever wished it, and for a tense moment, I thought those nomads would tempt fate.

Before anyone could move, though, a stern voice stopped the blood in our veins. A girl called out, "Lieutenant!" and I turned from my adversaries to see Amethyst staring at me.

She said nothing else. She only looked at me. It wasn't really a glare or a scowl. In her eyes, I saw something else. Something worse. I saw regret. Disappointment. Frustration. It was the look she had given Damascus when she had reluctantly disregarded his wishes, defied Uriah's orders and sent us after Irrideous. It was the look she reserved for those who forced her hand. And only minutes before, she had been smiling at me. She had implied she was happy she brought me along.

Firmly convicted, I swallowed uncomfortably. I lowered my sword and softened my stand. I didn't sheath my blade, though. That would have invited disaster. Thanks to Amethyst's words, I would not attack needlessly, but I doubted the Samarans shared my temperance. They would have killed both of us if given the chance, so I kept my sword visible and flipped them a coin from Amethyst's purse. "Sorry for the mess."

Before we left, I did one other thing. I reached for the shelf behind the counter. I grasped a water jug, that simple request the tavern keeper had denied. I don't know why. Maybe I wanted to gloat, to prove I could do what I wanted, when I wanted. Maybe I wanted to show that we were indeed better than they. Maybe I was just thirsty. For whatever reason, I lifted the jug to my lips. With one eye on my enemies, I took a long draft and delightfully discovered that there was indeed water inside. It wasn't quite pure, but it was refreshing and satisfying all the same, like the spoils of war.

I took one final glance at the man lying unconscious behind the counter. I kept an eye on the three men in the corner. Then I walked out with Amethyst, and I took the water jug with me.

Answers

"Unbelievable," was the only word Amethyst could say once we returned to the hot streets of Severance. "Unbelievable."

I didn't answer. I took the moment instead to tuck away the purse, sheath my sword, and wipe the tavern keeper's blood from my fingers.

"I thought you were a Vanguard agent," she said once she calmed her nerves. "Didn't they teach you restraint? Discipline?"

"I'm not some fancy citadel sentry," I shot back. "I spent half my career fighting pirates and marauders. That line of work usually requires boldness and initiative, not restraint."

"That kind of boldness will not help us find Irrideous. Or the harbor, for that matter."

The harbor. Right. I had quite forgotten we were still lost. "At least we have water now," I boasted, holding out the jug.

She glared at me, gritted her teeth and pulled anxiously at her scarf. All the same, she did eventually take the water and swallow a cool draught, and in the lull that followed, we heard something unexpected. A raspy voice suddenly said, "Rideous?"

At the name, we turned and saw nothing. Then we glanced down and noticed a filthy beggar dressed in gray rags. He was the same beggar we had passed when entering the tavern. His long hair was matted with sweat and dust. His dirty nails were chewed down to stubs. But he had lighter skin, like us. He had been born in Estavion and had likely lived there for some time in his unfortunate life before somehow ending up here on the cobblestone streets of Severance. He was staring up at us with inquisitive eyes, and we stared awkwardly back.

"Ya knows 'im?" His outstretched hand curled into a single crooked finger. "Ya knows Rideous?"

"Maybe." I leaned down. "The better question is, do *you* know Irrideous?"

The beggar smiled a wide, toothless grin. "Maybe."

At last. We had found someone who lacked the fear to keep quiet, even if his mind was half gone. At least I wouldn't have to beat the truth out of him. I just needed to learn his price, so I held out Amethyst's bloated purse.

"Migrant scraps, that is. No good 'ere," he spat, swatting my hand, but then he noticed the water jug in Amethyst's hands and licked his cracked lips. "What's there?"

"This?" I reached for the jug. Then I tilted it over, dribbling some water into the dust.

"Miscreant!" The beggar bent toward the ground and pushed his mouth against the stones to suck moisture from the cracks.

"No!" Amethyst cried out, pulling him up. "Don't do that. Please! We'll give you the water," she promised, wiping his cracked lips with the hem of her dress.

"*After*," I clarified. "What do you know about Irrideous?"

"Not much. Not much a'tall. Little to know, that is," he babbled eagerly, his tongue loosened by our offer.

"Do you know him?"

He cackled. "Knows 'im? Ha! No one *knows* Rideous. No one nears a prince like 'im —no one sane, that is. No one who likes their insides on the inside."

"But he lives here?"

"Um—no. Well, sometime hence, maybe. Don't know. Just heard of 'im, that is. We all heard of 'im. Hard to forget, stories like 'is. Hard to hear."

I had to close my eyes and think to make any sense of the beggar's incoherent babbling. "So—wait. He doesn't live here?"

"Um—no. No."

"So he's left?"

"Maybe."

Answers

I knelt down and talked slower, trying to put ideas in his head. "Did Irrideous move someplace else?"

"Maybe, maybe." The beggar squinted, not liking my choice of words. "Not 'xactly. More *left* left, that is." He jerked his chin sideways as if we knew the secret destination to which he referred. I looked, half expecting to see Irrideous walking toward us down the winding street.

Amethyst, however, understood the beggar's ramblings. She leaned closer. "You mean he died."

"Died. That's it."

She glanced at me. This wasn't the answer she wanted.

"I thought he was building an army," I said, trying to redirect the beggar's thoughts. "Have you heard anything about that?"

"No. Dead, he is. Hard to hear."

I stood back up and groaned. I tried to rub some of the sweat from my eyes. Maybe this was a waste of time. The beggar was obviously missing a few chinks from his chain.

Amethyst kept prying, though. "When did he die?"

The beggar scraped some crud from the edge of his mouth. "Oh, uh, ya knows. A while. Sometime hence, maybe."

That meant he didn't know. Probably because it never actually happened.

"What happened?" Amethyst persisted. "How'd he die?"

"Killed 'im wife, he did," the man nodded sadly. "Went mad. After that, who knows. Not me, that is."

Amethyst glanced at me again, her eyes fraught this time. Then I remembered. Damascus had told us that Irrideous may have regained his sanity after the tragedy with the Cornerstone. He had returned to Severance and had the frame of mind to fall in love and marry. Had he then regressed again?

"How did his wife die?"

The answer didn't come right away. For the first time, the beggar delayed, his face contorted with grief.

I shook the water jug in his face, sloshing the contents within. "Did you hear me? How did she die?"

"Burned," came the reluctant answer. "Burned her, he did. Burned 'imself."

A chill ran up my spine. Did Irrideous use a firebomb? Did he torch his own home the way he incinerated Amethyst's chambers in the citadel?

The heiress thought the same thing, I could tell, but she stayed focused. "Did they find his body?" she pressed. "How do you know he's really dead?"

"Left her," he insisted angrily. "Left her behind, he did."

Amethyst glanced at me once again, her hazel eyes drowned in confusion.

"You said he killed his wife," I reminded the beggar.

"Not her." He shook his head. "*Her.*"

Amethyst knelt and grasped the beggar's hand. Her voice softened to a whisper. "A daughter?"

"*Her.*"

"Irrideous had a daughter?"

"Pretty. So pretty." The beggar stared off into space, as if he could see the daughter of Irrideous standing there in the street, dejected like him. "But he left her, he did. No man sane could do that."

"What happened to her?" I asked.

The beggar shrugged. "Gone."

"Where?"

He had to think long about that one. "Sold, like the orphans, sometime hence, I think. Raised by whores, maybe."

Amethyst turned to me a fourth time, her voice strained. "Isn't slavery illegal in Samara?"

I nodded. "So is prostitution. And murder. But it happens." Then I turned to the beggar. "Is that it?"

"Maybe. Maybe."

Answers

"Do you know where she is now?"

"Who?"

"The daughter," I said.

He shrugged. "Gone."

"Gone where?"

"Somewhere hence. Gone."

I groaned again, more frustrated this time. "Do you at least know her name?"

"Who?"

"The daughter of Irrideous!" I clenched my fist again. It was all I could do to avoid knocking him out like the tavern keeper.

The beggar didn't notice my anger, though. He just thought about my question. For a long time, he stared at the dusty street, then his bare feet, then my tall boots. He noticed my broadsword. My hands. Then maybe he saw my fingers still stained crimson by the tavern keeper's blood, because he blurted out, "Red!"

"Red? Her name is Red?" Amethyst asked.

"Red 'air," he exclaimed, his lips parting in a toothless grin.

"But what about her name?"

"The whore. Ha! The redheaded whore. Ha ha," he cheered, nodding his head and singing along to some old song suddenly remembered. *"The whore, the whore, the redheaded whore!"*

I stepped back. We wouldn't learn anything else from this beggar. We had already lost him to the music in his head. So I said to Amethyst, half joking, "I can go back into the tavern. I can probably pound something out of the owner."

She didn't laugh, and she didn't seem to mind our dead end either. We had learned something new. Therefore, she took the water jug from my hand. She leaned down again and held out the promised payment. "Just one last question. What's your name?"

The beggar was still singing:

The whore, the whore! The redheaded whore!

Her beauty deep, her old son adored,
She'll raise the lash, and cry, 'Never more!'
And crush the Damned, the redheaded whore!

"Sir?"

Through gales of snow, she'll follow the Ghosts!
In halls of gold, she'll proclaim the boast!
Through streets of stone, she'll confound the hosts,
And scorn the Thief, that—

"Sir?" Amethyst tapped his shoulder this time, stopping him mid-line. "Your name. What do they call you?"

He leaned back in amazement. "Me?"

"Yes, *you*," she insisted. "What do they call you?"

"Crazy," he laughed. "Crazy. Crazy!"

"Crazy," she repeated softly.

"Crazy," I said to myself, completely agreeing.

But then Amethyst reached out—I'm horrified to say—and she touched that filthy man. With elegant hands, she brushed the greasy hair from his face. She pushed the water jug into his hand. "You're not crazy," she whispered, though somehow I suspected she wasn't addressing the beggar anymore. "You know a man should love his own daughter, don't you?"

"The whore?"

"Yes, even a whore."

The beggar slurped a hasty drink, dribbling water onto his matted beard. His dull wits returned, and his eyes grew sad again. "Not right. Not sane, what he did."

"No. No, it's not," she managed to say.

Then she stood and left. She started walking without me.

I followed after a bit, quite confused. Had I heard correctly? Had her confidence faded again? What had come over her? I had never

Answers

seen before her like that. Suddenly, she seemed unraveled. The mere suggestion of an unloved daughter had broken her.

I meant to ask why, even though it didn't seem proper, but I didn't get the chance. At that moment, a loud shout echoed in my ears instead. Answering the call, I turned in the narrow street just in time to see the furious tavern keeper stomp around a corner.

"What's this?" I smiled to myself. "Back for more?"

The large man was indeed back, but this time, he didn't come alone. Nor did he bring his three friends from the tavern. No. In the five minutes since I had left him unconscious behind his counter, he had apparently awakened and slipped out the back door. Rather than face me alone, he had sought out reinforcements.

He had brought ten imperial guards to arrest me.

SURGE

There were ten imperials, I'm sure. I had time to count, and my senses were heightened by the adrenaline surging through my veins. A towering man led them, and he had sleek black hair that fell over his shoulders before it faded against his black uniform. In their hands the soldiers clutched spears twice as long as my Vanguard broadsword, and tucked through their belts they held short swords in reserve. They marched around the corner, their eyes focused, their boot stomps loud on the cobblestones, and the tavern keeper pointed them toward Amethyst and me.

"There he is," the man spat. "He's Vanguard for sure. The girl too. Migrants, both of them, asking about Irrideous!"

My grip tightened around the scabbard in my hand, but I didn't draw my sword yet. The imperials still seemed doubtful. The leader approached slowly down the dusty street and watched us carefully. Maybe he didn't want to spook us and cause an unnecessary chase. Perhaps he doubted whatever story the tavern keeper had told him.

"You there," he called cautiously. "Migrants! Stand fast."

I did hold my ground. I used those moments to think. I tried to imagine talking our way out of an arrest, but that didn't seem likely, considering the intolerance we had endured thus far. Then I thought about spending the next few days in a Samaran prison in the catacombs beneath Severance. That didn't seem so bad. At least it would be cool and damp down there—much preferable to those hot trenches they called streets.

But then I glanced at Amethyst, and in her frantic eyes I saw a different truth. How a fourteen-year-old girl might not last long against all the murderers and rapists and thieves in the dungeons.

How it might take Damascus days or weeks to secure our release. How Irrideous might find us there. Or how the Samarans might learn her identity and demand a ransom for an heiress.

So I made my choice. I wrapped my fingers around the hilt of my sword, and I spoke quietly to Amethyst. "Now might be a good time for those lace gloves."

"I agree," she whispered back, "but I didn't bring them."

I turned, horrified. She couldn't be serious.

But she was. And then she turned and bolted down the street.

"Narrow girl," I muttered.

At Amethyst's flight, the imperial captain surged forward in pursuit, and since I hadn't moved yet, he assumed I would come quietly without a fight, and he tried to pass me without a word. I had no such intentions, though, and as the tall imperial flew by, my right arm shot out. My clenched fist broke his jaw and shifted his momentum sideways. Then he dropped his spear, tripped on the uneven cobblestones, and cracked his head against the brick wall. He slumped to the street and stopped moving.

"Halt!" another soldier shouted. "Stop!"

I didn't check if the imperial captain lived. I sprinted after Amethyst, and the nine remaining men followed. I soon caught the heiress, and together we led the Samarans on a reckless chase through the city. We were still lost, and we could never avoid the entire imperial garrison, but that didn't matter. I was a slave to my instincts and training, and both of them were screaming to flee. To run and never stop.

But running proved difficult. The winding streets suddenly grew crowded. Maybe they had always been that congested, and we just didn't notice before because of our leisurely pace. As we ran full speed, though, we couldn't help but bump into loiterers. Crash into parked carts. Trip over wooden crates. Slip on refuse and filth overflowing the gutters. I tried to turn that clutter to our advantage. As often as I could, I yanked a cart or knocked down random refugees

Surge

so they would fall in the street and hinder our pursuers, but my efforts seemed pointless. The imperials closed the distance.

To make matters worse, we still didn't know where we were. We didn't even know what direction we should go. I knew that we had to push west somehow, toward the coast and the harbor where the *Solution* waited, but in those crooked, narrow streets we never traveled in the same direction for longer than a few steps, and we couldn't see above the buildings to spot any landmarks. We couldn't even glimpse the sun. We could only keep running until…what? Until we reached the northern wall and the wide Rapha`Dim? Until we stumbled out the eastern gate and into the desert? What then? I couldn't take Amethyst out into those shifting sands. There was a reason the nomads called it the Impasse.

I tried not to dwell on that. We just had to escape somehow, so I just pushed myself harder. I pumped my arms and ignored the sweat dripping into my eyes. I sprang quickly each time my boots slapped the cobblestones. I shoved a peasant aside and shot through another intersection. I think I actually increased the distance between myself and the imperials.

But then a desperate plea reached my ears. "Mordecai, wait!"

I slid to a halt. I paused a moment to glance back.

Amethyst was still coming, but she struggled to keep pace. When she reached my side, she bent over and heaved in gasping breaths. Sweat already soaked her frock. Blood flushed her face. She couldn't keep going like that, I realized then. Perhaps I could outrun the imperials. I was a trained soldier, after all, a strong man in my prime, but she was just a girl. Without her gloves, she was a fourteen-year-old weakling. And I couldn't leave her.

"Stop! Halt there! Halt in the name of the Empress!"

The imperials were still coming fast. They would catch us in seconds. All the same, I paused to suck in a deep breath and clear my mind. But then I choked on the stench. The rancid smell of refuse and sweat and filth. How had I ignored that stink before? Was it always so overwhelming?

No. The smell was stronger in that street. It came from somewhere close. From my right. From an alley.

I saw then our answer, or a temporary solution at least. There was a narrow alley blocked with refuse. A trash heap with crates and debris stacked halfway up the brick walls. A small area only a few paces wide, where there would be no room to escape.

Exactly what I needed.

Without a word, I grasped Amethyst's wrist and pulled her into the alley. Without explaining myself, I lifted and tossed her effortlessly onto the trash heap. "Climb!" I ordered, and she did. Without questioning my plan, she clambered up the pile, grasped the ledge above, and pulled herself up to the roof of the adjacent building. Then she looked down and saw me kicking over the wooden crates so she couldn't be followed.

That's when panic came. "Lieutenant! What are you doing?"

"Just stay there! Don't worry."

Then the imperials rounded the corner.

There were still nine of them, and like me they didn't seem winded from the pursuit. But I meant what I said to Amethyst. There was no need to worry. Because these weren't dreadnaughts. They didn't wear lace. They didn't have firebombs or brimstone. They were only men, and I can handle men.

My heartbeat hardly quickened. As they caught their breath and entered the alley, I even had time enough to close my eyes a moment. Calm my mind. Think back to my training. Remember Uriah's sage advice, his techniques for such a scenario against multiple enemies with long weapons. *Divide and conquer,* he would say. *Eliminate the range advantage.* Then my eyelids snapped open. I dropped my sword and proved my worth.

I charged straight into the nine, twisting past two spearheads thrust at my chest. I pushed into the fray, where their long spears proved a curse instead of a blessing, and I used the narrow alley to my advantage. I drove my shoulder into the first man's chest, pushing him until his back crashed against vertical bricks and his head bounced against the wall. I kicked a second man in the ankle, and when he stumbled I snapped my knee into his chin. A third man pushed me, trying to hold his spear shaft across my neck, to choke me out, but my clenched fist found his stomach. Then his neck. Then his left eye. He fell back into a fourth man.

"Behind you!" Amethyst shouted from above.

The warning was unnecessary. I could already smell and even feel the fifth Samaran behind me. I heard him drop his spear because I was only one pace away. Then his bulky arms wrapped around me, pinning my arms to my chest. He forgot about my head, though, so I snapped it back and caught his teeth with the back of my skull. When his grip slackened, my elbow found his lower ribs. My heel crushed his groin.

Imperial number six came next. He had entered the alley behind his allies, guarding the rear, and now he screamed at them to step back so he could employ his long spear. He thrust that weapon at my neck. I only twisted slightly in response. I let the sharp spearhead pass a finger's breadth from my skin, and then I reached up and caught the shaft. With one hand, I snapped the pole, removing the point. With the other hand, I yanked hard, pulling the sixth imperial forward until my knee emptied his stomach, and as he doubled over to vomit, I whipped the spear pole like a staff and cracked it against the base of his neck.

With six down, the narrow alley grew less crowded, so the remaining three rushed together. They dropped their spears and unsheathed their short swords. They still had a hard time of it, though. They had to take care not to accidentally impale each other while I could flail indiscriminately with my new staff. The unconscious bodies of their allies cluttered the cobblestones and tripped their feet, but I danced around the fallen. I twisted past thrusts and whirled my staff against wrists, disarming the last three. I spun and leapt, my pole a mallet of rhythmic precision, and when the music ended, only the ninth imperial remained.

He didn't continue the dance, though. He fled from the alley to alert reinforcements.

I stooped to pick up the fallen spearhead, and I followed him.

"No! Don't kill him," came instructions from above, as if I didn't have enough to worry about.

But Amethyst was right. I was risking too much already. The Samarans would demand blood for this, and if I didn't show some restraint, we would never be able to convince the Empress that this was all a misunderstanding and not a strategic attack. So I relented. When I turned the corner, I didn't hurl the broken spearhead into the soldier's back. I sent the staff instead, throwing the shaft like a javelin and striking the ninth man in the back of the head so that he slumped into the street unconscious.

Then I took a deep breath and looked up.

For once, the heiress didn't have any words. From her perch on the rooftop, she only surveyed the scene below. She double-checked that each of the nine were incapacitated and would not rise again to challenge me—not in the next few minutes anyway. Not until we were far from that alley. Then her gaze widened. She studied the Samaran civilians and refugees still crowding the street. She looked for glinting swords, hidden knives. She listened for cries of alarm.

I listened too. I spun round to see if any of the people in that narrow street would dare attack me. All those men and women and children only stared in abject terror, though. Their eyes drifted from their unconscious soldiers, their fallen heroes, to my bloody hands. They stared horrified at the Estavian soldier, at the Vanguard agent, at the monster who had wounded so many of their men, their brothers and husbands and fathers. They looked at me, and they shrank in fear.

Good.

Surge

Convinced of our momentarily safety, I glanced at the roof again where Amethyst waited.

"Is it safe to come down?" she asked.

"Wait! What can you see from up there?"

Amethyst stopped and straightened. She spun around slowly, her eyes scanning the horizon. "I can see the Towers," she called down, "and the ocean!"

My heart fluttered. "Can you make it there? Can you stay on the rooftops?"

To test my suggestion, Amethyst tiptoed along to top edge of the wall. Then she made a short run, jumped, and leapt over the alleyway where I had fought the imperials. She landed safely atop the next building and smiled down at me.

"Good," I called up. "Then go. I'll follow."

She did go, and I only delayed a moment. I lingered long enough to slip into the alley and retrieve my unsheathed sword, and then I chased after the heiress.

It was like tracking a falcon on a cloudy day, following Amethyst through that city, and I had to watch my path ahead so I didn't crash into refugees, bump into children, or trip over beggars lying in the street. When I could glance up, I seldom caught more than a fleeting glimpse of her boots flying between rooftops. Sometimes I only saw the tail of her crimson scarf fluttering behind a high brick wall. I kept up, though. I often tripped over the uneven cobblestones. My heart knocked against my ribs. But I kept up.

It probably helped that Amethyst made slow progress. The streets weren't straight, after all, and she could only leap over the narrow side alleys, so she couldn't blaze a direct path to the sea.

Instead, she had to scamper diagonally back and forth across the rooftops. Occasionally she even had to backtrack. Once she had to stop entirely, climb down, and then ask for my help to scale the next wall. But only once.

"We're almost there!" she called down a few minutes later. "I can see the market and the harbor wall."

Almost at that same moment, though, I heard something else. From somewhere behind us, a distant horn resounded. A trumpet call echoed throughout the city.

"They found the soldiers in the alley," Amethyst said.

"It doesn't matter. Keep going!"

But it did matter. After a few seconds, another horn answered the first. Then a third sounded to the south. Then the north. Then from somewhere dangerously close, almost on top of us. Then to the east ahead of us. And then we heard frantic voices shouting.

Worse than that, an older man ahead of me suddenly turned, ducked into the nearest building, and slammed the door behind him. Then someone else closed a small window. A woman shoed her children into another home and shut them all inside. Curtains slid closed. Shutters slapped.

In about fifteen seconds, the crowded street emptied.

"It's an alarm," I realized. "They're signaling an intruder! They're warning the residents and sealing the city!"

"Then we should hide! Get out of the streets."

"No!" That wouldn't work. We would be caught in minutes. "Keep going! Faster! We must reach the harbor before they seal the gates."

Amethyst didn't argue. She took off again, leaping from rooftop to rooftop, and I followed, appreciating the empty streets for the moment. After another minute, though, we encountered a new obstacle ahead. The buildings abruptly ended. The narrow streets opened up into a wide square crammed with carts and stalls and scurrying merchants.

Surge

We had returned to the market.

We were close, then. I could see the outer wall just past the open square. I could see the gate through which the *Solution* lay moored to her dilapidated pier. But the imperials were close too. Atop the outer wall, I saw archers and spearmen. At the gate I saw seven other soldiers, one of them mounted, and I couldn't guess how many more patrolled the harbor beyond the wall. If we stepped into the market, there would be no protection from arrows or spears if they fired upon us.

We still had a chance, though. The market hadn't yet cleared. The merchants were still frantically packing their wares, refusing to abandon their livelihoods, so we used them to our advantage. As soon as Amethyst shimmied down from the last roof, we entered the square and slipped among the crowded stalls. We forced ourselves to move slowly and casually, hoping that no one would realize who we were and where we were going until it was too late.

But as we passed the last cart and approached the final gate, the mounted imperial did notice us. I noticed her too. She was the same woman who had stopped us after we left the *Solution*. We had spoken to her about Irrideous. And when she saw us coming, still breathing hard, our clothes drenched with sweat, our eyes darting from the archers to the guards to the harbor beyond, she recognized us and realized the purpose for the alarms. She pointed her spear at us.

"Halt! You there, migrants!"

At her call, the six imperials guarding the gate instantly formed a tight line. That mattered not, though. We were already close to the outer wall, well under the line of sight from the archers above. So I attacked.

When the mounted soldier changed with her spear extended, I ducked under the tip, grasped the shaft, and pulled the woman from her saddle. When she fell to the ground, I put my boot into her face for good measure. Then I turned to face the last six, and I dropped the spear.

I finally unsheathed my broadsword.

They came all at once under the gate. Five hurled themselves at me with spears and sabers while the sixth circled around to capture Amethyst. The heiress stood fast, though, and when the imperial only tried to knock her down instead of taking her head, she used his leniency to her advantage. Remembering Uriah's secret techniques, she snapped her fingers tight as daggers. She easily sidestepped her opponent's thrust, and she sent a shot under his lamellar armor and into his ribs. When he bent over in pain, she spun behind him and followed fast with more strikes to his lower spine and neck. She hit five separate nerve clusters in two seconds, and the imperial fell in a wave of spasms.

Then she looked to me.

"Go," I shouted. "Get to the ship!"

Amethyst didn't question me. She bolted past the last five through a narrow gap in their defense. She slipped through the gate, entered the harbor, and began her final sprint south along the outer wall toward the *Solution*.

Ahead of her, the harbor was strangely clear of civilians and soldiers, and the ship was miraculously already prepared. After hearing the alarms, Abner must have guessed our peril and taken the initiative to clear his moorings, secure the ramp, and ready the oars. Damascus had also returned, and he waited with the captain to haul us up, cast off and escape the harbor. We only needed to reach the ship, and Amethyst was already on her way.

I intended to follow in a moment. I had already knocked the first imperial against the gate, and I had cornered the last four against the wall. But then the first man noticed Amethyst and took chase, and I had to break form to catch his shoulder from behind, twist him around, and slam my hilt against his temple. A second man took advantage of the distraction, though, and swept my leg with a spear. For the first time that day, I fell to my back.

Then it all fell apart.

Surge

Two men threw themselves onto me, pinning me under their weight. Then the woman somehow roused herself from where she had fallen off her horse. She chased after Amethyst, and I could not stop her. Then from atop the city wall, archers noticed Amethyst's desperate sprint, and arrows rained down. They intentionally missed, thankfully. They showered the boardwalk ahead to scare her off, to slow her down so she could be captured, but it worked.

It happened in a terrible instant. Amethyst skidded to a halt to avoid the arrows. The chasing woman crashed into her. From the *Sole Solution*'s bow, Damascus cried out. Amethyst screamed in response, and the surge filled my blood again.

I was still pinned, but my flailing arm finally caught one of my attackers in the eye. When he fell back, I had room to snap my forehead up and catch someone else in the nose. Then I was on my feet, and I forgot Amethyst's previous warning about not killing anyone. As a third man swung his sword at my head, I ducked underneath and thrust my blade upward. The tip found a chink in his armor scales, and my broadsword went through his stomach and out his back.

I didn't realize then what I had done, though. All conscious thought had fled my mind. I was a machine, a soldier protecting my liege. By pure instinct, I pulled the sword from my enemy's belly, and as a fourth imperial attacked I whipped my wet blade overhead. Blood spattered. Bones crunched. The fourth man's head fell from his shoulders.

I looked south and saw the woman dragging Amethyst to her feet. I heard shouts somewhere overhead. I glanced up and saw imperial archers perched atop the wall, their composite bows ready and their strings taut. Then somehow my hand found a spear. My arm went back, then forward. The javelin flew straight and pierced an archer's chest. But his finger slipped. The bow released. An arrow shot down.

And the girl screamed.

The Spider's Claw

I didn't see what happened exactly. I only heard the scream, like a banshee in the night or the cry Amethyst had unleashed in the citadel when the flames came. Like the hopeless shouts of our soldiers slaughtered in a courtyard. Like the shrieks my sister must have made when her murderer struck.

I moved forward in a daze. One of the imperial guards was somehow back on his feet. Though he could barely stand, he held his spear horizontally in a defensive stance to block my escape. I had no restraint left, though. My bloodstained sword sliced his spear in half. My free hand wrenched the weapon away. My fist broke his jaw. Then my arm wrapped around his neck, grasping his throat like a vice. I squeezed until he stopped struggling, and I let him fall.

Then a searing spike of pain burst through my shoulder.

It was an arrow, I realized. Nothing more. A bolt shot from the ramparts overhead. It pierced my left shoulder, rendering that arm almost useless. No matter. It would take more than that to stop me. When I glanced up, though, I saw the countless archers on the wall preparing more. Much more.

So I looked for a shield, and I found another imperial.

He was the second guard, the man I had struck with my elbow before casting him aside. He lay where he had fallen among the other six guards I had crushed. I shifted my sword to my injured left hand, and then I grabbed his collar with my right. I hefted him up so he stood between his allies and me.

"Walk," I growled in his ear, "or perish."

He walked. We both walked slowly toward the spot where Amethyst had fallen halfway to the *Solution*. Far overhead, the archers followed us with drawn bows, ready to fire the instant I released my hostage. From behind, additional imperials swarmed through the gate and into the harbor. They kept their distance, though. No one approached or fired upon me. They just watched as I dragged my captive toward Amethyst.

Finally, after an eternity, I reached her. She was alive. Better than that, she seemed unharmed. But the woman was dead. The female officer who had chased Amethyst now lay over the girl's legs with an arrow lodged in her neck and blood dripping from the wound. Amethyst was still weeping, though. For some reason the sight of the lifeless woman had overwhelmed her. She was useless, and I couldn't lift her, not while I carried a hostage with one arm. Not with an arrow stuck in my other shoulder.

So I raised my voice and cried toward the *Solution*. "Help!"

Two things happened next. First, Damascus stepped forward on the *Solution*'s bow and raised his arms, and suddenly a strong wind rose over the waters. It grew fast and powerful into a gale that brought blinding mist and stinging rain. The storm became so thick I soon couldn't see the ship or the walls or the soldiers behind me. Of course, they couldn't see me either.

At the same time, two of Abner's crewmen leapt off his ship and down to the pier. They sprinted toward Amethyst and me. I lost sight of them almost immediately in the gale, but I cried out repeatedly, screaming over the howling wind until they found my location. They pushed off the dead woman, picked Amethyst up, and carried her back to the ship.

I followed close behind. Since my hostage no longer seemed necessary, I tossed him aside and followed the crewmen and the weeping girl. Once we reached the pier, hands stretched down through horizontal sheets of rain. Someone lifted Amethyst onto the deck. I climbed up without help and found Abner waiting for me.

"I see you've been making friends," the captain laughed.

"Just get us out of here!"

The Spider's Claw

Abner only laughed harder.

I'm not sure exactly what occurred after that. As the rush wore off, I felt the imperial arrow still lodged in my shoulder. The kite runner was listing violently in the crashing waves. We still had to somehow escape the crowded harbor of Severance and avoid their frigates and catapults and who knows what else. But that was Abner's problem, not mine. My task was complete.

So I collapsed onto the wooden deck and lay on my back. I dropped my sword. I closed my eyes and breathed deep. After decades of drought, I stretched my arms wide and embraced the saline rain, and I hoped the terrible storm would never pass.

Damascus kept the gale going a while longer, but once we cleared the harbor, he lowered his miraculous hands. The winds dissipated. The sky cleared. The rain stopped.

The rain. Did it actually rain?

"You made it rain," I managed to say. "I thought you needed a catalyst to make it rain."

Damascus stood over me. "That wasn't rain, my boy. I'm sorry. It was only mist whipped up from the harbor."

He could have fooled me.

"Can you walk?"

I wasn't sure, but I tried anyway and found that I could, so Damascus helped me off the main deck, through the door, and into the captain's cabin. He guided me until I fell into the bed at the far end of the stateroom. Then he tended my shoulder.

He ripped open my wet tunic. Yanked at the arrow. Tore the tip from my flesh as I cursed in agony. But then the old words followed. My sinews and skin wove themselves back together. Everything felt right, better than new. My exhaustion vanished. Even my thirst disappeared.

Then it all came rushing back. The chase. The screaming girl. The dead woman. The murdered Samarans. Our narrow escape. Suddenly I sat up and stared at Damascus, completely confused.

How was he so calm? Why wasn't he rebuking me?

Amethyst was there too, I noticed. She stood in the doorway, her frock soaked with salted rain and sweat. Her damp scarf clung to her pale face. She clutched my sword and scabbard in her trembling fingers. Her eyes were downcast, her spirit fragile.

That's why.

No one spoke for a long moment. I half thought to escape, to make up some lie and excuse myself from the room. But I didn't. That wouldn't be right. Not that I had done anything else right that day, but still. I couldn't leave Amethyst alone. Not after all we had suffered together. So I waited until Damascus gently asked the dreaded question.

"What happened?"

"I'm sorry," I blurted out automatically. "It's just—"

"I didn't ask you, lieutenant," Damascus snapped. Then he asked Amethyst again, even more gently, "What happened?"

She sniffed loudly and kept her face downcast. "I wanted to look for Irrideous."

"And?"

Her volume fell. "I only wanted to find the stone."

"And?"

"I took Mordecai. We left the ship and explored the city. We spoke to a few soldiers. A beggar. Some refugees."

Damascus nodded thoughtfully. "And?"

Amethyst finally didn't answer.

So I risked speaking again. "I lost my temper."

Damascus turned and considered my words thoughtfully.

The Spider's Claw

I took that as permission, and the rest of the story tumbled out. The first female soldier who questioned us. The refugees crowding the city. The chaos. The tavern keeper. My unprovoked attack. The threats of arrest. The chase through the streets. The market. The flight through the harbor. I forgot some details, I'm sure, but Damascus heard the basic idea.

"It's my fault," I added after finishing. "If I hadn't struck that tavern keeper—" I shook my head at the thought of what might have been, but I couldn't change that anymore. I could only do my best to make it right. "We should go back. I'll surrender to the Samarans and stand trial."

"No," Amethyst insisted. "You can't do that. You were only helping me. I should never have left the ship in the first place, but I couldn't wait. I wanted—" Her voice trailed off, unable to find the words.

Damascus knew what she meant, though, and he stepped close enough to rest a wrinkled hand on her shoulder. "Come now, my dear. It's all right. The responsibility does not rest solely on you. I share the blame also. My mistakes with the Cornerstone started this foul tragedy, and I brought us here. At least for your own part, your heart was in the right place. You were only trying to help, to do what you thought was right.

"But sometimes our hearts can deceive us." He knelt down so he could gaze into her eyes. "Sometimes reason and logic fail, and learning only confounds the matter. In those times, you must be cautious, remember? In those times, you must look to someone other than yourself. You must look to me, to Abner, to those others you love. To those who care about you. Sometimes you must listen and obey, even when your heart says otherwise."

"I must trust the ones I love," Amethyst whispered.

"And trust the ones who love you," Damascus added.

Then the room fell silent.

This was not some sudden epiphany, I realized. It was an old lesson learned anew, a sacred refrain she had memorized and oft repeated. The teacher was reminding his student about something he had taught her long ago, and she obviously hadn't mastered it. Not yet.

But Damascus didn't press the matter. After that painful reminder, he ended the lesson and turned back to the more urgent matters at hand. He looked to me, the murderer, and pursed his lips. The disappointment returned.

I waited a long time for him to pass judgment.

"You might think," Damascus finally said, "that I would like nothing more than to be rid of you, lieutenant. The idea is most tempting, I assure you, and not without merit. The Samarans would prove harsh, I imagine, and you would receive no mercy from them. Not that you deserve it. You would be executed within hours of your surrender."

No argument there.

"But that seems an unnecessary waste at the moment, and I do not believe you've served your full purpose, not yet," Damascus added. "Amethyst may still need her guardian if we continue our course, and the plan—"

"Wait." I couldn't believe my ears. "You're letting me stay?"

"Make no mistake. You *will* serve sentence for the deeds you committed today," Damascus promised me, "but that will come later, after the more pressing dangers have passed. And your judgment will not pass from the Samarans. No. The Vanguard discipline their own. Isn't that right? Once we return to Tel Tellesti, you will be reported and charged. The matter will be thoroughly investigated. The Imperial Empress will be notified and consulted, to appease her wrath, and you will pay your debt, whatever the arbiter deems fit and proper. But as I said, that must all come later."

My heavy heart lightened. I could scarcely imagine a more welcome respite. Amethyst also breathed a little easier.

The Spider's Claw

"There are more pressing matters to address at the moment," Damascus continued. "Our endeavors in Severance have proven futile, and we are no closer to finding Irrideous or the stone. Therefore we must determine a new course."

My spirits sank again. "So you didn't find anything either?"

"I'm afraid not," the tutor confessed. "I visited the imperial archives. I found my old friend. She granted me permission to search the official records, and I did find some information about Irrideous. It was all circumstantial, though—nothing of relevance. I found only dates for his marriage and the birth of a daughter, Bethel Emm." He sighed. "Such a wonderful name."

I didn't comment.

"But there was very little after that," Damascus continued. "Nothing at all except—"

"A fire?"

He nodded sadly and sat in a chair next to the table. "Their home burned to the ground eighteen years ago. Irrideous and his entire family perished. Bethel was only two."

Amethyst and I glanced at each other. Neither of us was surprised. Despite the extra details, this was the same story we had heard many times in Severance, and it was a tale neither of us believed.

So I asked Damascus, "Are you sure that's what the records said? Is there any chance they could be wrong?"

The old man scratched his head. "I suppose there is a chance. A slight chance. There *were* some strange omissions from the record. There is a rule in Severance, you see. A scribe cannot notarize a death unless he sees the body himself. And while there was a signature next to the death record for the wife, there was no signature next to Irrideous's name. Or Bethel Emm's."

"What does that mean?"

Damascus shrugged. "It could mean any number of things, but mostly likely it means their bodies were never found after the fire. They were only *assumed* dead, consumed by the flames."

"So they may have escaped," I guessed. "Irrideous and Bethel may still be alive. He may still have the stone."

"Do you think we can still find him?" Amethyst asked.

"I'm sorry, my dear, but no," Damascus said. "I wouldn't have the slightest idea where to begin. Even if we knew for sure he still lived in Severance, it could take weeks to search the city. Months maybe."

"If the Samarans didn't arrest us first," I joked. No one laughed, though.

"I'm afraid we have nothing," Damascus said instead. "No location. No occupation. Nothing. We can only run and hide and hope my fears about Irrideous prove wrong."

Amethyst hung her head dejectedly.

But I wasn't ready to give up. Not yet. Not after risking so much and earning such a price on my head. "Wait."

Damascus raised his eyes.

"There *is* something we can do."

Amethyst narrowed her eyes. She hadn't guessed what I was about to say. Maybe she didn't remember. A lot had happened in the last few hours.

"Well, out with it," Damascus said impatiently.

"We learned a few things ourselves," I explained, "mostly the same as you. Some things were different, though. We heard rumors about an army, some kind of recruitment Irrideous is conducting, but we also heard something interesting about the daughter, the, um—"

"Bethel Emm?"

"Yes. Her. We talked to this one man and, well…" I thought back to the crazy beggar. Could we really trust anything he said? "We heard that Bethel was sold into slavery. Sold as a whore."

Damascus's eyes brightened. "Bethel is alive?"

"Maybe, though that doesn't help much, does it?" I suddenly felt foolish. I should have kept my mouth shut. "It's not like we could find her, not without visiting every brothel in Samara."

The Spider's Claw

"Indeed," Damascus agreed. "Such a task is far beyond us, and somewhat inappropriate, mind you, but maybe..."

His voice trailed off and his brow furrowed. His mind raced, considering possibilities outside my scope of experience. He was recalling his research, I suspect, searching the archives in his memory for some ancient solution. Finally, at long last, he found it.

"Starlight."

I blinked twice. I glanced sideways out the window. "It's not quite dark yet. Maybe in another hour or two."

He didn't hear me. He leaned over the octagonal table and pushed aside the parchment rubbings from Ballabor until he reached the cracked vellum underneath, the old map of the Inheritance I had noticed before. His finger found Severance along the eastern Samaran coastline, and then he traced north across the Rapha`Dim.

I stepped closer. "Damascus? What is it?"

A smile creased his lips. "How would you like to visit another Ascendant sanctuary, lieutenant?"

A few minutes later, Damascus and I exited the stateroom so Amethyst could change into something fresh and dry, and then Damascus climbed the steps to the quarterdeck above to speak with Abner. "Captain, would you kindly change your course?"

"Where to?"

"Just north of the delta, please. We wish to make landfall and visit Spiderclaw."

The captain laughed. "You're going back into Samara? Now? Haven't had enough excitement for the day?"

"Just set the heading, captain. There's no need to complain."

"It's my ship. I'll complain all I like," Abner jested. "It's the only fun I get."

I left the two men still arguing and slipped through the hatch. Once in the cargo hold, I found my satchel and stripped off my wet clothes, that useless disguise I had worn in Severance. I retrieved my Vanguard uniform. It was soothing, I must admit—the smell of tanned leather, the cool touch of chainmail, the soft folds of the vermilion mantle. It all smelled right, like home. For a moment, I felt safe. It was only a moment, though.

I didn't take the whole uniform. It was still too warm for that, but I pulled on the boots, pants and tunic. I buckled the wide belt around my waist. I wiped the Samaran blood from my sword and returned the clean blade to the scabbard hanging at my side. Then I returned to the main deck and waited.

For the next half hour, the *Sole Solution* sailed north until we crossed the wide mouth of the Rapha`Dim River. Abner dropped anchor in the shallow waters off the coast, just past the surf line. The crew produced a tiny boat from the cargo hold and lowered it overboard. It seemed hardly large enough for two people, let alone three, but all the same I climbed down and secured the oars. Damascus and Amethyst soon joined me, and I rowed the few hundred paces to shore and beached the small craft.

When I stepped onto the soft sand, a chill ran through me. I hadn't expected to return to Samaran soil so soon. I wondered what the imperials would do if they knew I was there.

I suppressed those thoughts quickly and secured the tiny boat on the nearby dunes. Then we set out walking with Damascus in the lead, Amethyst in the middle and myself at the rear. We crossed the white beaches. Then a rocky shoreline. Then flat, sandy fields with sparse grass.

It was a risky path. We were shadowing the Rapha`Dim's northern banks. The waters flowed only a few hundred paces away. In the fading twilight, we could actually see the walls of Severance to the south just across the broad river. It's possible their archers were watching us. If they realized who we were, and if they thought to follow us, they would have little trouble with the chase.

No such pursuit occurred, though, and Damascus seemed unconcerned. He pressed on. Then twilight turned to sunset, and sunset fast turned to night. The old scholar had brought lanterns for each of us, and he lit them just by snapping his fingers. Then we walked some more as the half moon rose and the twinkling stars dotted a cloudless sky. No one spoke.

After two hours or so, Damascus abruptly turned us north, away from the river. The ground grew sandy again, almost worse than the beaches. Our pace slowed to a crawl. Amethyst and her tutor seemed to manage well enough, but I got sand everywhere. Somehow the grit even invaded my boots.

But then the sand disappeared. I felt solid rock underfoot—and not just any rock. It was polished smooth like the courtyard at Ballabor. Like the ancient walls in Tel Tellesti's citadel. Like Ascendant granite.

Like a sanctuary.

Exhilaration rippled through me. Then I lowered my lantern and saw a floor spreading before us in the midst of the wide-open floodplains. This was no typical floor with stone tiles and seams between, though. No. The pavement was one continuous slab of granite worn perfectly smooth. It stretched far into the darkness around us, boggling the senses.

"Amethyst! Look!"

"Seen it," she replied. "We've been here before. Twice."

It was strange, the way she answered. I had heard that tone of voice before in the guest quarters after the dreadnaught attack. Then I remembered. She had just watched a woman die in her arms not four hours earlier, and she had been despairingly quiet during our conversation in the stateroom. I'm sure she would have rather spent the night alone in the cabin with her grief.

I kept asking questions, though. Maybe I could help her forget her sorrows for a while. "What is this place?"

"It's an Ascendant sanctuary called Ur Thourou."

I balked at the odd name. "Or throw?"

"No, listen. *Er tha'row.*" As she spoke, I raised my lantern and watched her lips curl unnaturally to form the sounds.

"Er-thru-thru," I tried again.

The heiress laughed a little at my incompetence. "Exactly."

"It's lovely," I said. "Rolls right off the tongue, doesn't it?

She smiled. "That's one of the reasons why the Samarans call it the Spider's Claw."

I shivered a little. "Somehow that's worse."

"But it's easier to say. Isn't that the point of a nickname?"

I didn't have an answer for that. I just glanced down again at the polished pavement. "Wait. What's the other reason they call it the Spider's Claw?"

Amethyst shrugged and pointed. "Because of those."

I looked and noticed something else in the distance that had escaped me before. This new sight didn't spur the imagination, though; it sent shivers down my spine.

I couldn't see everything clearly in the darkness, but from the faint moonlight I could roughly make out a circular formation of monolithic spires rising from the polished granite floor. They reached up, far up into the heavens, higher than the Towers of Samar probably. There was an outer ring with perhaps ten or twelve spires stretching skyward, and an inner ring with another eight or so about half as tall. Each skeletal spire curled slightly inward as it rose, almost like the fangs of a snake or the petrified talons of some titanic arachnid beast.

"This place is rather disturbing in daylight when you can see the spires," Amethyst continued. "They do somewhat resemble spider's legs, at least if the spider was colossal and prostrate on its back…and dead and half buried so only its curved legs were protruding from the ground. And if the spider had twenty legs instead of eight."

"That's enough," Damascus suddenly said, irritated that our conversation had slowed our pace. "Come now! Keep up! We're almost there."

We walked on, and I tried not to imagine what the spires resembled during the day. I especially tried not to think about the fact that we were fast approaching the focal point where the monster's maw was most likely located. I just tried to focus on the fact that Amethyst seemed marginally better.

Soon after, we reached the exact center where the spires reached up around us like splayed fingers grasping at the sky, and Damascus finally stopped. He didn't produce any scrolls or parchment, though, nor did he approach the stonescript that covered the ancient granite. Instead, he opened his lantern and snuffed out the flame. Then he turned and told us, "Douse your lights, please."

I blinked, confused. "How will you read the inscriptions?"

Damascus only glared at me impatiently.

"Aren't you here for research?"

"Of course not, you thoughtless twit. I've already been here countless times. Besides, who does research in the dark?"

"Then why—"

"I mean to summon a friend, that is all. Now please, be quiet. I must concentrate. Oh, and—" he glanced down at our legs, "—move back a touch."

Amethyst and I glanced at each other doubtfully, but we retreated and snuffed our lanterns. We gave her teacher a wide berth, and there in the dark, far away from civilization and any prying eyes, Damascus began a most peculiar dance. Illuminated only by innumerable stars and a half moon, the old man shuffled his feet, taking the smallest steps possible without ever raising his sandals off the floor. He waddled in circles for perhaps five minutes and muttered to himself as he watched the speckled sky, and as he danced, I noticed white sparks arcing between his feet and the granite floor.

"There we are," he announced after those long minutes.

I raised my eyebrows. "Finished?"

"Yes. Ready?"

"For what?"

"Just stay back, please," he warned, "and cover your ears."

I glanced at Amethyst again, even more doubtfully this time, but I covered my ears all the same. It's a good thing. No sooner had we protected our hearing than Damascus thrust his arm up. From the focal point at the sanctuary's exact center, he reached skyward, his hand imitating the claws of the temple spires as if grasping the stars with splayed fingers. What shot from his palm, however, was no less than a streak of lightning. With a tooth-chattering crash and a blinding explosion of light, the old man hurled a thunderbolt into the veil.

Fourteen

"Lieutenant, please. You're trying my patience."

I stop and hold my breath. Did Rehoboth just interrupt me again? I had half forgotten she was there.

"Damascus threw lightning into the sky?"

I shrug. "That's what happened."

Rehoboth sighs and glances sideways at Uriah. "Are you sure he wasn't struck by lightning instead?"

I frown. She can't be serious.

"It would explain a lot about the odd man, wouldn't it?"

"Why don't you believe me?"

"I am trying to keep an open mind," she smiles, "but you're not making much sense. You must admit that. You've been through a lot. Your memories are inconsistent, perhaps. And considering everything you've seen, it's very natural for you to—"

"Lose my mind?"

"Exaggerate," she says. "Take the gloves, for instance. Maybe they amplified Amethyst's strength. I admit that's possible. It's also possible, though, that you were weakened from the uncomfortable weeks at sea, and when the girl demonstrated unexpected dexterity, your mind invented a justifiable excuse. You choose to believe in mystical gloves rather than accept the difficult truth that you lost."

Her explanation makes me laugh. "That's good. Keep going."

"Well, there's the dreadnaught, who you described as immense and demonic, but you fought at night in an unfamiliar place with unfamiliar allies, and you received a very serious head wound after falling from a wall. Any of those factors could explain the anomalies in your memory."

"I suppose."

"And this gale that helped you escape Severance," she added. "Similar events have been reported by mariners in the past. It's possible it was just an immense wind storm."

"And it *just happened* to strike at the same moment Damascus raised his arms?"

She smiled at me. "Stranger things have occurred."

I change the subject. "How did the Samarans respond to that incident, by the way? Do they still want me dead?"

"We'll get to that, lieutenant. Don't worry."

I can't wait.

She extends an inviting hand toward me. "So, the lightning…"

"Yes?"

"Are you certain you don't want to change your story? Tell me what actually happened?"

I don't bother answering. Why waste my breath? Instead, I gaze again at the fold of velvet on the cedar desk.

Rehoboth sighs again and glances at her notes, though she doesn't seem to be looking for anything. Perhaps she's merely tired of asking all the questions.

Uriah leans forward to try his luck. "You do realize that no one can corroborate your testimony?"

"You could always ask Damascus."

The comment produces a laugh from Rehoboth. A real laugh. "You really expect us to believe anything that man says?"

"You don't trust him?"

"After what happened in Del Solae? No, I'm afraid we can't."

"That's strange." I lean forward. "Then why are you only wondering about the lightning and the gale and the gloves? If you can't trust Damascus, how can you ever believe a single word I'm saying?"

STARLIGHT

Damascus did launch a thunderbolt from the sanctuary of Ur Thourou. Believe me. And that lightning strike was only the first. For the next hour, in fact, Damascus hurled streak after streak into the dark sky, waiting perhaps five minutes between volleys.

Amethyst and I only observed. We retreated a fair distance, sat near one of the claw-like spires and rested our backs against the warm granite. Under a speckled night sky and a half moon, we watched the old man shuffle and dance in little circles while mumbling incoherently, and whenever he reached upward, we clapped our hands over our ears to muffle the blast.

It was quite the spectacle—almost enough to make me forget about Irrideous and the fatal mistakes I had committed at Severance. Almost.

"He's crazy, isn't he?" I said to Amethyst during a lull.

"A little," she admitted with a sad smile, but the strain still lingered in her voice. She hadn't yet forgotten our mistakes from the day either.

I did my best to distract her. To distract myself. "Has he always been like this?"

"Eccentric? Yes."

"How long have you known him?"

"Four years."

"Four years," I repeated. "Four years of lessons and research and expeditions." I shuddered at the thought. "Sounds tedious."

"It's better than the alterative. Better than the citadel. The empty rooms. The lonely meals. Better than the academy and all the—" But she stopped. In the dark, I heard her sniff and wipe away some tears.

"I'm sorry," I said quickly. Then I also fell quiet.

I didn't speak for a long time after that. I felt like a fool for trying to improve the silence; I just sat quietly, and Amethyst sat quietly. And when Damascus reached up again, we covered our ears and closed our eyes for the blinding white flash and the reverberating thunder that shook the sanctuary like a giant drum.

It was still nice, though, to have a moment's rest after such mayhem. I had spent the last few weeks brooding and fretting about Irrideous and the Cornerstone. I had spent most of the day terrified about what we might find in Severance. And I had spent the better part of an hour sprinting for my life out of that dusty city. So I didn't mind just sitting there in the dull heat on the edge of the desert.

The solace didn't last, though.

My thoughts soon wandered, as thoughts are apt to do when given the opportunity. They wandered unconsciously back to the events of the day. Before I knew it, I was reliving everything in my mind, and worse than that, I was finally realizing what I had actually done—who I had killed and what irreversible damage I had caused. In a parched world already teetering on the brink of war, I had somehow made our situation worse.

Then I was trying to wish it back, as if such a thing were even possible. I renounced every action. I wondered if I could visit the families of the men I killed. Would they listen to an apology, or would I only fuel the smoldering bitterness that was tearing the Inheritance apart?

And Amethyst. What had I done to her? I had been assigned to protect her, but instead I had only caused her more pain.

No. That wasn't right.

I stopped to consider that notion more carefully, and at last I found a slight distraction from my self-condemning thoughts. I *did* share the blame for Amethyst's current mood, but just a part. Something else was also contributing. Something beyond me. Something beyond the threat of Irrideous and the drought, even.

Starlight

I ran through the sequence again, but this time I focused on Amethyst. Various events coalesced. I remembered how the girl had frozen when the Samaran woman died. Before that, I recalled how Amethyst had withdrawn when the beggar had mentioned the daughter of Irrideous. Were the two events connected? And what had she lamented to the beggar? *A man should love his own daughter.* That was a little unprovoked, wasn't it? Unless…

I had chanced upon it, then. I knew that somehow the tragedy in Severance had unearthed a thorn in Amethyst's heart. I didn't speak of it, though. Not at first. I did not believe I had the right to say anything. After all, I was still only a soldier. I wasn't her teacher. I wasn't even her friend. She hardly knew me. She didn't trust me.

Or did she?

She had been surprisingly gracious toward me, I had to admit. Maybe she felt indebted since I had saved her from the firebomb, or perhaps she was just being a silly teenage girl who always had to speak her mind. Perhaps she lacked the experience to know when to stay quiet and save her secrets for someone more trustworthy. For someone besides me.

I felt there was more to it than that, though. There was some basic human connection between us—like father and daughter perhaps? No. Like brother and sister. She seemed invested in me, like she had been determined to redeem me since the beginning. She had gently opened my heart to the Ascendants and gradually introduced me to their wonders. She had heeded my counsel even when I had been wrong to offer it. She had left Ballabor because of my suggestion, and we had battled the demon and the soldiers of Severance together.

That, more than anything else, convinced me of the bond. I'm not sure I can describe it to someone who's never endured such a trial, but let's just say there's a reason why the Vanguard call each other "brother". When you fight alongside someone, when you're on the battlefield straining for your very life, when you're desperately fighting to extend your wretched existence for another day, for another hour...well, there's a bond that forms with those beside you.

It's a bond stronger than blood or oath. It's a trust that exists because you've seen the same things, committed the same sins, shared the same curse. You have shed the same blood, and now you're trapped in the tempest together, and you'd best hold on tight. Because everyone else will hate you for what you've done, and they'll never understand why you didn't have a choice.

I reached out for Amethyst and touched her hand. I tested if the bond existed. My life was already forfeit, so what could I lose? Besides, it wasn't like we were going anywhere soon.

"Amethyst, may I ask you something?"

She answered with silence, but she didn't flinch at my touch.

"You don't have to talk if you don't want to," I said quietly. "I won't think ill of you. It's just—I can't help but wonder about the woman on the docks. The effect she had."

More silence.

Was I pushing too hard? I couldn't tell. Without the lanterns, I couldn't see her face. I could only make out a faint silhouette in the night. "Her death wasn't your fault. You know that?"

She held her breath a moment.

"I know it's hard to watch such things, but—"

"I've seen people die before, Mordecai," she said softly.

Good. She wasn't mad. "Then what is it?"

More silence. Then a tooth-rattling crash as Damascus hurled another thunderbolt toward the heavens.

I waited a long time afterward without an answer. I started to think maybe I should have asked about the beggar first. It didn't seem right to go back, though. "I'm sorry. Forget it."

"She reminded me of my mother."

A sad story followed. It took some gentle prodding on my part, but over the next thirty minutes, Amethyst shared the many reasons for her sorrow. It was confusing at first, disjointed. I could tell she had never shared these facts before. She dumped all the pieces in my lap like a shattered vase, and it took some time to fit everything back together. It didn't help that she was intentionally vague about specific names and places.

I eventually learned, though, that Amethyst was born into a small noble House, one of the oldest and most esteemed in Tel Tellesti. Her line stretched back to the glorious years of the great King Viticus and the First Alliance. She could name forefathers who served in every major battle in the past millennia, in fact, from the Ambush at Del Solae to the skirmishes at Alzeer. Her House was fast fading, though. A slew of accidents and untimely deaths had whittled the male heirs, and few sons had been born in recent generations. As such, her own father was actually the last lord in their proud lineage.

When Amethyst was born, her parents considered her a great blessing, the promise of more children to come. But then tragedy struck again, and her mother died during the first years of the drought when Amethyst was still very young. To make matters worse, her mother was pregnant at the time, and the second child was never born. Amethyst was left alone with her father.

The man did not adapt well. To lose a wife was bad enough, but somehow her father convinced himself that the unborn child was the son he wanted so badly, a male who could continue the line. Now only Amethyst remained, and despite her casual title of *heiress*, she could not legally inherit the House or pass on her name. She could not join the Vanguard and serve Estavion. Her best hope was to marry well—to find someone gracious enough to merge their names so her House would not be forgotten forever.

But that seemed doubtful. To many, Amethyst's House seemed cursed. Few families entertained the notion of betrothing their son to the heiress, and no one committed.

Her father grew desperate. He withdrew her from the academy, from her peers. He hired a private tutor, hoping that an accelerated education might make her more desirable as the noble wife of some future lord. He worked tirelessly to improve the family's reputation and cement those friendships that remained.

It had been difficult, she confessed, growing up with such a singular purpose. She had no childhood, no friends. She was only a symbol of her House who could never make mistakes or disappoint, and whenever she needed her father most, he was always absent. He left her alone in the citadel.

"Did you notice that?" she asked me. Had I noticed that her chambers in the old palace were *her* chambers? Had I noticed she lived alone despite being so young? Had I noticed that after the Summit, when she had spoken so well in that great hall, her father never applauded her? He had been there, she assured me. But he didn't offer his praise. The Lord of Near Thunderlun, our dreaded enemy, had offered kind words, but her own father had remained seated and focused on the proceedings. He hadn't even visited her after I took her to the infirmary, and on the morning of her departure to Ballabor, in the hours before she was to leave and flee for her life, he had not come to wish her well. Instead, her father had only sent a servant with a note that read, "Be good. Remember to do as you're told."

No wonder she had trouble trusting the people she loved.

Eventually, this did all come back to the events in Severance. Amethyst admitted that it hadn't been easy to hear about the Irrideous abandoning his daughter. That struck a bitter cord too familiar. And the imperial woman, the female soldier who had accidentally been shot and incidentally saved Amethyst's life? She had been slightly past middle age, Amethyst noticed. She had been just about the age her own mother would have been if she were still alive, and the woman had died in Amethyst's arms.

At all this, I had no answers. No words. I just offered my arm around her shoulder, and she didn't push away. We sat silently as Damascus split the speckled sky with spider webs of light.

Starlight

Amethyst and I leaned against the spire at Ur Thourou for an hour perhaps. I couldn't rightly tell. In the dark, I couldn't see the distant horizon, so it was difficult to guess how high the half moon climbed during the time we waited.

Sometime later, though, after Amethyst confessed her family history, Damascus grew weary. Or at least I assumed he had grown weary, because he suddenly stopped. We were still alone, and the friend he meant to summon hadn't come, but he stopped and stood motionless in the focal point.

"You look like you could use a rest," I called over to him. "I would suggest that you pull up a chair, but—"

Damascus called back, "There's no need, lieutenant. She's almost here."

Curious, I stood and glanced into the darkness past Damascus. I searched the endless granite pavement and the curved spires of Spiderclaw, but I saw nothing, not even the faintest shift in the shadows. Then I turned behind me, but saw nothing again. For another few seconds, I tuned my ear and listened for the slightest scuffle or footfall, but I heard nothing. "How do you know she's coming?"

Damascus didn't answer. He only stood with his head tilted back slightly as he gazed into the night sky. Silly old man.

Almost without thinking, I also tilted my head back, content for the moment to watch the stars and listen to the silence, but as I looked I noticed something strange. I saw a pinprick of light drifting across the sky, a dim streak falling to earth.

A shooting star.

No. It couldn't be. It moved too slowly. Its path was too erratic. And this wasn't a fast streak of light passing overhead and vanishing in an instant. It was a bright speck, a white flame descending toward us.

"What is that?" I asked Amethyst.

She didn't answer. She had already risen to her feet. With tears still in her eyes, Amethyst watched transfixed as the speck descended and stopped at the focal point. Damascus didn't seem surprised, though. He addressed the floating speck as casually as he might speak with a person. His friend, apparently, had arrived.

"It's a fairy," Amethyst gasped.

"Fairies don't exist," I answered automatically.

"Of course they do, or they *did*," she clarified, "just like elves and dragons and angels and demons and all those other creatures. People don't just make up things like that. They were all quite commonplace long ago when the Ascendants created the Inheritance, but they died out over the ages, and—"

Amethyst's focus collapsed as she crept toward Damascus and his friend. I followed, and the nearer we dared, the clearer we glimpsed the pixie. At first she seemed only a blur of white light against a black curtain, but as we drew closer, I could see transparent, moth-like wings, dazzling hair white as lightning, and golden arms that shown like the sun. And her voice? I heard a high-pitched coo, almost like a whisper, and when she spoke, Damascus laughed heartily. They were indeed old friends. The kindred spirit knew exactly what cords to strike. She knew just how to touch his heart.

Then, in a dazzling moment, the pixie turned. She noticed Amethyst, and time slowed to a halt.

It's crazy to suggest such a thing. I know—I'm sorry. But I can't describe it any other way. The fairy looked, noticed Amethyst and gasped. She blinked out sparkling tears, like frost on frozen caronaria, and suddenly—I don't know. It seemed I was outside my own body, watching myself. Watching her. I couldn't move. I couldn't think. But time passed. I'm sure of it. Whole minutes evaporated as the tiny fairy gazed at the heiress, rapt by her presence.

Starlight

Then the creature blinked. Her eyelids brushed away the tears. Time resumed. She spoke in a whisper that snuck past my ears and pierced my mind. She said to her friend, "Dayspring, is that *her*? The one you've told me about? The Immortal?"

Damascus turned and noticed Amethyst.

"Amethyst! I'm sorry. How terribly thoughtless of me." He stepped forward, grasped her hand, and pulled her closer. "This is Starlight, an old friend."

Amethyst could only answer with a trancelike stare.

"My name is Aurorealla, actually," the fairy said, her distant voice a nervous jumble, "but you may call me Starlight. That's what Damascus calls me."

"Fewer syllables," Damascus chuckled.

The heiress swallowed and managed to find words. "You—you know Damascus?"

"Yes, of course I do. Why else would I—" But then the fairy stopped. She turned to Damascus and read his thoughts as easily as reading a note. "You haven't told her about me."

"Of course not."

"Then you haven't mentioned the last Artifice yet." The fairy grew excited. "You haven't told her about the Seraphim, or even the Fulcrum."

"Will you still your thoughtless tongue? She's not prepared," Damascus sputtered. If Starlight had been a normal person, he might have clamped her mouth shut.

But the tiny Whisper floated beyond his reach. "May I ask her something then?"

"What? No!"

"Oh please? I'll be careful," the fairy promised.

"This is neither the time nor place for such foolishness."

"You brought her here. When will I have another chance?"

The old man clenched his jaw until his lips twitched. He stared down the fairy, hoping to override her stubborn will with only a stern

233

expression. Then he glanced at his student and gave her the same treatment. Both remained hopeful, though, so eventually he relented. "If you must, I will allow it, but keep it brief. And *simple*."

Delighted, the fairy drifted closer toward Amethyst.

The girl stepped forward as well. She had quite forgotten her sorrow by then, I suspect, with such a creature offering her such interest. "*You* want to ask *me* a question? About what?"

"About your heart, silly. What else?"

"My—my heart?"

"Yes. I was just wondering, what do you want?"

Amethyst glanced at me as if she hadn't clearly heard the question. She glanced also at Damascus before turning back to the fairy. "I'm—I'm sorry. I don't understand."

"What's to understand?" the sprite laughed. "It's a simple question, isn't it? It's *the* question—the most important question. *What do you want?*"

Amethyst gave it a moment's thought. "You mean, what do I want right now?"

"What else would I mean? *Right now* is all that ever exists."

Amethyst slowly dropped her gaze and licked her lips. For a long while she pondered the question while the fairy hovered nearby, entranced by her consternation.

"I suppose, if I think about it," the girl eventually said, "I want to find the Cornerstone. That's why we're here."

"Why?"

"To prevent war, of course."

"Are you certain? Do you even grasp what war means?" Then Starlight said quietly to Damascus (so quietly I almost didn't hear), "She can't fathom it yet, can she? She's a child."

"Excuse me," Amethyst interrupted. "I *do* understand."

"You understand war?"

"Yes."

Starlight

The fairy shifted closer again. "And you understand what the Cornerstone is?"

"Yes."

"Then why seek it? You know how treacherous it is, how dangerous and powerful. It has only brought grief to everyone who has ever touched it, yet you still want it. Why? Just to prevent a war? To stop some faceless strangers from dying?"

The heiress didn't answer. She just lowered her head again.

Starlight pushed further. "Why? There must be another reason, Amethyst. Something deeper. Why risk so much?"

That's when I realized the truth. All at once I understood.

This was all for her father.

No. It was even deeper than that. This was for her family. For her House. For Estavion too, I'm sure, and Talsadar and Gideon and the other Vanguard who had died protecting her at Ballabor. For all those who still suffered from the long drought. But in the deepest parts of her heart, she wanted to restore her House, cement their name in the annals of history. She had to redeem her mother. Prove her worth to her father.

She needed to earn his love.

Suddenly I knew why she had invested so much time and effort into her Ascendant research. I understood why she had overruled Uriah's orders and risked our lives for the slim chance of finding Irrideous. It wasn't because of some childish fixation on magic or some strange historical obsession. Amethyst needed the Cornerstone. She needed to believe it existed. That she could find it. That she could fix everything wrong with her life. Because what was the alternative?

Amethyst didn't say all this, of course. I'm not sure she even thought it. I suspect her emotions and motives were just a swirling windstorm. She only knew she wanted the stone so badly it hurt, even if she didn't know why.

But I knew. Damascus knew.

Even Starlight knew, I suspect, because the fairy dropped the matter and didn't ask the question again. Sensing Amethyst's pain, she hovered close and whispered, "It's all right, child. I know. I know better than you, and believe me, it's okay."

Slowly, Amethyst raised her trembling head.

"It's a good reason."

The girl wiped a tear from her eye.

Then the fairy turned. She drifted back toward the old man, her tone cordial and professional again. "So *Damascus*, why are you here? It's not time yet."

"I know," Damascus said, "but I'm afraid we've encountered a problem." He glanced at us as if he didn't want anyone to hear what followed, but since he had no choice he reluctantly admitted, "I need help finding someone."

"Someone?"

"Bethel."

His revelation threw the fairy into a fit. "Oh! Goodness, Damascus! How could you?"

"Starlight, please!"

"How could you lose that girl?" the fairy cried. "She's your favorite part of the protocol!"

"Will you desist?"

Starlight threw a tantrum while Amethyst and I watched, completely baffled. "This is absolutely absurd! How could you forget about her?"

"Why do you think I asked you to keep track, you intolerable moth?" Damascus seethed. "I knew I might forget."

"You—you did?"

"Yes!"

"Oh!" Starlight calmed. "Good, then. Good. Quite clever."

"Thank you," Damascus groaned. "So what of it?"

"Well, I don't know where she is," the fairy confessed.

Damascus's head sank.

Starlight

"But I can find her," Starlight added quickly. "Is she still in Severance?"

"I doubt it. We believe she was sold," Damascus said. Then he lowered his voice and added, "Sold as a harlot."

"The whore," Starlight mused. "The redheaded whore."

I held my breath. Did she actually just say that? I glanced at Amethyst; her eyes confirmed my suspicions. She had heard that sentence too, and thought it strange.

"If I remember correctly, she may be in Heda Fare," Starlight said, "but I should check and make certain."

"Very well," Damascus answered.

"How did you come this way? By boat?"

"Yes."

"The *Solution*?" she guessed.

"Indeed."

"Then return to Captain Abner. Head northwest for now. I'll learn where Bethel is, and I'll find you on the Mediate."

"Very good," Damascus sighed, happy at last. "How long, do you think?"

"A few hours." Then Starlight drifted into the sky. "If you need me sooner, you know how to call."

Fifteen

"There's no need to stop," the arbiter says.

"You don't want to ask about the fairy?"

"Are you going to insist she's real?"

"Yes."

Rehoboth smiles. "Then why waste our time?"

"In that case, may I ask something?" I venture.

"If you must."

"Does Amethyst's father know how she felt?"

Rehoboth glances furtively at Uriah before saying, "How could I know that?"

"It's just—it seems that a lot could be solved with a very short conversation."

"That's not the focus of this inquiry."

"But if I could just speak with him—"

"Lieutenant," Rehoboth interrupts. "Let me ask you something. Do you have a daughter of your own?"

I lower my eyes.

"Do you have any family whatsoever?"

I don't answer, not to her. She doesn't need to know.

Rehoboth mistakes my silence as a negative response, and she leans closer. "Listen to me, lieutenant. Listen carefully. In general, most people do not listen to counsel, even wise counsel from close friends. And people certainly don't value the advice of absolute strangers. Especially strangers who know *absolutely nothing* about which they speak. Understand?"

"Of course," I say, though I know better than she ever will.

Epitaph

After Starlight drifted back into the heavens from whence she came, Damascus sighed. "That should suffice. Come now. Let's be off. Abner must be growing anxious." Then he lit his lantern and happily wandered away.

"That's it?" I asked. "Aren't you going to explain that?"

"Explain what, lieutenant?"

"*That!* Her!"

"Nonsense. The more I explain about Starlight, the less you will understand. It's best you simply accept that she is my friend, and she will help us. That is all you must know." He walked on as he spoke, leaving me more confused than before.

Amethyst seemed content, though. Better than content. She practically floated after speaking with Starlight. She had forgotten about the pains of that day, about her distant father and the dead Samaran soldier who resembled her mother, and she followed Damascus without complaint. They nearly left me alone in the dark.

Before they vanished entirely, I reminded myself that I was just the soldier, not the scholar. I didn't really need to know. It was a painful reminder after all that had happened, but it worked. I hurried after them.

We left the astonishing Spiderclaw, the Ascendant sanctuary of Ur Thourou. We walked south past the talons and across the polished floor and the sandy plains until we reached the muddy banks of the Rapha`Dim. Then we turned east and followed the riverbank back to shore. We launched the tiny boat, I ferried us back to the *Sole Solution*, and once our feet touched the main deck, Damascus issued our new orders.

"To the rolling headlands, captain. Set course for Heda Fare."

"Heda Fare." Abner hummed the name. "At last, a welcome haven. Why couldn't we'of started there? And stayed there?"

Amethyst giggled. Damascus rolled his eyes. Then the two disappeared into the cabin.

It was night still, the middle of the watch. Regardless, Abner roused half his crew and set course northwest through the tropical waters. He excused my duties temporarily since I wasn't yet proficient enough with the kites to launch them in the dark, and he let me sleep after the strange detour to Ur Thourou, but at first light the next morning Abner pulled me from my hammock and stationed me at the *Solution*'s bow.

I began my task, taking bites from my breakfast whenever the chore allowed. After a few minutes tending the kites, though, my eye caught a strange glare off the churning waves. I heard a faint buzz like an arrow whizzing past my ear. Then a streak of light burst from the horizon and veered toward us. I would have excused it as a wisp of foam or sun glinting off some ocean spray, but the streak flew straight for the rear of our ship and abruptly stopped outside a stateroom window. The window opened, and the light vanished inside.

Starlight had returned.

No. It couldn't be her. Heda Fare was far to the northwest at the headlands of the Chersonese peninsula. The *Solution* would require about a month to reach that destination, and she was the swiftest ship in Estavion. There was no possible way the fairy could have traveled that distance and returned—not in the few hours since she had left Ur Thourou. Was there?

I wasn't certain, but I couldn't concentrate on my task, not with my heart fluttering at the thought of Starlight's speed, so I left the kites half finished. I crossed the listing deck and knocked on the cabin door.

It half-opened a moment later, and the old man's head poked out. "Yes? What is it now, lieutenant?"

Epitaph

I tried to peak past him, but I could only see the edge of the table and part of Amethyst's leg hanging off the adjacent chair. She was talking eagerly to someone, though, or was she reciting some stonescript?

Damascus grew impatient. "Speak up, boy. What is it? We're very busy. Amethyst is quite behind with her lessons."

"I'm sorry. I just thought I noticed Starlight returning."

"Oh, yes indeed. She's just returned. I'm sorry I didn't think to tell you. Still, she's brought encouraging news. She found Bethel in Heda Fare. The girl is with a harlot known as O'dessa Fetch. Can you believe that? Such good fortune."

I didn't respond. I had stopped listening after Damascus mentioned Starlight's return.

"Is that all, lieutenant?"

"Yes," I blurted out. "I suppose so."

"Good. Thank you!" Then the door closed in my face.

I didn't see much of Starlight after that. She remained hidden in the stateroom with Amethyst and Damascus for the next few weeks as the *Solution* sailed toward our new destination, and she seldom left the cabin even when the teacher or the student came out for the occasional recess or meal. No one else saw her either. In fact, I'm quite certain Abner and his crew never realized they had a stowaway. Starlight had this remarkable ability to render herself nearly transparent, so whenever she did leave the room, I'm sure everyone else dismissed her (like I had) as a sun glare or a wisp of foam.

I'm glad Starlight accompanied us, though, despite the way she avoided the crew. Her presence soothed Amethyst. Almost immediately, the girl's confidence returned, and her optimism proved contagious. The spirit of the whole ship soon lifted. We quickly forgot the disaster at Severance and sailed toward the beautiful port of Heda Fare with light hearts.

We shouldn't have been so happy. We were still living off meager rations. Irrideous was probably still plotting his strange revenge. For all we knew, another dreadnaught was waiting for us at Heda Fare. And we hadn't heard any word from home, so we didn't know if Estavion had already sent her armies to war against Near Thunderlun. It seemed incredibly unlikely that we would find the Cornerstone with Bethel Emm, and even if we did, I doubted Amethyst could use it against our troubles. Part of me hoped she would never try.

But those concerns no longer seemed pressing. They were possible problems for the uncertain future. In the clear present, the crew and I were content to man the sails, fly the white kites, scrub the decks, fish for supper, and enjoy the salty air as we left the tropics and skipped northward into cooler waters.

Days turned into weeks. We traveled hundreds of leagues. Our high spirits endured. We detected no ships shadowing us. We hardly noticed any other vessels, actually. I manned the kites until it became second nature to find the slipstream. Abner whistled at the helm. Amethyst directed extra winds into our canvas sails, and she welcomed the sunrise every morning, often with Starlight at her side. Damascus didn't berate me quite as often, and each day brought us closer to Heda Fare and the lost daughter of Irrideous.

After about a month, the *Solution* entered the Mager Straits between the Chersonese headlands and the northern Oorameres. We spent a few days sprinting through those shallow channels with the precipitous islands to our left and distant snowcapped mountains to our right. Then we rounded the last point and entered the bay outside Heda Fare.

At some point a few days later, the last day of our approach, I was standing near the bow tending the kites. The sun was rising, I think, and I was alone. The rest of the crew was preparing for our

Epitaph

imminent arrival, but as the Ascendant port came into view, I paused to consider the spectacle. I saw the glistening granite spires of Heda Fare beaconing us closer, and framed behind the distant city I glimpsed the Silvertip Mountains at the edge of the horizon, the twilight glinting off their snowcapped peaks like jewels in a diadem. I noticed the rolling, green shores encircling us like a womb, and suddenly a tear rolled down my cheek.

That had never happened before.

The arrival felt profound, though, much like the moment when Amethyst had explained the Testament to me. I realized again the footsteps we were tracing, and that we were sailing the same waters traversed by the ancient Chersonese all those eons ago when they answered Estelle's invitation and followed the migrants to the Eastern Estates. We had finally returned to the path laid out for us so long ago, the path we had almost lost in Severance—the path we would have never found again if not for that strange fairy.

Starlight had fixed everything, or at least improved our situation. She was indeed our light in dark times. Like the northern star, she had guided our course. She had affirmed Amethyst's purpose and touched her heart. She had done wonders for Damascus too. For all of us.

And then, at that very moment, with gratitude swelling, I noticed a streak in my peripheral vision. A wisp drifted across the *Solution*'s bow. Starlight was leaving us.

Without thinking, I stepped forward. I called out, desperately hoping she wouldn't leave yet. Not until I spoke with her. Not until I thanked her. "Starlight? Wait!"

The streak shrank to a pinpoint of light. Then it arced and approached the bow. Starlight stopped just past the railing and out of reach, but close enough that I could make out her shape against the waves crashing ahead of us. She wasn't pleased to see me, though. When she saw who had called, a spiteful contortion curled her body. "What do you want?"

Maybe she didn't recognize me. "I'm sorry. I didn't mean to startle you. I'm Lieutenant Mordecai, remember? We met that night at the sanctuary. I'm Amethyst's escort."

"I know what you are!"

All right. I could have done without the hostility, though. "I just wanted to thank you for everything you've done."

"Someone has to clean up your mess."

Damascus must have mentioned my actions in Severance. "Yes, well, you've been most helpful. I don't know what we would have ever done without you."

"That's funny," she teased. "I know precisely what we'd do without you."

She was starting to get to me. I didn't know exactly what she was implying, but I had a feeling I wouldn't like it.

And she kept going. "I must confess, I don't quite see your worth, *lieutenant*. I know Damascus says you're necessary. He insists the plan is impossible without you, but I don't see it. I don't see how you can justify any of it."

My heart started racing. I nervously clenched my fist.

Still she continued. "You don't even know yourself anymore, do you? You think you're so clever. Somehow you've convinced yourself that *you're* the savior the world needs, but even you can't justify it anymore, can you? You've forgotten the reasons for the wars and the droughts, as if there were any in the first place. All you know is wrath and vengeance."

I didn't answer. I couldn't.

"Why can't you leave anyone alone? Why must you always poison our happiness? Won't you ever be satisfied? Is it really that impossible to forgive?"

I remained silent.

"Answer me!" She was suddenly screaming words that bore into my mind. "Don't you cower there! You're the One who called! You

Epitaph

started this anew and broke the truce. You dared question me, as if I didn't know, so answer me! She's not here. Why hold back?"

"I'm doing what's necessary," I blurted out. "I'm finishing what I started. I'm fulfilling the oath, whatever it takes."

"*Whatever it takes.*" She grew sad. "So began every injustice the world has ever endured."

Starlight seemed to fade away. Perhaps she lost her will to remain. She obviously wanted to be somewhere else, somewhere far away from me, but she didn't leave. Not yet. She had one last thing to say.

"Damascus probably wouldn't approve of me saying this," the Whisper said. "He believes you're irredeemable. He thinks that nothing we say or do will ever make a difference, not for you—but all the same, heed my words." She drifted closer, almost within reach, her voice an iron vice that choked the air from my lungs. "*Stay away from Amethyst,* lieutenant. Give this up. Go back to your hovel. Go back to the darkness and rot. Forget that the world exists, and let it forget you."

Her tone had changed, I noticed. Her purpose was different. She was trying to scare me off, to push me away, and I don't like being pushed. "What if I don't?"

Starlight smiled as if that was exactly what she wanted to hear. "Then you've already lost. You are nothing but a walking corpse, a loose thread that will be severed the moment your usefulness expires. If you continue this path, you will be nothing but a frail footnote in the margins of history, never to leave your lasting mark, and no one will mourn your passing."

That was the end of it. With that chilling epitaph, she left. She faded away, and her streak drifted up and vanished against the gleam of the distant sunrise. Or was it sunset? I can't recall.

I just knew the light was fading.

Sixteen

"That was the moment."

Rehoboth lowers her quill. "Pardon?"

"You asked me before," I remind her. "When did I first start suspecting Damascus? That was the moment."

"When you spoke with Starlight that evening?"

"Yes."

"Interesting." Rehoboth marks something in her notes. "Why?"

Isn't it obvious? "The things she said. The comments she made about Damascus. About me. None of it made sense, not unless something else was about to happen."

"Another attack?"

"No. Something worse."

ANGEL

I didn't see Starlight again after that conversation, not that I cared to. In those few moments, she had completely undermined my serenity. After a blissful month at sea, suddenly I was vexed again. Fear seized my heart. All at once I recalled the drought, the Summit, the firebomb, the looming war, the dreadnaught, Irrideous, the Cornerstone and my actions in Severance. To that disturbing list, I now added something else. Damascus thought me irredeemable, and Starlight said he had a plan.

A plan. A plan for what?

She had mentioned it before, I remembered. When she had appeared at Spiderclaw and asked Amethyst that strange question about her heart, Starlight had mentioned a protocol to Damascus. But what could it be? A plan for the stone? A plan to save Amethyst and Estavion? A plan to somehow escape the coming doom?

I couldn't begin to guess the answers, and to make matters worse, I had no time to consider the mystery. Mere minutes after Starlight disappeared into the sunset, in fact, the *Solution* entered the Chersonese haven of Heda Fare. Abner ordered the kites withdrawn and the sails retracted. We rowed into the expansive harbor among hundreds of ships of all shapes and sizes, and we zigzagged through the four granite breakwaters until the captain found an empty slip. He eased the ship closer so a few men could leap to the pier, and then he called to me.

"I could use you on the dock, pup. Unless you're busy."

I performed my duties. I hopped over the railing and down the wooden boards, and I helped with the *Solution*'s moorings. I tried my best to ignore my palpitating heart too, but for once the chores were not an adequate distraction. As I pulled on the ropes, I could only see the loose thread Starlight hoped to sever, and as I tied off the lines, my own stomach twisted into knots.

Vile fairy. Damascus had rightly chided her loose tongue.

The next hour passed in a blur. Two friendly ambassadors arrived to welcome us. Abner greeted the officials and graciously answered their questions, and since Chersonia was yet allied with Estavion, the process was smooth and effortless—much better than our arrival in Severance. There were no soldiers to inspect our ship, no subtle threats. The two ambassadors said nothing about my Vanguard uniform. They only charged Abner a modest fee for renting the pier before they left.

Damascus departed the ship soon after. He left alone, like before, but this time he did not explain why or where. I didn't bother to ask. I suspected he was leaving to find the harlot named O'dessa Fetch, and if I was wrong, I didn't care. I only knew I didn't want to talk with him. I didn't want to speak with anyone. I just wanted to be left alone with my thoughts.

Ten minutes later, though, a crewman found me brooding on the quarterdeck. "Amethyst wishes to see you, lieutenant."

I reported to the stateroom and stood just inside the doorway. I stared blankly ahead, trying to conceal the tempest within. Then I found my voice. "You called, miss?"

"Yes, I was—" But she stopped mid-sentence. "Lieutenant? What is it?"

Was I that terrible at hiding the truth? "It's nothing."

"Are you certain?"

Angel

No, I wasn't. I was rattled and taut. I wanted nothing more than to speak honestly, and I knew Amethyst would listen. Just as I had borne her burdens at Spiderclaw, I knew she would understand if I spoke my mind. But I couldn't confess yet, not there in the cabin where Abner might overhear through the thin walls. Not then, when Damascus might return at any moment. I had to sort my thoughts first. Wait for the right time.

So I took a deep breath and suppressed the nerves. "I'm fine. What do you need?"

She didn't believe my excuse, but she respected my privacy and dropped the matter. "It's—it's silly. I'm sorry I called. I only wanted to show you. To ask how I look."

An odd question. Was she offended that I hadn't yet looked at her? That I could only stare out the window as I tried my best not to curse her teacher and the cruel pixie that had offered her such encouragement? It was a simple enough request, though, so I turned and gave the heiress my attention.

Then my heart skipped another beat.

Amethyst had blossomed. How had I ignored this? She hardly seemed the same girl. She had changed into a shimmering velvet gown with matching purple slippers, but other things were different as well. Her straight brown hair had turned into golden tassels that tumbled over her slender shoulders, just like I remembered from the Summit. Her soft skin practically shone with warmth, and her lips seemed darker. Her sapphire eyes gleamed with confidence, and every other feature seemed pronounced. Enhanced. Even her chest had—well, the girl had suddenly grown into a woman, and I could do nothing but stare.

"Lieutenant? What do you think?"

I took special note of her tone. She wasn't inviting the expected response, like a noblewoman soliciting a servant's unneeded opinion. She was asking sincerely, like a child seeking her father's blessing. I couldn't think of an appropriate compliment, though. I could only stammer, "I, uh—"

That was perhaps the best answer I could have ever offered. At my words, she blushed and smiled. "Thank you."

"What did you—how did you—"

"It's just a little something Damascus taught me."

I let out a strained laugh. "More magic?"

"Not exactly. The other me—the muted, plain girl—that's the illusion, a disguise. But I thought I'd forgo it just for today. We don't have many enemies in Heda Fare, and—well, I wanted to look like me, the real me. I didn't want Bethel Emm to meet the shadow. She is quite important, after all."

"Yes, of course," I automatically answered, though I tensed at her words. Why was Bethel so important? Was she part of the plan? Did Amethyst know what Damascus was plotting? Did Captain Abner? Was everyone on that ship part of a conspiracy except me?

Amethyst instantly detected my concerns. "Lieutenant, are you sure nothing's wrong?"

I couldn't keep dodging her questions. I needed to distract her until I was ready. "I'm fine. It's just—I was expecting to see Starlight again."

"She left recently, just this evening. Damascus said she had important matters to attend to. Did she not say farewell? She suggested she might."

"It must have slipped her mind," I shrugged. "That's all right. I'll just speak with her when she returns."

This time it was Amethyst who tensed slightly.

"She's not returning, is she?"

"I don't think so. I distinctly got the impression that she would be leaving us after her business was concluded here. And then—" The girl shrugged and said nothing else, but I understood what she meant. Starlight had no immediate plans to return. In fact, we might never see her again.

Angel

"It's just as well." I stepped toward the cabin door. "Will that be all?"

"For the moment," came her reply, "but I need you to change as well. Find your best clothes. It wouldn't hurt to wash and shave, and be quick. We must be ready to leave when Damascus returns from his errand."

"Why the haste? We only just arrived." I glanced curiously out the door at the fading sky. "It's getting late. Shouldn't we wait until morning?"

"Fetch is a harlot, remember? I doubt she keeps normal hours. And as for the haste—" Her eyes turned toward the table, toward the parchment rubbings from the Testament. Her thoughts, I suspect, drifted back to those long days we lingered at Ballabor, and the price paid for our leisure. "Must I really remind you why it may be foolish to delay too long in one place?"

No, she didn't.

I left Amethyst in the stateroom and crossed the main deck, then descended through the hatch and into the cargo hold. I found my hammock and my satchel. I reached inside for the chainmail. The vermilion mantle. The leather bracers. I retrieved each part of my uniform, but when I finished the bag wasn't empty. Something else weighed it down. So I reached inside one last time and pulled out the final item—the dreadnaught vambrace.

I had forgotten about it. But I remembered then, and more importantly I remembered why I had brought it along in the first place. I had known I might need a reminder of what chased us, but more than that I needed to remember the blood that had already been paid, and how that costly price hadn't even been enough to secure our peace.

And there I was, worrying about my own skin.

A strange peace filled me. I had been so concerned about Starlight, about Damascus and his protocol. But why? What if they did mean to discard me the moment my usefulness expired? Did I deserve any better? My fate no longer mattered to me. I concerned myself only with my own duties and my promise to Uriah. Amethyst must remain safe. Let them kill me when this was over. I would not oppose them. Not if Amethyst got her chance with the stone first.

Damascus returned from his scouting trip a few hours later, and we left soon after. It was chilly that far north in autumn, and it was past midnight when we disembarked the *Solution,* but we were warm enough. Amethyst wore her beautiful velvet gown, her lace gloves and silver mirrored bracelet, and a sheer scarf. I wore my uniform. Damascus dressed in some pressed linen robes that somehow made him appear even older, and he carried the only lantern among us, but that was also enough. By that feeble light, we entered Heda Fare to find O'dessa Fetch and Bethel Emm, the daughter of Irrideous.

My nerves had settled by then, and instead of worrying about Damascus or Irrideous, I focused on our surroundings, not that there was much to see. The vast Ascendant city seemed nearly deserted by that late hour. As we slipped through the harbor, we passed Chersonese patrols wandering the wide granite walkways, and I noticed swordsmen and archers stationed atop the towering stone lighthouses that overlooked the docks, but otherwise we saw little life. The harbor was empty except for the soldiers and the moored ships. We heard no sounds except the lullaby of waves lapping against the breakwaters and our own feet scuffing against polished stone. By habit, I walked with my hand resting on the hilt that hung from my belt, and I scanned the shadows for any hint of movement, but I noticed nothing. No assassins or dreadnaughts. The Chersonese soldiers ignored us as well.

I only had Damascus to worry about, then.

Angel

If the old man intended to try anything, though, he masked his intentions well. He never acted suspiciously. On the contrary, as we left the harbor and entered the wide main streets of Heda Fare, Damascus held his lantern high and walked slowly, as if on holiday. He maintained the lead, trusting me to watch his back and keep up, and he pointed out various architectural features to his student. He spoke almost constantly, with a slight twinge of excitement, in fact, and I soon realized the teacher was actually enjoying himself.

Didn't he remember where we were, what we were doing?

No. To Damascus, this wasn't a desperate mission with little chance of success. He was on an expedition, nothing more, and the ageless city had lulled him into a false sense of security. He didn't notice the window shades pulled shut as we passed. He did not double-check each side street as we wandered down the granite avenue. He did not stop to think that if anyone ambushed us in the middle of the night, in the middle of that wide street, there would be no easy escape. He only knew he was visiting an Ascendant construct with his beloved pupil, and he couldn't have been happier.

"Heda Fare is situated perfectly," Damascus lectured. "Such precise harmony, as if the Ascendants built the landscape around the city instead of the other way round. There's the grand Tollah Bay, of course, which forms a comfortable western border. Then there's the cold waters of the Zuben'Ro, which flow swiftly down from the Silvertips, through the surrounding fields, and into the canals of the city. There are supplementary channels too. Did I ever teach you that, my dear? They can manage the influx even during the heavy floods. And there are secondary aqueducts that siphon water from the glaciers during the droughts. They thought of everything! Quite ingenious."

His fawning made me sick. "They didn't think of *everything*. They forgot an outer wall."

Damascus paused a moment and lifted his lantern so he could see my face. Had he forgotten again that I was there? His irritation returned. "They did not *forget*, lieutenant. Come now! Remember your history. The Ascendants enjoyed a serene existence. They did not build fortifications because they did not need fortifications. There are the unbreakable walls around Tel Tellesti, of course, and other cities besides, but *we* built those during the Thousand Year War and the Northern Invasion that followed."

"Then what about Ballabor?" I interjected. "Why carve an impregnable fortress if there was no need for it?"

Damascus huffed and continued walking. Apparently he had neither the time nor energy to explain that particular anomaly to an uneducated imbecile like myself.

"The strength of Heda Fare and of all Chersonia, in fact, lies solely in its geography," he continued for Amethyst's benefit. "The sea encircles the peninsula with its wealth. The Silvertips scrape moisture from the heavens. The wide streams frolic down from the mountains to irrigate the surrounding meadows.

"And you must forgive an old professor for such heresy," he added quietly, "but I dare say Estelle chose poorly when she arrived with the migrants. She was bewitched, I'm sure, by high Tel Tellesti clinging atop the granite cliffs and framed with falling water, and she claimed the illustrious city and the great Corde for her people. Had she explored the whole continent first, though, she would have seen what the clans later discovered. She would have found lush hills, rolling and green. She would have enjoyed the generous sea as her border instead of mountains and desert. And her descendants, I suspect, might have endured the current drought a little better."

"Then why did the Celadon Council attended the Summit?" Amethyst politely interjected. "Are the Chersonese not suffering as greatly as the other estates?"

"The years have been lean, I'm sure," Damascus answered, "but the Silvertip glaciers are still thick, and the sea remains bountiful. No. The clans attended the Summit because Estavion asked, not because they fear the drought. They came to offer aid, I suspect, and to honor our friendship. One should always respect the old alliances, remember, and the alliance between the clans and the migrants is as old as they come."

A dangerously simplified answer, I thought. Damascus knew as well as I that if Near Thunderlun and Samara broke the peace and destroyed Estavion, they would attack the clans next. The Council attended to Summit to protect their own interests, not to honor an obsolete treaty.

But Damascus didn't mention this. Instead, he returned to his lecture. As we turned a corner and started down one of the main avenues toward the city's central sector, the teacher began pointing out the similarities between Heda Fare and Tel Tellesti.

"The granite is a shade lighter here, you'll notice, but both cities—and every other Ascendant city, for that matter—boast the same efficient design. Tel Tellesti is almost twice as large, and it was raised in a semicircle against the cliff edge instead of a three-quarters disk hugging a harbor, but both rely on curved streets laid out in rings that circle a central feature from which radial avenues extend outward.

"Looking down from the Silvertips," he explained excitedly, "the whole city resembles a tiled mosaic of concentric circles, or perhaps a wheel with many spokes. An ingenious layout, I must say, so much superior than that lazy grid design the Samarans often employ. In an Ascendant city, the main avenues always lead either *toward* the center or *away* from center, and the curved streets circle *around* the center. So if you can't see the central construct, like the citadel in Tel Tellesti, then you know you're on a circular street, and you can often tell just from the bend how far out you are. As I said, most ingenious."

I groaned audibly, bored with the lesson. I didn't understand why Amethyst listened so intently either. She must have heard this all before, but she seemed content to listen again. If I wanted Damascus to pause, then, I had to speak, and if I wanted him to stop for good, I needed an appropriate complaint. I quickly found the necessary words. "Are you sure it's wise to speak so loudly?"

"Come now," he retorted. "Still worried about dreadnaughts, are we, lieutenant? No need for that. We're in the blessed haven. The first Chersonese claim. The one city in the whole Inheritance that has endured every war unscathed! This place has a sacred history, and I doubt even Irrideous would dare defile it."

"He defiled the citadel," I half whispered to Amethyst.

Damascus narrowed his eyes. "What was that?"

"I said, 'How much farther?'"

"Not far." Damascus pointed down a curved side street with his lantern as we reached another intersection. "Just beyond this next sector. I met a local smith, you see, while I was out earlier this evening. He provided sound directions, and he was such an interesting fellow. He had such a peculiar technique for stoking, my dear. Perhaps after this, we'll have time for another visit and I can show you his method."

He rattled on as we continued down the side street, his voice echoing off the ancient granite walls, and I thought that perhaps an early death would not be so terrible. At least I would escape his tedious company.

Sometime later, though not nearly soon enough, Damascus stopped his incessant rambling and paused in another intersection. He raised his lantern higher, checked the avenue numbers carved into the nearest corner, and muttered to himself, "The southwestern avenue. The thirty-eighth street." Then he turned to Amethyst and smiled sadly. "Nearly there. This way."

His mood changed. The lectures abruptly ended and the remorse returned. The tutor faded away, replaced by the foolish scholar who had once discovered a terrible secret. And now he meant to knock on a door. He meant to meet the daughter of a friend he had betrayed.

Such a strange plan.

We continued a little farther. We had barely entered the city, I knew. Though we had walked for hours, it would have taken us another half day to reach Heda Fare's center where the beacon stood. But Damascus did not take us deeper. He led us instead around one last curved street. His pace slowed as we continued past stone buildings, garden plazas, trickling fountains, and wide avenues illuminated with flickering lamps. We saw few people in that sector except for the occasional patrol, and in long overdue silence, we eventually reached our destination.

There, Damascus stopped before a typical door that seemed insignificant. In fact, it looked nearly identical to every other door we had passed that long night except for one feature. The old wrought iron latch had been painted white.

"Is this it?" Amethyst asked.

"If the smith spoke true," a weary voice replied.

"What are you waiting for?" I said.

The tired man reached for the white handle, then stopped. His fingers curled nervously.

"Damascus?" Amethyst inquired.

"I'm all right, my dear. I only fear—" He inhaled deeply and forced a smile to his wrinkled lips. "Well, there's much I fear."

"Would you rather we wait outside?" she asked.

"No," he said hastily. "No, I may require your strength."

Good. If this was going to be difficult for Damascus, I wanted to watch.

We entered. As Damascus took another breath and pulled, the door slid open silently on greased hinges. We stepped over the slate threshold into a dark room, and the gate closed behind us with a dull thud.

I briefly wondered if we had found the right place. There was no sign or other indicator except a white latch. Could such a thing be trusted so implicitly? What if we were invading some private residence? What if some poor homeowner rose screaming from his sleep and chased us from his abode?

No such incident occurred, though, and as our eyes adjusted to the gloom, I decided we were indeed where we should be. We stood in a foyer, a small sitting room. It was an eerie chamber, full of shadows that swallowed the light from our lantern, but a heavy perfume teased my nose and plush rugs welcomed my sore feet. Suggestive tapestries accented the walls, designed to stir carnal desires. Red silk curtained the windows with layers of privacy, and intricately carved tables and upholstered chairs beckoned us to stay forever.

A lavish room, I thought. A room intended for pleasure. A room funded by pleasure.

Damascus swallowed uncomfortably. He was unsure how to behave in such a place, but he stepped forward regardless. That's when I noticed her, the only other person in the foyer. She was an elegant woman who must have been exquisite in her youth, but she was faded and cracked now, like an oil painting left too long in the sun. She still adorned herself with sparkling jewels and flowing silk, though, and she sat knitting on a cushioned chair, her only light a solitary scented candle on a nearby sconce. On a low adjacent table she had a plate piled high with tropical fruits and pastries that would have embarrassed a royal baker.

Was the drought truly that insignificant in Heda Fare, or was she just wealthy beyond compare?

As Damascus drew near, the woman glanced up expectantly, but then her smile vanished. She was expecting someone, I think, but not us, and she bristled when she noticed three strangers in her establishment. "Who are you? What do you want? What do you mean, entering my home so late?"

Damascus abruptly stopped. "I'm sorry. O'dessa Fetch?"

Angel

The name sparked some recognition, a response practically undetectable. I noticed how her eyes widened slightly and her teeth clenched before she caught herself, though, so I knew she was lying when she said, "Never heard of her."

"Oh," Damascus replied, believing her answer. "Are you certain? This is most assuredly the right place. You see, O'dessa used to, um, *work* here."

"Maybe she did," the woman said before resuming her knitting, "but no longer."

"I see." Damascus sighed with relief. "Then I'm most sorry for our intrusion. But would you, perhaps, happen to know where we might find her?"

"She's not here. That's all I can say."

"But where else would she be?"

"I don't know. I don't concern myself with such things."

Damascus glanced back at Amethyst, a little frustrated and seeking help, so the heiress stepped forward and spoke instead. "Are you certain you've never heard of her? We believe she's rather well known."

"Not to me," the woman answered without looking up.

Amethyst shrugged. That was all she had.

"We're terribly sorry to have disturbed you then," Damascus apologized, "but could you at least point us toward someone else who might know where to find this woman Fetch? She's in a business most illegitimate."

"Oh, I wouldn't know much about that," the woman smiled.

"Ah." Damascus nodded. "Then I apologize again. We will leave you in peace. Good evening, ma'am."

"Good evening, sir."

Then he turned toward the door.

I couldn't believe it. Damascus actually turned to leave. This man, this same scholar who had decoded ancient languages and unraveled the mysteries of the Ascendants, had been duped by an old whore with a pathetic range of skill. Despite his measureless knowledge and unparalleled foresight, he had been bested by a lowly harlot feigning ignorance, and he seemed content to leave without forcing the issue. Was he that terrified to face his past? Was this part of his grand plan?

I didn't bother to ask. I just took the initiative. We had come too far and risked too much to be turned aside by a casual lie. If Bethel was there, if there was even the slightest possibility the Cornerstone lay hidden in that city, then we couldn't leave yet. I wouldn't leave without giving Amethyst her chance. So I stepped forward. As Damascus and Amethyst turned to leave, I brushed aside my vermilion cloak and reached for my broadsword. Without warning, I unsheathed that blade and thrust it toward the woman, stopping a mere breadth from her throat.

My companions cried out in alarm. Even worse, a burly man suddenly emerged from the shadows, a jagged dagger in hand. With flawless composure, though, the elegant O'dessa Fetch raised a commanding hand, keeping her bodyguard at bay, and she regarded my old sword with detachment before glancing up into my unwavering eyes.

"Vanguard."

I didn't answer. I only held the blade close to her neck and hoped it would loosen her tongue.

Damascus cleared his throat nervously.

Fetch ignored him, though, and talked only to me. "You're far from home, soldier. You have no authority here."

I leaned closer. "You think I mean to arrest you?"

"The thought occurred to me," she smiled.

I glanced at her bodyguard, who held his knife ready and eager. I then glanced at Amethyst, though, and gladly noticed the gloves still over her fingers. Damascus also had a hand inside his robe, ready to produce something fantastic if a brawl ensued. With such powerful allies supporting me, I stepped back and lowered my sword, hoping

Angel

the shrewd woman would respond to reason now that we knew each other's true identities.

"We just came for a girl," I said.

"Her name's Bethel Emm," Damascus piped in. "She's the daughter of Irrideous."

Fetch glanced behind me, where the teacher and student waited nervously. Then she shrugged. "Maybe she's here, maybe she isn't. But my girl doesn't work with groups."

"No! We don't mean—" I shuddered at the insinuation. "We just want to talk."

"Just talk?" She laughed at the notion.

"We can still pay, if we must, but we're only here to talk." To convince her, I sheathed my sword.

"That won't do," Fetch replied. "It's bad business to accept payment for services not rendered. It's even worse to service those I do not know. And I definitely do not know you. I'm not comfortable working with those with whom I do not share an acquaintance."

"But my dear Fetch, we *do* have a mutual acquaintance, don't we?" I reached for Amethyst's purse, which was still stuffed from our visit to Severance. I emptied the bag onto the table beside Fetch's chair, and as the coins rained down, I watched the silver reflect in her eyes.

"Yes," she said at last. "I believe we do."

"Good. Now go fetch the girl."

O'dessa Fetch didn't exactly live up to her moniker, but she did bring us to Bethel. Leaving her bodyguard behind, she escorted us through a dim carpeted hallway, deeper into the building, to another lavish parlor with a few additional chairs and two doors that led into rooms beyond. The left door she opened straightaway without knocking, though she stopped halfway through the doorway so we couldn't follow her inside. She spoke to someone within.

"You have more clients."

"You said I was finished for the night," a frail voice replied.

Fetch disappeared into the room. "Stand up! Put something on."

"No. Please!"

We heard an angry hand slap against soft skin. "Quiet! I'm not keeping them waiting. They've already paid for you."

"They?" The voice cracked. "What do you mean?"

"It's all right," Damascus called in anxiously. "We can wait. And we can visit within. A little privacy might be nice."

There was silence for a few moments. Then Fetch reappeared in the doorway, exasperated by her girl's behavior. All the same, she indicated for us to enter.

Damascus slowly stepped into the chamber first, followed by Amethyst and me. Once inside we found a typical room for such a place. There was a small bed covered with feather pillows and soft furs, a single window blocked by heavy shades, one rickety chair, a few candles for soft lighting, and a woman—no, a girl, no more than twenty.

But she was not typical.

Indeed, as soon as I noticed her sitting on the bed with a thin robe draped over her shoulders, I forgot about the dismal room. I forgot where I was and whom I was with. I forgot my identity and duties and fears. Faced with such an angel, I forgot to breathe. And yes, I know I've already said that Amethyst was lovely. That's still true. Starlight, too, with her mysterious radiance, had held me spellbound when she pierced the darkness of Ur Thourou.

But Bethel Emm, the daughter of Irrideous, far exceeded Amethyst, Starlight and every other woman who has ever graced this dismal existence. She was perfection, with flawless skin and lush copper locks framing a forlorn face. She had legs long and emerald eyes like a deep well of infinite mystery and sorrow. That sadness only accented her allure, though, like she was screaming for someone—anyone—to reach out, ransom her and be her savior.

To that end, Damascus forced himself forward.

In her presence, I was forgotten. Suddenly, Bethel was the only person—the only thing in the world that mattered. He no longer considered Irrideous or the Cornerstone or even Amethyst. He only saw the miserable girl, his last chance to redeem the sins committed against her father, and he stepped forward, his open hand outstretched as if approaching a wounded bird that might fly at the slightest provocation.

His caution was wisely founded. As he neared, the young harlot shrank back, dreading whatever the ancient man might require. "Who are you? What do you want?"

"Why, I'm Damascus, child."

"Do I know you?"

"No—no, you don't," Damascus choked on the words, "but I know you."

"You do? How?"

How indeed. How could he ever explain such a thing? I had supposed he would ease into the story slowly, but Bethel asked him right out. Now what would he say?

Damascus didn't speak at first. He instead reached into his robes like he had done when battling the dreadnaught. Instead of a miracle, though, he produced something common. He grasped an old book, the same leather-bound manuscript I had noticed so many weeks ago on the table in the *Solution*'s stateroom. He perched on the edge of Bethel's bed.

The book captured Bethel's attention, as the old man had hoped. She had probably never seen such a rare and valuable device before in her life. The book itself was not even the true surprise, though. As Bethel watched, Damascus laid the manuscript on her bed, unfastened the buckle, and spread the book slowly so as not to tear the brittle sheets. The parchment cracked as he flipped the pages, and he only stopped near the back when he found what he meant to show her. Carefully, he tore out a single sheet, and he offered it to Bethel.

Curiosity replaced her fear. The girl took the page reverently, holding out both hands to support it underneath like a thin sheet of ice that might melt or crack in her fingers. Then she looked at the page itself, at the image drawn there, and she saw a simple charcoal sketch of three people—a woman seated in a tall chair, an infant cradled in her arms, and a man standing behind, his hand resting tenderly on the mother's shoulder.

"I drew this a very long time ago." Damascus slid a little closer. "This is an old friend of mine, a man named Irrideous. That's him behind his beloved wife…and his daughter, a girl named Bethel."

The harlot didn't speak. Confronted by such lost reality, of a life she never tasted, she could only stare blankly at the sketch. For a long time, Bethel sat motionless and rapt by that colorless image, the only glimpse of her family she had ever seen, and I wondered if she could even comprehend what she was holding in her hands.

Until she began to cry.

I couldn't bear to watch. I didn't need another reminder of my wife. Of my sister. So I left. I stepped out of the small room, and this time Amethyst accompanied me. We closed the door and left Damascus alone with Bethel.

Seventeen

"What did you say?"

I look up from my evening meal, a thin bowl of stew that I can barely swallow. "Excuse me?"

"You were alone with Amethyst again," Rehoboth points out. "Didn't you discuss your conversation with Starlight? Did you ask Amethyst about the plan?"

The spoon slips from my fingers and clangs against the bowl. I close my eyes and stroke the stubble darkening my chin.

"You forgot, didn't you?"

RANSOM

I forgot. That's an understatement, but yes, I forgot Starlight's epitaph and the protocol she had mentioned. I forgot that Damascus considered me irredeemable. But Bethel had that effect. In her enchanting presence, Damascus forgot about Amethyst. The heiress forgot about that beautiful city, her quest for the Cornerstone, and the madman hunting her. In that young harlot's arms, I suspect countless other men had forgotten their debts, their children, their wives and their every care.

How else could Fetch afford such decadence?

For once the intentions were different in that room, though. Damascus had not come to forget. He came to remember Irrideous and the tragic history of which Bethal was unaware, so he resisted her spell and forced himself to speak.

I'm not certain how he did it. As I said, Amethyst and I had left him alone with Bethel, and we waited awkwardly in the parlor, just the two of us. Fetch had vanished to check on another client, so we sank into the provided chairs, and we didn't talk.

It would have been a good opportunity to ask Amethyst about my concerns, I admit, but they were the farthest thoughts from my mind. Amethyst also remained silent. Neither of us said a single word for the next ten minutes, in fact, because we soon realized that if we didn't speak, we could hear Damascus and Bethel's conversation through the door.

"You knew my father?" her voice said, barely audible.

"I did," came the answer. "I still do. Quite well."

"He's—he's alive?"

"Yes, my dear. I'm sorry to say, he's still alive."

She grew slightly excited. "He sent you?"

Damascus made no reply. I wish I knew what he did instead.

"What? What's wrong? He's not afraid, is he?"

"No."

"Is he—is he exiled? Why can't he come? Does my mother still live too? Tell me!"

"Bethel, please stop. Sit down, child. Just listen. Please stop and hear me."

There was a long pause—a painful, dreadful moment during which Amethyst glanced fretfully in my direction. Then Bethel's accusation broke the silence. "You said you were sorry. Sorry that he's still alive."

"Yes."

"Why would you say such a thing? And why can't he come? Doesn't he know how long I've waited? Does he know what's happened to me? Why would he leave me here if he could come rescue me? Am I that detestable?"

"He *can* come, child. That's just it. That's why I'm sorry," Damascus insisted. "He could if he wanted, if he knew what was best for him—for you. But your father—" The old man paused to muster his nerves again. "Your father is lost, my dear. He could come. He could step through that door any minute, any second, but he won't. He doesn't want to find you. He—he doesn't want to come. I know that makes little sense. I know you can't fathom such a thing, but there's no other way to say it."

There was another pause before Bethel's weak voice reached us in the parlor. "It's because of the stone, isn't it? That—that shard."

Amethyst and I shared another wide-eyed glance.

"So you've noticed it?" Damascus said. "Yes, this is because of that shard, *the Cornerstone*. And that is where I share the blame. I'm the poor fool who discovered that power, my dear, and I offered it to your father. It is because of me that he fell, and he has continued falling to this day.

Ransom

"But that was never the intent," Damascus insisted. "You must believe that! I never wished for this. I never wanted any of this. And I tried to save him. Even though I gave him the shard, even though I let him fall, I hoped he would learn from his own faults, as all men must. I thought he would reach bottom and realize the emptiness of all that narrow ambition. I meant to return to him then, to offer him forgiveness when he needed it most.

"But Irrideous—" Damascus stalled, his voice still labored. "Irrideous never bottomed out. That's the problem. That's what I never could have anticipated. He kept pushing deeper, further, seeking that which was never meant to be found. He fled past my reach, and now he's truly lost far beyond hope. Beyond reason. And yes, I fear it would be better if he were dead."

There was a third pause, longer and more agonizing than the previous two. When I glanced sideways at Amethyst, she did not meet my gaze, and I noticed tears in her eyes. Was she thinking of her own father then? Was Bethel weeping on the other side of that door?

"So that's it," the harlot finally uttered. "I *am* alone."

"No!" came the ardent reply. "No, my dearest. I have found you now, and *I* will never leave you alone."

There was silence again in the harlot's room. A long silence. It was a good silence, though—the calm after the tempest, or the quiet moment when two long lost friends lock eyes in the street and smile.

Eventually their private conversation continued, but with less tension. They discussed personal history and things like that, but few matters of significance. Damascus mentioned the war and our mission to stop Irrideous. He told Bethel about Amethyst and his life as

273

her mentor. He spoke often of the shining citadel in Tel Tellesti, a wonderful city he promised Bethel would soon see. Strikingly absent from their conversation, though, was any further mention of the stone. Indeed, I realized that since arriving in Heda Fare, Damascus had hardly mentioned the catalyst. In the lovely face of that child, the old man had seemingly forgotten why we were there and what was at stake, and despite her familiarity with the relic, he didn't bother to ask where it was.

I couldn't blame him. The man had been handed a rare opportunity. Why waste it on such dreadful business? How many other men, I wondered, had wished for a chance to undo mistakes from their pasts, and what would I do if given a similar chance? Not much, probably. I could never bring myself to beg pardon from the families I ruined in Severance, nor could I redeem myself from the countless lives I extinguished in the fields around Veldt. And if the situation were reversed—if my sister's murderer somehow found me so he could confess and repent—I would not show mercy. I could never forgive him, not if I had a thousand years.

Still, I couldn't fault Damascus for losing focus. I myself was lost in thought. Amethyst was mentally absent. Neither of us said a word while Damascus visited with Bethel, in fact, so when Fetch returned, she found us sitting silently and staring at the floor. It must have been a perplexing sight, because when she emerged from the dark hallway with an oil lamp carried before her, the elegant woman grew concerned.

"Something wrong?"

Startled, I looked up and tried to offer an explanation.

Amethyst beat me to it. "They just wanted privacy."

"I see." Fetch tilted her head. "Will you require anything else then? I don't have another girl available, but I could bring some wine."

I raised a hand. "We're fine, thank—"

That's when I saw it.

Ransom

I couldn't believe I hadn't noticed it sooner, but when I had met Fetch earlier that evening, she had been seated below me with only a single candle for light. Later, when she had escorted us to Bethel's room, I had followed Fetch from behind with Damascus and Amethyst between. At that moment, though, sitting in that chair and looking up from that angle at Fetch standing nearby and holding that lamp so near her face, I noticed her necklace—a black, iridescent necklace. A shard of rock, framed with silver wire and hanging from a shining cord.

"The Cornerstone," I whispered.

"What?" Fetch asked.

Amethyst glanced at me, but when I nodded toward the necklace, she abruptly stood, her eyes fixated on the relic.

"What is this?" Fetch asked nervously. "What's wrong?"

Amethyst pointed her gloved finger at the woman's neck. "Where did you get that?"

"My necklace?"

Amethyst nodded and bit her lip.

The woman stepped back and reached toward her throat, though her fingers never touched the stone. Then she spit out a convincing lie. "I've—I've had it forever. I don't remember where I found it. Maybe at the market street."

"That stone belongs to Bethel," I said.

"*Nothing* belongs to Bethel," the old harlot countered.

"You stole it?" Amethyst asked.

"How could I steal it? I own her."

Her statement made complete sense, of course. Fetch had purchased Bethel years ago in Severance, right after Irrideous had torched his home, murdered his wife, and disappeared. Fetch had taken a considerable risk buying a girl so young, not knowing how she might develop, so she probably held the mysterious necklace as collateral. That way, if her investment in Bethel failed, the shard might at least prove valuable.

As Fetch withdrew, I suspected something had changed since that day nearly twenty years ago. No doubt Fetch originally purchased the Cornerstone as part of an estate. She had likely bought all the earthly possessions of Irrideous in one lot without knowing what a catalyst was or what it could do. Since then, however, I could tell she had touched it. She hadn't dared as far as Irrideous or lost her sanity. She feared its power, so she only kept it nearby, but she was still attached. She wouldn't surrender the stone. Not willingly.

Amethyst had not yet realized what I had already surmised, so she kept pressing. The girl foolishly stepped closer to the elegant whore and reached out an open hand. "Would you at least let me look a little closer? Just for a moment?"

"No."

"Please?" Amethyst softened her tone as if she were soothing a crying baby. "It's so unique. May I just see it?"

Fetch only bristled. "I think it's time you left."

"Would you sell the necklace? I could make a generous offer."

"It is *not* for sale," Fetch answered, pushing past us and toward Bethel's room.

I almost intervened. I was already fingering my sword. If she offered the slightest reason, I was prepared to take her head, but Bethel's door opened before I could act, and Damascus emerged. He looked surprised at Amethyst, who had grasped Fetch's hand. He glared at me, at my hand gripping my sword, and his countenance hardened.

"What's the meaning of this? What's wrong?"

"Her necklace," Amethyst exclaimed.

Damascus only sighed. "Come now! Is that all? Didn't you notice it before?"

Amethyst didn't respond. She only released Fetch's hand and glanced at me, silently asking the question already at the forefront of my mind. *If Damascus knew, why didn't he say anything?* I couldn't answer, though. I could only watch and listen as Damascus defused the situation with perfect decorum.

"I must thank you, my dear lady, for accommodations so immaculate," he said. "The room was perfect, and your grace has far exceeded your well-deserved reputation."

"Thank you," Fetch replied automatically, but cautiously.

"But now, I must ask one final request." Damascus pushed Bethel's door shut and lowered his voice so the girl would not hear his next words. "We've traveled far on a vital mission, you see, with singular purpose. We must ransom what Irrideous lost."

"You want Bethel?"

"And the necklace," Damascus added.

Fetch laughed in his face. I tightened my grip on my hilt.

The experienced tutor seemed unconcerned. "We can pay handsomely, of course. Whatever price you name, we are prepared to double it."

"That's completely out of the question, I'm afraid."

"Triple?"

"No."

"Oh? Come now. Surely we can reach some agreement."

Fetch shook her head. "Bethel is priceless. She's the most famous girl in the whole city—in the whole estate. They call her the Angel of Heda Fare. Did you know that?"

"I'm certain you can find another girl, one just as stunning."

"It's not just that," Fetch said. Then she paused to ensure her next words struck with enough force. "She's barren."

Damascus physically recoiled. Amethyst cast a forlorn glance at me. I swallowed a lump in my throat.

"Do you know what that means?"

Damascus didn't answer, but he knew. We all knew. Bethel could work twice as often as most, and always without risk. She would never carry a child, which meant her shape would never change from birth and nursing. For far longer than most in her line of work, she would remain tight. Firm. How fortunate for Fetch, and how wretched for Bethel.

The thought left me nauseated.

Damascus must have felt something similar, or something much worse. In that moment he probably realized he could never keep his promise to Bethel. She would indeed remain alone in that brothel forever, and there was nothing he could do. He masked his despair well, though, and he only paused briefly before simplifying his request. "The necklace, then."

Fetch laughed again. "I'd rather slit the girl's throat."

"Dear woman," Damascus protested, "you cannot be so unreasonable! There must be some satisfactory arrangement."

Fetch leaned against the paneled parlor wall, closed her eyes and wrinkled her nose. Then she tossed out a number, some random price she plucked from the ether. "Ten thousand."

I nearly gagged on my own tongue. Amethyst guffawed at the outrageous figure.

"Ten thousand, all in advance, *just for the girl*. And I would need a replacement," Fetch added, glancing at Amethyst. "She might do, I suppose, if you added some meat to her bones."

Amethyst clenched her gloved fingers. I half thought (and silently wished) she might strike the woman, but Damascus only bowed diplomatically and promised, "We'll be back." Then he headed for the door, and we followed.

"Merciless roach," Damascus raged once we exited Fetch's brothel and returned to the curved granite street of Heda Fare. "To hold such a precious child against her will. To extort her very life! And for what? For money? For comfort? Bah!"

Ransom

"And for the Cornerstone," I reminded him. It seemed he needed the reminder, although from the glance he shot at me I doubt he appreciated my initiative. He just snapped his fingers to light his lantern. Then he huffed off toward the harbor.

"It's not past hope. We can return," Amethyst chased after her tutor. "We only need more money."

"Forget the money," I said. "Just make her agree. Force her hand."

"And how do you suggest we do that? Hmm?"

"I don't know. Amethyst has all the authority. Why can't she command Fetch?"

"Because we're not in Estavion, lieutenant. Amethyst has no influence among the clans. Neither of us can order anyone to do anything whatsoever."

"So we do nothing?" I thought back to my tense conversation with Starlight. "Is that your *plan*?"

Amethyst narrowed her eyes curiously.

Damascus only sighed sadly. "We must return to Tel Tellesti. That is the only course left. If we explain the situation to the king, perhaps he'll appropriate the necessary funds. Then we can return."

"That will take months. We need a faster solution."

"There is none," Damascus answered. "In better times perhaps something else could have been done. Not so long ago, the king could have simply written a letter to his allies here, but now with the drought and a war brewing…" He let the sentence hang in the air, unfinished and dreadful.

Amethyst perked. "We can still go to the Council here, can't we? Fetch *is* working illegally. If we report her, she might be arrested, and we could ransom Bethel."

"And take the Cornerstone," I added again.

"No," Damascus answered. "We cannot indict Fetch. We have no evidence. We have only our word, the word of visiting migrants against a Chersonese citizen. And even if the authorities believed our accusation and raided the brothel, they would arrest Bethel too. She may be a slave, but she's also a harlot. She would be detained, just like Fetch.

"As for the stone," Damascus glanced sideways as if he were adding the thought solely for my benefit, "Irrideous and I never reported that particular discovery. As such, there is no record connecting it to me or Irrideous, or especially Bethel. As far as anyone knows, the catalyst belongs to Fetch, so if she's arrested the Cornerstone will be confiscated along with her other possessions. Then who knows what will become of the relic, or who might find it after that." He shivered at the idea. "No, better to let it stay where it is. Better to let it hang where it can do no more misfortune than it's already done."

Damascus finished with a decisive wave of his hand, and that was it. I couldn't argue further. Neither could Amethyst. We could only follow Damascus down the cold street to the nearest intersection and turn southwest down the radial avenue that led toward the harbor. We could only move silently through that sleeping city as our hopes slipped away.

We were finished, I realized. Damascus was right. We had lost. Despite all the chances we took, the orders Amethyst defied and the lives I wasted, our efforts had been futile. We couldn't safely win back the stone, so we had no choice but to return home empty-handed. Perhaps Damascus would order us elsewhere for the time being. Perhaps the *Sole Solution* would endlessly circle the Mediate Sea. There seemed little point in delaying the inevitable, though. Eventually, war would devour the Eastern Estates. Eventually, Irrideous would win.

Irrideous.

The mere thought of his name made my blood boil. He was still out there somewhere plotting his revenge against Damascus and planning Amethyst's death, and our every strategy against him had proven fruitless. Our escape to Ballabor had caused the needless death of hundreds, and our detour to Severance had only escalated the tensions between Samara and Estavion. In Heda Fare we had reached another impasse, and now we had no choice but to abandon an innocent girl to her voracious mistress. It was almost as if—

It was almost as if Irrideous had planned all this.

My throat tightened. Despite the chilly night air, I suddenly burned feverishly. I couldn't stand to consider such a frightening possibility, but once I started down that path, I couldn't stop. Was that why we hadn't been attacked again since Ballabor? Had Irrideous ignored us in Severance because he knew the Samarans would try to arrest us? And was it possible that even here, in Heda Fare, Irrideous hoped we would find his daughter? Did he expect us to find O'dessa Fetch and the catalyst? No, it couldn't be. Because if that were the case...

If that were true, then Irrideous already knew exactly where the stone was.

He left it there, I realized. How had I not guessed that before? Irrideous didn't lose his precious Cornerstone or abandon the girl. He had crafted the entire dilemma. He torched his home and left his daughter. He probably personally convinced Fetch to buy Bethel and the relic and carry them both off to Heda Fare. He carefully secured the treasure not in a dungeon guarded by traps, where Damascus might outthink him. Not in a fortress defended by dreadnaughts, where Amethyst's gloves might overwhelm him. No. He hid the prize in another country where simple laws would protect it. He positioned Bethel Emm in Heda Fare, where her anonymity would imprison her.

He hoped Damascus would find the girl and the stone. That much was certain. He drove the old man from the citadel, from his refuge at Ballabor. He lured us to Chersonia with promises of redeeming Bethel or finding the stone just so Damascus would witness torture meticulously prepared. Irrideous wanted Damascus to taste Bethel's pain, to stand in her room and watch her cry. To weigh his ethics against his guilt, choose between desire and duty. To once again fail. To encounter such injustice, and to walk away without being able to lift a finger.

If that was the plan, Irrideous had succeeded. He had cruelly dangled the solution before Damascus. He had tempted his old friend with his only possible salvation to the approaching doom. Perhaps he was in the city at that very moment, watching us slink away defeated and hopeless. Perhaps he would return to the brothel that night, retrieve his heirloom, and unleash the true might of his long-festering vengeance.

Why wouldn't he? There was nothing left to stop him.

If only we were like him, I wished. If only Amethyst weren't an heiress and I not Vanguard. If only we weren't bound by oaths and laws. If only—

I stopped walking.

Amethyst paused a moment later. "Mordecai?"

"There's another option," I said quietly, my heart pounding like the demon of Ballabor against the gates. "There *is* a solution, though you may not like it."

"Then do not say it," Damascus suggested, irritated that I had stalled us. He obviously longed to return to the ship, where Abner kept the captain's cabin warm.

"Wait," Amethyst said. "I want to hear."

I smiled. At least I still had her trust. So I spoke, my voice low and ominous in the dark avenue. "It's just—well, Fetch could meet with an *accident*. Despite its reputation, Heda Fare isn't perfectly safe. There are still dark alleys and disagreeable sorts. I doubt Fetch often leaves her home, and when she does I'm sure she brings her bodyguard, but that doesn't mean she couldn't unfortunately encounter some band of thieves."

"And die?" Damascus asked.

"It needn't come to that," I shrugged. "We would just rob her, that's all. Steal the stone. We'd take everything else of value, just so the crime would appear genuine."

Ransom

"We will not violate Chersonia's laws," Damascus insisted.

"Damn the law," I shot back. "Did Irrideous consider the law when he abandoned his daughter? Did Fetch honor the law when she purchased Bethel's life?"

"Their crimes do not justify our own," Damascus retorted.

"What of Bethel and your promise to her? You would break your word to spare Fetch?"

He sighed but offered no reply.

"What of the famine and Near Thunderlun? What about the Samarans and Irrideous and his invincible dreadnaughts? We stand on a precipice with all our old allies ready to betray us, but you think we should return to Estavion? Tell the king about the stone and beg a ransom? Hope he doesn't laugh in your face?"

"That is our only choice," Damascus said quietly. "That is the path we must take. We will not take a single step down the other road, not without knowing where it leads."

"We could save Estavion," I seethed.

"Perhaps," he admitted, "or we could end up like Irrideous. Perhaps we would make everything unimaginably worse."

I didn't have an answer to that, and before I could formulate another argument, Damascus turned and walked away again. Just as simply, he ended the argument. He continued down the dark street, carrying our only lantern with him, and he left Amethyst behind as if he expected her to choose between himself and me—nobility and necessity, the light and the dark.

Between good and evil.

Amethyst did choose. After a lengthy, excruciating gaze into my eyes, she chased after her teacher. She left me in the dark.

I shouldn't have been shocked. I shouldn't have felt betrayed. She had known Damascus a long time, much longer than she had known me. He had taught her every good thing she believed. He had been her father and friend when all others had abandoned her, so why would she do anything except blindly follow him?

Her choice proved irrelevant, though, because a raging blaze consumed the brothel that very night.

Eighteen

Rehoboth leans closer. "Did Damascus burn the brothel?"

"What? No!"

"We know it wasn't Irrideous. Who else could have done it?"

"It wasn't Damascus," I insist.

"How can you possibly be certain?"

"He didn't have the opportunity."

Rehoboth checks her notes. "According to Abner, after the three of you returned to the *Sole Solution*, you and Amethyst went straight to bed, but Damascus left again."

I have to think back a moment. "Yes, but he left *with* Abner."

"In the middle of the night?"

"It was nearly dawn by then. They meant to visit the market at first light and purchase supplies."

"And you accompanied them?"

"No. I was exhausted. I had been up for nearly twenty hours at that point."

"Then how can you know what Damascus did or didn't do?"

"Damascus opposed the entire idea!"

"In front of Amethyst? Of course he did. It never occurred to you it might be an act? You already suspected him."

"Yes, but not for that. I didn't think him capable of arson and—and murder."

Rehoboth rolls her quill in her fingertips. "What about now?"

I pretend to consider the possibility. I wring my hands together with an exasperated sigh. Soon, though, I shake my head. "Why don't you ask Abner?"

"We already did," Rehoboth smiles at my predictability, "and Abner insists Damascus never left his side, but this *is* Abner we're talking about. He bought the *Solution* from Damascus."

"What?"

"He never mentioned that?"

"No."

"Of course not. Why would he? But the truth is that Damascus and Abner are old friends. They'd traveled often with Amethyst and Avram, and I wouldn't put it past the good captain to lie about his friend's whereabouts."

"That's absurd."

"Is it? Considering the evidence, isn't it possible that Damascus asked Abner to cover for him?"

"No," I say.

"Then perhaps they burned the brothel together and stole back the Cornerstone?"

"Definitely not!"

"Then what, lieutenant? What other assumption can be made?" She laughs as if the entire situation is the setup for some distasteful joke. "Surely you don't expect me to believe it was all a coincidence? That the brothel just happened to burn that very same night?"

I close my eyes. "Of course not."

"So what other explanation is there?"

"It wasn't Damascus."

"How can you know that? How can anyone prove that?"

"Because—" I swallow a long breath. There's no turning back after this. "Because I did it. I burned the brothel."

Ruined

We left the concentric streets and radial avenues of Heda Fare. After trudging for hours in defeated silence with me trailing far behind Amethyst and Damascus, we returned to the expansive harbor, to the *Sole Solution*, and boarded the ship. Damascus and Abner left again, and Amethyst disappeared inside the captain's cabin. I went below deck, where most of the crewmen slept in their hammocks. I found my place among those beds and reached for my satchel. I meant to return my sword to storage, I suppose, along with my gilded mail and vermilion mantle, but as I pulled open the leather bag, I saw it. I noticed the dreadnaught vambrace again, and it all came flooding back.

I remembered Talsadar and Gideon lying broken and dead in the courtyard of Ballabor. I remembered the Samaran woman hunched over Amethyst, the arrow lodged in her neck. I recalled all the other men I had killed and the additional men I would kill, if war came. I remembered the drought. The famine. The failed Summit. The Samarans and Glacians eager to seize our portion.

All because of an insidious stone.

I wished there was something I could do. I wished there was something Damascus *would* do. He still had a plan, didn't he? Didn't he have some idea how to use the Cornerstone again? Or let Amethyst try? Isn't that why he let her chase Irrideous in the first place? To give her that opportunity? It wasn't for me. No. Damascus was right about me. I could never use the relic safely. But maybe—

Maybe I could offer that chance to someone else.

So I removed my Vanguard uniform. I took off the restrictive coat of mail. I cast aside the cloak, the armor and my oath. I took the dreadnaught vambrace and stole off the ship.

Somehow—I don't even know how, since I had hardly paid attention to our route before—I found my way back through the Ascendant city. Through the dark and cold, I avoided the few Chersonese patrols. I found the right street. I found the door with the latch painted white.

I stood motionless for a moment and stared at the latch, the slate threshold, the point of no return. But I did not linger long. The sun would soon return. Light would bathe the ancient streets, and I would see things differently. So I swallowed my fear. I slipped the armor onto my forearm.

I became a demon.

I can't recall exactly what happened next. As the vambrace affixed to my skin, its intoxicating elixir overwhelmed my senses and tainted my memory. I know my body changed, though, and my strength increased exponentially. I did not open the harlot's door then. I smashed the thick wooden boards, I thundered over the threshold, and I found Fetch.

I murdered her there in the dark sitting room in her brothel. Without explanation or warning, I snapped her neck, and when her bodyguard rose from the shadows to avenge his mistress, I killed him too. I slit his throat with his own knife, I think. Then a fire came. Perhaps I knocked a candle onto the rug, but soon my skin was burning. Somehow I pried fingers under the vambrace. I peeled off the armor, and as my senses returned, I found myself in the midst of a consuming blaze.

My legs moved. In a stupor I fled from that burning hell. I forgot about the stone and the young redheaded whore. I just ran. I took the vambrace, knowing enough not to abandon it in the street where some child might find it, and I returned to the harbor, the ship and the hold. I hid the vambrace back inside my satchel, hid my face in my hands and fell into my hammock.

But rest never came.

Dawn broke an hour later, and I gave up my futile effort to sleep. With bloodshot eyes and a heart of lead, I climbed through the hatch to the *Solution*'s main deck, and I found that Damascus and Abner had returned from the market with fresh provisions. They also brought disturbing rumors about home.

"There is talk in the city this morning about Estavion and Near Thunderlun," Damascus mentioned bitterly to me as the captain climbed toward the helm. "The brooding threats have finally turned to thoughtless actions. A Glacian host is massing near our northern border, near Esker and ruined Del Solae, and we are mustering all our strength to answer." He cursed in a strange tongue before adding, "That narrow fool, Masada! The student should know better."

If my heart was not already in my boots, it would have fallen there. At last the dreaded war was certain. "Should we return home, then?"

"I have already given Abner the command. I wish we could stay longer, but we must leave before Amethyst awakes. She will insist on returning to the brothel, I think, to try some new argument against the old harlot, and I admit nothing would please me more, but that door is closed now," Damascus said wearily as he gazed longingly toward the ancient granite of Heda Fare. "There is nothing left to do except—"

Then he saw it, a black pillar of smoke reaching into the sky.

"No! This cannot be. Not today!" He dashed across the deck and pounded against the cabin door. "Amethyst? Amethyst! Get up at once!"

Damascus and Amethyst never suspected the truth. I doubt they suspected anything, in fact. They were so concerned about Bethel's fate that their feet seldom touched the polished stone streets. They flew fast back to the brothel with me in tow, never stopping to question how or why, and when we finally slid to a stop in the intersection where the southwest avenue crossed the thirty-eighth street, they still couldn't think.

Amethyst could only gasp, "No! Damascus?"

"Hush, child. Hush." He grasped her hand and coughed as a cloud of acrid smoke wafted over us. "Quiet now, and steady. Steady, girl!"

They slowly moved forward through the smog, each cautious step measured and deliberate. I followed at a distance, and soon we encountered a gathered crowd choking the wide street. We pushed through that obstacle, past the merchants and neighbors and various other citizens of Heda Fare, but in their eyes we saw reflected horrors never imagined. They had thought themselves safe, I realized then. They had never guessed the distant dangers might threaten even their fair haven, but now they knew the awful truth. There was no shelter from this storm. Not for them. Not from me.

After much pushing and rude shoving and hasty apologies, we breached the edge of the crowd that had formed a rough semicircle a safe distance from the brothel, or what remained of the brothel. The building still stood, since old granite has little to fear from fire, but the gray stone walls had been scorched black. The door with the

Ruined

white latch had been burned away, the silk window curtains had been vaporized, and through those gaping wounds we saw not a sitting room adorned with lavish fixtures, but a furnace chamber filled with putrid smoke and ash.

The smell alone nearly made Amethyst wretch.

It must have resembled her own chambers, I suppose, and I felt horrid for bringing her back to that place, for creating such a haunting reminder. I could never have warned her, though, not without revealing my involvement, so I instead sought for a distraction, and amazingly I soon found the best one imaginable.

"Look!" I pointed out. "Look there! She lives!"

Amethyst and Damascus turned a little to the left, to a nearby station where some Chersonese soldiers had gathered. The clansmen had come to investigate the crime, I suspect, and to clear the mess. They had two bodies with them, cocooned in bloody sheets and lying in the street, but they also had a beautiful girl wrapped in a warm blanket, a redheaded woman not more than twenty.

"Bethel!" Damascus ran forward. In a sight unmatched he folded the harlot into his arms. The girl hugged back, desperately sobbing as she clutched her only friend in the world.

Amethyst and I kept our distance. Bethel was not our prize.

The intimate embrace between the old man and the young harlot attracted the attention of soldiers, though. Every single person in that street, in fact, stopped and gazed in wonder at the strange reunion, and one specific soldier—the officer in charge of the investigation, I assume—approached us fast.

"You two! Migrants!"

My throat tightened as he neared.

He didn't ask about the murderous fire, though. He only said, "Do you know this woman?"

"Bethel?" I nodded my head nervously.

The investigator's face brightened. "You're related?"

I glanced cautiously at Amethyst and answered, "Yes."

"Is she a suspect?" Amethyst interjected.

"No. Certainly not," the inspector replied.

I breathed easier. "This was an accident, then?"

"I didn't say that," he answered. "This was malicious and foul, certainly, and warily done. Someone invaded the woman's home. Whoever he was, he broke her neck and stabbed her companion. Then the murderer set the fire to cover his crime."

I bristled upon hearing my secret actions described in such precise detail. I also gladly noticed, though, that the inspector mentioned no names. Perhaps he didn't yet know who Fetch was and why someone might wish her dead. Perhaps he would never think to detain some visiting migrants.

Amethyst had a different question, though. "How can you know Bethel didn't do this?"

The soldier smiled. "Look at her."

I did look. I saw Bethel sitting there in the street, a blanket wrapped around her delicate beauty. I saw Damascus nearby, whispering ancient words into her ear, filling her with strength and comfort, and I knew the inspector was right. Bethel seemed hardly able to sit up straight, much less break Fetch's neck and overpower a thug twice her size.

"How did she escape then?" I asked.

The inspector's smile grew wider. "She said she heard a soft voice. Can you believe that? She said—" He laughed a little. "She said she saw a dim light outside her window a moment before the fire started. She heard a whisper urging her to climb out from her bedroom."

I forced out a nervous guffaw for the inspector's benefit. Out of the corner of my eye, though, I noticed that Amethyst's eyes were already scanning the morning sky for shooting stars.

"Bethel said she didn't know where to go after that," the inspector continued. "She doesn't know her way through the city. She had

Ruined

no money, so she never went farther than a block from the fire, and after she returned, she's stayed here with us."

"This was her home, terrible though it was," I said.

"But now," the officer said hopefully, "you can take her?"

I didn't answer. At the startling idea, I could only stare at Amethyst until the girl blurted out, "Yes, I suppose we can."

"Wonderful!" The inspector produced a scroll and quill from a shoulder bag. "Would you mind if I listed your names to that effect? For my report? You understand. I can't leave her here unattended."

"Yes, of course."

With fresh purpose, I stepped closer and quickly conjured up some false names, though now I can't remember what they were. I only remember that I invented a whole identity for us. I told the inspector that Amethyst was my daughter and Damascus was my uncle. We were merchants visiting from Paggat, and Bethel was our kin, I explained, the daughter of my cousin or something to that effect. It all came easily, I must admit, much more easily than I expected. I didn't think I possessed such creativity.

Then again, before that bitter night there were many things I thought beyond my reach. Like murder. And desperate sacrifice. And the Cornerstone.

The stone.

While I stood there speaking with the inspector, I remembered the catalyst, the reason for this madness. I couldn't end my conversation and start searching the bodies, though, not without calling attention to myself, and Damascus had already lost himself in Bethel's company again. I'm sure the stone was the furthest thing from his mind.

But Amethyst still stood idle nearby as she listened to my lies, so during a brief lull, I caught her attention. While the investigator was engrossed in his report and copying whatever details seemed pertinent, I reached out and nudged Amethyst's arm. She turned confused, but then I mouthed a word. Silently I said, "the stone," and tilted my head toward the dead.

Amethyst understood the hint, and while I distracted the inspector with my story, she meandered toward the stained sheets that covered the bodies. She moved past the other soldiers and nonchalantly lifted the smaller shroud that covered Fetch's scorched body. She covered her nose momentarily in response to the stench, but then, with a convincing display, she lowered her eyes as if mourning a dearly departed friend. Tenderly, she kissed her fingertips, and with that anointed hand she reached down and stroked the unrecognizably charred face of O'dessa Fetch.

In the same movement, Amethyst grasped the necklace and snapped the charred cord with an unnoticeable tug. Despite the numerous soldiers surrounding her and the countless curious spectators crowding the wide street, the heiress stole away the Cornerstone and slipped it unseen into her pocket.

Soon afterward, once I satisfied the inspector and Bethel found strength enough to walk, the four of us started back toward the *Sole Solution*. Amethyst and I led the way, walking slowly, and Damascus followed with Bethel, his arm cradling her weak form. He led her like a cripple, as if she might trip and shatter to pieces if he didn't support her, and during our whole walk back, he spoke with her about—well, I'm not quite sure.

This time, I couldn't eavesdrop because Heda Fare had fully awoken. The broad streets were bustling with commerce. Merchants and residents walked to and fro before and behind us. Carts rattled down the avenues. Mounted riders and patrolling soldiers moved throughout the squares and plazas, and except for the thin smoke still hanging over the city, I noticed little evidence of the coming war or the long-standing drought.

We were also ignored in that chaos, thankfully. We were not approached by soldiers or peddlers. No one thought us suspicious because of our clothing or accents. No one even seemed bothered by the beautiful, sad woman being led away by a power not her own, so we reached the harbor without incident and easily found the *Solution*'s pier.

There, however, we stopped, because as soon as Bethel noticed the kite runner that would bear her hence, she lost interest. Indeed, the moment Amethyst and I ascended the ramp and stepped aboard the main deck, Bethel froze. She even took a step back. "You're returning to Tel Tellesti?"

So Damascus had already explained about the city. Had he also told her about the life she might find there? How strange and different and wonderful it would be?

"You're welcome to accompany us, of course," he said.

"To a glorious citadel? To a life in court? Somehow I don't think I belong there," the harlot confessed.

And amazingly, Damascus didn't contradict her.

I really must stress that. Even now, so many weeks later, it makes absolutely no sense. Damascus had formed an attachment so immediate and intimate that he seemingly forgot about Amethyst. He was no longer the old scholar, but like someone enlightened, content to enjoy his few remaining days in Bethel's presence. He seemed like an ancient sage who had waited ten thousand years for this very moment.

Yet when Bethel suggested she stay behind, he didn't argue. Instead, when she said, "I don't think I belong there," Damascus only smiled and replied, "No, I suppose you don't."

Amethyst shifted uneasily beside me on the *Solution*'s deck. I almost cursed the old man's narrowness.

"I *do* appreciate everything you've done," Bethel stressed.

"My dear child, there is nothing you must say. I understand." Then, as if to prove his point, he reached into his robes and said, "I only ask you take something, wherever you might go."

Damascus produced two items from his mystical inner pockets. The first was a small coin purse, but the second was that book—the manuscript from which he had torn the sketch of Bethel and her parents. As they stood on the pier, he pushed the leather-bound volume into her hands first.

"No!" Bethel adamantly shook her head. "I can't."

"Come now, I've already read it countless times. It won't help to keep it longer. But you? You will find it most useful."

"I can't read it."

"Oh, I'm sure you'll decipher it soon enough."

"You don't understand," Bethel said. "It's all scratches to me, even the common dialects. I can't read *anything*."

His smile deepened. "Don't worry, child. You will learn soon enough, and this book will answer all the greatest questions of your life."

She didn't seem convinced, but she accepted the gift. Then Damascus offered her the small purse. Flustered, Bethel tugged at the string and opened the pouch, but when she peeked inside, her eyes widened and her head shook more adamantly than before. "No!"

"Bethel, please."

"It's too much!"

"For one life? No, it is not nearly enough." He grasped her hand tenderly. "I know it's hard to accept. I know that you've never tasted happiness. You've never known grace, so it's hard to believe that you—even you—are prized by anyone. But you are, my dear! To me, a single lock of your hair is worth all this. You are worth the entire world and infinitely more."

Bethel broke down again. She cried in her redeemer's arms, and he wept as well. At my side, I heard Amethyst sniff, and on the quarterdeck Abner sighed. The whole world paused for a spell, and even my own anxious heart relaxed a little.

This was because of me, after all.

I could never utter such a boast, though, so I remained silent. I stood motionless on the *Solution*'s deck, watching and waiting while the old mentor sent off the beautiful girl. And when Bethel left, and when Damascus ascended the ramp, we finally started for home.

It took forever to leave Heda Fare's expansive harbor. It was a crowded port that day—perhaps the most crowded I've seen—so the crew rowed cautiously along the four colossal granite breakwaters that crisscrossed the green waters like interlaced fingers, and Abner stood at the helm to maneuver us safely through the liquid switchbacks.

"Take it slow, lads," the captain said. "No need for haste."

Wise words for anxious times, I thought.

I turned to say something to Amethyst, but the girl had left my side at some point in the last hour. When I looked, I found her on the quarterdeck behind Abner, standing beside Damascus and leaning over the railing. They both seemed lost in thought, maybe, or transfixed by something in the distance. Or someone.

They were searching for Bethel.

She was hours away by then. She had left the pier soon after the *Solution* had cast off, and by that time I imagine she had used her new wealth to buy a horse, purchase some provisions and leave the fair haven. At that very moment, I suspect she was racing over the rolling eastern hills, the cool wind combing her bright hair, a strong steed carrying her fast away, and freedom—freedom beckoning her toward the lofty Silvertips and the distant horizon beyond.

All the same, I didn't blame my companions for searching backward a little longer.

We had accomplished a great thing that day, and we deserved that blissful moment. We had discovered a slave and released her from captivity. We had outwitted a madman and ruined his plan. More importantly, we had at last found the long-sought prize, the lost Cornerstone, and we could return victorious to Tel Tellesti and present the catalyst to the king. Perhaps then we could even avert the coming war, and maybe, just maybe, Amethyst might win her father's trust.

I shivered at the thought. Or perhaps from the autumn air that swept over the tranquil bay. Amethyst must have also noticed the chill, because she left her teacher's side and wandered across the quarterdeck, down the steep stairs and into the cabin.

I followed. I had nothing better to do, so I entered behind the heiress as she collapsed into a chair. She gazed out the starboard window, I stood motionless near the door, and for a long while neither of us broke the satisfying silence.

But eventually, Amethyst spoke. "I can't believe we did it."

I smiled and nodded.

"I never believed we'd succeed. Did I ever tell you that? The Inheritance is so incredibly vast, and Fetch was so—" She lost her voice momentarily. "It's amazing, isn't it? How perfectly everything fell into place? How it all worked out? Who would have thought?"

Perfectly isn't the first word I would have chosen, but I just said, "We got lucky, that's for sure."

"And helping Bethel—" She sighed. "That feels good."

"What of the stone?" I asked, suddenly anxious to know my effort hadn't been wasted.

Amethyst flinched at my words, almost as if she had forgotten our primary objective, but she reached into her pocket and slowly lifted out the ancient relic by the blackened chain. She held up the catalyst without touching it, though whether that was intentional or not, I cannot say. I only know we both marveled at it.

I had not yet seen the Cornerstone so close or in such good light. I had only heard vague descriptions from Damascus and noticed it hanging around Fetch's neck in her dim brothel. Now that I had the chance to study it, though, I saw that it indeed appeared like a flat black stone with four sides. It was slightly wedge-shaped, somewhat like an actual cornerstone an architect might fit into a building's foundation. Two edges were straight, ground perfectly smooth, while the other two were jagged and rough, as if they had been broken.

All that seemed normal, even expected. What surprised me, though, was the color. The stone was black, as I said, but black doesn't seem sufficiently emphatic. It was deep. Empty. Perilous. Staring at it, I felt I was gazing into a bottomless abyss, knowing full well that whatever tumbled into that void would be lost forever. It felt treacherous and enticing all at once, and I confess my first impulse was to touch it. Despite knowing that I could never manage such a test, I still yearned to learn for myself if all the terrible stories were true. To discover if our sacrifices were justified.

But Amethyst moved first.

My hand instinctively grasped my sword. I don't know why. I didn't mean to stop her. In fact, I wanted her to try. That was why I'd done everything, wasn't it? I still felt threatened when she reached for the stone, though, because somehow I knew that *this* was the moment of truth, the decision that would determine our destiny. When Amethyst grasped that timeless power, she would either somehow control it, or it would overwhelm her as it had so many others. She would either prove me right or destroy us all.

If the girl was fearful, she didn't show it. She instead seemed determined to conquer the impossible. The catalyst was there—dangling from its cord, cloaked in forbidden beauty—and this was Amethyst's moment to prove herself worthy of her existence. Others take easier routes. Some climb mountains, swim oceans or pursue love despite the risks just to show it's possible. Little boys sometimes explore dangerous places, especially after they've been warned explicitly not to. Young girls often rush to the side of a rebellious man they've been told to forget just to be caught up in his adventures. I suspect all of us possess some insatiable seam that must test how tenacious the world really is.

So she touched it. With one hand, Amethyst reached for the Cornerstone. With a single finger, she stroked the catalyst, and it ruined her.

Nineteen

Rehoboth reaches for the velvet scrap lying on the cedar desk. Carefully, she lifts the folded fabric. She glimpses the Cornerstone for herself, but she doesn't touch it. Instead, she says, "What did it do to Amethyst, specifically?"

"If you would stop interrupting me—"

"Answer the question, lieutenant."

I clench my teeth and close my eyes. "I don't know."

"You saw so much. You learned so many strange things. You must have some idea about what it did to her."

I lower my voice. "You won't believe it."

Rehoboth only smiles. "That hasn't stopped you yet."

She is right, of course, but this is different. I'm not sure I can ever find words to describe that effect. Rehoboth is patient, though, and so is Uriah. They both endure an intolerable silence while I search for an adequate explanation.

"Have you ever realized," I eventually say, "how we're such good liars? I mean, maybe not you, your grace, but people. I know myself...I lie every day. When Caleb asks about the famine or the war, I tell him everything will turn out right. When Amethyst asks how I'm doing, I nod and say everything's fine, even when that's the furthest thing from the truth.

"But most importantly, I lie to myself," I confess. "Every night when I lie down and try to sleep, I can't help but feel like I haven't done enough. I haven't been good enough. There's so much more I could have done—*should* have done—and every morning when I wake, the first thought in my head, the first emotion in my heart... you know what it is? I feel like a failure. I see an impossible task before me. Countless duties unfinished. Promises broken. A better man, I know, wouldn't live this way. He wouldn't suffer so many mistakes. He wouldn't tolerate so many compromises.

"But then before I lose my sanity again, you know what I do? I lie. I tell myself it's okay. You're still a good man, I say. Stick another man in your place, give him your history, your regrets, your experiences, and he would perform just as badly. He might even do worse. You're not a failure. You're a victim of your circumstances. You are a god trapped in a weak, mortal body. You're capable of anything. You can accomplish the impossible, if only the world would awake and realize your worth."

Rehoboth narrows her eyes. She hasn't been notating any of this. "Is that truly what you tell yourself every morning?"

"Well, not *every* morning. Sometimes I wake up half drunk from the previous night," I smirk. "Those are the good days."

The arbiter glances down and checks her notes. "What does this have to do with Amethyst?"

"Well, as I said, I'm a good liar," I continue. "I'm so good, in fact, that I don't know if I've ever confronted the truth. I've never looked deep, past all the excuses and justifications. I've never truly faced the person I actually am.

"But Amethyst? When she touched the stone, *she knew*. For a split second, she understood who she truly was. She glimpsed her deepest nature. And she was never the same."

Dichotomy

For a brief moment, Amethyst touched the Cornerstone. She felt the infinite void.

I felt something too. I don't know how, but when Amethyst made contact, something inexplicable and dreadful emanated like a shockwave. Colors vanished. Sounds faded. When she touched the stone, she touched the whole world, or at least the men on the *Sole Solution*. Most importantly, she touched her own heart. She found something black.

"Amethyst?"

She didn't answer. Tears flooded her eyes, and she recoiled as if she had brushed a glowing coal. A paroxysm swept through her, and she dropped the scorched necklace in a trembling, hyperventilating fit.

"Amethyst!" My grip tightened on my sword.

As the stone struck the floor, Amethyst's eyes raced from me, to the open door, to the window, and to her bed. She had the eyes not of a young girl, but of a wild, trapped beast that might lash out any second at me. Or at herself.

"Stop!" I stepped forward, my free hand outstretched. "Listen to me! Calm yourself! Look here!"

She didn't respond. She couldn't hear me, I suspect. Perhaps she couldn't even see me. Amethyst was already lost in a vicious tempest, and I could never reach her.

I could reach the Cornerstone, though, and remove that menace from her presence. It still lay where she had dropped it on the wooden floorboards, and she was shrinking backward. If I moved quickly, she might not react soon enough to injure me, and even if she did, she wasn't wearing the gloves. So I reached out and prepared to spring forward.

But I moved too late. At that moment frantic footsteps approached behind me. Then Damascus and Abner burst through the open stateroom door.

They had felt Amethyst's attempt with the stone from the quarterdeck, and in the fifteen seconds since they had rushed down to prevent whatever might happen next. Now that they stood in the doorway, they saw a girl panicked and stricken. Damascus especially saw the Cornerstone lying on the floor, and he noticed a Vanguard agent leaning forward with one hand outstretched toward the forbidden relic and his other hand tight around the hilt of his sword.

"What have you done?" Damascus demanded.

He didn't wait for a response, but dashed toward his young student. She cried out, screaming at him to stay back and leave her alone. She seemed terrified by some invisible fiend, terrified of herself perhaps, but Damascus still approached. She struck at him next, attacking her own tutor with dagger-like fingers, but he deftly skirted the assault and reached for her. With two outstretched fingers, he anointed her temple, and simultaneously he grasped her neck. He spoke something ancient and potent, and Amethyst fell limp.

Damascus caught the girl, who seemed small and frail. He lowered her gently to the floor and positioned her arm under her head like a pillow. His attention turned fast to the stone after that. He grasped the sleeve of Amethyst's purple gown, tore a scrap of fabric from the hem, and bent toward the object. Like a baker using a rag to pull a pan from an oven, Damascus wrapped the catalyst in a velvet sheath without touching it, and he tucked it within his linen robe.

Then he turned toward me with blazing eyes. "Get out."

"Let me explain. This is not what you think."

"I said *get out!*" he bellowed, rising to a height that crowded the room.

Dichotomy

I foolishly resisted, stepping forward to defend my actions. Before I could speak, though, a gentle hand grasped my shoulder from behind, and Abner's voice slipped reason into my mind. "Come on, pup. Now's not the time for words."

So I saved my breath. I released my sword. I backed out of the cabin with Abner, and we locked Amethyst away.

The captain was right. That was not the time for talk. So I slept instead, finally resting after nearly thirty hours, and I awoke the subsequent afternoon feeling slightly better. But the proper time didn't come later that day or that night. Or the next day. Or the following week. It was time instead for the *Solution*'s crew to focus on their task while Damascus focused on his. So while the mentor worked privately with his pupil, we worked with the wide canvas sails. I launched the silk kites. Abner directed our course from his helm. He brought the ship back across Tollah Bay and south through the Mager Straits. Once we rounded the headlands, he turned us east along Chersonia's southern strands toward Paggat and Tel Tellesti beyond. He set our course home.

On that final leg of our journey, however, we lacked our usual speed. I tended the kites like before, and I had become quite the expert by then, but without Amethyst guiding the wind into my flying sails, the kites hung low and flaccid in the cloudless sky. Likewise, our spirits sank. The crew hardly talked. Abner leaned against the helm like a cripple propped against his cane. I neglected my swordplay. Damascus kept his student sequestered in the captain's cabin, and the ship plodded along like driftwood in a current.

Still, I thought our progress too swift. Each day, every single hour, brought us closer to the citadel. Within three weeks, the *Sole*

Solution would return to its slip in the harbor. Amethyst would return to her life in court. I would return to my recruits, to my training yard. I would soon report back to General Uriah.

And then what?

We had hoped to return as victorious heroes. Indeed, even then we sailed with the Cornerstone, but it was not the salvation we had sought. Amethyst could never present the stone to her father, nor could Damascus offer it to the king as a tool against our enemies. I could not even claim success in my personal mission. I was bringing back Amethyst alive, yes, but not safely. I had left as a trusted lieutenant with a confident heiress, but I was returning as a murderer with only a hollow shell. At least I hadn't been forced to kill her.

I wished we could go back. I wished Damascus would avert our course and delay our homecoming. I just wanted to return to where I felt safe, back to Heda Fare, perhaps. But no. I had never felt safe there. Back to Ballabor then? Or the citadel? Or Veldt? No. How far back did I need to go? How long had it been since I truly felt safe for longer than a fleeting moment? Had I ever existed without resentment and regret?

It was when my sister still lived, I realized. Incredible. I was a young man then. Had it really been that long since I knew true peace? No wonder I felt exhausted.

After two long weeks, Abner noticed my deepening melancholy and decided to intervene. The usually jolly captain could hardly ignore his own despondency, but nonetheless he left his helm and approached the bow. He noticed me wrestling with the tethers, wasting so much time and effort on such a useless endeavor, and he smiled knowingly. "It's okay, pup. You should rest. You've done your best, and there's no shame in that."

"I was a fool, captain. A narrow fool."

"No argument there."

I glared at him cautiously. Did he somehow know about my secret actions in Heda Fare?

Dichotomy

"We were all fools," he continued, "and glad fools at that. Not a man on this boat who didn't believe in that girl. Or *want* to believe."

So he didn't know. All the same, I hung my head. I knew he was trying to cheer me up, but he only made it worse. I had shattered many hopes then, not just my own. Why hadn't I left everything alone?

I tried to change the subject, to think of anything besides the Cornerstone and Amethyst. Only one other thing came to mind, though, and it was no less disheartening. "What of the rumors, the news you heard in Heda Fare? Did Damascus speak true? Are the Glacians moving against us?"

"Damascus only spoke half the truth," the captain answered. "The Glacians are moving, yes, and Masada is personally leading the horde, but the Samarans are rallying, too. We heard reports of cavalry massing near Alzeer."

I swallowed a rising lump in my throat. "How many?"

"No way to tell, not from gossip, but after our visit to Severance, it wouldn't surprise me if the Empress assembled the whole Tay`Jeen."

The Tay`Jeen, the western company. The last time Samara rallied that host, the armored cavalry had numbered ten thousand strong, and that was many generations ago. The mounted army couldn't defeat our corps, perhaps, but it was swift and mobile. With so many horses, the Samaran riders could travel thousands of leagues, circumvent our Vanguard, strike an unguarded target and retreat—all in a single day. They could destroy an entire city and withdraw before our reinforcements arrived.

"Uriah faces an unwinnable war on two opposite fronts," I groaned, "and the weapon we hoped to use against them lies useless on the cabin floor."

Abner shrugged and slapped my shoulder. "At least we're still ahead of Irrideous."

If only he had been right.

We sailed onward along the southern coast of Chersonia for another week. The ship trudged east through murky waters under a gray sky. Then we dipped through the Straits of Nore Mere. We entered Adis Bay and started the final stretch home.

During that whole time, I didn't see Amethyst once. Her tutor emerged from the stateroom occasionally for fresh air and meals, but the girl stayed locked away. Whether this was her idea or his, I'll never know. I didn't give it much thought, either. I just sat at the bow tending the kites and watching the waves break against our hull. I halfheartedly scanned the horizon for signs of other ships or streaks of light, and when that grew old I sat alone in the cargo hold with my broadsword. I didn't practice my form, though. I sat for hours sharpening the blade with my whetstone, and as I ground away the folded steel, I stared at my satchel, at the vambrace hidden within, and pondered how everything had fallen apart.

I understood my part, at least. I didn't like it, and I regretted my choice, but I understood why I had made it. Part of me even suspected I would do the same thing again if given the chance. I'm a soldier, after all. I swore an oath to protect Estavion. My life was already forfeit after Severance, and I had promised Uriah I would keep Amethyst safe no matter the cost, even if I had to surrender my own life. Even if I had to corrupt my own heart.

But Amethyst. She was meant to be our salvation. She was supposed to justify the cost. Even Damascus had believed her capable, hadn't he? Isn't that why he agreed to send us after Irrideous? So why had she reacted the way she did? She wasn't a Vanguard agent with red hands and a black heart. She wasn't an old mentor filled with

Dichotomy

regret or a villain bent on vengeance. She was a mere teenager. A delicate flower. A precious jewel. So why couldn't she use the stone?

I didn't know, but I had to find out.

I left the hold, therefore, and I returned to my place at the bow. Then I watched out of the corner of my eye, and later that evening I noticed Damascus emerging from the stateroom. I didn't act then, though. Not yet. I noted instead how Damascus took his evening rations with the crew and spoke with Abner. I counted the twenty-three minutes until he returned to the cabin, and I stayed up long into the night in case he reappeared.

The next day, I repeated my vigil. Then I carefully spied for another three days after that and soon discerned a predictable pattern. While Amethyst remained hidden, Damascus usually left the cabin at least for the morning, afternoon and evening meals, and occasionally he would come out for a late night pipe as well. For the morning and midday rations, the old man only collected a portion for himself and Amethyst to carry back to the stateroom, but for the evening meal Damascus usually lingered on deck to encourage the crew. He often brought out his vellum map and advised Abner about our course, and during these recesses he usually left Amethyst alone for almost half an hour.

I made my choice, and I watched two more days to verify the mentor's habits. I waited until we were only a few days from Tel Tellesti. Then late one afternoon, I positioned myself under the quarterdeck stairs only a few paces from the cabin entrance. I turned and leaned over the railing, facing away from the door where Damascus would emerge. I scanned the foaming waves, noticing a distant eastern shoreline, the gray cliffs coming into view, and I waited.

An hour passed. Then another. The sun fell toward the horizon. I heard movement above me as the crew gathered on the quarterdeck for the evening ration. Somber words were spoken. Someone asked about Amethyst, but I don't remember the reply. I was too busy wondering if Damascus had somehow anticipated my actions and changed his schedule for that day just to spite me. Such mockery didn't seem beyond him.

My stomach started growling. I almost abandoned my post. Then I finally heard metal scrape against wood. A wrought iron latch lifted and a hinge squeaked. Footsteps circled behind me, and boards creaked as someone ascended the quarterdeck stairs. A few moments later, an aged voice greeted Abner. Damascus even asked about the weather.

I turned and slipped through the door like a thief.

I found a dark room with windows shut and curtains drawn tight. The air felt thick with sweat and tears, and it actually took my eyes a minute to adjust from the daylight outside, so I spoke before I even saw her.

"Amethyst?"

I heard no reply, but once my vision cleared, I saw her sitting cross-legged on the floor not two steps before me, her skin pale, her elbows resting on her knees, her chin cradled in her hands, her eyes pressed shut. Her hair remained golden, though it was tangled and greasy from weeks of neglect, and she wore the same velvet gown with the torn sleeve. She sat in almost the exact spot where she had fallen, actually, and I half thought she hadn't moved in all the days since.

I noticed one last thing, though, that convinced me otherwise. Amethyst was surrounded by white shards. She had broken her porcelain horse again, but this time she hadn't asked Damascus to put it back together. She had smashed the figurine apart, and she now sat among the pieces. Was she that shattered herself?

Dichotomy

"Amethyst?"

She didn't speak, but she sucked in a quick breath of air, so I guessed she heard. I reached forward then and touched her shoulder. That finally prompted a response. She flinched and whispered almost unintelligibly, "Go away."

"I must speak with you."

She stayed silent again.

"Where's the stone? Does Damascus have it?"

She didn't answer that either.

I surveyed the room, searching for anything to discuss. If I could persuade her to speak about something else, maybe I could redirect the conversation back to her experience with the catalyst. My eyes soon settled on the small table and the rubbings lying there. "What have you been studying recently? Anything new?"

Still no answer.

"Amethyst, please. You must talk about this."

Nothing.

"You can't hide in here. Not forever."

She cracked one of her knuckles.

"Can't you just tell me what happened?"

"Nothing happened," she whispered.

"You really think I believe that?"

She didn't bother to answer.

"It's okay. You can tell me. You can trust me with anything."

"Just leave me alone."

I considered her request, but I didn't like it. In fact, I grew irritated. I shouldn't have been so impatient, but I had sacrificed so much for her, and she had only failed me. All I wanted now was a simple explanation, and she couldn't even offer that.

So I lost my temper, I'm sorry to say, and as I considered my next words, I chanced upon something unkind. It was downright cruel, and I should have never said it, but I couldn't help myself. I needed her to talk. So I leaned close. I spoke slow and clear. I said insidious words she never wanted to hear. "You want me to ignore you? Just like your father does?"

Her head rose suddenly, her eyes livid and bloodshot. I'd never seen her like that.

"That's it, isn't it?"

"You really want to know?"

"*Yes.*"

Amethyst wiped her raw nose, sniffed in another deep breath, and glanced up at the ceiling. Then she closed her eyes and said with quivering lips, "I saw him."

Her father, I assumed.

"I saw him. At my feet. Dead."

"You saw a vision?"

"No. When I touched the stone, I saw—I don't know. I saw *everything*. I saw you and Damascus in some far off place sometime long past, and you seemed different somehow. Older. Then I saw myself here in the ship. In this room. And then—" She shivered at the thought.

"And then?"

She wrung her hands. "I saw what I want most."

"I don't understand."

"No, I don't suppose you would." She brushed some stiff strands of yellow hair from her eyes and tried to explain anyway. "I'm not sure I can describe everything, but I know at least that I didn't have an accurate idea of how a catalyst works. Maybe Damascus didn't explain it well enough, or maybe I never paid attention, but for some reason I always thought a catalyst was something like—like a wishing stone. That I only needed to touch it with a certain thought in my mind. If I just told it what I wanted, it would make my wish happen."

A reasonable hypothesis. I had half assumed the same thing.

"But it doesn't work that way," she continued. "It doesn't listen to conscious thought. It responds to desire and raw instinct. So when I touched it, it searched the deepest parts of my heart. It showed me

Dichotomy

what I really wanted, even though I hadn't realized the truth myself. It tried to manifest my desire, and if I hadn't dropped the stone when I did—" Her voice cracked and she fell silent again. A tear streamed down her pale cheek.

But I wasn't about to let her stop. "Why did you drop it? What did you see? What did you want?"

"*What do I want?*" she repeated sadly. "Starlight tried to warn me, lieutenant. I can't believe I didn't realize. She asked me that question when we visited Ur Thourou. Remember?"

I did remember. I also remembered other things Starlight had said that I wished I could forget.

"I lied. I didn't say anything, but still I lied to her. I lied to Damascus. I lied to myself, even. I convinced everyone I wanted the stone for Estavion, for my father, but that's not true. Not really. I wanted it for myself. And my father…I don't want him to learn from his mistakes. I don't want to prove myself to him. I'm tired of trying to make things better, and I just—I want to be finished with him, Mordecai." She swallowed painfully. "I want my father dead."

She fell quiet, and for once I didn't goad her. I had the truth, at last, the answer to my burning question, but it failed to satisfy. On the contrary, it left me more lost than before. I had placed so much faith in that girl, in her innocence and privilege. I had believed her more noble, but I was wrong. When pressed, she proved no better than I.

What hope was there for any of us, then?

She was right. I should have left her alone. I wanted to run, leap off the ship, swim to shore, and never look back. I couldn't abandon her like that, though. Not after forcing that confession. I had to say something, to offer some kind of hope to her, to myself, so I reached out. I touched her knee. I softened my voice.

I told her lies.

"It's okay," I promised. "It's understandable, what you felt. Anyone else would think such things. That doesn't make you evil,

Amethyst. It makes you human. You must understand that. *Accept that.* There are horrid parts of you, yes, parts you may never change, but that's okay. You can hide those desires. Learn to control them. No one must ever see that side of you, not if you don't wish it."

She didn't answer.

I continued. "You know what you should do? Take back some control. You feel lost. Guilty. But you're focusing on the negative. You just need some perspective. You need to do something good, and you'll feel infinitely better." I playfully nudged her shoulder, hoping to prompt a reaction—any reaction—but I received none. "Come on. It's a new day. Why don't you come out? The fresh air might do some good. We can spar, you and I. You can toss me around the ship, show everyone just what to think of you. How about it? And when we get home, just think. You can still present the stone to the king. You can still be the hero. The whole nation will have you to thank. *To esteem.* Who then would dare suspect you're anything but a saint?"

"I would."

"But you can *choose* not to believe that," I told her. "You can believe about yourself whatever you want to believe. And when your father asks about this day, you can tell him anything you want. You can still earn his respect."

"Lieutenant?"

My heart fluttered, and I nearly jumped. I turned to see Damascus in the doorway, far ahead of schedule and glaring with utmost disapproval. He didn't say anything else, but he didn't have to. I knew what he demanded. So I stood. I leaned down for one final word. "Just believe what you want." Then I slipped out the door before it slammed behind me.

I almost stepped away, but before I could move I heard quiet voices seeping through the panels. Once more I listened through a door, wondering what the old mentor would say to his student. How would he fix her now?

Dichotomy

"I'm sorry," I heard her say too quickly, as if everything were always her fault.

"Come now. There's no need. I let him in, didn't I?"

She didn't reply.

"Besides," Damascus continued, "maybe it's good you heard the lieutenant, because now you have a choice. He *is* right. Do you realize that? You can, if you so choose, lie about who you are. You can try to *earn back* your honor, and you can pretend to be a better person until you think you deserve what's already been freely given.

"And there's second option too. Did you know that? You could *shift the blame*, as so many others have done. I'm shocked the lieutenant didn't try that argument, come to think of it. It would be easy. With little effort, you could convince yourself that the fault lies elsewhere. You could believe that Irrideous tricked you. That I allowed you on this quest. That the lieutenant stole the stone and placed it in your hand. That the whole world conspired against you, and it's not your fault for failing.

"But there's a last option, my dear—the best option—and it's my favorite of the three. It is the one thing in the world powerful enough to change a person forever."

"And what is that?" Amethyst asked halfheartedly.

"Come now," came the shrewd reply. "I wouldn't be much of a mentor if I gave you *all* the answers, would I?"

Twenty

"He didn't tell her the last option?"

I shrug. "He wanted her to figure it out for herself, I guess. Either that or he wanted to *show* her instead of only telling her."

Rehoboth mutters something about a silly old fool, but Uriah smiles slightly. Maybe the general appreciates the mentor's reasons.

"May I continue now, your grace?"

She waves me on.

"Thank you. So that brings me to our final approach, which happened the next day. I did spend that night contemplating the last option and Amethyst's failure with the Cornerstone, but once we returned to Tel Tellesti's harbor, Damascus and Amethyst left the *Solution*, and I didn't see either of them again for, let's see—a few days—"

"No, wait."

I silently curse her for these disruptions. "What now?"

Rehoboth checks her notes again. "You're forgetting something."

Have I? "No, I don't believe I am."

"Here we are!" She proudly holds up her rediscovery. "You and Damascus spoke."

I chuckle. "Yes. We spoke on many occasions."

"I mean on the *Solution*, before your return." Rehoboth points at the parchment. "Abner said he saw you and Damascus speaking late one night, just the two of you."

Did the captain spy on us? Did he overhear *that* conversation? The possibility makes me shudder, but I shake my head and insist, "Abner's mistaken. He must have imagined it."

"He was quite certain. He mentioned specifically how unusual it was." She starts reading from the page. She even imitates Abner's inflections. *"An odd sight, Mordecai and Damascus talking. They hardly spoke to the other, even with others about, and they never talked alone."*

"That's certainly true."

"Lieutenant," Uriah interjects. "You're hiding something."

"I'm—"

"Mordecai, out with it."

My palms are sweating. I don't know how or when the general learned to read me so easily, but I don't humor him. I can't answer this time, not about that. They'll never understand.

The arbiter tires of my silence. "What's wrong, lieutenant? How bad can it be? You've already confessed to arson. Insubordination. Treason. Assault."

"Don't forget murder," Uriah adds.

"How much further could you possibly incriminate yourself?"

I don't dare speak.

"Wait," Uriah says. "This isn't about you anymore, is it? You're trying to protect someone else."

A bad guess, but I could pretend it's true. The general usually has such good insights.

"Is it Damascus?"

I bite my tongue. Too soon.

"Abner?"

Stay quiet.

"Amethyst?"

"No!"

"Who, then?"

I take a deep breath. "Damascus."

Epiphany

Abner spoke correctly, I'm sorry to say. About everything. I didn't speak with Damascus immediately after my conversation with Amethyst, though. In fact, I didn't see Damascus again that evening. He didn't come out for his usual pipe. He stayed with his student well into the night, and had I gone to bed with the rest of the crew at my usual time, I probably would have never spoken with him again. Everything would have turned out immeasurably better.

But when the light faded and Abner started the night watch, I didn't descend to my hammock. I couldn't. I was too angry. Too disappointed in myself, in Amethyst. I had sacrificed everything for her. I had bought the stone with my honor. I had given her the chance of a lifetime, and what had she done with it? Nothing. For some stupid reason, she couldn't bring herself to forgive her own father, and for that selfishness the entire continent would suffer. I would also soon face judgment, and I despised her for that.

I hated Damascus too, because he meddled with ancient and supernatural powers. Because he introduced a girl so young and broken to such dangerous devices. Because he offered false hope in desperate times. And most of all because he didn't force Amethyst to try the Cornerstone again, but decided instead to turn her pathetic failure into a didactic opportunity, as if this were all just a fable and our lives didn't matter.

So I hated him. I hated the girl and myself. I hated the whole world, and I couldn't sleep, so I stayed brooding on the deck late into the night. The crew descended one by one to their beds in the hold, and all the while I lingered at the bow near the tethers and winch. As Abner briefed the night watch, I fingered the slack lines. While

Amethyst and Damascus slept in the cozy cabin, I stood in the damp cold and contemplated the drifting kites that reluctantly dragged us toward our doom—the kites that refused to soar high without Amethyst's help.

We were somewhere in the northeast quadrant of Adis Bay by that point, and though our pace was slower than usual, we had made decent time. We would probably reach Tel Tellesti within a few days, then Amethyst would resume her neglected life in the citadel. I would be imprisoned and brought to trial. The Vanguard would face the Tay`Jeen without me, and our other armies would confront the pale hordes of Near Thunderlun. Caleb and my trainees would be sent to battle prematurely. In every way that I could possibly imagine, my life would soon grow incomparably worse, and there was nothing I could do to delay the inevitable for even one hour.

Or was there?

I glanced behind me. It was past midnight. I could see little on the deck, and I could barely focus with all the fear and loathing clouding my vision, but I could see enough to spy Abner at his helm. There was another sailor high above and half asleep in the nest at the top of the main mast, and a third man was adjusting the riggings for the secondary sail. None of them were watching me, however, and even if they were, there was no lantern near the bow to illuminate my actions. Nor could they reach me fast enough to prevent any scheme I might try.

I made my choice. I reached inside my tall boot for the dagger always hidden there, and I grasped one of the slack lines. That was the only option that made sense. The speed gained from the kites was nearly negligible at that point, but still, we might gain a few hours or even a day if I cut them loose. Then who knew what might happen? Perhaps Amethyst would get a second chance with the stone. Maybe I could sneak an attempt while Abner replaced the kites.

As my blade touched the rope, though, a powerful gale rose over the waters and swept across the *Solution*'s deck. The line jerked from

Epiphany

my grasp, burning my fingers and yanking me off balance. I crashed into the railing and nearly dropped my knife, but I soon regained my footing and reached for the tether again.

But then I noticed something odd. The rope was no longer slack. The line was creaking loudly and pulling hard on the iron winch. The deck was bouncing under me, and we were skipping over the waves, churning up a fine spray that chilled my bones.

The kites were flying high again, I realized. Our speed had vastly increased. We were traveling faster than ever before, and it wasn't Amethyst's doing. No. On her very best day, the heiress could never produce such winds.

Then a voice leapt from the darkness, and I guessed who had commanded the wind. "Did I surprise you, lieutenant? I'm so sorry." As Damascus emerged from the shadows, though, I could tell he wasn't repentant.

"I'm fine." I massaged my raw palm. "Leave me alone."

He eyed the dagger still clutched in my hand. "Come now! That wouldn't be prudent. I can't have you causing any more mischief. Not yet. Besides, there's something I've been meaning to discuss with you."

I slipped the knife back into my leather boot. "I have nothing to say to you."

"Then you can listen."

I stepped toward the hatch that led below deck. "Perhaps another time."

"*Now*, lieutenant. There will not be another time."

A strange choice of words, but I couldn't ignore a direct command, even from him. I stood livid on the bow with arms crossed. Damascus made no effort to calm me. Even in the dark, he must have suspected I would have torn him asunder if not for his position, but he only rested his elbows on the railing so he could stare off into the surrounding void. Then he sighed and waited a long time before speaking.

As the minutes crept by, I imagined grabbing his leg and pitching him overboard.

"Something's been puzzling me," he eventually confessed in a cordial tone. "Something about you. For the most part, you've been strangely predictable. Ever since you weaseled your way into Amethyst's life, in fact, you've failed to impress. That nonsense at Ballabor. Your *mistakes* in Severance. That violence against Bethel. All quite disappointing. I thought you would have improved by now."

My pulse quickened as he spoke. Did he know about the fire in Heda Fare? Had Starlight seen me?

"There have been some surprises," he added dryly. "Not many, mind you, but some. The way you ignored Captain Abner and Avram, for instance, though you must suspect their significance. And this—this tiptoeing around Amethyst. I must say I didn't want you anywhere near her, despite our agreement, so I watched you closely, but again you surprised me. You didn't try anything, despite all the opportunities presented. You only *talked* with her, as if that could accomplish anything."

"I wouldn't be so sure," I interjected, wishing he would just make his point and leave. "Talk can change a lot of things."

"Not with her. Not anymore. She's far past that, I'm afraid, far beyond your reach, and surely you must have suspected that. But you kept trying, beating your head against the granite, and I believe that leaves only one possible explanation." He slowly turned from the turbulent sea and regarded me curiously. *"You haven't figured it out yet."*

That was an understatement.

"Ha! That's it then, isn't it? Ha ha! You—you think you can turn her, don't you?" He doubled over in a fit of laughter.

I fantasized again about tossing him overboard and watching him disappear beneath the black waves. I even glanced at Abner, who was still standing behind the helm at the opposite end of the ship, and I wondered if he could see us.

Epiphany

"Oh! Oh, my dear boy," Damascus sputtered after catching his breath. "Oh—you must forgive me. I'm sorry. But there's so little that surprises me nowadays."

"Glad to help," I said mockingly. "Perhaps there will be more surprises to come."

"No—no, there won't," he promised, his solemnity returning. "There's no stopping this, not now. You're too far behind, I'm afraid. The pieces have been set already. The plan is in motion. We're far past the tipping point. It's best you just lie back. Rest a while. Enjoy the peace while it lasts."

"What do you mean?" I leaned closer, suddenly remembering my last conversation with Starlight. "What are you planning?"

"You haven't guessed that either? Pitiful."

"That doesn't mean I can't stop you," I said, wishing I hadn't put away my dagger.

"You've never been able to stop me before. What makes you think you can start now? And besides," he smirked, "all this—this *fuss* about the Cornerstone. This isn't even half of it. This is just the beginning, the first act of my masterpiece, my magnum opus. This is all but a prelude to an extraordinary symphony that will forever alter the fabric of humanity.

"And I must say, lieutenant," he sighed, "I *am* sorry for excluding you. I didn't want to. I don't want anyone to end forever, even you, and I especially didn't intend to turn your own hand against you. But you left me no choice. I'm sorry. You had your chance. You decided not to trust me, *to in fact oppose me*, despite the alternatives I provided. And now there is no forgiveness left. Not for you."

His words seemed like stonescript, cold and final, immutable and eternal. He sounded like a supreme arbiter passing judgment on a convicted traitor, and my fury yielded to dread. "So that's it?" I swallowed nervously. "You're just going to let me die?" Then another chilling thought occurred to me, and I retreated a few steps. "That's why you're here. You intend to kill me yourself."

"Come now! Don't be absurd. If it was my place to kill you, I would have done so long ago."

I sighed in relief.

"No," Damascus added before leaving me, "I'm going to let Amethyst kill you—with an arrow through the heart."

A strange verdict, I thought. Estavion usually beheaded her traitors. The Vanguard hung war criminals. I was both, though. Perhaps that's why Damascus believed I deserved a unique execution at the hands of the heiress. Still, it seemed like a waste. Shouldn't we save our arrows for the battlefield?

I was too spent by that point to care. Bitterness swelled in my heart. My every muscle twitched with fear. Confusion clouded my mind. I fretted again about Damascus, about his protocol, but I could posit no explanation. I couldn't think straight about anything, in fact. I clenched my fingers until my knuckles turned ash white, and I crashed my fist down on the *Solution*'s railing with enough force to crack the weathered board, but even that failed to clear my mind. I only felt a fresh paroxysm of agony that further fueled the tempest within.

My previous idea about severing the kites seemed pointless then. Every tortuous breath felt like a futile exercise. I couldn't avoid the coming doom. I couldn't rescue Amethyst or save myself. So why try? Damascus was right. There was no use beating against a granite wall.

Nature itself seemed to confirm my epiphany. As I submitted to my fate, a pale radiance appeared beyond the distant horizon. A violet glow grew in the east. An ominous light illuminated the bay and stung my weary eyes. I left my post and crossed the bouncing

Epiphany

deck as the *Sole Solution* sped homeward. I stumbled through the hatch to the dark hold. I fell into my hammock, and I wept until the tears ran out.

Troubling dreams pulled me into a restless slumber. I saw my murdered sister among other memories long ignored. I saw an empty Inheritance and fields black with ash. I glimpsed visions as well—images of Estavion burning and Near Thunderlun's ghosts shouting a mighty cry of victory. Perhaps I saw Damascus too. I'm not exactly sure who it was, but I saw someone like Damascus dancing at a celebration with a leather-bound book clutched in his hands and a fairy hovering near his shoulder. Lord Masada was there too, speaking kind words, though his mood quickly changed when he noticed me, and he uttered a name fleeting and unfamiliar.

Mordecai.

But it wasn't Masada's voice. It was someone closer.

"Lieutenant?"

My eyes open. The trance dissipated. I saw a rugged face bent over me. "Captain?"

"Ha! So your wits returned, have they? Damascus said you lost them last night."

I groaned, rubbed my eyes and sat up. When I looked again, I realized the hold was nearly empty. Light poured down through the hatch in a bright beam that illuminated swirls of dust. And Abner was there—Abner, who had never bothered to rouse me before. I had never even seen him below deck.

"What's wrong?"

"You overslept, pup. It's nearly dusk."

I cursed and fell from the hammock as Abner returned to the main deck. I followed him up the ladder, and when my head popped though the hatch, I glanced eastward to guess our new position. My mouth instantly fell open, though, because I didn't see the bay stretching before us, nor did I see a faint shoreline in the far distance. I didn't see the kites overhead or the sails fluttering in the wind.

Instead I saw empty masts and a vacant ship, and just off our bow I saw granite cliffs stretching into the sky. A bright citadel clutched the edge of the precipice high above, and from either side two glistening streams tumbled down until they dispersed into a white mist that blanketed the docks below: the sheltered harbor of Tel Tellesti that the Ascendants carved into the base of the bluffs.

We had returned home. We were moored to a pier amidst the Estavian fleet.

"How?" I said aloud. "I thought I had three more days."

"Damascus provided some extra wind." Abner shrugged and shifted some supply crates. "He thought haste was justified, given the circumstances."

I surveyed the empty deck and noticed the stateroom door leaning open, the cabin vacant. "He's gone?"

"He left the moment we docked this afternoon. Seemed quite impatient. Went to the citadel with Amethyst, probably to report to Uriah or the king. The crew's gone too. I thought they could use a short leave."

"But you stayed?"

"Someone had to watch the sleeping dog lie." He chuckled and wailed on my shoulder.

"I'm sorry."

"Why? Best afternoon I've had in months, all alone with the girl." He stroked the *Solution*'s weathered railing as if brushing a cherished horse. "We'll get new orders soon, sending us south again or up to the Glacian coast perhaps, and I thought she could use a tender touch before then."

I smiled. *Tender* was not the first word that came to mind when I thought of Abner.

"I wouldn't delay, though, if I was you. Once Uriah learns you're back, he'll expect a visit. You know how he is."

I did know. I knew all too well how Uriah would react after Damascus informed him about my failures. I would be fortunate to

Epiphany

leave his office on my own two legs, and in any event I would never see Abner again, or the *Sole Solution*. Or the blue sky.

So I nodded sadly and extended a weary hand. "It's been a great honor, captain. I'm sorry it had to end."

Abner reached for my wrist, and we grasped each other's forearms like old friends. "You stay out of trouble, lieutenant."

Abner returned to his chores, whistling while he worked, and I slipped below deck one final time to pack my things. Over my shoulder I slung my satchel, a heavy burden, and I climbed back up the creaking ladder. I took one last, long glance at the swift ship, at the kites folded in the corner near the bow, the wide quarterdeck where Amethyst had bested me with those gloves and the stateroom where I had learned so many secrets. Then I descended the ramp and entered the harbor.

The lower docks of Tel Tellesti were crowded with soldiers, sailors and merchants all preparing our fleet for war, so I passed unnoticed among the walkways and soon reached the foot of the cliffs. I groaned at the sight of Estelle's Ladder—the famed 3,333 steps carved into the granite. On my best days, I dreaded that laborious path, and that was not my best day.

I then remembered the lifts, though, and realized they must have been working to lower all the cargo down to the harbor, so I circled the western waterfall's undercutting and gladly found my assumption correct. I needed only to wait a little and help unload the next shipment, and then I rode the empty iron cage up the entire distance.

Once at the top, I exited the cage and passed the waterwheels and gears that powered the lifts. Then I entered the city near the outer ring and walked for hours along the ageless streets. I could have made better time, I suppose, if not for the evening crowds—if not for the fear that made each step heavier than the last—but eventually I reached the central circles and approached the inner gates. After I identified myself to the guards, I was welcomed back to the citadel of Estavion, and after a few more dozen steps, I stepped aside to vomit in the gutter.

That's when I decided to delay a little longer.

I should have gone straight to Uriah's office upon my arrival, but I couldn't. Nor could I flee, despite the fact that I probably could have walked out Tel Tellesti's gate and vanished forever before anyone knew I was missing. I was bound by oath, bound by blood, and at the very least I owed Uriah an explanation. He would soon hear the facts from Damascus, if he hadn't heard already, but he would not hear the reasons, and he needed to know those.

I couldn't bring myself to tell him, though. Not yet. Once I reported to his chambers, my life would be forfeit. I would never walk anywhere again without thick chains around my ankles and a Vanguard escort surrounding me. So I bided my time. I savored my freedom while it lasted.

I returned to the barracks, which seemed unusually empty. I dropped my satchel on my bunk and enjoyed a hot bath. I shaved my beard and washed months' worth of grime and fatigue from my skin. I changed into a new uniform with a freshly pressed vermilion cloak and polished mail that glinted like a golden coat. I wandered the empty dormitories, puzzled by the vacancy, and soon my feet found my favorite place in the whole citadel: the Vanguard training yards.

I could not linger long, but I wanted to see the open square, the polished pavement and tall pillars. I needed to see Caleb and all the other trainees who had excelled under my tutelage. Maybe I could give them one final lesson and hear the steel echo off the walls. It was time for the evening drills, after all. But I was disappointed. The yards stood empty and quiet. I saw no trainees and no instructors. They had already left for war.

Epiphany

I could delay no longer then. There was no one else to see. I could have visited Amethyst, I suppose, but I doubted Damascus would allow me near her. So I turned toward the inner halls and sought Uriah's office.

When I reached the general's door, it was already wide open. I heard restless voices inside as well and entered slowly. I found Uriah leaning over his desk, speaking with someone, but not Damascus or Abner. No, this was another man, someone I hadn't met before. He wore no uniform, but he was Vanguard surely, judging from his mighty stature and assertive composure. He was fingering the map on Uriah's desk and sharing something about the ruins of Del Solae.

It occurred to me this could be Amethyst's father. They did possess the same subtle resolve. But then Uriah noticed me, his squint narrowed, and he interrupted his visitor with a name that sounded familiar. "That's enough for today, Avram. Thank you. May we continue tomorrow morning?"

"Of course," the man replied, "though I still insist Damascus would be a far better consultant than I."

"I'm sure you're right. Perhaps tomorrow you will advise me together with your old mentor. Regardless, I'm thankful for your assistance, especially now, at such a difficult time."

"It is my pleasure and honor," Avram answered. Then the valiant man tilted slightly and departed without acknowledging me. He shut the door and left me alone with Uriah.

I immediately sought escape. "I'm interrupting. I apologize. I can return later."

"Nonsense! It's good to see you, lieutenant." Uriah circled the desk and grasped my hand. "Captain Avram was only helping with strategy, that's all. He's visited Del Solae with Amethyst and Damascus, so I requested his opinion about the lay of the land."

That's where I knew the name. Avram had been Amethyst's escort before me, and he had only stopped because of his wife's death. I wondered if he knew his duties would soon resume.

"If I had known you and Damascus were back," the general continued, "I wouldn't have bothered Avram at all. Why question the student when you can learn from the master?"

I blinked, not truly understanding and only half listening. "You didn't know we had returned?"

"Course not. How would I?"

I glanced back at the door and nervously fingered my sword. "Didn't Damascus—hasn't he come?"

Uriah shrugged and circled back around his desk. "He hasn't come here, and I haven't left this room all day."

"So—" I held my breath. "So you don't know."

"Know what?" Uriah tensed. "What happened, Mordecai?"

I sighed with relief. I had previously cursed Damascus's procrastination in Ballabor when he had delayed explaining our business to Talsadar, but now I silently blessed his oversight. Then I settled into a chair and explained everything to Uriah—except that I actually explained nothing. I spoke like a typical lieutenant giving a typical report, but in my excitement to postpone the inevitable, I lied about almost every part of our adventure.

The core details were the same, if I remember correctly. I did tell Uriah that we had left Ballabor and wandered throughout the Mediate for the better part of four months, and I included our detours to Severance and Heda Fare. I invented new reasons for our actions, however. I had grown adept at lying by then, so I quickly conjured up plausible threats. Instead of a dreadnaught, I claimed that a master assassin had snuck into Ballabor and killed General Talsadar before being caught and executed, and I said that Damascus had insisted we leave because our refuge had been compromised.

Epiphany

Then I explained how we had briefly visited Severance and Ur Thourou and Heda Fare, never lingering long in one place just to avoid possible pursuers, but throughout my story I somehow never mentioned Irrideous, the Cornerstone, my crimes, or any word about Bethel Emm and all the other miracles I had witnessed at the hands of Damascus and his protégé.

As for our untimely return? My trembling voice and fearful gaze? I blamed those on the imminent war. We had heard rumors of escalation between Near Thunderlun and Estavion, I said, thankful to finally tell the truth. We had heard reports of Samaran cavalry massing near Alzeer, and we had hastened back to Tel Tellesti to offer our assistance.

"So is it true?" I asked after finishing my story. "Are we preparing for war?"

"We are already engaged," Uriah answered gravely. "The Samarans haven't yet ventured beyond Alzeer, thankfully, but the Glacians are moving. They've eliminated three outposts around the Cradle, and they've captured every scout we've sent north of Esker. Even as we speak, a great host is massing in the mountains past ruined Del Solae."

A new terror seized me as Uriah spoke, though the words seemed familiar. The same thing had happened before the last Northern Invasion. The Glacians had assembled their armies on the mountainside and swept down like an avalanche. We had reacted too slowly to stop them, and it had taken us decades to drive them back.

"So that's why the barracks and yards are empty."

Uriah nodded. "I deployed the entire reserve three days ago to reinforce the companies I'd already sent to Esker. I'm sorry you arrived too late. I know you would have liked to bid your men farewell."

"It's no matter. I'll see them soon enough on the battlefield."

But Uriah stopped me with an upraised hand. "No, lieutenant. You will remain here with the heiress."

"What?"

"You eliminated one assassin most admirably," Uriah said, "but you never identified the conspirators. As such, Amethyst's life might still be at risk, and someone must protect her."

I laughed slightly. Uriah still believed I was a valuable asset to Amethyst. He didn't know that Damascus could confound an army with his tricks, and with her lace gloves, Amethyst could overwhelm the entire Vanguard corps.

"Something amusing, lieutenant?"

I couldn't admit the truth, so I just shrugged and said, "It's just— I mean, I didn't prove very helpful on our trip. I think Damascus is better off protecting Amethyst by himself."

"You may be correct, but Damascus isn't staying."

I blinked, befuddled. "I'm sorry. Why not?"

"He's leaving with me tomorrow."

I didn't like the sound of that. "Why? You're not expecting him to use the Cornerstone, are you?"

Uriah furrowed his brow. "The what?"

I paused, confused. Then I remembered I hadn't informed the general about the catalyst yet.

Uriah didn't wait for my answer. "I'm taking Damascus with me because he personally knows Masada."

I slowly rose from my chair. "Excuse me?"

"That's the only reason I haven't already left," Uriah said. "I've been waiting for your return, waiting for Damascus. He lived in Stonemoor with the Glacians, sometime ago. Didn't he ever mention that? He was part of Masada's council. He knows these barbarians and can think the way they do, anticipate their actions. Who knows? Maybe he can speak with Lord Masada. Talk some sense into him. Perhaps we won't have to slaughter the pale bastards and drive them back to their burrows, or maybe he'll have another plan how to stop this, something I haven't considered…"

Epiphany

The general continued, I think, but I was no longer listening. My attention had evaporated as soon as Uriah said that the old tutor knew Masada. Then my mind flashed to something else I had recently heard. I remembered how Damascus had told me there was no stopping him, not anymore.

"So what of it, lieutenant?"

I tried to focus. Was Uriah still speaking?

"Where's Damascus? You said he returned with you this afternoon," someone said. "Why hasn't he reported yet? Is he with Amethyst?"

I didn't answer. I just left. As another epiphany struck, I flew out the door without another word.

Twenty-One

"I remember that," Uriah says. "You frightened me, leaving so suddenly like that."

"I'm sorry, general."

"Oh, it's all right. Compared to everything else you've done, it's quite forgivable."

"Why did you leave?" Rehoboth interjects. "Why didn't you accuse Damascus or request an official investigation?"

"I don't know," I say. "I wanted to be sure, I guess. I only had a suspicion at that point. Nothing more. I just knew that something didn't feel right. Something didn't add up.

"But that," I continue, "that itself troubled me. After all, if Damascus *was* hiding something, and if he had any experience pretending to be something he wasn't, then figuring out the truth would be incredibly difficult, wouldn't it? I mean, Damascus is widely educated and well traveled. He's perhaps the smartest man I've ever known. So if he had some ulterior motive, he would have worked tirelessly to conceal that purpose. He would have buried it under pretense, hidden it behind half truths."

Rehoboth seems impressed with my analysis. "You believed the good tutor was capable of such deception?"

"*Any* man is capable of such deception," I stipulate. "Anyone is capable of great evil, if pushed far enough. It may take a while, and some crack sooner than others, but yes. If he believes strongly enough in a cause, a man can live a lie. He can indefinitely deceive those around him. He can invent a convincing identity, live in the midst of his mortal enemies and harbor a secret agenda for years."

"What kind of agenda? What was his plan?"

"I couldn't say. Not yet. It didn't add up."

"That's because you're only a soldier," Rehoboth reminds me with that stupid smile. "You're only a drone—a cog in a machine. You couldn't envision the big picture because that's not your job." She pauses long enough to scribble something on her notes. "You should have stopped and reported to your superiors. You should have followed procedure and trusted the system to work."

"Yes," I concede, "I should have."

ESKER

Perhaps I was only a small part of the machine, but I knew more than anyone else. I had seen and heard many phenomena unknown to Uriah, Abner or even Amethyst, and now that I had a full night's sleep and a mind racing with fresh fears, the various pieces coalesced of their own volition.

I remembered how Damascus had steered our suspicions away from Masada, though the alkali had clearly implicated the Glacian lord, and I remembered that I had never managed to explain how the dreadnaught somehow knew we would escape to Ballabor. I recalled how Damascus had conveniently offered Irrideous as the mastermind behind the attacks, even though the evidence hardly supported that assumption. I remembered Talsadar, who had first suggested that some other villain was directing Masada's actions. I thought then of Starlight, who could cross an entire continent within hours and find long lost friends, or inform assassins. And finally I remembered the plan, a protocol mentioned by both the mentor and the fairy.

I had dismissed the plan before, believing it irrelevant or at least inexplicable. Even when Damascus and Starlight had called me expendable and irredeemable, I had disregarded their cruelty. Whatever their plan might be, I had assumed it was designed to protect Amethyst and Estavion; if a worthless lieutenant had to be sacrificed in the process, so be it.

But what if I had guessed wrong?

I didn't know but I had to find out, so I rushed from Uriah's chambers. I turned left, ran down a granite corridor, and slipped into the labyrinthine hallways of Tel Tellesti's ageless citadel. I marched toward the atrium, the indoor garden where Damascus usually conducted Amethyst's private lessons. I doubted I would find them there, given the late hour, but that's where I would start. Hopefully, I would find the girl with her tutor, and I would question him thoroughly about this whole debacle. And if not? I would check his chambers. Then her chambers. I would check the royal court and the dining hall. I would search the whole palace if I had to. I would confront Damascus, beat a confession from him, and make him explain why he had never bothered to mention that he personally knew Lord Masada, our first suspect and the greatest current threat to our safety.

I never made it to the atrium, though, because halfway there I literally ran into Amethyst. Of all the soldiers, councilors and servants in those hallways, I bumped into the heiress as she was walking briskly in the opposite direction.

"Lieutenant! How are you?"

She seemed better, I immediately noticed. She was a brunette again with muted features, and though her confidence hadn't fully returned, she bore little resemblance to the frail girl I had left broken in the *Solution*'s cabin. She was also alone, though, so I ignored her inquiry and demanded, "Where is he?"

"What?"

"Where's Damascus?"

"Damascus?" Amethyst smiled at the name. "He's gone. He left soon after we returned."

"Why? Where did he go?"

"To Esker. To the battlefield," she answered, confused by my urgency. "Uriah requested his help."

How could that be? Uriah hadn't left yet. The general had specifically told me not fifteen minutes prior that he hoped to leave tomorrow with Damascus.

"Mordecai? Is something wrong?"

There was indeed something wrong, but I wasn't ready to say it yet. I needed to ask one last question, though I dreaded the answer, so I grabbed her arm, pulled her aside in the hallway, and whispered, "What about the stone, Amethyst? Tell me he didn't take it."

She physically recoiled. "I don't know."

"You didn't give it to the king?"

"No. There wasn't time. He hasn't summoned us yet."

My heart rate accelerated. "But that was the whole idea. To retrieve the Cornerstone. Present it to the king. Stop the war."

"I don't—I don't know," Amethyst insisted. "I thought we abandoned that plan after—after what happened."

Maybe she was right. Perhaps her teacher had abandoned the idea. Perhaps he had wisely realized just how perilous the stone was before locking it away forever.

But maybe not.

My thoughts swirled uncontrollably. My pulse raced. The fog lifted, and though I still wasn't certain, I strongly suspected Damascus hadn't abandoned the plan after all. Perhaps he still meant to use the stone. Perhaps he had learned how to wield it at some point in the past twenty years. But if that was true, why hadn't he told Amethyst, the king or Uriah? Why had he behaved as though he still feared the stone's power, and why had he allowed our armies to march toward a battle they could not win? It seemed pointless to withhold this incredible gift from everyone in Estavion unless—

Unless he had other loyalties.

That explanation made complete sense. Why hadn't I seen it before? How could I have been so idiotic? And I had helped the old traitor! I had murdered Fetch for him, for Estavion, but now he had the Cornerstone, and he was taking it north.

"Lieutenant?"

Amethyst's voice jerked me back to reality, and I blurted out, "Damascus is taking the stone to Masada."

"What?"

"That's why he's going to Esker."

"Lieutenant, you're not listening," she explained. "Damascus left to help *Uriah*, not Masada. He said the general requested his presence."

"Amethyst!" I seized her shoulders. "Uriah hasn't left yet."

She fell quiet. She didn't blink. The blush drained from her cheeks. "What do you mean?"

"The general isn't leaving until tomorrow, and he hasn't spoken to Damascus. Uriah hasn't seen him since our return."

"But—but Damascus—this morning."

"Listen to me. Think carefully! Are you absolutely certain you know where the stone is? Is it possible Damascus has it? Could he have taken it with him?"

Amethyst's eyes flitted from my face, to the pavement, to the ceiling. Her doubt melted into suspicion and then dread. She never answered my question, though. As soon as she understood the truth, she twisted from my grip and fled down the hall.

In a split second, the heiress disappeared down the corridor, her padded slippers silent on the stone floor. She took the first left down a winding staircase. I called loudly after her, but when I noticed how everyone else in the hallway stared at my outburst, I decided against another shout and instead chased her discretely.

I had a difficult time keeping up. Amethyst was petite and nimble compared to me, and she could slip down the crowded staircase easily while I seemingly bumped into every person between us, so by the time I reached the next level down, I had lost her. Fortunately, I had already guessed where she was going, so I didn't panic. I instead strode calmly through the next hallway, around a corner, and into the great hall. I passed the Foundation, the great table of arbitration, and exited through the hall's eastern entrance. I walked through the narthex, past the exact spot where I had stood guard those many months ago. I continued down another hallway, around a second corner, and then I arrived at my destination.

Amethyst's chambers.

The door was ajar, so I slipped inside without knocking and instantly noticed that her quarters had been beautifully restored since the explosion. There was a new cedar door, of course, and new tables and chairs all intricately carved and upholstered with satin and velvet. The granite floor had been scrubbed clean. The silver mirror and stately wardrobes had been replaced. As far as I could tell, everything was restored to its perfect condition.

Well, almost everything.

As I entered the room, I saw Amethyst scurrying about. She had already changed into a faded riding dress, and she had traded her slippers for her tall buckled boots. She had a scarf around her hair, and she was shoving various provisions into saddlebags.

It seemed pointless to ask, but I couldn't stop myself. "What are you doing?"

"What do you think?"

"You can't be serious." I stepped forward and snatched away the lace gloves she was stuffing into her bags. "You can't leave. If Damascus has stolen the Cornerstone, we must report him."

"No."

"That is our duty."

"No! You don't understand. This happens all the time."

She wasn't helping him. "What do you mean? What happens all the time?"

"This—these disappearances. These *interventions*. This isn't the first time Damascus has disappeared. He's always sneaking off to meddle. Don't you remember what he did in Severance?"

"That was different. He was visiting the archives."

"No, he wasn't," she confessed. "That's just what he told you and Captain Abner. He knew you would be suspicious, that you wouldn't understand. But Damascus didn't go to the archives. He went to see the Empress Yuridonna. He wanted to tell her about the trouble in Estavion and ask for help finding Irrideous."

"He spoke with the Empress?" I laughed and tried to imagine the old man explaining his way past the tower guards.

"You underestimate him, lieutenant. Damascus has traveled far and wide. He is renowned as the greatest mind in the Eastern Estates. His research has brought him to the attention of every ruler in the Inheritance. There are many lords who have *begged* for a few hours of his time."

"Like Masada?"

She shrugged and tossed a plump purse into her saddlebags. "Perhaps. I think that's why Damascus left. If he can speak with Lord Masada, maybe he can dissuade him."

"If he's trying to help, why keep it a secret? Why lie about leaving with Uriah?"

"Because I am an heiress to the greatest House in Estavion," Amethyst reminded me. "Think about it, lieutenant. How would it look if anyone knew my mentor was speaking with the other estate leaders at such a time?"

"It would look like treason," I said plainly.

She nodded.

I leaned closer. "Amethyst, what if this *is* treason?"

"Damascus would never hurt me, Mordecai. You know that. You've seen how he is around me. He's like—he's like a father, and he would *never* do anything to harm me."

"Perhaps," I admitted, "but what if you're wrong? What if there's even the slightest chance he's been lying? What if these visits were meant to organize something else?"

She didn't answer immediately. After a long pause, though, she stepped closer. With complete resolve, she reached for the lace gloves and pulled them from my hand. "Then I'm the only one who can stop him."

Finally.

"I'll need your help," she continued. "I can sneak out easily enough. There are secret passages Damascus showed me, but they will only take me outside the city. To reach Esker in time, I'll need a horse."

"Consider it done."

"Good. Meet me in the western fields at dawn."

I should have second-guessed her, I suppose. I should have warned her that if we were wrong, we would both be guilty of insubordination and conspiracy. I would be guilty of abduction.

But I was panicking. I wasn't thinking clearly. I only cared to stop Damascus before he could reach Esker, so I left Amethyst's room and returned to the barracks. I spent little time preparing since my satchel was still packed from our previous journey. I needed only to check that the dreadnaught vambrace remained hidden within the bag, and I slipped my dagger inside my boot. Then I visited the empty mess hall and stole a few days' worth of rations and some water skins.

After that, I snuck into the stables to find two horses, which proved the hardest part of the assignment. It was easy to move about unnoticed since I was still a trusted lieutenant and the stables were practically deserted because of the late hour and the looming war, but I had a difficult time finding two mounts suitable for the long ride ahead. Almost every animal left behind seemed sickly or small. In fact, after a thorough search I only found two horses ready for the course, and unfortunately the regal animals belonged to King Everett and his only daughter, the princess Evelyn Viticus. I couldn't steal them, could I?

Why not? I thought. Might as well add theft to the list.

I stole the two mighty horses, fit saddles onto their backs, and loaded them with my provisions. I mounted the stallion, guided the mare by its reins, and left on that mission—the last and most important errand of my life.

I rode fast through the dark, horseshoes echoing on the city pavement. In the middle of the night, I passed unchallenged through the inner gates and out of the citadel. For another hour, I galloped up the western radial avenue toward the west gatehouse. When I approached the exit, a few dozen city guards with torches and pikes stopped me, but when they saw a rider cloaked in vermilion and sitting high atop the king's horse, they forgot their questions. They offered a salute and lowered the great lever bridge; I rode across the western course of the Corde.

It was a short ride then through the hamlets and villages that hug the western limits of Tel Tellesti. I passed like a fleeting shadow along granite roads and dying farms. I soon reached the distant fields, the patchy barley crops Amethyst had chosen as our rendezvous, and I dismounted. I tied the horses to a nearby fence. I sat amongst the thin sheaves of a dismal harvest, wrapped in the Vanguard mantle to ward off the autumn chill. I watched the eastern road and waited.

I sat motionless a long time, watching for the faintest trace of Amethyst's approach. As dayspring broke the pale horizon and silhouetted the city, I watched the ancient Ascendant construct slowly awake. I studied the gray winding roads that splayed in all directions for countless leagues. I considered the majestic spires that rose high over the city like a jeweled diadem. I marveled at the mighty Corde, how the waters split into two separate courses that circled the walls before hurtling fearlessly over the towering cliffs into the bay far below. For the first time in my life, I doubted I would ever see that sight again.

And I was glad.

It was strange, how different everything seemed. How once, not so long ago, a girl had convinced me the Ascendants were venerable and benevolent, that they had left behind a birthright greater than we could ever fathom. That everything would turn out well if we only trusted and persevered.

But so much had changed since then. The innocent faith of a girl now seemed like the naïve hope of a neglected child. The wisdom of the aged now felt like a conspiracy. And the gift of our forerunners seemed more like a curse.

I used to think it breathtaking, how the river diverged into two graceful channels at the city's narrow northern edge, but it looked unnatural then. Grotesque. And just as the city split the placid river, the other gifts of the Ascendants would soon cleave the Eastern Estates. We had been lulled into false security, seduced by empty promises that left us ill prepared for the trials that followed. Instead of being strengthened by the blessings, we had been weakened and degraded until brother turned against brother, migrant against clansmen. Until a teacher betrayed his student.

And there she was, walking confidently toward me in the twilight, still believing this was all a misunderstanding.

Amethyst didn't speak when she emerged from the barley fields. Like a specter, she half floated toward the white horse, her slender arm outstretched, and the animal bowed as if they were old friends.

"Careful." I offered her the king's mare instead.

She still reached for the stallion.

"That's Princess Evelyn's horse," I warned her. "He's too spirited. I think the mare would be—"

Without answering, the heiress flung her saddlebags over the stallion's back. Then the girl climbed into the saddle. Surprised by the weight, the horse reared slightly and nearly bucked her off, but she held firm.

Once the stallion calmed and accepted its burden, Amethyst regarded me where I stood on the ground, my cloak moist with the morning dew. "Ready?"

"Not especially."

I climbed into the king's saddle regardless. Then we were off, galloping as fast as the horses could manage. I deferred to Amethyst since she knew the highlands better, and when we reached the edge of the barley fields, she turned us north toward Esker and ruined Del Solae.

We rode in silence for most of that first day, an unbearable tension weighing us down. Not that Amethyst noticed. Instead of pushing our limits, she stopped often for food and rest, and whenever we passed peasants on the road or farmers in the fields, she diverted our course to speak with the migrants. Mostly the detours were inconsequential and brief, but sometimes she would stop for whole minutes at a time to ask about troop movements or anything else out of the ordinary, and she would always superficially inquire, "You haven't, by chance, noticed an elderly gentleman riding this way, have you? You couldn't have missed him. He would have passed only yesterday."

Amethyst never received a positive answer to her question, but her confidence endured regardless. And when the sun dipped low in the cloudless sky, she reared up in a shaded glen under a great oak and announced, "We should spend the night here."

I eased my horse beside hers and glanced at the sky. "There are still hours of sunlight left. Shouldn't we press on?"

"This will suffice for today. We mustn't exhaust the horses."

I silently cursed her caution. "This is a race, Amethyst. Do you think Damascus stopped this often?"

Esker

"Damascus is innocent, lieutenant. You'll see. We must only find him before Uriah arrives."

I faulted her logic, but I couldn't argue even then. She was still my lady and my charge. I could not force her to see my point of view. I could only remain at her side, or press on alone.

I dismounted and prepared camp.

Over the next week, we pressed northward across the eastern highlands of Estavion. We made dismal time and stopped far too often, but nevertheless we reached the lower foothills and started the steady climb toward the glaciers on the morning of the sixth day. We found the tributary late that afternoon, crossed the frigid waters, and by evening we came within sight of the city of Esker and the migrant legions encamped outside the southern limits.

"Have you ever seen such a sight?" I heard myself say aloud. "Look at them!"

She did look, though she was not as easily impressed as I. From atop her panting horse she saw countless white tents spread across the rocky fields like snow on a winter's morn, like herds of sheep waiting for the harvest slaughter.

"How many, do you suppose?"

She shrugged. "If this is the whole First Company, then it's one hundred thousand. Another twenty if the Vanguard have already arrived."

Then I noticed something else in the fading light. Farther up the mountainside, passed Esker and ruined Del Solae, another massive army waited to engage ours. In the freezing twilight, innumerable torches flickered like fireflies blinking in a summer field, and they illuminated our enemy, the ghosts of Thunderlun.

"And how many are there, do you think?" I asked anxiously.

"More than enough."

Amethyst was right, of course. The outcome seemed already decided. Some day very soon, the pale Glacians would sweep down to bury our waiting host. Perhaps it would be tomorrow. Perhaps they would wait another day until Uriah arrived with our last reinforcements. Once the battle began, though, it would not end quickly or well. Casualties would number in the hundreds of thousands. The fields surrounding Esker would drown in blood. Countless fathers and brothers and sons would never return home. And when our legions failed to contain the ghosts there, conflict would spread throughout the Inheritance. Our country would write its final chapter unless we could stop the war before it started.

So Amethyst and I approached Esker.

We didn't enter the city, for there was no need. Instead, we rode directly for the nearest patrol. Amethyst in particular boldly advanced toward the picket line where twenty shivering men guarded the rear flanks, and she called, "You there! Valiant soldiers of Estavion! Hear me. We are Vanguard sent from the high general, Uriah. We bring an urgent message to Commander Lanxe. Let us pass!"

I cannot say how she already knew the commander's name, but her words won the soldiers' trust and an escort through the lines. We then passed rows and rows of tents where soldiers old and young alike huddled around pathetic campfires and waited for death in the shadow of the mountains. I looked carefully into the eyes of each man as we passed, thinking I might find Caleb. I never saw him or any of my other men, but I did notice that every soldier gazed back in wonder as we rode past. They especially noticed the proud heiress on the flashing white horse, and a hushed murmur spread throughout the gathered host.

"It's her!"

"No, it can't be. Why would she come?"

Esker

"Who else could ride that fair horse? Who else can command the White Stallion? She has come to lead us!"

I ignored the whispers. I pulled the king's horse alongside Amethyst's and spoke cautiously. "Damascus won't be here. We're wasting time."

"He's here, lieutenant," she answered, "or he would have passed through. Trust me."

I groaned. The last time I had trusted her, I had walked into a Samaran city stricken with fear and drought, and I had murdered at least two imperial soldiers before leaving. I again didn't argue, though. It was not the right time. Soon we reached the largest tent in the middle of camp, and there we dismounted and handed our reins to our escorts. I held aside the flaps so Amethyst could enter the command tent, then ducked in after her.

A blast of hot, dry air welcomed me, and my face instantly flushed. I soon noticed a tall man with sideburns standing there amidst a gaggle of tables and chairs and various other officers. They were all bent over a tattered map lying flat on a low table, doubtlessly studying the local terrain to prepare for the imminent conflict. A nearby fire provided the abundant heat and light, and when our arrival was announced, the tallest man turned and welcomed us with warmth that rivaled the hearth.

"What's this? More Vanguard? I am honored. Uriah must consider this front important indeed."

Amethyst spoke before I could. "We are only messengers, Commander Lanxe."

"A *Vanguard* messenger, and a girl at that?" Lanxe smiled. "Are the days so dire?"

"Better to be over prepared, wouldn't you say?"

The commander nodded and duly offered us some tea in porcelain cups.

"Thank you, but no," Amethyst refused. "We're on an urgent errand, one that requires utmost secrecy and haste."

"So that's why you neglected to introduce yourself," Lanxe deduced. Then he turned and instructed his supporting officers to vacate the tent.

"Oh, no," Amethyst clarified. "The message we've brought isn't for you. We've come to see Damascus."

The commander stiffened. "Who?"

"Damascus," Amethyst repeated, her voice growing strained.

Lanxe scratched his sideburns. "I'm afraid I don't know the name. Is he a captain?"

Amethyst's mouth opened but made no sound, so I spoke. "Damascus is a historian, actually. An Ascendant scholar."

"A civilian? Here?" Lanxe stifled a laugh. "Definitely not. We evacuated Esker weeks ago. We escorted the refugees to Le`Hai before we established camp."

"Damascus isn't from Esker," I explained. "He's a former resident of Near Thunderlun who now lives in Tel Tellesti. He would have come from the south, like us. General Uriah sent him ahead as a consultant."

Lanxe searched his memory but came up empty handed. He turned to his officers and relayed the name to them. I had already guessed the outcome of our visit, though, so as Lanxe conferred in private for a few moments, I reached toward a nearby table and snatched up a sheet of papyrus and a quill. While Amethyst stood in dumbfounded unbelief, I scrawled a single word on the note and folded the papyrus into my palm before anyone noticed.

"I'm sorry," Lanxe eventually said, turning back from his conference. "We haven't seen this Damascus or heard any mention of him. Are you sure you didn't overtake him?"

"It's possible." I stepped toward the exit. "We'll search the road again."

"You could also search Esker," Lanxe suggested. "I wouldn't endorse such action, not with the ghosts lurking so near, but if you would like, I could spare a small escort. It shouldn't take more than a day to cover the area."

I shook my head. "That won't be necessary. Thank you. If he's not here, he must have gotten lost along the way. We'll retrace the road and find him. Don't worry."

"As you wish," Lanxe conceded, "but be careful. And do not venture near the ruins."

I nodded thankfully and backed out. Quite abruptly, I pulled the absentminded heiress from the command tent. I paused long enough to drop my note on the dirt floor behind me, but then I pushed Amethyst out into the cold.

She seemed paralyzed at that point, stricken by her failure to find Damascus where she expected. Somehow I lifted her into a saddle, though, before mounting the king's mare and grasping her reins. Slowly, I rode us out of camp, and once we passed the final picket line, I reached over and nudged her shoulder.

"You all right? Amethyst?"

Something stirred within her. She blinked.

"Can you hear me?"

"You were right. I'm sorry, lieutenant, but you were right."

Of course I was. I didn't celebrate, though. In fact, I tried to disregard her conclusion. I couldn't have her giving up. Not yet. "Maybe I'm wrong. Maybe we outpaced Damascus."

"No. That's impossible."

"Then he's here somewhere. We just need to find him." I glanced around in the darkness to the campfires in the north and the pale outline of Esker beyond. "We could still search the city, I suppose."

"He won't be there."

"Where else then?" My eyes drifted up past ruined Del Solae. I focused on the distant torches that dotted the mountainside like stars in the cloudless sky. "It's not like we can check the Glacian camps. Even if we surrendered, they would condemn us as spies and kill us on sight."

Amethyst wasn't listening to my argument, though. She was gazing halfway up the barren mountainside—at the ancient ruins.

"Amethyst?"

"There's one more place we must look."

"Where?"

She shrugged. "Where else would an Ascendant scholar go?"

Twenty-Two

"What did you write?"

I sip a steaming cup of fragrant tea, my last delicacy before the plunge. "I'm sorry, your grace. You were saying?"

"The note you dropped for Lanxe."

I'm honestly surprised by her inquiry. "He didn't tell you?"

"No."

"Curious."

Rehoboth tries to wait, but her patience is thinning. "Answer the question."

"I had already trusted that girl with my fate once. Do you think I would make the same mistake twice?"

Del Solae

Dusk had fallen, but we lingered longer. We waited until utter darkness descended, then we started. For two hours, we followed the tumbling tributary west and north, far past the First Company's left flanks. We circled around Esker through vast, parched fields of barley and rye, and when the slopes grew too rocky for crops and the incline rose too sharply for cart or plow, Amethyst stopped and dismounted.

"We should leave the horses here," she announced sadly. "I think we've evaded the scouts thus far, but we'll never reach Del Solae unnoticed if we ride any farther."

A wise precaution. I dismounted as well, and after a brief pause to untie my leather satchel from the saddle, I chased off each horse with a slap to its rear. As the loud animals snorted and galloped away, Amethyst and I continued on foot.

Thankfully, the conditions favored our dangerous mission. There was no moon that night, and a wisp of mountain fog veiled the stars. We still crept slowly over the foothills toward ruined Del Solae, however, ever fearing the distance our sounds would carry in the crisp air. We constantly scanned the darkness ahead, always expecting at any moment to glimpse a shifting shadow or a pale, ghostly patrol.

I did not fear the Glacians. We were well prepared for such an encounter. I wore my gold-plated chainmail under a steel breastplate, and beneath my vermilion cloak I had a broadsword hanging from my belt and a dagger tucked inside my boot. There was also the satchel slung over my shoulder, of course, and the vambrace hidden within, though I desperately hoped I would never have to use that last resort. Then there was the heiress beside me, and though she looked harmless in her plain blue dress and faded woolen cloak, I knew she carried the lace gloves inside some pocket.

Those armaments would serve little comfort, though, if we were detected too soon. Our errand relied on stealth—on finding Damascus and learning his intentions before either army discovered our presence—so we crept quietly toward the ruins, and whenever we noticed movement or heard sound, Amethyst held up her hand, knelt to the ground, and patiently waited until the threat had passed.

But as we neared the ancient construct, her steps grew heavy. We slowed to a crawl, and after another hour, when at last we reached the outskirts of the ruined city, Amethyst stopped beside a crumbling column and did something I wished she hadn't. She spoke.

"How did you do it, lieutenant?"

"I do not think now is the—" but I stopped when she turned toward me and I saw the terror in her eyes. She was not afraid of the Glacians. No, she feared she might find something else, someone else, and she dreaded the choice she might soon face. So I dared to whisper, "What do you mean?"

"The fields at Veldt. Your entire unit was killed. You faced a mob of Samaran marauders all alone," she explained quietly, as if I needed the reminder, "but you didn't flee. You knew you might die, you knew it was hopeless, but you fought anyway. How did you do that?"

An apt question, considering her dilemma. I debated telling her the truth, the *real* truth about what happened—the details even the official records didn't contain. But that wouldn't help. She wouldn't understand that decision.

I thought then to tell her about Fetch. About the terrible risks I took for her, for Estavion. She might not understand that choice either, and even worse, she might blame herself for my mistakes and lose focus on the present crisis.

I had to go further back, then, and share my oldest secret, something I'd never confessed to anyone. I only needed to find the words.

Del Solae

"Veldt was easy," I stalled. "I was backed into a corner. There was no option but to torch the fields, so I don't think that story will do you much good to hear."

Her eyes fell.

"I have another story, though," I added quickly, "one that may prove fitting."

"Another battle?"

I shook my head and sat on a nearby heap of rubble. "The reason I joined the Vanguard."

She pulled her cloak tighter around her neck, and I took that as an invitation to continue.

"There was a time, you see, when I was not so different from you. It was many years ago, a different life, it seems, but once I was young too. I was the eldest son of a renowned nobleman who lived a lavish life in an old city. I wasn't a soldier then. I was an architect. And I had a sister."

"A sister?"

"Yes, a precious creature. Beautiful and fair. Graceful as a snowflake, and just as delicate. She was adored by everyone, and she was married young to a good friend of mine—my very best friend. For many years, everything was perfect, until—" My voice failed. I paused to swallow the lump forming in my throat. When I inhaled, my chest burned and my heart raced. Was this how Damascus felt when he confessed about Irrideous?

"Until?"

"She was murdered," I said. "I'm sorry to be so blunt. I don't know how else to say it. She was betrayed, and I'd rather not explain the details because—because I was the one who found her body, broken and burned."

"I'm so sorry."

I shrugged off her sympathy. "Pain eventually finds us all, Amethyst. There is no escaping it. And I accepted it, for a time. My sister would have died ultimately, as we all must when our days expire, so I did my best to move on. I left my home, to begin with, to escape the memories. I moved south and found work. I met a wonderful woman named Dinah, if you can believe that. I got married. Settled down. Started a new life."

"But it didn't last."

"It would have, I suspect, if the details had been different. I could have accepted losing my sister, even at such a young age. Many others have suffered far worse, and I didn't expect better. But my sister didn't die from drought or plague," I said, specifically referencing the reason Amethyst's own mother had perished. "My sister was *murdered*, and the killer escaped. Though he was diligently pursued throughout the Estates, he was never captured, and to this day justice has not been served. To this very hour, he walks free among us.

"I tried to forget him. I tried to ignore the ache. I couldn't do anything about him, so I focused on my new life. But the grudge festered. A darkness spread within me. And one day—" I paused for a deep breath, reluctant to continue. Though I knew Amethyst would understand me more easily than anyone else I could imagine, I still didn't want to say it. "One day my wife and I had an argument. I don't remember what it was about anymore. I don't know who started it, but I remember that I struck her."

In the dark stillness, I heard Amethyst inhale sharply, but she didn't interrupt my confession.

"That's when I realized the truth," I continued. "That's when I realized that sometimes…sometimes we can't fix the things that are broken with us. I know that's not what you want to hear. I know that's not what Damascus would tell you, but sometimes we can't fit the pieces back together. We can only push forward and try our best to survive. Sometimes our only hope is to stop the same thing from happening to someone else.

"So I left my wife. I knew I couldn't have justice *and* peace. I couldn't have happiness *and* vengeance. I made a choice. I decided what mattered most, and I abandoned all else. I left my wife and searched for my sister's murderer. And after exhausting my personal resources in that effort, I joined the ranks to survive, and—well, you know the rest."

My story abruptly stopped, and I grimaced. I wished I could have ended with the epiphany instead of burying it in the middle. Damascus would have never concluded a lesson so awkwardly.

But the heiress didn't seem to mind, and she asked almost immediately, "Did you ever catch him? The man who murdered your sister?"

"No," I shivered in the cold. "Not yet."

Amethyst hung her head, and for a long while she didn't move. But then her hands slipped inside her cloak. She fumbled with something inside her pocket. And when her slender fingers emerged again, they were gloved in lace.

"We should go."

Amethyst crept forward, and I followed like a shadow at her side. Together we approached the crumbling wreck of Del Solae, stalled at the city's edge, and stared at the desolate destruction.

It seemed strangely appropriate, I must say. It almost felt fitting that her friendship with Damascus might dissolve amidst those ruins already so familiar with betrayal. After all, it was in that very city that the Glacians had instigated the last war nearly a thousand years ago. On that dark day when the Inheritance still seemed new, the ghosts of Thunderlun had swarmed from the north and shattered our fragile peace. In a matter of hours, they had pounded the proud Ascendant construct of Del Solae into rubble before moving onward to threaten our blissful existence.

Still, if any lesson could be learned from history, I knew the dissolution of Amethyst's relationship with Damascus did not necessarily mean the end of her. Like the great king Viticus, she could assemble her strength. He had miraculously survived the long siege of Tel Tellesti, and more than that, he had created a new precedent. He had rallied the southern estates, convened a Summit, formed a new alliance and repelled the invaders. From seemingly hopeless defeat, he had risen triumphant. With the ruined granite of Del Solae, he had even built a new city of the Inheritance and proudly named it Esker.

In similar fashion, I hoped history would repeat. I hoped Amethyst would prove strong enough to salvage the fragments of her life. I hoped that she, like our lauded ancestors, would gather the rubble, start fresh and build something better. But to do that, she had to survive the next few minutes. To be reborn, she must first perish. So when she hesitated at the city's edge, I silently moved ahead, and the heiress followed me into that graveyard.

The little warmth remaining in my blood immediately stole away. In the late watches of the night, a choking fog descended. The ruins of Del Solae seemed then like a haunted forest of cold granite, eerie and silent.

We crept even more cautiously than before, picking our path through the rubble under half-collapsed arches and over fallen walls. We stalked through spacious homes with walls and roofs smashed apart from an ancient onslaught. We walked over long radial avenues and curved granite streets that mirrored so many other Ascendant cities. We crept through empty squares where markets had no doubt been held, and we passed fountains and pools long since quiet and dry. All the while, we searched for signs of her tutor or a Glacian patrol, but we found nothing.

The minutes turned into hours, and still we continued in vain. My stomach tightened with hunger. My freezing lips cracked with thirst. Amethyst must have felt even worse than I, but she diligently pressed deeper into the city and closer to the Glacian camps on the opposite side.

Then a faint glimmer appeared in the eastern sky, and new fear seized me. I abruptly turned in the dark, and when Amethyst noticed my reversal I explained, "We've gone too far. We must go back. Sunrise cannot find us still in the city, not with the horde so near."

"But we're almost there."

"What?" I scanned the dark streets again for any trace of movement or glint of torchlight. I listened for voices too, or for the clink of armor. "I can't hear anything."

"Nor I, but I think—I think I can *feel* something."

"The stone?"

"I hope not." She moved forward regardless.

I followed, and for the next few minutes Amethyst tracked an invisible trail like a hound. She strode straight down a corridor and turned left into a crumbling alleyway. We crossed through the next intersection, detoured left around a ruined home, and squeezed through a cracked wall.

Then I saw what Amethyst had felt—a faint glimmer in the distance. A fairy perhaps? No. As we drew closer, I saw a warm glow dancing in the freezing night. A campfire.

Without a word, Amethyst and I crept closer, always hidden behind some rubble. We stepped over debris and crawled under a fallen tower that blocked half an avenue. We reached a wide, dry canal with a broken bridge, so we slid down one embankment and clambered up the other. Our progress slowed considerably, but we still neared the light sooner than I desired. Then we stopped, knelt behind a toppled pillar, and peaked over the edge into the empty avenue beyond.

We couldn't hear much at that distance, but we were close enough to see two men. One sat with his back toward us, a white hooded cloak draped over his head and shoulders, so we couldn't guess who he was, but the man across from the stranger was easy to identify. The flickering flames clearly illuminated his white beard and twinkling eyes, and when he chuckled at something his mysterious friend said, the laughter bounced from wall to wall until it rang in our ears like a bell.

"Damascus."

As I said his name, panic gripped my heart, and though we had dared the ruins to confront the old man and wrest the Cornerstone away, the idea now seemed suicidal. How could we ever defeat that wizard? What if he turned the catalyst against us? What if that was Lord Masada sitting across from him, and what if there were other ghosts lurking nearby in the shadows?

I almost suggested we leave. I nearly told Amethyst that we should retreat and notify Lanxe. As I opened my mouth to speak, though, I thought of the First Company. I remembered Caleb and all the other soldiers encamped beneath Esker. I imagined what might happen if Damascus used the stone against them.

So I reached for my sword. I drew slowly so the folded steel would not ring against the sheath. I whispered, "Ready?"

Her hand grasped my shoulder. "No! Not yet."

"Amethyst, this is why we came."

"Is it, lieutenant? Look at them."

I did look again, and I had to admit this hardly seemed like a clandestine meeting intended to transfer a deadly weapon. There was no haste, no secrecy. They were laughing. Sharing old stories. "But what else could it be? Why venture this far?"

"We must be certain. We will not attack. Not until I know."

She was still unconvinced. A part of her still hoped he had only come to talk. Very well. We would sneak closer then. We would wait while Damascus meddled with Masada or whoever his strange friend was. We would stay until we heard the teacher speak clearly of the stone, and then we would spring my trap. To that end, I sheathed my sword, lifted the satchel's strap higher onto my shoulder, and stepped around the toppled pillar.

That's when the ghost moved behind us.

He timed his surprise perfectly, I must say. He waited until my sword returned to its scabbard and I was mid-step and off balance. Then he moved like a cloud in a night sky, and before I could cry a warning, the Glacian warrior ambushed us.

I realized then why we call them ghosts. Besides his silent approach, this enemy indeed resembled some ephemeral spirit clad in silver. He wore ceramic armor beneath sheer, billowing robes that fluttered in the cold wind, and he towered over me, strong and deadly, with even his face painted white. Or was that his actual skin color? I couldn't tell. I wasn't paying attention to those details. I was distracted by the long battle-axe in his hand, its razor tip a mere handsbreadth from my throat.

Worse yet, he wasn't alone. After the first ghost emerged from the shadows, a dozen more appeared and surrounded us with axes, maces and war hammers. Hands assaulted us. Something hard struck my skull from behind, and when I bent over in pain, someone swept my sword from its sheath while someone else yanked the satchel from my shoulder.

Through it all, Amethyst did nothing. She still wore her lace gloves, and she could have effortlessly flung off our adversaries, but she surrendered and offered no resistance.

"Why are you stalling?" I growled. "Do something!"

Before she could answer, another blow struck my head and everything went black.

I regained my senses only a few moments later, I believe. I felt two strong arms under mine. I heard my boots scraping the granite streets. I was being dragged, I realized, toward a faint light. Toward a campfire.

I found my footing and managed to half-walk, half-stumble the last few paces. Then I raised my head and saw Damascus still sitting behind the small fire, though his strange companion had vanished. Before I could guess where the hooded man had gone, my support suddenly disappeared. I tripped and almost fell into the glowing embers. My head bounced against the pavement, and when I picked myself up, I could feel the heat from the flames singeing my hair.

"Thank you, lieutenant," an old voice said. "That will be all."

I blinked, confused by his statement and half-blinded by the blood trickling from a gash on my forehead. As I wiped my eyes and looked again, though, I realized Damascus wasn't speaking to me. He was addressing someone behind me, issuing orders to the ghost who had captured us.

As if to confirm my suspicions, the Glacians moved away. They vanished again into the shadows, taking my broadsword and satchel with them. They left me alone with Damascus.

No. Not entirely alone. Amethyst was beside me, in body at least. Her mind seemed lost, though, confused and horrified by these new facts: her Vanguard escort was so easily fooled; her mentor commanded our enemies; we had been left unguarded, our hands and feet unbound; and worst, I might have been right all along.

Damascus did not clarify these strange matters. He was not embarrassed or surprised that we had caught him. Nor was he angry that Amethyst was here or had not trusted him. He was not even gloating at his victory over us. Instead, he was cautious. Reserved. It was almost as if he'd been expecting us. As if he had known all along what we would do, though he had hoped for something better.

Then he spoke, and his words confounded her further. "You disappoint me again, Mordecai. You still think you can turn her against me?"

Del Solae

I could not answer or understand his reference. My recent injuries still left me unfocused.

"And you, my child. We are beyond this, aren't we? You have witnessed my methods time and time again. You know why they are necessary. Must I prove myself once more?"

"Yes." I finally lifted myself up. "Prove it. Prove that the Glacians don't follow your orders."

"I do not answer to Vanguard, least of all you."

"Then answer to her." I wobbled to my feet. "Tell her that Masada didn't bomb the citadel at your instruction. Convince her you didn't bring the dreadnaught to Ballabor."

He sputtered at the absurd suggestion.

"Did they burn the brothel," I asked, adding my own crimes to tip the scales. "Did they kill Irrideous?"

"Come now, lieutenant! You know full well what happened to Irrideous," Damascus spat, almost losing his temper.

"Stop! Stop it, both of you!" The girl stepped between us. "I swear! If you two don't stop arguing, I'll have you both imprisoned for insubordination."

Her authority silenced us momentarily. Damascus especially hung his head with unexpected shame.

"There is no time for this," Amethyst started again, "and I'm sorry we interrupted your—your meeting, Damascus, but we must leave before we're found. Uriah may have already arrived in Esker. War may come with the morning, and we cannot be caught in the ruins."

The heiress took a decisive step away from the campfire and toward the direction from whence we had come. I followed after her, my legs still unsteady.

But the old man held his ground.

"Damascus?"

"I'm sorry," came his reply, "but we cannot leave. Not yet."

Her voice rose hopefully. "You can stop this?"

"No, that's not it. There's no stopping the war, I'm afraid."

"Then we must go." Amethyst took another step backward. "Why else would we stay?"

Still her tutor stayed near the fire, his expression strained.

Amethyst's voice cracked. "Damascus?"

He didn't answer.

"Can't you see?" I whispered. "Here's your proof."

"No."

"Ask about the Cornerstone," I suggested.

"No! Damascus, tell him he's mistaken!"

Again, her mentor's silence contradicted her words.

"No," she said, her voice barely audible above the cold wind. "Damascus? Please!"

"Amethyst, listen. This is not what it seems."

"NO!" she suddenly shouted. "No more games. No more lessons! Stop treating me like a child and tell me the truth. Tell me you don't have it."

I held my breath. For an interminable moment, no one spoke. Amethyst glared at her tutor while he considered the dying fire.

"But I do, my dear," Damascus finally confessed, a tear streaking from his eye. "I took the stone with me, since I could not leave it unattended. I brought it here, because there are some things that cannot be left to chance."

Her hand rose to cover her mouth.

"But this is for your good, Amethyst! For the greatest good of the world! You must believe me."

She began to weep.

"This—this is the only way!"

The girl stepped back, almost as if she meant to flee into the darkness. Sensing her panic, Damascus stepped forward as well, his hand outstretched as he called her name.

I stepped between them.

Del Solae

I had expected this outcome, after all, and now that Amethyst knew the terrible truth, I meant to force her hand. So I stepped forward. Though I could never hope to counter Damascus without my sword, I stepped between that villain and the heiress. I offered myself as the bait, hoping that Amethyst would rescue me the way I had rescued her from the Samarans. The way she had saved half of Ballabor's garrison from the dreadnaught.

I was still dizzy at that point, and I doubted my ability to throw an effective blow, so I threw my weight into Damascus and pushed him with both arms. He stumbled and almost fell backward into the fire, but he regained his footing. Quickly I pressed forward again, hoping he wouldn't have time to reach into his robes and produce some artifice to annihilate me.

The old man had no need for such tricks, however. He still had other sentinels waiting in the shadows. As soon as I rushed, in fact, Damascus spoke a single command, and pale figures leapt from the darkness. Strong fingers grasped my wrists from my left and right, and two enemies yanked me back.

I was expecting their ambush this time, so when a third ghost emerged, my boot snapped up and found his jaw. Then somehow I twisted free from the man on my left, and my fist found his eye. The third man also fell once the odds were even and the fear of death cleared my senses.

There were countless other ghosts lurking in the ruins of Del Solae, though, and no sooner had I defeated the first three than a dozen more took their place. They instantly surrounded me, their white cloaks forming a billowing wall that trapped me alone with the fading fire, and they attacked without pause or warning.

I moved fast and well. If Uriah could have seen me, he would have been impressed. These were not starving imperial guards, though. They were Masada's elite, and while the first three had seemed content to merely restrain me, the reinforcements were determined to break me. They swung hammers at my head and axes at my neck, and when I ducked under those, they kicked me with studded boots and struck me with maces.

One ghost in particular broke formation. This was the same Glacian lieutenant that Damascus had addressed before, I think, judging from my satchel still hung from his shoulder, and he knocked me backward and raised his axe for a deadly blow. I leaned forward desperately, hurtling my fist into his stomach before he could land the stroke, but I somehow forgot about his armor. Instead of hitting chainmail or leather, my clenched fist slammed into a hard ceramic plate, and fingers broke. I stumbled back, hunched over and cradling my splayed hand, and then his axe pommel struck my skull again.

I collapsed in a heap, my face fallen against the pavement and my limbs limp. Somehow I kept my eyes open, but I could not focus on anything distinct. I could only see a flickering light somewhere close by, and I could hear laughter and footsteps closing in around me. Then a boot came to rest on my back. An incredible weight pushed me down. A cold steel edge lightly touched my neck as if an executioner were lining up his swing.

"Careful," a mocking voice said. "This is the one Damascus warned us about."

My blood stirred proudly when I heard those words, and I wished I could prove Damascus right, but at that point I couldn't even stop my drool from dribbling onto the freezing pavement. I thought of Caleb waiting for war and death in the shadow of the mountain. I thought of Gideon and Talsadar lying unavenged in their graves. I even thought of my sister, and I imagined it was her murderer standing on my neck. But still I could not summon the strength to rise, and when the ghost lifted his deadly axe, I could only think to shout one name:

"AMETHYST!"

And finally, the girl came.

An alarm rose from the gathered enemies, and though I could see nothing, I heard ceramic armor shatter and maces clatter to the ground. Shrieks and war cries resounded all around me; I heard more boots in the distance dashing across the streets to reinforce the ghosts, and from somewhere nearby an old voice cried out, "Stop!"

His words went unheeded, though, and then the foot on my neck lifted as that enemy joined his comrades. I still could not stand, but I rolled onto my back and watched with wonder and horror as a blur of blue wool tore the Glacians apart. Though tears clouded my vision and a throbbing headache dulled my wits and memory, I'm certain that Amethyst stood as my sole shield as wave after wave of ghosts emerged from the ruins to vainly crash against her.

She spun like a bucking stallion, throwing men back into the darkness from whence they came. As Glacians screamed and charged, she neutralized their axes and hammers with lace. And when another dozen white-clad soldiers rushed from the north and into the dim firelight, she turned away from me to answer them with her own fierce cry.

But then soft feet stepped over me. Linen robes passed by. An old figure moved silently behind Amethyst, a withered hand outstretched toward her.

"Behind you!"

She turned just in time. Her gloved fist struck his shoulder like a battering ram. Damascus flew back, spinning like a top before he crashed into a ruined wall.

No sight had ever pleased me more.

When she saw who had almost surprised her, Amethyst turned and stood over him. While Damascus raised his arm in defense, the heiress raised hers to attack. When he again cried out for her to stop, she answered with a quivering voice, "Don't you dare! Don't you ever dare to command me!"

"But my dear girl, I was not commanding you."

Confused, she looked behind her and saw that the ghosts had ceased their assault. They held a line near the limits of the light, their pale faces furious at the sight of a slender migrant heiress standing above the old man—at the sight of the numerous injured and fallen that already littered the ruins. But they obeyed the voice of Damascus.

Then that voice spoke to the girl. "Have I ever commanded you? Have I ever overstepped my bounds? Have I ever taught you falsehood or given you reason to doubt?"

"Don't listen to him!" I pleaded.

She hesitated, her fist still raised high. I saw her consider me, then the anxious ghosts, and then her fallen teacher.

He tried again. "Amethyst, you must trust me!"

"But you took the stone!"

"I took it, yes, but not for the purpose you suppose."

"Then return it." She reached down with her free hand. "Give me the relic!"

"That would not be wise, I think."

"Damascus, what do you—no! Give it to me!"

"Take it!" I shouted. "What are you waiting for?"

"Be silent, lieutenant," she screamed. Then she pressed her eyes shut. "You will give me the stone, Damascus. Now! This is not a request. It's a command."

He nodded solemnly. Then, revealing a strength I didn't realize he still possessed, he managed to bring himself to his feet. "And if I refuse?"

"Please," she begged. "Do not refuse."

"But I'm afraid I must, my dear." He rose to his full height, his hands open and defenseless. "You cannot possibly survive the stone, not now. I am sorry. I will not surrender it to you. You are left, then, with one simple choice."

"No, Damascus—"

"Yes, my dear. You must trust me, or you must kill me."

War and Death

That was her moment of decision. As Damascus stood silent and defenseless, Amethyst had the chance to choose our destiny. Prove her worth. Take the stone. Save the Inheritance. All she had to do was strike.

"Take it!" I shouted. "Kill him!"

Amethyst tightened her gloved fist and held her breath, but Damascus made his own wordless plea. As the girl weighed her options and searched his eyes, her teacher stared back. He answered her anger with mercy and countered her doubts with assurance. With a look, he shattered her heart into a million fragments, and then he made it whole again.

"No! Don't you—Amethyst! Stop!"

But I spoke too late. Her clenched fingers relaxed. Her arm lowered, and her eyes slid shut. Tears poured forth, and the brave heiress reverted into a frightened girl. She wept aloud, buried her face into her mentor's chest, and held him tightly as sobs wracked her body.

"It's all right," he whispered, stroking her brown hair. "I'm here. Everything will be all right."

Then he noticed me again, and his fury burned.

I was still sitting on the cold pavement, my left hand broken and my spirits crushed. I was unarmed and alone, and the ghosts of Thunderlun were surrounding me again. As soon as Amethyst had surrendered, they had breached the limits of the firelight to tend their wounded and help Damascus. Within a few seconds the Glacian lieutenant was standing over me again, his battle-axe impatiently awaiting instruction.

Damascus nodded at me. "Get rid of him, Ataca." Then he turned and led Amethyst away. The teacher took his student north into the darkness toward the Glacian camps. He left me with the ghosts in ruined Del Solae.

"On your feet," the Glacian lieutenant growled.

When I didn't immediately comply, two other men reached down and jerked me up. Then a blade jabbed into my back with enough force to dent my steel breastplate. Soon I was walking forward, leaving the campsite, stumbling in the dark, tripping over debris, and wandering through the wrecked city with no clue as to my location or direction.

"Where are we going?"

A quick kick to the back of my knees was my only answer, and then I was pulled up again by at least three hands and pushed forward by another two. I didn't count the odds, though. Nor did I wonder where they were taking me or why they didn't kill me on the spot. I could only think of Amethyst, the heiress who had been betrayed by her greatest friend. I cursed the man who had won her trust and tricked her with love, and I hated myself for leading her into such a trap. I had let Damascus escape and now a murderer walked free.

Worse of all, her father would never know what happened to his daughter. He would never again know peace.

That thought finally ignited the rage. Fresh energy—or maybe it was the freezing cold, I don't know—set my hair on edge and raised bumps on my skin. When the enemy lieutenant shoved me again, I didn't stumble. I instead shot forward and bolted away from my escort and into the darkness.

Not ten steps later, a short axe spun past my ear, ricocheted off a wall before me, and clattered to the ground. Then the ghosts gave chase, but without a sword bouncing at my side or a satchel swinging on my shoulder or even a weapon in hand, I outpaced them. I leapt over collapsed walls and sprinted through the ruins.

War and Death

Help could not be far off. I only needed to escape the city. Surely if I reached the limits of Del Solae and entered the fields around Esker, the ghosts would cease their pursuit. They wouldn't risk being spotted by our scouts, would they? Surely they wouldn't start anything yet. Not in the dark, and not without Masada's express command.

So I ran. Within seconds I reached the ruined bridge and vaulted over the dry canal. I dove through a smashed window and fell through an empty doorway. I willed myself forward, pushing past the pain and disorientation of my previous loss. I promised myself I would see the coming sunrise.

But the ghosts had no intention of letting me escape, and despite my considerable lead, they closed fast. They knew the city better than I, and more importantly they were not alone. As they chased me, they cried alarm and blasted horns, blatantly disregarding their previous stealth, and from all around, more ghosts emerged from the dark ruins. They came fast, their pale cloaks billowing in the mountain air. From my left, twenty Glacians rushed from a wrecked home. To my right, twice that many climbed from another dry canal. My pursuers swelled to fifty. Then hundreds. Then thousands, or perhaps more.

Amethyst and I had somehow snuck past an entire army, I realized then. Or they had allowed us through. Under specific instructions, probably, the ghosts had assembled and hidden a whole company in the ruins. They had let us slip inside the city past countless waiting ambushes, knowing all along that we would be captured eventually.

Now I alone was escaping with a horde at my heels. I ran south hardly ahead of a line that stretched unendingly to the east and west. I retraced our steps. Though it had taken hours to sneak into Del Solae and reach the campfire, I reached the outskirts in a matter of minutes. There the ruins grew less frequent. The granite forest thinned. I reached the edge of that broken city.

And I found another great host waiting.

I slid to a halt, my boots slipping on the frozen pavement. With horror, I looked at a second line stretching far to the left and right ahead of me. It was difficult to discern anything specific in the pale blackness, but I could make out dark cloaks, polished mail, pikes that rose above the gathered men like grass in a field.

No. It couldn't be.

I heard a shout. At my arrival, an unseen officer ordered a distant marshal to fire. From far behind this new line, a trebuchet launched a burning missile into the sky. The flare arced high overhead, over the waiting army, over me, and into the ruins beyond. From that faint light, I knew that I stood at the shore of a vermilion sea.

Lanxe had come at last.

He must have deciphered my message. Though I had only written "ruins" on my note, the commander had guessed our destination (though I'm sure he never suspected the reason for our errand). He had even assigned his best trackers to follow us. He could not deploy the First Company, not without the king's permission, but he had done the next best thing. He had moved the Vanguard corps under cover of darkness. He had apparently positioned a few batteries of trebuchets and catapults as well, because as soon as the scouts reported movement in the ruins, he launched more brimstone flares. Flaming meteors filled the night sky. I clearly saw twenty thousand migrants waiting to welcome me.

But then I heard a dreadful roar rising close behind me, and I remembered why I had been running. I glanced back at the ruins and saw the massive Glacian horde still coming, undeterred by the missiles raining into their ranks. I bolted away again, flying over the barren fields and parched grass. I finally left the ruined city and led the ghosts of Thunderlun toward my brothers; as I approached the line, I cried out and waved empty hands.

"Stop! Don't shoot. Vanguard—I'm Vanguard!"

There was no need for such desperation. They had already seen my plight and noticed my uniform. The crest parted, and I plunged

War and Death

into an ocean of swords, shields, pikes, armor and men. Vermilion mantles enveloped me. For a fleeting moment, I was safe.

Then the horde crashed into the migrants. Del Solae hurled its hidden terror upon us. I witnessed the first battle of a war that would eventually consume the Estates.

A war I had started.

I can barely describe what happened next. The tide surged around me. Trumpets blared. The Vanguard pressed forward. More lights streaked overhead. Catapult shots crashed around us, crushing friend and foe alike. Arrows whistled. Spears were hurled. Shields were hewn. Thousands of men shouted and hacked and pushed and killed and died.

Both sides fought bravely. Within ten seconds, I saw deeds worthy of tale and song. But they were wasted. Though the ghosts and Vanguard had all promised to fight for king and country, for lord and estate, for families and friends, I knew the bitter truth. They battled and died because of a stone. Because of a girl who could not face her fears. Because of me. I wanted nothing more than to stop all of it, and somewhere in that chaos, I found a chance to do just that.

Somehow, either by fate or luck, I noticed a certain ghost among the thousands of Glacians who assaulted our line. He tore three of our men apart with a battle-axe, and he raised his arm in victory for a split second. Then he shouted some command to his own men before entering the fray again, and I couldn't hear what he said.

But I saw my satchel hanging from his shoulder.

I had no sword at that point. No spear. No shield. I only had a dagger in my boot, which hardly seemed adequate, but I didn't care. I would not lose her again, not to him. So I raced through the surging swells of men and steel. I reached the churning border between Estavion and Near Thunderlun. I hurled myself into that nightmare.

Using my shoulder as a ram, I crashed through the Glacian line. Then I ducked under a spiked mace and slammed my one good fist low into an enemy stomach where armor did not protect him. An axe struck my arm, but it glanced off my chainmail and only bruised the skin underneath. Then a war hammer bounced off the steel plate that protected my back. I somehow pushed on, though, and as I approached the lieutenant who had stolen my sword and bag, I leapt into the air, flung myself on top of him, grabbed the satchel, and pulled until the strap broke.

As I fell back hard on the pavement, the enemy lieutenant saw me clearly enough to recognize who I was. Then a cruel smile spread across his pale face, and he lifted his axe. In the same instant I lifted the flap and reached inside the satchel. I felt cold stone and drew out the dreadnaught armor. I slipped that damned vambrace onto my forearm.

I embraced the curse.

Instantly, an empowering wave of adrenaline surged through my veins. My pupils dilated and every hair on my body stood erect. The heavy obsidian armor grew feather light, and I became aware of everything around me. Despite the crushing darkness, I could *feel* the ghosts of Thunderlun surrounding me. There were twelve immediately behind me, and another eight before. Beyond them there were hundreds and thousands swarming through that ruined city. Then there was the Glacian lieutenant, of course, his sharp axe still flying toward my head.

I didn't pay him much attention, though. I was distracted by something else. I could feel something moving north. Something powerful and irresistible.

The Cornerstone.

I moved at last. With inconceivable speed, I turned toward the ghost above me, his axe still in hand. He had started the blow hours ago, it seemed, and even now his swing looked impossibly slow, as if pushing through mud. He stood motionless above me, an easy target, and when I drove my foot upward into his chest, I felt his ceramic armor crack and his sternum snap. Whether that killed him instantly, I cannot say, but he lost his grip on the axe as he flew backward and screaming into a dozen other men.

Then I was on my feet and charging north through the enemy ranks like a bull through reeds. The other ghosts shouted alarm and converged against me, but I cast aside whoever blocked my path. Though still unarmed, I possessed an excessive advantage. I had the vambrace, and that single piece of armor endowed me with the strength of ten men. Without hammer or mace, I flung soldiers left and right.

At last I understood how the dreadnaught had ravaged Ballabor's defenses so easily, and beyond that, I realized how much pleasure he must have derived from such destruction. I also took joy in that violence, and as the countless ghosts assaulted me, I laughed as they fell under the might of my arm. Blinded by such unprecedented power, I became a force of nature. Unstoppable. Undiscerning. Insatiable. Unrepentant.

Irredeemable.

I crashed northward through ruined Del Solae with no need for a sword. The entire city became my weapon. I scooped up pieces of rubble and hurled those blocks like catapult missiles, taking out multiple men at once. I disarmed ghosts with a slap of my hand and blocked heavy war hammers with an outstretched palm. I grabbed one man's arm and tossed him into the air, then seized another man's leg and wielded his entire body like a club to carve a path through the horde.

In the mayhem that followed, I honestly don't know how many I wounded and killed. The entire battle seems a blur, and I can't recall specifics. Maybe the bloodlust tainted my memory, or perhaps the vambrace poisoned my mind. Maybe the thought of rescuing

Amethyst blinded me to everything else. I only know that I crushed everyone who approached me as I retraced my steps, and sooner than expected, I reached the rear limits of the Glacian horde and burst free. Then I moved farther northward and returned to the campsite.

Damascus was no longer there. Nor was Amethyst. Even the fire had disappeared, leaving behind only a few faint embers and some gray ash as proof of its existence. That entire sector of the city now seemed desolate, but somewhere in those ruined streets an old man was still leading a frightened girl, and I finally had the means to oppose him.

I set off again, running faster than ever through the vacant ruins. I followed a vague feeling that pulled me like a compass needle. A few more patrols surprised me along the way, but I quickly destroyed them, and at last I came to the granite avenue.

I could see him ahead in the dark. Or I could feel him. There was little light in that section of the city, though the faint eastern glow was growing with a promise of sunrise and perhaps Glacian reinforcements. I would be long finished and gone before then, however, especially since Damascus hadn't yet noticed me.

He was walking slowly, moving between two long, high walls that flanked the wide street. His back was turned toward me, and I could not see Amethyst with him. He still had the stone, though. I knew that. And I would take it from him. I would do what Amethyst could not, and more. Then I would somehow find the girl afterwards and escape.

I don't know how I was thinking so clearly, especially with the vambrace wrapped around my forearm and its elixir poisoning my

War and Death

veins. Its effects had previously only confounded my judgment and clouded my mind. Somehow I could see clearly this time, and I even knew enough to fear Damascus. Or maybe I feared his knowledge. In any event, I didn't engage him directly. Even with the obsidian armor, I suspected the old man would offer an adequate counter offense if given the opportunity to defend himself, so I sought a way to deny him that chance, and I soon remembered the dagger in my boot.

I reached inside the leather and grasped the carved ivory handle. I took a few more steps, trying to judge the distance in the dim light. I flipped the knife around and fingered the blade. Then I took two long strides forward and hurled the dagger with all my might at the mentor's back. It flew straight and true with the speed and accuracy of an archer's arrow.

I made too much noise, though, and Damascus somehow heard. He pivoted and stepped to the side, turning curiously toward the sounds. My knife flew past him, toward the person walking directly before him—the girl I had failed to notice.

And I heard her shriek as the dagger struck.

"Amethyst!"

I rushed forward. What had I done? How could I have been so inept? I had misjudged every turn, wasted every opportunity. Even when Damascus had his back turned, I couldn't fulfill my promise. I couldn't protect my charge.

I could still kill the man responsible, though.

So I surged down the avenue, crying out ravenous threats. I promised to rip Damascus apart and make him suffer. He would answer that day for the Vanguard of Ballabor. For Talsadar and Gideon. For Caleb and the men who were dying that very minute in the southern part of the city. He would pay for my sister, even, and at last I would take vengeance on someone.

Damascus never answered me. Nor did he mourn Amethyst. He only stood motionless in the dark and considered me with strange pity as I advanced. He moved neither to the right nor left, forward nor back. And when I drew close enough to gather momentum, he only shifted his feet. As I lifted my fist, he raised an open palm. As I prepared a deathblow, he whispered an ancient curse.

And a bolt of lightning exploded from his hand.

It wasn't as large as the thunderbolts at Spiderclaw, but it was enough. The blast struck my chest and spread through my armor. The vambrace leapt off my arm. My gilded chainmail became a glowing coat of torturous agony, but I didn't feel the pain for long. There was only a violent jerk that emptied my lungs and snapped my back. Then nothing. No pulse. No breath. My vision blurred. My arms stopped moving. My legs buckled, and try as I might, I could not will them forward. I couldn't make any part of my body do anything whatsoever.

I could only fall dead on the pavement.

Twenty-Three

"Dead?"

"Dead," I repeat.

Rehoboth glances at Uriah, but the general only stares back. She tries again. "You mean you were knocked unconscious."

"I was dead, your grace."

Rehoboth marks her notes, but she doesn't argue. Instead she casually asks, "What was it like?"

"Excuse me?"

"Being dead."

I laugh awkwardly, comb my fingers through my hair and stroke my chin. All the while, I avoid eye contact with both the arbiter and the general, and I wonder how I can explain it. If it can even be explained.

Eventually I just say, "It wasn't like anything. I was dead. I felt nothing. I *was* nothing."

"No bright light? No tunnel? No chorus of angels welcoming you to paradise?"

"No."

"Not even fire or brimstone?"

"Nothing."

Rehoboth doesn't bother to copy that down.

"Then how do you know what happened next?" Uriah asks.

"Amethyst told me."

"And you believe her?"

"Why wouldn't I?"

THE LAST OPTION

Amethyst lay where she had fallen in the avenue, my dagger lodged in her shoulder, grinding against muscle and bone. After ensuring I would not threaten her again, Damascus approached the girl and held her down.

"Shhh! Quiet now. It's all right."

"Damascus?"

"I'm here. Steady, girl. Hold tight. This will hurt a little."

With great pain, he pulled the knife from her flesh while the girl screamed in agony. After he removed the long blade, he flung it into the darkness where it clattered against an old ruined wall in Del Solae. Then he lifted Amethyst.

"Not too quickly. Carefully now! Hold my hand."

Amethyst noticed blood gushing from her wound, and her head grew light, so she tightly grasped her teacher's right hand while his other made short work of her injury. His gentle touch stopped the bleeding, and a few mystic words closed the wound. She still breathed hard for the next few minutes, but the pain eventually passed.

Then she lifted her eyes. She saw my body in the avenue with a smoldering hole burned through my breastplate, mail and tunic, and a different pain welled in her heart. "Mordecai?"

"It's done, my dear," Damascus answered. "Finished."

She tried to crawl toward me, but her teacher held her back.

"No, child. There's nothing you can do."

"But Damascus, you didn't—"

"I'm sorry, but I did. I had no choice. He attacked you."

"He didn't mean it."

"Oh, he did, in fact. He meant it more than you can yet grasp. But it's finished now. He can't hurt you anymore."

"He was my guardian," she lamented. "How will I ever explain this? How can I ever—"

"You must accept this. You can't change it."

"But can't we do something? Can't you help him?"

"What?"

"You've fixed me so many times. Can't you do the same for him? Just once?"

Damascus lowered his eyes. "It doesn't work that way, I'm afraid. This is different. I can repair a damaged cup so it no longer leaks, but I cannot replace the water once it has run out. That power is far beyond me. It is beyond any of us."

Amethyst hung her head as the sounds of distant battle reached her ears. Soon the ruins would be filled with more blood, and she was just as powerless as I had been. She couldn't stop any of it.

But then she remembered the reason for all this.

"Damascus?"

"Yes, my dear?"

"Do you still have it?"

"Do I have *it*? You mean the stone?"

"Yes."

For a brief moment he kept silent while Amethyst shivered in the cold, but soon he confessed, "Yes, I have it."

"Do you think—"

He waited for her to find the words.

"Do you think it can work?"

"Perhaps. Perhaps not. I don't think it's a good idea to try."

She knelt beside me. "But it *might* work."

"It's possible, but would you really have me try it again, despite the risks? Would *you* touch it again, despite the trouble it's caused? Despite what happened to you last time?"

She didn't answer.

The Last Option

"And would you do it for him, of all people?"

Amethyst looked Damascus straight in the eye. She showed him the confidence that had inspired the Fifth Summit.

"My dear child. Come now! You cannot be serious. He has caused so much suffering. He has started a war that will leave countless dead. He is *a bad man*, Amethyst. Completely irredeemable. Of all the people who have died tonight, he at least deserves his fate."

"I know," she admitted, the tears welling in her eyes, "but—but I don't have to treat him as he deserves, do I? Can't I choose to forgive him? And maybe—might that change him?"

Damascus knelt beside her, his eyes wide with wonder. "So you've learned it, then."

She stared blankly, not catching his meaning.

But the old man grasped her tight and hugged her close. For a long while, he did not let go.

"Well, then," he said when he finally released her, "let's have at it, hmm?" Then he reached into an inner pocket of his robes. He produced a small black stone hanging from a burnt chain, and he held it out for Amethyst.

"You want *me* to try?"

"You think I can do it again? After what I did? At my age? No, you must take it."

She reached out but then hesitated. "Are you sure it's safe?"

"Safe? Of course not! There's no part about this that's safe. If you cannot guard your heart, it will utterly consume you. You will never be the same again."

She withdrew her hand, and Damascus didn't chastise her. Instead, he reached toward the hole in my armor and my burnt flesh underneath. He dropped the stone on my chest, where it nearly disappeared against my blackened skin.

"Now remember, you must focus," he cautioned. "You must banish all else from your mind. Every desire. Every wish. You cannot think about the war or long for your mother. You must forget the anger you feel toward your father. You can only think of the lieutenant. His ransomed life must be the only desire in your heart."

"I understand."

"Good." He took a deep breath. "Then you may try whenever you are ready."

Amethyst closed her eyes and tried to focus. She reached for my chest, lowered her hand, and felt again for the relic that had nearly destroyed her. She touched the Cornerstone. And me.

All at once, her thoughts penetrated the city. In the southern sections where the war still raged, the thousands fighting amidst the ruins stopped. The battlefield fell silent. Vanguard and ghosts alike paused with terror as some inexplicable power pierced the heart of every person on that mountainside.

Suddenly the conflict seemed useless. Against such power, all effort felt wasted. A fragile peace settled in Del Solae, and each man implicitly understood that his deeds mattered not. The whole war mattered not.

Kneeling next to my corpse, Amethyst felt no such peace. Because her actions did matter. Her desires mattered. Her choice would change the world, and she was still conflicted.

"Amethyst?"

She sensed her name, but she could barely hear it among all the other internal voices screaming at her. Tears streamed from her eyes,

The Last Option

and five seconds passed. Then ten. Still she held the stone, though each moment grew more unbearable than the last.

But then a hand grasped her shoulder, and a voice stronger than all the others gripped her heart. "Amethyst!"

"I can't—I can't."

"Focus, my girl! Focus! Think of Mordecai."

"But my father—"

"You cannot help that now, but Mordecai, my dear. He's gone forever. You will never again hear his voice."

"No."

"You will never speak to him again. *Is that what you want?*"

"NO!"

"Then do something about it!"

"I can't!"

"You must. If you cannot do this, no one can!"

Amethyst almost lost her focus, but Damascus meddled once more. The old man placed his frail fingers over Amethyst's trembling hand. He touched her mind and spoke potent words to strengthen her will and guide her heart. And for a moment, for a fraction of a second, her heart grew pure. The conflict vanished. She wanted a good thing.

And the Cornerstone answered.

A blinding radiance surged forth. The dark moments before dawn turned into brightest day. The whole mountain trembled, and the few walls still standing in Del Solae cracked and fell. The armies of Near Thunderlun and Estavion reeled and marveled at sights and sounds unrivaled in all the annals of history.

Then the light subsided. Night endured. The tremors creased. The battle ended.

And I gasped for air.

Twenty-Four

"After that? Well, you know the rest. Drawn by the light of my resurrection, both assembled armies advanced into the ruins, but no further fighting occurred. Instead, Damascus summoned Lord Masada and Commander Lanxe. He explained everything to both sides. He told them about the assassination attempt, the attack at Ballabor, the needless escalation, and he pinned it all on Irrideous. Most ingeniously, Damascus argued that this was all the plot of his demented protégé, who wanted us to annihilate each other so he could step into the void and rule the world.

"Amazingly, Masada bought that explanation. He apologized for the battle and cancelled his planned offensive. He even promised to attend another Summit, if our king invited him. Then he left. He gathered his dead and retreated with the ghosts of Thunderlun. He left Del Solae and the rest of the Vanguard corps unscathed.

"As for Damascus, Amethyst and me? We stayed long enough to help the wounded and fallen, but then we returned to Tel Tellesti. Damascus finally presented the Cornerstone to the king. He even offered to try using it again, if requested, to end the famine that has plagued the Estates.

"But the *good* King Everett did not make that request," I seethe. "For some foolish reason, he confiscated the catalyst and imprisoned Damascus for insubordination. He opened a formal investigation. So here we are."

Finally finished, I lean back and fold my arms over my chest.

Rehoboth eases forward. "That leaves *many* unanswered questions, lieutenant."

"True, but that's life, isn't it?

Rehoboth glances at Uriah, annoyed.

I stand from my chair. "Is that all?"

"Not quite." Rehoboth raises a hand. "I have one last request."

"Yes?"

Her smile returns. She motions to the two guards posted at the entrance, and these men promptly exit the interrogation room and leave me alone with the arbiter and the general. Then Rehoboth moves around the desk. She stands next to me and quietly says, "We need you to indict Damascus for sedition."

I clench my jaw until my cheeks turn red. "What?"

"According to our statutes, a traitor must be publicly accused by a witness—"

"I know the law. What I don't know is why you want Damascus to hang for treason."

"We can't just banish him," Rehoboth answers. "Who knows where he might go, what he might say?"

"Why do anything? Just release him."

"Impossible."

"He hasn't done anything wrong!"

I wait for a response, but Rehoboth doesn't answer. She just glances back at Uriah.

The general tries his luck. "Lieutenant, this is a direct order."

I laugh in his face.

"We can give you a full pardon. Purge your record."

"You could make me king. I won't do it."

"This is for the greater good," Rehoboth says.

"I won't condemn an innocent man!"

"Please," Rehoboth scoffs. "You still believe he's innocent?"

"He helped Amethyst save my life!"

"After he killed you," she jests.

"I had it coming. Weren't you listening? Damascus saved countless lives. He redeemed me, a murderer who deserves no forgiveness. He's a good man. The best man."

Twenty-Four

"Are you certain about that?"

"There is *nothing* that will ever convince me otherwise."

Rehoboth doesn't respond, but she glances at Uriah again.

"For pity's sake," the general answers. "Just tell him."

I glance at Uriah. Then at Rehoboth. "Tell me what?"

Rehoboth sighs and drops her trademark smile. She walks behind the desk, to her notes, and starts flipping through pages.

"Tell me what?"

"Lieutenant," she begins again, her lips dripping with disdain, "throughout this investigation, there has endured one persistent defect in your otherwise adequate logic. Though you correctly suspected Damascus, you never doubted him for the right reason. All along you thought he meant to use the Cornerstone as a weapon to somehow sabotage Estavion and throw the Inheritance into war. Am I correct?"

"Yes."

"Therefore," she continues, "when Damascus prevented the war, you changed your mind about his morality. You then told us this whole story just to prove his innocence and validate your own doubts. But what if Damascus never desired a war in the first place? What if he wanted something else? Something far better?"

"Like what?"

In response, Rehoboth lifts a sheet of parchment to show me a simple sketch. On the brittle paper, the arbiter has drawn a small black square.

"The Touchstone."

"The—the what?" I assume a confused expression. "Another stone? Like the Cornerstone?"

"Not quite." Then Rehoboth launches into a well-rehearsed explanation she has apparently saved for this moment. "You see, there's another part of the Ascendant myths—one not as famous as the rest, though I'm still surprised Amethyst never told you. According to this particular legend, the Touchstone was a small, flat, square stone—smooth on one side, coarse on the other. The Ascendants built it to test their purity of will or something to that effect. They endowed it with extraordinary, limitless powers, and they used it to mold the Inheritance as they saw fit, so it was with the Touchstone and *not* the Cornerstone that the Ascendants carved the valleys, lifted the mountains and built their cities."

"How?"

"Specifically, the legend claims that anyone who holds the Touchstone will possess infinite power."

"Infinite power? What does that even mean?"

"It's hard to imagine, isn't it?" Uriah interjects. "Let me put it differently. Do you remember when Amethyst touched the Cornerstone? How she *envisioned* her father dead?"

"Of course."

"If she had been using the Touchstone instead," Uriah says gravely, "she wouldn't have just imagined that desire. She would have *made* it happen. Her father would have died right then, no matter where he was."

"That's what the Touchstone does," Rehoboth clarifies. "It creates whatever you want most. It manifests desire—any desire whatsoever—without regard to good or evil."

I laugh.

"Yes," Rehoboth agrees. "Sounds preposterous, doesn't it? Perhaps that's why this particular legend isn't especially popular. I myself never believed, nor did I know anyone who did. But there's one last part of the legend, lieutenant. Supposedly, when the Ascendants left this world behind and rose into the heavens, they couldn't take the Touchstone with them. It was a physical construct, you see, so it couldn't exist in the ethereal, but neither could they destroy it. Nor could they just leave it behind where some foolish girl might find it, use it, and accidentally murder her father.

"So they did the next best thing. The Ascendants broke the Touchstone. They shattered it into pieces and hid those shards in

Twenty-Four

various sanctuaries around the world. Over time these fragments became lost, but the legend endured, and those small pieces—those shards of black rock—became known as Cornerstones."

As she says the last line, Rehoboth leans forward and reaches for the scrap of velvet lying on the cedar desk. Reverently, she pulls the fabric back. As if for the first time, she gazes again on the catalyst, a shard of the omnipotent Touchstone.

I think again of the dagger in my boot.

"As I said," she continues, "I never believed the stories. They always seemed impossibly illogical. But now? You've reported that Damascus found a Cornerstone. He used it. He restored your life."

I close my eyes, and for almost a whole minute, I stay silent. Both the general and the arbiter patiently allow me to choose my next words carefully.

"Let's make sure I follow you," I say, feigning ignorance. "You think Damascus planned the whole war just so he would have an excuse to find a piece of the Touchstone?"

"No, not Damascus," Rehoboth admits. But then she leans in again, dangerously close. Her smile returns, her eyes dance, and she whispers, "Irrideous."

I shift nervously in my seat.

"Tell me. When did Irrideous abandon Bethel Emm and leave Severance?"

"What?"

"Answer the question."

I stop to think. "Well, it was after Bethel was born, so maybe eighteen years ago?"

"Eighteen years? How interesting. And when did Damascus first come to Tel Tellesti?"

"I honestly don't know."

"You don't? Well, I do. Would you like me to tell you?"

Do I have a choice?

"About fifteen years ago."

"That's circumstantial. It doesn't prove anything."

"No, but it's a strange coincidence, isn't it? It's also a strange coincidence that Irrideous possessed intimate knowledge of the Ascendants, just like Damascus, and he left behind a daughter, a girl that Damascus was quite attached to."

"Damascus felt responsible for Bethel's situation," I remind her. "Weren't you listening?"

"I was listening. Were you? Or were you too distracted by the heiress to realize what was happening under your nose?"

"What?"

Rehoboth waves off her own allegation. "Let me tell you about another disturbing coincidence. Do you remember how this whole catastrophe started?"

"With the Fifth Summit."

"Not exactly," she corrects me. "This all started with a bomb. An alkali bomb built with materials only Damascus knew about."

I laugh again. "That bomb almost killed Amethyst. Damascus wouldn't risk her life like that."

"Was it a risk, though?"

"She almost died. If it hadn't been for me—"

"Yes, I know," Rehoboth cuts me off. "You saw that ribbon she dropped, and you chased after her. That was most heroic of you, lieutenant. But please remind me, why did she drop that ribbon in the first place?"

"I don't—I don't remember."

"You don't? Well, let's see." Rehoboth lifts her notes and flips through some pages until she finds what she's looking for. Then she reads my own testimony back to me. "*As he spoke, Damascus pulled a silk ribbon from Amethyst's hair...*"

I fall silent. I harden my eyes. This is all too perfect.

"Let me explain what actually happened," Rehoboth finally offers. "I think Irrideous wanted the Touchstone. He wanted it so desperately, he was prepared to do *anything*. He was willing to change

Twenty-Four

his appearance and invent the false persona of an old scholar with a strange name. He was willing to painstakingly work his way into the citadel and earn a trusted position as Amethyst's mentor, and he used that influence to travel the world. He disguised his true intentions quite well. As far as anyone knew, he was just letting the girl travel, see the world and learn a bit of magic. Seems rather harmless, doesn't it? All the while, though, he was secretly studying Ascendant temples and searching for clues about the Touchstone. He kept looking until he exhausted every possible resource except one—the Testament at Ballabor.

"But he couldn't visit that site without just cause," Rehoboth continues. "Ballabor is the king's personal retreat. It's strictly off limits. So Irrideous invented a crisis. With his unique knowledge and experience, he built an ingenious bomb and planted it in his student's own chambers. It wasn't really a risk. He could have healed any injuries she would have sustained, but to 'save' her life and clear himself of any possible suspicion, he also provided a solution. He dropped her silk ribbon just so you would pick it up and follow her.

"In the investigation that followed, Irrideous cleverly pinned the blame on Lord Masada, thereby allowing him access at last to Ballabor, but there he learned something most surprising. He discovered that the Cornerstone had already been in his grasp once before. So he improvised again. He summoned a dreadnaught to Ballabor. He created another threat just so Amethyst would have no choice but to defy Uriah's orders and send you on a vain chase. He took you on an intimate tour of his own tragic life, all while impersonating a sputtering old man."

"That dreadnaught nearly killed everyone at Ballabor, including Damascus," I remind her. "You really think Irrideous would risk his own life like that?"

"I don't know, but I do find it curious that Damascus didn't immediately use his lightning against the dreadnaught, even though he could have saved the whole garrison."

I don't have an answer for that.

"In the end," Rehoboth continues, "once Irrideous had the stone again, he no longer needed a war to justify his actions. So he visited Esker. He provided a convenient solution and avoided a catastrophe. And no doubt he expected to return home a hero. Maybe he thought he would be granted even greater leniency than before, which he would use to search out the remaining Cornerstones. Regardless, I'm certain he never expected that we might guess who he really was and what he was truly after. But in the end, he couldn't hide from me."

Confident in her summation, Rehoboth settles into her chair, her smile stretching from ear to ear.

"You're wrong."

"Please, lieutenant. You already said Damascus is capable of anything."

"That was different. I questioned his loyalty, nothing more. I thought perhaps he had a secret allegiance, but you're describing him as if—as if he's a monster. As if he heartlessly sacrificed thousands of lives for his own personal agenda. And Damascus is not such a man."

"Are you certain?"

My fingers curl into a fist. "I was there, your grace. I saw him with my own eyes. I saw him stand against a demon. I saw him caress Bethel and—and touch her heart. He healed eighteen years of loneliness in an instant. I saw him rescue Amethyst from madness, and Irrideous—Irrideous could never do such things."

"You also heard Damascus say that you would die with an arrow through the heart."

"That doesn't change anything. Not anymore. Not after he saved my life. Go ahead—accuse him all you want. Invent your theories. I won't believe any of it."

Rehoboth just shrugs. "I don't care if you believe, lieutenant. I don't need you to believe. I only need you to follow orders, because despite everything else that has happened, you *did* start a foolish war with both Near Thunderlun and Samara, remember? The Empress

Twenty-Four

wants blood for your unprovoked attack on Severance, and own our people are demanding an explanation for the lives lost at Del Solae. They all need someone to blame, Mordecai."

"And you intend to give them Damascus."

"Damascus. Or an expendable Vanguard lieutenant. Either will do, I suspect, and quite honestly I don't care which it is." She leans in closer again. "I'll let you choose, lieutenant. You can either indict Damascus, or you will face the gallows yourself for arson, murder, insubordination, and theft."

"Don't forget treason," Uriah adds.

"And treason."

Twenty-Five

The interrogation room door creaks open, and I shuffle out. I must look terrible, because one of the guards posted outside offers to escort me to the barracks. I shrug him off, though, and turn left down the long hallway. Slowly, I glide down the ageless corridor without stopping to think. Soon I reach an intersection and turn a corner, and there I stop.

I lean against the cold granite. I close my eyes and ignore my racing pulse and churning stomach. Instead, I listen. Without speaking or breathing, I wait. It can't be long now.

My patience is rewarded. I hear the interrogation door open again, and two pairs of footsteps emerge. The door closes behind them. A key scrapes into the lock and turns the bolt with a clank. Then quiet voices drift down the hallway and around the blind corner, never suspecting that I can perceive every syllable.

"I don't like this," the general says. "I'd rather he make his choice in a cell."

"He has much to absorb, and I don't want him distracted. Just give him until morning," the arbiter answers. "He'll come around."

"And if he doesn't?"

Rehoboth only laughs slightly. Though I don't peek around the corner, I can imagine how she must be smiling at Uriah's doubts as she spins to leave in the opposite direction.

The narrow fool.

She thinks she's trapped me—forced me to choose between saving myself or the man who redeemed me. She thinks she's won, and she's confident enough to set me loose for the night. She's even willing to leave the stone behind in the interrogation room with the rest of the evidence, all guarded by only two men. No doubt she hopes the king will honor her great victory with a new title, like viceroy or chancellor perhaps.

She'll never see that promotion, though. I'll make certain of it. She doesn't deserve it anyway. She still hasn't grasped how dangerous I am. She has underestimated my capabilities. Even worse, she's offered me new information. She's revealed her knowledge of the Touchstone.

She's given me a third choice.

This is unexpected, I admit. I had long assumed I would be finished after my testimony. I wanted only to clear Damascus before vanishing, since I couldn't let him die unceremoniously at the hands of these ingrates. I had thought I might have to fight my way out of the old citadel, but I had no intention of dying for my crimes. Not here. Not ever.

But everything is different now. Rehoboth knows about the Touchstone. Uriah does too, judging from his composure during that revelation. And if he knows, Damascus must have told him. That's the only possible explanation. It's also probable, then, that Uriah isn't the only person he told.

So I leave the Cornerstone behind one last time. I ignore the dreadnaught vambrace and everything else locked in that room. I leave the guards untouched, and I sneak deeper into the citadel.

Thirty minutes later, I climb one last staircase and enter the hallway adjacent to Amethyst's chamber. It's nearly midnight now, and the construct is practically deserted, but as I round the corner I still find four Vanguard watching the girl's door.

Twenty-Five

They are dressed in the ceremonial uniform of gilded chainmail, polished breastplates and vermilion mantles, and they carry broad swords in ivory scabbards. Even thusly arrayed, though, they aren't a noteworthy threat, despite the fact that my only weapon is the dagger inside my boot, so I approach boldly.

The guards tighten their formation when they notice me.

"I must speak with the heiress," I explain.

"I am sorry," one of them replies. "She is resting."

"This matter is urgent. It cannot wait until morning." I try to step around the Vanguard and reach for the door.

The armored man cuts me off. "We have been given explicit instructions. No one sees the heiress, least of all her tutor. Or her previous escorts."

I almost open my mouth to argue, but I don't waste my breath. It's useless. These are Vanguard, after all, each of them conditioned and perfectly loyal. I probably trained some of them myself, and I know they would defy even the ocean if it flooded the highlands and swept through Tel Tellesti.

I have no choice, then, but to force the matter. There is no other way. I suppose this is Rehoboth's doings, but if she truly wanted to deter me, she should have posted more than four. These men will not be a challenge. I must only move quickly enough to silence them before they can alert reinforcements.

How should I handle them? I couldn't pretend to accept their refusal and leave. They would suspect a surprise, and their senses would be heightened. I must act at once, then. It will be best to eliminate the leader first. I can hook my elbow around his neck before he can unsheathe his blade. Then I can use him as a shield while I kick the second man in the throat and crush his windpipe. At the same time, I can steal the leader's weapon from its sheath and whip it toward the last two men. They are standing close together. One careful slice might sever both their throats before they know what's happening.

As I plan my attack, the leader watches my eyes drifting from him, to his sword, to his men. Perhaps he guesses what's about to happen, because he fingers his hilt. "Didn't you hear, lieutenant? No one sees the heiress."

That's it. Go ahead. Loosen that blade. Make it easier for me to pull once I've crushed your neck.

I flex my fingers, stretching out the kinks from a long day of sitting in a chair and talking to dust. I shift my weight onto my left foot, ready to spin and coil my arm around my target. But then a rusted iron latch creaks and scrapes. A door slides open. Drawn by the sound of our voices, the girl appears at her threshold.

"Captain? What is it?" Amethyst immediately notices me. More importantly, her keen instincts detect the tension, and she commands the other Vanguard, "Let him pass."

I relax, but my opponent grips his sword tighter. "My apologies, milady, but I have specific orders from Rehoboth—"

"And now you have orders from me," Amethyst interrupts impatiently. "Choose carefully whom you will obey."

The captain looks at Amethyst, and then at me. He considers his next move. In the end, he chooses wisely. He saves his life and his men. He releases his sword and steps aside, so I follow Amethyst into her room and shut the door.

Once inside, I close my eyes, trying to focus on the reason I came. Trying even to remember. How can I get her to talk about the catalyst?

Amethyst speaks too soon, though, in a hoarse voice. "I'm sorry for that. They've been there since we returned from Esker, and they

Twenty-Five

don't take kindly to my instructions. It's like they've forgotten who I am."

I let that comment slide, despite my lingering curiosity about her true identity. Now isn't the time.

"They've also confined Damascus to his quarters," she adds without looking at me, "but you already know that, don't you?"

"I'm surprised he's not in the dungeons."

"Rehoboth is too smart for that. She wants to keep Damascus calm. Unsuspecting. She can't have him trying to escape before he's taken to the gallows."

"They can't execute him. Not yet."

"Who told you that?"

"Rehoboth said—" but as I say the words, I realize they're false. The arbiter lied to me. She wanted my cooperation, yes. She wanted me to indict Damascus. It would be easier that way. People would ask fewer questions. Even if I wouldn't frame the old tutor, though, Rehoboth must have other ways to prove his guilt. She likely has additional evidence stacked against me as well. "How could I have been so blind?"

"This isn't the first time Rehoboth has done this, lieutenant," Amethyst explains. "She gave you a choice, didn't she? She said you could pick between yourself and Damascus?"

I nod.

"It's a nice gesture, isn't it? The illusion of control, of choosing your own fate? Damascus actually suggested the idea in another trial not so long ago, though I doubt he ever guessed she would use it against him. Or you."

"So there was never a chance. The conclusion was already determined. My testimony, the whole—" I squeeze my fingers into a fist. "Rehoboth and Uriah never wanted the truth."

"They were only following procedure, nothing more. They never had any intention of letting either of you live."

I sink into a chair, forgetting why I came. This is absolutely astonishing. I expected such behavior from Rehoboth, of course, but Uriah is a Vanguard general. Doesn't he know better?

Then my mind drifts back, far back. For some reason I'm suddenly back in the narthex and listening to Damascus after the opening ceremony of the Summit. After a pause, I bring Amethyst back as well. "It's true, isn't it, what Damascus said? Even the best of men with the best intentions can commit great evil."

She turns toward me with a folded garment in hand, her bloodshot eyes wide with confusion.

I try again. "Even a great general can condemn a guiltless man."

"Yes, I'm afraid he can."

"I hope you don't blame me."

"What? No!" She reaches for my hand. "Why would you say such a thing?"

"I caused this. If not for my actions with Fetch or at the ruins of Del Solae—"

"But you prevented so much else," Amethyst insists. "Have you already forgotten?"

"Amethyst—"

"No, Mordecai. Listen to me." She kneels at my feet. "You must understand! This is not your fault. It isn't even Rehoboth's fault. *This is Irrideous*. He played you like a harp. He played all of us. He chased us from the citadel and Ballabor and Severance. He drove you like a wedge between Estavion and Samara and Near Thunderlun. He used us all to start a war."

It's strange how much she sounds like Rehoboth right now.

"But you stopped him," she continues. "Don't you realize that? You didn't mean to. You didn't even know what you were doing. But because of you, the ghosts retreated. The Tay`Jeen disbanded."

I look away. This conversation is veering out of my control.

She waits patiently. She mistakes my frustration for remorse. She carefully considers her next words, and eventually she says, "You

Twenty-Five

know, it *is* true, what Damascus said. Even good men can commit horrendous evils."

I still refuse to meet her gaze.

"But the reverse is also true," she adds. "Did you ever realize that? Even a fool with wrong intentions can accomplish great good. Even a wicked soldier can accidentally save his country."

Her kind words reach for my heart. They nearly penetrate the crushing darkness, and when I finally raise my head, I must seem a different man. A better man.

The girl smiles. How can she still be so confident?

Then I notice saddlebags on the table behind Amethyst. I also notice other provisions scattered about her room, and I see the folded dress clutched in her hands. "Wait? Where are you going?"

"I'm leaving with Damascus." She stands and pushes the final garment into her bag.

"What? Now?"

"He's scheduled to be executed. Haven't you heard? So we're escaping tonight. We're going west. There are some ruins in the Vale we've never visited. Who knows? Maybe we'll find Bethel. Start a new life."

I rise from my chair. "But—but what about your duties? Your responsibilities?"

"I won't serve a country that doesn't trust me."

Neither of us speaks again for a moment.

Then I say, "What about your father?"

Amethyst only answers, "Damascus is my father now."

Her resolve strikes like a hammer. She allows no hesitation. Unable to speak, I watch silently as she packs.

Amethyst, however, effortlessly continues. "You could come along, if you like. I could use a servant."

Her joke makes me smile. I have already considered leaving, but coming from her, the idea seems so simple and logical. I can envision myself visiting Chersonia with the young heiress and her ancient teacher. I can imagine watching, bored out of my mind, while they research Ascendant ruins. I can even picture Damascus growing excited at some new discovery, like the long-lost location of another Cornerstone.

Then I remember why I came, and another idea occurs to me—a thought that never would have occurred if Rehoboth had proven less talkative. It's a terrible idea that I'm certain Amethyst never considered, but she must face the possibility before she leaves forever. I must know her answer.

So I say, "I'm not sure that's a good idea."

Amethyst stops, confused by my heresy.

"It just—it seems an unnecessary risk," I blurt out before she can respond. "What if Rehoboth is right about Damascus?"

"What do you mean? What did she say?"

"She said the same thing you did, that Irrideous planned all this, but she took it a step further. She suggested that Damascus and Irrideous are the same person. She said he's searching for something called the Touchstone."

"That's absurd."

"I know. Trust me. But still, what if it's true? If there's a chance, even the slightest chance that Damascus lied about all this—" I purse my lips. "You'd be taking a terrible risk, Amethyst. Let him go, by all means. Trust him that much. But don't go with him. Don't put yourself in his hands."

"He saved your life, Mordecai, and still you doubt?"

"I don't want to, but I can't help it. I only have accusations and theories. There is no solid proof about anything."

"Is that all you need? Proof?"

"Is it so much to ask?"

"You could try having faith."

"*Faith.*" I cough out the word as if it's poisonous. "Faith is for good men, Amethyst. Noble men who still believe in humanity. Not

Twenty-Five

men like me. Men like me, we need proof." I hang my head. "And that's the one thing you can't give me, isn't it?"

The girl doesn't reply. She only wrings her fingers together.

She's close. So close. But I can't push any further. She'll panic and flee. I can't force the issue, either. She's not a weakling who might succumb to threats. I have no choice, then, but to leave, so after a long pause I sigh and step toward the door.

"Wait."

I stop.

"What if I could provide the proof you require?"

"You can't."

"But if I could," she says, "would you fight for him? Would you try to change Rehoboth's mind?"

"That's not possible."

"Then speak to Uriah or the king. Please! There must be someone who can overrule her decision."

"Why me? Why don't you try yourself?"

"They won't listen. I've spent too much time with him. They think—" She squeezes her eyes shut. "They think he's *corrupted* me, lieutenant. I have the proof. I have compelling, indisputable proof, but it doesn't matter. They won't listen."

I step closer, my pulse racing. This is what I came to hear. What I never expected to hear. "You can prove his innocence? Beyond doubt?"

She nods.

"How?"

Amethyst bites her lip. Suddenly ashamed, she turns away, her eyes downcast.

"Amethyst?"

"No. I'm sorry. I promised."

"Promised who? Promised Damascus?"

She doesn't respond.

407

"What did he tell you?" I press even closer. "What could he have possibly told you?"

For an eternity, the heiress doesn't answer. She keeps her back toward me and sucks in deep breaths. She clenches her fingers into fists and then stretches them out again, all without speaking a word.

This time, I wait. I hold the air in my lungs until it burns, but still I wait. After all I have endured for the past few months, for the past long decades, this is effortless. I wait for many minutes while Amethyst painstakingly wrestles against some internal foe.

My patience pays off again. Amethyst wins her internal conflict. Or she loses. Regardless, she turns and desperately whispers, "You must swear, Mordecai. Swear to me you'll never tell."

"I swear."

Amethyst leads me through a hidden back passageway so we can circumvent the Vanguard posted outside her door. Then we silently slip through the citadel halls. I follow her to the atrium where she finds a lantern, lights it by snapping her fingers and passes it to me. Then she pushes on an inconspicuous section of wall to reveal another secret tunnel descending into blackness. She leads me down a cramped staircase, and eventually we enter a vast, underground chamber, the likes of which I've never before seen or imagined.

Instinctively I raise my lantern high, but the infinite darkness swallows the meager light, so I have no choice but to ask, "What is this place?"

"Damascus calls it the Vault. It's an Ascendant sanctuary."

"Another sanctuary? Here? Beneath Tel Tellesti?"

"It's the foundation for the entire city."

"That's impossible," I gasp.

Twenty-Five

My senses confirm Amethyst's claim, though. The chamber does indeed seem incomprehensibly massive. Furthermore, under my feet I can feel smooth stone, just like the polished floor at Ur Thourou, and along the nearby wall (or at least the small portion of the wall visible), I notice stonescript carved into the granite, just like at Ballabor.

I approach the ancient inscriptions and reach out reverently. "This is your proof?"

The heiress only laughs slightly. "Don't be silly."

"Where is it, then?"

"This way." She leaves the tunnel entrance and steps into the blackness. "Follow me."

For a moment, I hesitate. I'm perfectly comfortable in the dark, but it still feels unsafe to leave behind our only passageway to the world above. How will we ever find our way back? Before me, I can see nothing no matter how high I raise my lantern. I see no other wall, no ceiling, and no other distinguishing features of any kind. There is only the granite floor stretching forward into blackness. Suddenly I'm back on the *Sole Solution* at midnight under a starless sky with nothing but bottomless oblivion stretching out forever before me, and she wants me to leap from the boat.

"Mordecai?" Amethyst's voice reaches out from the void. "It's okay. You can trust me."

I'm not so sure, but I put one foot in front of the other. By faith I follow her voice, and when I find her, I do not stray.

We venture deep into the vault. We walk for hours, maybe more. It's hard to tell since we don't pass a single marker, and I can't imagine how Amethyst knows where we're going or how far we've traveled. My feeble lantern only illuminates a few paces in any direction, and there is no other light in the underground chamber. For all I know, we are walking in circles. We may be utterly lost despite Amethyst's unyielding confidence.

"How do you know where we're going?"

She stops and stares at me. "Can't you feel them?"

"Feel who?"

She shakes her head. "We're almost there. Come on."

Apparently "almost there" means another thirty minutes, and I grow wary. If we dare much farther, we may not have enough lantern oil for the return trip. Just as I'm about to say something, though, I do feel *something* drawing me closer. It's not unlike the effect I felt in Del Solae when I wore the dreadnaught vambrace and chased the Cornerstone. At the same time, I finally notice something ahead. I spy a small, vague shape. At first I think it's a wall or perhaps another exit that leads upwards to safety, but as we near, I can see that this object is just a simple wooden table, no wider or taller than a nightstand.

On this humble pedestal, however, I discover something else. Hidden in the darkness far under the citadel, I find three small objects—three shards of black rock.

"It can't be," I gasp. "More Cornerstones?"

Amethyst doesn't answer, but I'm already transfixed. Quite subconsciously, I step closer and closer. And closer. Mesmerized, I lick my parched lips. I swallow in a vain effort to soothe my throat. Then, noticing how my fingers are shaking involuntarily, I place the lantern on the polished floor, and with my free hands, I reach for the forbidden relics.

"What are you doing?"

I flinch back.

"No touching."

"Of course," I say, blinking my eyes to force concentration.

I lean a little closer. With significant effort, I suppress the compelling urge to reach out, touch the catalysts, and satisfy my heart. Instead, I familiarize myself again with their size and shape. I notice that, as Rehoboth so precisely explained, the shards still have jagged edges on the inside and smooth edges on the outside. I can even imagine how the pieces fit together into a square stone.

Twenty-Five

"It's the whole Touchstone," I realize. "I mean, if you had the other piece—the Cornerstone we found."

"Yes," Amethyst answers solemnly.

A terrible thought comes to mind. "You—Amethyst, please. You haven't told Damascus, have you?"

The question makes her smile. "Who do you think showed this to me?"

I reel backward.

Then Amethyst offers a final explanation. "Rehoboth is wrong, Mordecai. All wrong. She thinks Damascus is a horrific villain. She thinks he started a war just so he could find the Touchstone shards and wish himself immortal or worse. But she's wrong. Damascus doesn't want the Touchstone. He's known its location all along, even before we left for Ballabor."

An insuppressible smile spreads across my lips. "So he spoke the truth, didn't he? When Damascus stopped the battle at Del Solae and explained everything to Masada and Lanxe?"

"It was all indeed a plot by Irrideous," Amethyst confirms. "An ingenious plan to take revenge on the mentor who failed him. He meant to frame Damascus and throw the Inheritance into war. He wanted Damascus to watch his world collapse. Perhaps he wanted Damascus to witness my death, or perhaps he even wanted me to turn against him."

"He almost succeeded."

"That he did." Her voice quivers at the thought. "Can you imagine it, at the ruins, if I had not stayed my hand?"

"And to think I encouraged you." I shudder. Then something else strange occurs to me. "Wait. How long have you known? Were you feigning ignorance the whole time?"

"No. Damascus only brought me here a few weeks ago after we returned from Heda Fare. I was still recovering from my experience with the Cornerstone, remember, and all his other labors had failed, so he showed me." Her voice softens. "He showed me the Touchstone. The whole thing. Do you realize that? He had the Cornerstone and these other shards. He could have used them before we chased him to Esker. He could have done *anything*. But he didn't, and do you know why?"

I shake my head. I honestly can't even guess.

"Damascus stood here," she says as a single tear streams down her porcelain cheek. "He looked at me, and he said the Touchstone was useless. He said he already had what his heart wanted most."

I don't answer. I can't. I can only stare at the heiress, the girl more valuable than omnipotence. The child for whom Damascus surrendered immeasurable power. The cornerstone on which the old fool built his every hope. The same student who almost killed him at Del Solae.

Then that priceless treasure turns away.

"I hope you can convince Rehoboth to see reason. I really do," Amethyst says through her tears, "but if you can't, I'm not waiting to see what happens. I won't watch him die. You have until dawn, lieutenant, and if you can't change her mind, then I'm leaving with Damascus. And there's nothing you or anyone can do to stop me."

With that solemn promise, Amethyst leaves me behind with the Cornerstones and the lantern. She vanishes into the endless void.

Twenty-Six

I can hardly believe my fortune. She did it. Prompted by her love for Damascus, Amethyst disobeyed him. She did it before, yes, when she left Ballabor despite his council, but this is different. She broke a promise—the only promise she ever made to him. She refused the one command he ever issued. To protect her beloved mentor, she betrayed his greatest secret.

And Damascus said she would never do it. The old fool.

He vastly underestimated me, just like the others. He idiotically assumed I had not grown or learned from our last encounter, and even though he knew—even though he recognized me from that first moment when he saw me standing in her blasted chamber—he never bothered to tell anyone else the truth. He went along with the illusion, with the game, thinking I would honor the agreement. He even let me close to the girl, his masterpiece, believing she was beyond my reach.

Now he would suffer for his mistakes. They would all suffer.

There's no rush, though. I've waited a long, long time for this moment. Why let it pass so quickly? Why not savor the victory?

I leave the other three Cornerstones. They'll be safe in the vault. I give Amethyst a long lead so I don't catch her, and then I venture back into the crushing darkness, into the void from whence I came. It's a difficult path, walking such a straight line without the slightest bent to the left or right. I've truly never been down here before—I never even knew this vault existed—and I do not wish to linger long. I can still feel the stones, though, tugging at my heart, so I keep them directly behind. With resolute strides, I push toward the outer wall with lantern raised high. I drift slightly to the right, thinking that if I don't arrive precisely at the exit when I reach the perimeter, I can backtrack left along the granite wall.

After two hours, though, the lantern light fades. The flame flickers. Then it dies.

No matter.

I hold the lantern aloft and feel for the old frame. It's made of wrought iron, a good material for a little trick. The metal is cold and rough against my fingers. It's completely useless as it is, so I grasp the iron firmly. I close my eyes and concentrate. I think ancient words learned from an old master—*illicai aga scheel*—and the iron grows hot until it glows like an ember.

With this new light I continue onward, ignoring the burning sensation that penetrates my leather glove and sears my hand. After another hour, I reach the perimeter. I don't arrive at the tunnel entrance, of course, but I don't panic. I simply follow my plan, like so many times before. I toss the lantern away, since I don't need its faint light any longer. By touch I follow the wall left, my fingers tracing the endless lines of stonescript carved into the granite, and soon my hand detects a missing section of wall. I find the exit.

I climb up the secret passage, and eventually I reach the hidden door that opens into the atrium—that same indoor garden where Damascus taught his pupil so many secrets and mysteries over the past four years—and I laugh. He should have told her more about me. A lot more.

There isn't time left for that education anymore. I will soon have the prize I seek. Though it is still dark with a few hours left until morning, the citadel halls are mostly empty. There are few to oppose me, few to even see me. I can march unchallenged through the corridors without care if my footsteps echo against the granite. I can skip down staircases, if I felt like skipping. But I walk easily. No need to disturb the Vanguard honoring their posts. Not yet. Let them walk their routes a little longer, for they will never make their rounds again. None of them will live to see the sunrise.

Twenty-Six

I pass many soldiers on my walk, recognizing most of them. I see some who live in the same barracks as I, and I recognize others whom I trained. Most know me as well, and a few salute as I pass. Why wouldn't they? I am cloaked in vermilion, like them. I am the famous Lieutenant Mordecai, sole survivor of Veldt.

The survivor. I suppose that's one way to put it. But it was easy to survive after planning the city's destruction. It was easy, luring the hungry Samaran cavalry to Veldt with rumors of an abundant harvest. It was just as easy to exterminate the few people still living after the nomads and migrants ripped each other apart. And when everyone else was dead—when every man, woman, and child in that city had perished under the sword—it was easy to burn the harvest fields and convince General Uriah that I only survived by chance and guile.

It would be just as easy to sack Tel Tellesti.

There is now no need for war and deceit. I will soon have something greater. I need only to circle down another spiral staircase and move through the lower levels. I must only turn one final corner to my destination.

Rehoboth's interrogation chamber.

There are still two guards posted outside the room. A pitiful defense. One of them is shamefully sitting cross-legged and sleeping on the floor, his back resting against the cedar door. The younger man, though, stands alert, and as I saunter down the hallway, his eyes perk. Strangely, he reaches out and grasps my hand.

"Lieutenant Mordecai, you're back!"

"Caleb?" I take a closer look, but this is indeed my favorite student. "Caleb! How are you? How long has it been?"

"Five months since you left. You didn't even say goodbye."

"Oh—I was under orders. I'm sorry."

"Of course, sir. Just giving you grief. We heard what happened, or part of what happened. What they told us, I mean."

"You'll hear the rest soon enough, I expect, but look at you!" I lean back and pretend to appreciate the sight. "They commissioned you already? Gave you a post even."

"This is just temporary. After the investigations are finished, I've been promised a place on the outer wall. There are many gaps after the mess up north."

"Right. The mess." I point at the locked door. "That reminds me. I left something in there earlier."

"Oh?"

"An old trinket," I laugh. "Something a friend gave me long ago. This is silly. But the questions just went on and on. I was in there all day. At some point I started playing with it, just to pass the time. You can imagine, can't you? But I left it in there on the table somehow. I only realized it now when I went home."

"That's unfortunate."

I grasp his shoulder. "But you can let me in? I only need a few seconds."

The young soldier firmly shakes his head. "I'm sorry, sir, but no. It's not that I don't trust you, but we've been given strict instructions. The royal arbiter herself told us that no one was allowed inside. You understand. And even if I could let you pass," he adds hastily to excuse himself, "I don't have the key."

"I guessed as much." I raise my foot toward the hand hanging behind my back. "And don't feel sorry. I'm proud of all you've accomplished. You performed your duty well, brother. You done exactly what I needed you to do," I say.

Then I shove my dagger into his belly.

It's hard work, pushing the blade through chainmail, leather, cotton, skin and ribs, but I manage easily enough, and as Caleb falls, clutching at his stomach and gasping for air, I turn toward his partner who has just awoken from his slumber. The second soldier is still on the ground, so he is even easier to kill. After a sharp kick to his

Twenty-Six

throat, then his temple, he slumps onto the granite. Soon after, Caleb stops struggling as well. The hallway grows silent.

Only the door opposes me.

It's heavy, just as I remember, and thick enough to repel a battering ram. The lock is also complex, far beyond my abilities to foil. It's possible Caleb was lying to me. There may be a key hidden somewhere on his body, but I don't feel like searching for it. I've waited long enough.

So I reach out. I place my bare hand on the door and close my eyes. In my mind, I recite an ancient curse that even Damascus doesn't know, and the door explodes with a tremendous crash and a shower of splinters.

Not very subtle, perhaps, and not nearly as impressive as the impossibly intricate plan that brought me this far. The noise will undoubtedly draw Vanguard to my location. I will be long gone before reinforcements arrive, though. They will find only two dead soldiers and an interrogation room raided.

They will fetch Rehoboth and Uriah, I expect. Though it is the middle of night, they will rouse the general and the arbiter. Those who dared to question me—to judge me—will find only shreds of parchment.

Will they guess then? Will they realize at last how I knew Irrideous so completely? Maybe I should leave them one final note. A confession, but a real confession this time. No more lies about my motives and reasons.

I could tell them how I faked every emotion and spun the truth in my favor. That I changed my aged appearance so I could appear young enough to join the Vanguard. That I betrayed the garrison at Veldt just to earn a transfer to Tel Tellesti. That I planted the firebomb and summoned the demon. That I leapt on purpose from the barrier wall in Ballabor and shot the arrow that killed the female imperial in Severance. That I burned the brothel not just because I hate Bethel, but because I couldn't pass an opportunity to watch

Damascus suffer. That I slowly crept into Amethyst's heart to learn her weaknesses and fears. That I manipulated her faith, stole her trust, and used her love for Damascus against him. That I gambled the Cornerstone for the chance at a much greater prize, and I won.

Such a confession would be fun, but I don't waste my time. They don't deserve to know. And besides, if I did mean to tell them, I wouldn't confess with a note. I would speak in person so I could watch the blood drain from their faces. I would reveal my true identity just so they would beg for mercy. And I wouldn't honor such requests.

No, if they want to know the truth, let them ask Damascus. He envisions himself as their messiah, so let him explain how he underestimated me at every turn. How he assumed I was still mortal, with human weaknesses like guilt and shame and doubt. How he thought I only wanted revenge, and how he forgot that with the catalyst, with the divine Touchstone, I could have the whole world. I could destroy migrants, nomads, clansmen, and ghosts. I could wipe humanity from the Inheritance and start again in my own image.

I could become a god.

All I need now is the last Cornerstone, the same relic Damascus offered all those years ago. The price for my temporal forgiveness. And when I find it, he will not die. Not yet. Such irrelevance is too good for him. He will endure a while longer, as long as it takes to find Bethel and Amethyst and tear them apart while he watches. Then he will burn as my trophy, and maybe after a few millennia, if my wrath is ever satisfied, I will let him slip into oblivion.

I search the room. It's here, I'm sure, buried under the splinters of the demolished door. Rehoboth left it behind with every other shred of evidence, never guessing that it wasn't safe behind an iron lock. Somewhere amidst the comfortable chairs, the cedar table, and those infuriating, meticulous notes, the last shard is waiting for its rightful owner.

Twenty-Six

It takes a minute, but soon I find it under a chunk of lumber, still sitting on the table and wrapped in its little scrap of velvet. Without reservation, I unfold its sheath. With bare fingers, I grasp that shard. I let the forbidden relic touch my unprotected skin, and I breathe in a deep, satisfying sigh. It's been far too long since I've tasted such power, such clarity.

I leave, stepping over Caleb's body, and emerge from the interrogation room as if from the womb, dirty and reborn.

Without thinking, I turn down the hallway. By rote memory, I return to the Vanguard barracks while sentries finally respond to the noise of my theft and scramble in the opposite direction. I enter the barracks, find my bunk, and there in the darkness I throw off my vermilion cloak and breastplate. I strip off the chainmail and the engraved bracers. I gladly remove the elements that so readily identified me as a loyal Vanguard agent, shedding the false skin that hid me for so long. I discard even the folded-steel sword and keep only the leather boots, suede pants, and linen tunic.

As I walk through the training yard, I glance up at the empty sky and wonder if Damascus ever guessed that part of my plot. Did he realize I had surpassed him? When he taught the girl how to steer the winds and shift the currents, did he know I could command the climate? That the debilitating drought was my idea, my masterpiece, and it had proved far more effective than his?

I suppose I could end it now. Why not? A little rain might prove amusing. Let the migrants glimpse the heavy clouds again. Let their hearts finally rise just before I crush their hopes forever. I turn my eyes upward and lift the curse. I remove the front so the rains will return in the morning, and I change the pressure so they will never leave again.

Delighted by my own genius, I turn toward the western inner gate, the closest path out of the citadel. I will only slip outside long enough to gather my full strength. Then I will return to claim the Touchstone and finally overthrow Damascus. As I turn a corner and sight the gate, however, I see that the entrance is still guarded by nearly two dozen soldiers, some of the best in the Vanguard. They pose no threat, but still I hope they have not yet heard—that they will let me pass unchallenged. I am tired of dealing with these bleating goats.

I meet no such luck. As soon as I come within view of their lanterns, I am commanded to halt. When I refuse to comply, the captain approaches with a hand outstretched. So I seize his wrist and twist until I break every bone in his arm. Then I use his own broadsword to murder his men, and when every last one of them is dead, I drop the useless blade next to the useless guards. I pass through the citadel exit and enter my old city.

For the next few hours, I meander through the dark streets and wide avenues, enjoying the walk and the freedom. I wander the familiar causeways and pass raucous taverns where soldiers and wenches carouse the night away, never guessing the horrors I will soon bring. I glance through other windows as I pass, and inside I spy innocent children sleeping in warm beds, never anticipating that this quiet night will be their last. I slip through empty markets and abandoned alleyways, through the worst parts of Tel Tellesti, until at last I reach my final stop, a simple stone house.

I fiddle with the rusted latch before entering, and once inside I pay no attention to the fact that the home contains no family, no furniture, no adornments, and no other evidence whatsoever to suggest anyone ever lived here. Instead I reach down and toss aside a burlap rug to reveal a hatch hidden in the wooden floor.

A simple trick, I know, but sometimes those are the best.

I lift the hatch and pass through, and after entering my bunker I take a brief inventory. Near the ladder, I check to ensure that the vermin haven't eaten holes in my sacks of alkali powder, and I shift the dangerous accelerant away from some water dripping from the leaking roof above. Against the far wall, I survey the dreadnaught armor I have carefully stacked there, and I find exactly what I left

Twenty-Six

before: hundreds of enchanted nephilim armor suits, each one smuggled piece by piece into the city over decades and saved for a special day. Saved for this day.

I solemnly kneel before the nearest suit of armor. Carefully, I lift the heavy obsidian breastplate, hoist it over my shoulders, and slip it into place, where it sticks firm. As its power fills my veins, I again sigh with deep satisfaction.

Then I hear a dull thumping, the echo of footsteps. Judging from the severity, this is no mere man, but a giant. A demon. Sure enough, when I turn toward the sound a juggernaut emerges from the shadows—a man almost three paces tall, bursting with strength and brutality, with a flaming spark in his yellow eyes.

When he notices me, the colossus bows and speaks in low, reverberating tones. "Prince Irrideous, my apologies. I wasn't expecting you."

"Neither was I, but things have worked out, Edo. My plan has succeeded better than I could have ever imagined, and the time has come to summon the others."

The demon of Ballabor smiles. "She killed him?"

"No." I present the Cornerstone. "She has done something immeasurably worse."

~~ End of Prelude ~~

Want more? Have questions? Then visit TOUCHSTONESERIES.COM where you can browse an FAQ, subscribe for updates and write a review. Most importantly, you can read PROTOCOL, a short letter that explains the dramatic events immediately following CORNERSTONE.

ACKNOWLEDGEMENTS

I must thank my family, friends, co-workers and everyone else who has encouraged me over the years.

I am truly blessed that Andrew Samuelson rallied my family so the first manuscript could be professionally critiqued, and I'm grateful that David Pomerico boldly suggested that I scrap that first draft and start over from an earlier point in the story.

I'm so proud of my beta team: Rachel Nyssen, Susan Gregory, Sarah Moore, Dan Bruno, Chris Kountz, Sarah Farber, Rebecca Towery, Shane Oldenburg, Kate Givens, Lauren Benere, Matthew Beaulieu, Damien Brooks and Ethan Zwerg. They graciously devoted time and effort to an unpublished author with an unproven story, and their feedback proved invaluable. I can't wait to start the whole process anew with the sequel.

Finally, I'd like to thank Rebecca Heyman, my indespensible editor who finalized both CORNERSTONE and PROTOCOL. I hope we can work together again soon.

Oh…and John Boggs. He helped too.

Made in the USA
Lexington, KY
12 January 2014